Keonah Days

A NOVEL

BY

M. Paul Chinitz

Order this book online at www.trafford.com
or email orders@trafford.com

Most Trafford titles are also available at major online book retailers.

Printed in the United States of America.

ISBN: 978-1-4269-4030-9 (sc)
ISBN: 978-1-4269-4096-5 (e)

Trafford rev. 12/15/2010

 www.trafford.com

North America & international
toll-free: 1 888 232 4444 (USA & Canada)
phone: 250 383 6864 ♦ fax: 812 355 4082

Dedicated to Betty Jo--

We met when young, were cleft when old,
and all those years between were gold.

Chapter I
THE ELKTON LODGE

If you leave the Interstate at exit 9, a short drive of about 10 minutes brings you to Elkton, Indiana, and a chance to get a peaceful night's rest away from the noise and exhausting hassle of 10 hours of turnpike traffic. The worst of which was being tailgated by big semis. I didn't know Elkton; it was just a signpost at the exit that coincided with a dejected wave of travel weariness that finally got to me. Certainly, I had only myself to blame for this. The sensible rule for travel is to go east in the afternoon and west in the morning, but if west is where you want to go and east is where you start in the morning, then you'd best get used to driving into the late afternoon sun and stop squawking.

Now Elkton is only a small town, and all I was looking for was a quiet room and a simple meal before the next day's 10 hour driving ordeal and its end to this escape—hopefully an end. But the road became main street even before I had started looking for motels, and there, just ahead, was the hotel, the Elkton Lodge. It seemed a bit large for the subdued late afternoon commerce on the main street, but I figured that Elkton, just as I, had once seen better times. Going down in life had one advantage though, I could park right in front.

The lobby was also large, but empty except for the desk clerk, and I had no problem getting a room and a rundown on the dining room schedule. Now this might seem like needless description to you when I haven't said anything much about who—make that what, rather—I was, and where I was going, but the fact is that the lobby had two, make that three, objects that demanded my attention. First, at the base of a column near the middle of the lobby, was the skin of an elephant's foot encasing a can and obviously intended as a spittoon. Now no bar; hotel lobby; or airport, bus, or train station that I have been in, in New York, has spittoons anymore. Granted there may be some, since New York must have nearly everything tucked away someplace, but I haven't been there, and even if there were such places, would you expect to see one made in such a fashion? I looked around for the other three feet, but the clerk, guessing my intention, said this was the only one left, and it was kept chained to the post to prevent its being coaxed away by another guest.

If I hadn't looked for the other feet, I would probably have missed the other two items, a pair of chairs along the far wall. Well, they really were chairs. You could actually sit in them, and I did; they almost demanded it. The seats and backs were carved in the shape of a cupped hand, one left and one right. I could see each was carved from a single piece of wood, probably a length of tree trunk as there were no joints visible, and the seat and back were a little on the narrow side. I couldn't make out what kind of wood was used, since they were finished in a black stain. The wrist of the hand was slanted back, forming a pedestal for the seat.

Definitely a lobby with character, I thought, and later perhaps I'd take a good look around, especially the pictures, hung rather high on the walls; landscapes mostly in rather ornate frames. The lower half of the walls were paneled in a dark wood, while the upper half was covered in a burnished gold paper with pink floral design accents. There were also the obligatory potted plants, two fig trees I believe, and oriental-looking ceramics.

My room was clean, but very ordinary as to furnishings, but I wasn't much interested in that. I was interested in a warm shower to get the kinks out of my back and legs from nearly 600 miles of alternately boring and harassing turnpike travel; then to eat and then to sleep.

Chapter II

Mrs. Adamson

By 6:30, I went down to the dining room on the mezzanine floor. There was something early 1940's in the style of this and the lobby. Surprising really, that it had outlasted what must have been many owners and remodeling. The dining room had originally been fairly large, but now a curtain brought the seating area down to a more intimate dozen or so tables, befitting the number of guests the management could reasonably expect, even on a busy night.

The menu was unpretentious, thank goodness, and when the waitress approached I was about to order a drink, but instead she asked if I was dining alone, and if so, the lady at a side table by a window, a Mrs. Adamson, she said, asked if I would join her. This had never happened to me before and I was uncertain on what to say, when, sensing my hesitation, she added that Mrs. Adamson was the owner.

"So kind of you to join me, Mr. Borden, we have very few new guests at dinner nowadays, and I like to make them feel a little more at home than they would at some diner. Besides, company may help atone for our rather limited weekday menu." Her voice was pleasantly soft and seemed sincere.

"Thank you, Mrs. Adamson, that is most thoughtful. I presume you knew my name from the register in the lobby?"

"Oh yes, but it was your inquiry about the missing elephant's feet that brought you to my attention. I was in the manager's room behind the desk when you asked. You see, very few guests even notice the oddities in the lobby anymore, so I was curious why you did." Mrs. Adamson appeared to be near my age, perhaps 5 years older. Blond hair originally, but graying rapidly and cut in a short bob. Her face was somewhat narrow for its length and had a strong nose. Pale skin, still mostly smooth but with an appropriate number of small wrinkles about the corners of her eyes and mouth for her age, which I judged to be about 50 or so. Since she was seated, I couldn't judge her height, but her light tweed suit and silk blouse suggested a lean, not thin, size 14 build.

A half-filled cocktail glass was by her plate, so I ordered a Scotch and soda from the waitress who had remained by the table. "Well you must admit ma'am," I replied, "that a pair of amputated hands bent into the shape of chairs and a novelty spittoon—even any spittoon these days, is not an every day encounter by a traveler; and even though I've been driving for the last several hours into the afternoon sun, I'm not too dulled to notice the unusual." I kept my voice light and casual so there would be little reason for her to take offense, not knowing whether the items were her own prize heirlooms or came with the hotel.

"Oh yes, you are quite right, Mr. Borden," she laughed. "You won't find furnishings like those in many hotels—excepting of course the other feet that were stolen, but only the left front one was after I acquired the Lodge." She cocked her head slightly and looked at me, a little quizzically I thought, before continuing with the obvious question: "And what do you do, Mr. Borden?"

"Nothing." It startled her a little. I suppose she expected to hear I was a sales representative, or even better, an advance man for a major company planning to move to Elkton. "Well not quite that bad," I continued after a sip of Scotch. "I used to do things, but I'm retired now."

"Well, what did you do and what are you doing here?", raising her brows to show maybe a little exasperation. "Unless there's some reason for you to be secretive." Her voice remained quite casual, and finishing her drink, signaled the waitress for another round by circling the tabletop with her finger.

"No, no," I apologized, "I didn't expect you would be interested. But actually, while I'm not really good at making entertaining small talk, I guess that to a stranger, anything about me is news. You must just promise to let me know when you've heard enough, and not let me babble on."

After the fresh drinks were served I told her the little I thought she'd be curious about, that I was an engineer working just outside of New York until two years ago when I decided to take an early retirement from a down-sizing company. That I had shut myself up in my house until a month ago, when I finally faced the fact that continued idleness and seclusion was going to wreck my health, both physically and mentally. I couldn't step back into my former friends' circle; it would be, well, painful. So I decided to rent my house, store most of the furnishings, and move out for a fresh start. I had been raised in Iowa, I explained, and rather liked the small towns. Not really a retreat to childhood, but I needed a sense of community again. So after much debate with myself I started out.

"And here I am," I finished, "my first stop on, hopefully, my way to renewal."

Mrs. Adamson did not seem to be bored, even though she must have felt some disappointment that I wasn't bringing hope that the renewal I was seeking would bring a financial renewal to Elkton and its lodge. I finished my drink and started scanning the menu, when she asked me in a low voice "You're wearing a ring, Mr. Borden, is it impolite to ask where your family is during this trip?"

"I have no family, Mrs. Adamson," I replied, and added after a moment, "my wife, Francis, died of cancer several years ago. It was a lingering death for both of us I guess. Her pain is over but mine is not. She gave me this ring when we married, you see. I wear it to keep her with me. I was trained to be practical and analytical, an engineer should be, and I was fairly successful as one. But when she died, I was left with nothing but grief and I indulged in it."

I stopped, but after a moment she said "But your children, Mr. Borden. She left you that, a better memory surely than a ring, and ones that needed your support and consolation even more than you."

I looked down at the menu again. I didn't want anyone to see my feelings being stirred-up again. "I have no children, Mrs. Adamson. Francis had three miscarriages. The doctors advised her not to try again, so I have only this ring, you see. Of course there are pictures and memorabilia, but I left them behind. I will get them when I can look and not be reminded of how she was at the end. But enough of that!" I said, a bit too loudly. The waitress must have been alarmed and started toward our table. Mrs. Adamson saw

5

it, but waved her away. "I'm sorry ma'am, I was trying to keep hold of my feelings but I seemed to have dropped one."

"My fault, Mr. Borden, I had no idea you were under such stress. But let's order, perhaps our kitchen can provide the right medication." The waitress returned when she opened her menu. She ordered number 3: breast of chicken marsala, rice, and a lettuce and cucumber salad. The entrees seemed a bit more interesting to me after the second Scotch, but I still felt prime rib with au gratin potatoes, peas and carrots, and her salad my best choice. It should be edible even if the Elkton Lodge was more talented in menu writing than in cooking. As it turned out, the food was much better than I had expected, especially the potatoes and salad, which was actually romaine, not lettuce, with coarse diced and seeded cucumbers, sweet onion rings, and a very light dressing of olive oil and fresh lemon juice, not vinegar.

We ate in silence for a few minutes. She seemed to be waiting for me to initiate conversation; perhaps my sudden outburst made her wary. "Did you acquire the Lodge recently?" I finally asked. Mrs. Adamson seemed unconcerned about her privacy and talked for some minutes about herself while we ate. She said she had married young to an Air Force pilot who was killed in a plane crash about 12 years ago. Her grandfather, who had built the Lodge had collected those oddities in the lobby, plus others, she said, asked her to return to Elkton as housekeeper for the Lodge. Her two children, now grown and married, lived away. Her son, the eldest, had entered the Air Force, like his father, and was stationed in Germany. Her daughter lives in California, where her husband practices medicine. Her grandfather died 6 years ago and left her the Lodge.

"My grandfather collected many unusual objects in his lifetime," she added. "He traveled a lot and regularly brought back things that amused him or added interest to the hotel, or even outraged or flabbergasted the townspeople. I've kept some of his more private ones in his suite—which is now mine—but most are in locked displays in the meeting rooms—safe from damage or theft," she added.

"Are there more things like the chairs in the lobby?" I asked.

"A few," she laughed, "but not furniture. Perhaps you'd like to see some of Rodde's Oddities—that's what I call them. Grandfather never really considered them high art, but many were things that he felt enhanced his image as an adventurer and world traveler to his business associates in Elkton. I suppose some of the items are valuable examples of the customs and craftsmanship of the places he visited."

I nodded a yes, and was about to signal the waitress for the dessert menu, when Mrs. Adamson suggested we have dessert and coffee after she showed me the collection. "Clarissa," clearly meaning the waitress, "will put your check on the room bill, the dessert and coffee will be free," she said, "but we'll split the tip which should be about $2 each." I saw my hostess was used to leading.

Chapter III
Rodde's Oddities

She took me across the hall to a meeting room where several large glass cabinets lined the inside wall, opposite the windows. One cabinet contained Indian items, the usual artifacts: feather headdresses, bows and arrows, bear claw necklaces, tomahawks, calumets and wampum belts. All labeled and separated by tribe. I feigned polite interest, scanning the labels, until in one corner I was startled to find what appeared to be, and was labeled as, scalps.

"That takes the ordinary out of this cabinet, doesn't it Mr. Borden?" she chuckled. "It's rather gruesome when you come across it unexpectedly. Grandfather Rodde was delighted in shocking visitors; the townspeople were used to it. That's why he needed to add new items to his collection from time to time."

"Did you accompany him on his trips?" I asked, still examining the hairpieces.

"Only on a few," she replied, "when the children were away in college, and then only to the more civilized places. I never tramped the jungles with him," she smiled. "I find roughing it distasteful. But actually, Mr. Borden, Rodde's real purpose in these displays was not malicious. He wanted to show human vanity and barbarity and any cultural trait he thought ridiculous superstition. Perhaps being with him so long at the Lodge, some of his attitude toward human foibles rubbed off onto me. You can see that these scalps, dried and shriveled as they are, are very old. The tragedy of their true owners, that terrible emotion, has by now been diluted to nothingness. So too has the boastful strutting of the murdering brave who took and displayed them. He too is dead, and maybe his scalp was also on display in some Indian's belt or lance. So now they are rather impersonal, for the little we know of their origin, aren't they? We can't recreate their owners' images, no grimacing scalpless heads to haunt us, so I left them in the collection after Rodde died. But he also had in this cabinet, on the shelf just below, some shrunken heads from the Jibaros Indians, South American you know. I had those sent back to a museum in Brazil. They were too much for me, and Elkton as well, I think."

Mrs. Adamson, I decided, was not as easy to understand as I had first thought. I was intrigued but cautious. She dressed well, the suit and blouse were well tailored and expensive. Feminine but not flowery. She wore earrings that dangled a bit, handsome ornate gold pin over the collar button of her blouse and a broad gold bracelet on her left wrist. She was just a couple of inches shorter than me, but I noticed she had flat shoes. There was nothing frail about her appearance, neither fat nor excessively thin, but perhaps a little bulgy in the abdomen, which was probably under tight control by the usual means, and adequately but not amply endowed above. She was aware I was inspecting her, but did not seem either offended or appreciative, just observant.

We moved on to the next cabinet which contained oriental ceramics, fans, calligraphy items, small wall hangings, and several richly embroidered jackets and robes. "No grisly items here," I commented.

"No", she smiled, "Mr. Rodde was not very successful in his oriental acquisitions. He told me that he had to compete against too many professional collectors, and travel into the interior villages where he might find something unique was too difficult and politically risky."

We moved on. The last cabinet contained African artifacts. Spears, knives, headdresses, baskets and masks. Again, separated and labeled by tribe. I passed over these quickly, but was stopped by some very fine stone sculpture by the Benin and Yoruba people. "I think they are first rate," was her comment. "In fact, several university museums have asked me to donate them, but I'm not certain I should do that yet. It would leave the African cabinet without much interest."

"I suppose not", I replied, "though there seems to be a revived interest in tribal masks. Although magical items don't impress me much. I guess as an engineer I'm much too matter of fact for that. Frankly, Mrs. Adamson, except for the rather macabre scalps and the absent shrunken heads— which I'm glad not to have seen—these cabinets have nothing as unique as the chairs, in my mind."

"Well, you are probably right," she responded, "but these are displayed in the public rooms; Grandfather Rodde kept his more bizarre things in his private suite." We walked back toward the elevator. Mrs. Adamson said something to Clarissa as we passed the dining room, and then turning to me, said "Clarissa will bring us coffee. We'll have it in my suite. Is that all right?"

I nodded agreement and we took the elevator to the 5th and top floor. Her suite, she explained, was originally Mr. Rodde's, which she found convenient and comfortable for her own use, since she had most of her meals in the dining room, and the hotel maids took care of most of the cleaning. "It is really rather luxurious for me not having to maintain a house, and yet having as much privacy as an outside apartment could offer. The other suites on this floor are closed," she explained as she unlocked the hall door. We entered a small room that contained a coat closet, a side table, and two perfectly normal chairs. A door, opposite the one we entered, led us into a larger room, furnished, it seemed to me, like a parlor. A round table was in the center with straight-backed chairs around it. At my right, on the far wall, was an around-the-corner sofa. Windows indicated that it was an outside wall for the building. A low side table with several pots of bright flowers decorated the rest of that wall. Continuing around the next corner to the wall on my left, were three doors. One just past the corner which could be for a closet or vanity, and two adjoining ones near the middle of that wall. Bookcases lined the remaining portion of the wall and continued around the near corner behind me at my left, ending near the door from the foyer.

Overall, the room was furnished in a mix of Danish modern and traditional styles. The drapes and rug were in earth tones with geometric patterns. It was a warm and comfortable appearing room, not overly masculine, and definitely not frilly feminine. Probably most of the furniture was Mr. Rodde's, but the modern pieces and the fabrics were most likely selected by Mrs. Adamson.

Several pictures, framed reproductions, were on the left wall, between the single and paired doors, above the bookcases, and on the right wall. They were a mix of popular post-impressionists. Still lifes and scenic views, but no portraits. I was especially attracted to a large print in muted tones of green and yellow. The subject was a fleet of small fishing boats at anchor in still harbor waters.

"A favorite of mine," she said, and in response to my question, "the artist, Palue', is not well known in this country. He titled it 'Approaching Twilight, Arcachon'. I found it in a Paris museum shop some yeas ago. There is a quiet peacefulness of the scene. I often find its calmness therapeutic when things get hectic. Does it have that same effect on you, Mr. Borden?"

"Um," was my noncommittal response. "Perhaps it's due to the absence of people. Faces almost always produce strong reactions in the viewer. Good or bad." I did find the picture's mood affecting me, but I had no desire to reveal more of myself than I had already done. I tend to subscribe to something I read once on the Anglo-Saxon theory of the treatment of emotions and desserts: 'Freeze 'em and hide 'em in your belly', though I'm more eclectic about the latter.

My hostess excused herself for a moment, disappearing through an archway opening from a short alcove on the right of the entrance door and extending behind me. I inspected the bookcases. There were a number of old books on travel and geography, obviously belonging to her grandfather. Others must have been Mrs. Adamson's: some modern novels, current biographies, a few on the women's movement, and a number of history and military books, possibly her husband's, since they were published in the 50's and 60's.

A muffled clank told me the elevator had stopped on this floor, and also that the suite was fairly well insulated from both inside and street noise. Voices from the direction that Mrs. Adamson had disappeared indicated that Clarissa had probably arrived with the coffee. Confirmed in a moment, when she brought a tray in from the alcove, followed by Mrs. Adamson with another tray containing cups and saucers, sugar, creamer, and plates and silverware. The ladies set up service on the parlor table and then Clarissa left, the elevator clank a moment later suggesting she was returning to the dining room.

"I didn't see Clarissa enter this room," I remarked as my hostess indicated a chair for me.

"Oh, no, there is a separate door from the hall to the kitchenette, just through that archway. Usually I like to make my own breakfast so I don't have to bother the kitchen staff if I rise late or very early, as sometimes happens. Also, of course, I serve tea to my bridge club meetings here, and it is easiest to make it myself." She poured coffee and offered me a slice of chocolate rum cake. It was delicious and I told her so.

"I'm glad you like it, Mr. Borden. Frankly, I thought your taste in food was rather limited, judging by your dinner selection, so I was sure this would appeal to a man."

I laughed, "no ma'am, you've misjudged me. I enjoy variety and many styles of cooking. In fact, Francis—that was my wife—and I used to share cooking meals on weekends and trying new recipes. Afterwards, though, she had little appetite and could tolerate only the most bland diet. No, my order tonight was in part a long delayed desire for Midwestern beef and in part, if you'll pardon me, a somewhat quizzical feeling about the capability of your kitchen staff on the more demanding concoctions. After all, Elkton is not a metropolis and the Lodge is not bustling with business."

"No offense Mr. Borden. If I had driven all day and ended at a somewhat sleepy town I might also be cautious about the menu. But as a matter of fact, I brought Mr. Chang Sou with me when I took over the Lodge. He had been chef at the officer's club at my husband's last base, and we became good friends. He is an excellent chef. I pay him very well, and he prefers the slower pace of the small town."

"But surely the Lodge doesn't do enough business to pay for that kind of help," I responded. "I saw only a half dozen diners tonight, and I'm sure not many travelers leave the interstate to spend the night here."

"You did, Mr. Borden, if I can believe your story." It was clearly an amusing retort for her. I could tell by her smile. "But of course you are right, Elkton is not what it was when Grandfather Rodde built the Lodge. Even in those years, when I was the housekeeper, we didn't have many overnight guests, but the Lodge did make expenses and a little more through its meeting rooms for civic and business meetings, and the dining room for wedding receptions and parties. We drew business from the entire county, not just Elkton. That hasn't changed. You're just here on a slow night, usual for a Monday. But to be totally frank with you, though I'm not sure why I should be, I have other investments which provide me with the same opportunity Rodde had to run the Lodge almost as a pleasant hobby, and at the same time give me a voice and position in the community. I like that very much."

We finished a second cup, and I rose to go, but she asked me if I'd like to see the more private cabinets in Grandfather Rodde's collection. She led me through the right-hand door of the adjoining pair. "This was Rodde's card room," gesturing with a sweep of her arm, "he had his poker friends here twice a week. They're mostly all gone now too, but I use it for my bridge club. We meet once a week here—my women friends welcome the opportunity to get out of their homes and socialize without having to spend the day before cleaning and preening if we met as a round robin."

There were a pair of tables, big enough for 8, when separated, so two games of bridge could be played. Straight-backed upholstered chairs, a side buffet along one wall, and two cabinets along the opposite wall. The cabinets were closed with rather ornately carved wooden doors. Mrs. Adamson crossed to the buffet, opened it, and asked if I'd like a nightcap. I'm not a big drinker, but politeness suggested I should accept her offer.

"Do you care for another Scotch, or perhaps a liqueur or brandy? I have Cherry Herring, Kaluah—a great favorite of my bridge girls—but perhaps too sweet for you. Oh, here we are, Drambuie, for a Scotch drinker!"

"Thanks, Mrs. Adamson, but only if you are having something too." She bent down, looking through the bottles. Finally she straightened up and turning towards me with a bottle, said she would join me, but would have an Irish Mist for herself. She poured from that bottle, and then poured my Drambuie.

"I haven't had this for years," she said raising her glass. "It was Grandfather Rodde's favorite."

We clinked glasses, and jokingly, I remarked "Scotch and Irish, but they don't really get along do they?"

"Perhaps not," she laughed, holding the glass up to the light. "But then my ancestry is English, an anathema to both. Please go ahead and look through his private collection; the cabinets are unlocked. I'll be right back."

I waited a moment after she left. I could hear her speaking to someone faintly, probably on the phone.

I opened the first cabinet and nearly dropped my glass. If this was Rodde's private collection, O.K. for a man's poker room, but for a women's bridge club? I had seen pictures of New Guinea tribes before, but none that so concentrated on their genital ornaments. There were about a dozen framed photographs hung on the back wall, obviously enlarged, single individuals from the front and side, and groups with spears and battle regalia. Leaning on one side of the cabinet were four actual penis sheaths of different sizes and shapes, similar to those in the pictures, and bone and bamboo nose ornaments of bizarre shapes. All labeled as to tribe. Of a less flamboyant style were pictures of New Hebrides natives wearing palm leaf coverings.

"My bridge club finds them very amusing." My hostess had returned quietly, I was bent over reading the labels. "It tickles them to imagine that underneath their husband's suits and civilized ties, there probably lurks a primitive urge to flaunt and exaggerate their sexual features."

"But women do too", I countered dryly, pointing to some small Minoan figurines of bare-breasted women. "The whole fashion industry depends on it."

"Yes, we are guilty, but you see there is a difference which is what Rodde meant with this cabinet. Women, mostly, display their female features— more discreetly to be sure—to attract desirable men, whereas these," waving a hand across the Melanesian display, "were meant to intimidate other men." I wasn't sure I fully agreed with her analysis, but said nothing. She seemed to have a theatric streak, as her comments on the Indian scalps suggested.

In the next section of the cabinet, Rodde had found some medieval cod pieces and chastity belts. I had never seen real ones before. Pictures of how they were worn were posed of course by models in medieval costumes. When she shut the cabinet door I noticed half a dozen oil paintings high on the wall above the cabinets. All nudes, none really pornographic, but the artists relished in portraying voluptuous female anatomy. "Appropriate for Mr. Rodde's poker club," tipping my head towards them, "but for your bridge group?"

"Rodde's saloon art," she said dryly. "He collected them from a bar in San Francisco and from the best—or worst—in Berlin and Marseille, so he said. I scolded Rodde about them," and then after a pause, "there is more to a woman than her body, and there should be more to a man than his cock." Her sudden use of a vulgarity startled me, but she still seemed cool and detached. Ignoring further the paintings, she went on: "Rodde liked to remind his guests about the foibles of mankind, though I know some of them felt smugly superior after seeing these cabinets. Why they don't seem to recognize that beards, mustaches, long hair, and now earrings are just another manifestation of primitive sexual display escapes me. Why do we need to continue carrying that jungle psychology with us in these times?"

Her voice remained at a normal speaking level, but I could sense she felt strongly about it. Perhaps as a businesswoman she had been put down by her male associates. Or was there some deeper resentment that had peeped out. "You may not have noticed, Mrs. Adamson, that I am clean shaven—well it's probably a stubble by now, but I shave every day. My hair is cut short as I believe befits one who must bear, however unwillingly, a male sexual display of incipient baldness, and there are no bangles in my ears, nose, or lips, and further, though you can't verify it, I have no tattoos of any kind: mom, roses, or belly dancers."

"But I have noticed, Mr. Borden," she laughed, "and I sympathize with the fact that you are an unwilling participant in the parade of pattern-bald males. I also accept your assurance that your skin is as nature made it—and aged it, nor will I ask you if you also display this other male fetish," opening the other cabinet.

"Grandfather Rodde certainly had a strange sense of humor," I mumbled, staring at the display. Several stone knives were displayed, labeled 'beriths, circumcision knives from Egypt and Morocco'. Next to them was a small decorated pottery dish containing what looked like little scraps of brittle curled paper. The label said 'foreskins'. I looked with raised eyebrows at my hostess.

"Actually I think they're fakes," she said. "Rodde bought the knives from an Arab shop in Cairo, and when he told the owner what he wanted them for, was offered these at a rather stiff price. Rodde said they were sold under the counter as aphrodisiacs and he believed him, but I still think they're fakes and told him so."

I heard the elevator clank to a stop, and decided it was a polite suggestion that the tour was over. I glanced at the other items in the cabinet. They were mostly Egyptian amulets and other magical items, and turned to go. Closing the doors, Mrs. Adamson led me back to the parlor. Clarissa was there gathering up the coffee cups and cake plates. I nodded to her and went through the foyer to the elevator. I thanked Mrs. Adamson for the most unusual hour I could remember. "But I'm curious," I added, "why would you keep that display," gesturing vaguely toward the inside of the suite. "It must be embarrassing for some of your guests and cause a few raised eyebrows among your Chamber of Commerce associates?"

"Actually it hasn't had much negative effect," she said. "I've already told you my bridge club is tickled playing cards in that room knowing what's in the cabinets and taking a peek now and then. But as a matter of fact, I can't really dispose of it. Rodde's will stipulated that I keep those cabinets in his suite and unlocked as a condition for receiving income from his trust. The trustee, who happens to be head of the Elkton National Bank, and husband to one of my club members, must formally check it once a year. The terms of the will are public knowledge, so no real stigma is attached to me. Rodde was well known for his eccentricities, but generally well liked in the community. Of course, my own behavior is always proper. Some thought they could add me to their own collection, but a subtle hint that their wives would hear about it soon disabused them of that idea. Goodnight Mr. Borden, I hope you find what you're looking for."

I bowed slightly and turned to the elevator. "And thank you for not abusing my hospitality," she added.

I looked at her for a moment before responding. "Mrs. Adamson, you have been most gracious. It would have been quite out of character for me to have repaid you in such a manner." I was about to push the floor button, but stopped and added, "and you can understand that Francis is still very much in my heart and thoughts."

"I respect your devotion, Mr. Borden. Some years ago I would have been envious of the kind of fidelity your wife inspired, but surely she would want you to go on with your life, not crippled by a memory that cannot be brought back to life. But excuse my impertinence, please. Goodnight and thank you again." She turned to enter the foyer and at that same moment Clarissa, carrying the tray of dishes entered the hall from a door to the right of the elevator, apparently a second door to the suite. I held the elevator for her and then pushed '1' and looked at her. She smiled and said "mezzanine please."

I said goodnight at my stop and she replied "Goodnight, Mr. Borden." Did Mrs. Adamson tell her my name? And, was Clarissa brought up to the suite as insurance that nothing would happen? Mrs. Adamson was not easy to understand. She seemed very self-assured, emotionally controlled, apparently educated and very much a mature businesswoman. But still, exposing me to Rodde's weird treasures, while each separately could be considered a cultural curiosity, yet when put together as a collection, they seemed somehow pornographic. Surely there were several ways she could satisfy the will without actually having to display them. In some sense I felt she had been testing me, but for what? And why me, I couldn't figure it out? Nor did I know if I had passed or failed her test.

I got to the dining room at 8:30 the next morning, later than I had planned. A lighter breakfast was called for as penance after the beef and drinks of last night. My waitress was not Clarissa, who did not appear at all. Perhaps she had only the dinner shift. Mrs. Adamson also was absent. Just as well, I thought. The woman disturbed me because I didn't understand her. Not exactly mysterious, but more like the clues to her thoughts and motives were offered stingily and even those she did display were ambiguous. My musing was interrupted by the arrival of soft-boiled eggs, dry toast and a very good marmalade. After three cups of coffee I was ready for travel. My bags were already packed, and after a short stop at the bathroom I took the elevator to the lobby. Another quick look at the chairs and spittoon was warranted on my way to the front desk. I gave the clerk my room key, told him I paid in the dining room for my breakfast, had no outside calls, or room service and asked for the bill. "You forgot to add last night's dinner bill," I said after a quick scan.

"Yes, Mr. Borden, I was instructed to mark that as a complimentary meal on the Lodge. There is no charge."

The inscrutable Mrs. Adamson again. I asked him to thank the management for its hospitality. I didn't want to directly refer to Mrs. Adamson. It might cause her some embarrassment with her staff. I paid and started to leave when he called out "Oh, one moment sir, the chef asked me to give this to you." He handed me a small paper sack. Putting my bags down, I opened it. Something was wrapped in foil inside, along with a slip of paper. I thanked him, picked up the bags. I pulled out the slip of paper. She had written in a small, neat hand: "I had an extra piece of the cake you seemed to enjoy last night. Please have it when you take a rest stop on your trip. Good luck. Mrs. Edith Adamson, 'Edie'."

So that was her name. And she had added her familiar too. Formality and casualness tossed together. More conflicting images.

Chapter IV

KEONAH

Leaving the widow Fashlich's rooming house for the second time that morning I wandered down Elm Street toward the Keonah Diner for lunch. Breakfast, lunch, and dinner at the diner were turning into the only purposive parts of my day. Something got done there, turning eggs, bacon, mashed potatoes, and chops into more Emmett Borden, late of Mamaroneck, N.Y. Nothing else I did could match that marvelous transformation, though why more of me was needed escaped me at the moment. I seemed to be superfluous to everybody and anybody, except my landlady when the monthly room rent was due.

My reasons for stopping at Keonah, a little town a few miles south and east of Cedar Rapids, Iowa, seemed sound during my drive from Elkton. It was small, very small, but close to two bigger cities and the cultural life of the state university. Beyond that I hadn't given it much thought. Culture was O.K., if you didn't encounter so many incredibly grungy students, smug with youth, yet too often spoiling its beauty with sloppiness, hypocrisy, and incredibly banal noise masquerading as music. An intolerant view by an old engineer on the vibrant and daring young liberal arters you will say, but haven't I seen it all before. Indeed, didn't I have some of it once myself? Impossible, engineers of my generation were always solid, not flaky; practical, not dreamy with the fictions of conceptualism and deconstructionism; rational, but aware of fallibility. Ah!, am I feeling pride in myself again? Smug in comparison to those campus tramps, shame on you Emmett Borden, Fran deserves better. There must be something for me to do, more than remaining passive, visiting galleries, seeing plays and movies, eating, sleeping and walking around and around the town.

Lunch was not very good today, it put me squarely into the sour and combative mood my pointless daily activity had been leading me. I stomped up the front steps to Mrs. Fashlich's porch, glowering at the cracked glass in the front door. She was sitting in the front room, looking through her album of photographs. Probably of her absent family and youth, I thought. Not time for her afternoon soaps on TV. Existing, not really living, just like me. I barked at her "Mrs. Fashlich, that glass on the front door, the cracked one you've put scotch tape on, why don't you get that fixed? You know someone's going to slam that door sometime soon and it's going to break all over the floor. Probably cut somebody. They may even get tetanus if they don't bleed to death first."

"What do you expect an old lady to do Mr. Borden? I've called Diehl's Hardware for two months to come and fix it, but he don't come." Mrs. Fashlich looked hurt, then worried, maybe the image of a bloody porch had entered her mind.

"Well for goodness sake, if you pay for the glass and putty, I'll fix it for you. Tetanus doesn't appeal to me much right now." I blurted it out from the frustration of my boxed-in life. It surprised me. Here was something I could do for an hour or two, and then go to sleep with a feeling of accomplishment and a godsend to all old widow ladies with cracked glass in their doors. Well, at least one. Why hadn't I thought of this before? Maybe I should check if there were more waiting for my help!

But Mrs. Fashlich was skeptical. After all, she hadn't seen me do much of anything for weeks. "Well, all right, but don't leave things half done the way my husband used to do, with no glass at all." That's the spirit, I thought. The widow Fashlich doesn't stay cowed for long.

I got my tool kit out of the car trunk and pulled out the broken glass, cleaned the rabbets, measured, and marched down to Diehl's Hardware.

Old Mr. Diehl, well certainly some years older than me, but lame with arthritis or lumbago or something, limped up to me from behind the counter. I told him to cut me a piece of window glass, get me a can of putty, and some glazier's points.

"Can't cut glass anymore mister," he mumbled, "arthritis has been acting up something awful for months now so's I can't grip the cutter."

I told him I had to have the glass now because the window was shattered. I looked around and found the glass racks. "I'll cut it," I announced and went back to the glass bench, Mr. Diehl shuffling after me.

"You'll pay for it if you break it," he warned. I ignored him. Somehow that bad lunch had fired-up my adrenal glands. Now I have hand-cut glass. I don't like to. If you don't do it every day it can be nerve wracking, keeping the straightedge from slipping while you press down on the cutter. Then tapping just so hard on the backside to crack the glass nicely, but only along the score line. "You ought to get a glass cutting jig," I told him. "It's quick and arthritis won't stop you."

"Won't pay," he replied, watching me. "People want me to install it too. I can't leave the shop to do that."

Fortunately, the glass broke along the score lines for me. "There," I announced smugly, "ten minutes time. How much are you going to charge me for that? Include the putty and points now." He turned back to the front counter and I dumped the cut-offs in the scrap glass can, wrapped my pane in newspaper, and headed for the cash register. "I want a receipt," I told him, "this is for Mrs. Fashlich."

"Oh, you a relative of hers? I haven't seen you before, have I?"

"Nope, I'm new in town, renting a room there, and just got tired of not being able to slam her front door because you wouldn't come up and fix it for her."

"I know," he sighed. "She's been pestering me for months. I had a helper, but he left me for school and my arthritis you know--."

I paid him, got the receipt, and an hour later had fixed the door and swept up the mess. Mrs. Fashlich was surprised and pleased. "My lord, Mr. Borden, you were fast. I thank you for that. I sure wish you were handling the hardware store. There must be lots of people that need things done like that around here."

At the diner next day, Mr. Diehl came in, nodded to me, ordered coffee from the waitress at the counter, and then came over to my booth. "Can I talk to you for a minute? It's Borden, isn't it?" I nodded, swallowed a bite of poached egg on toast and waved him to sit down.

"Widow Fashlich called me." He didn't look straight at me. "Said I ought to get some help at the store before some chain opens up a franchise here and shuts me down. She said I should talk to you, as you seem to be doing nothing—her words mind you—and might be interested?"

"Are you offering, Mr. Diehl?" I countered. "The thought hadn't occurred to me, but come to think about it now, I might be. Yes, I might be."

"Do you know anything about the hardware business, Borden?" He could look at me now that the matter was broached.

"Can't say that I do," I told him, "I've only been a customer, not a seller, but I know tools and how to do the usual home repair jobs. I've done it a lot for myself, for twenty years. I'm an electrical engineer by training, retired a few years ago. I grew up in Iowa, so I know what a gunny sack is, and oakum, and other things most chain store clerks back east never heard of. Do you want help Mr. Diehl?" I confronted him.

"Can't pay much, business isn't that good, but it might get worse if it gets around that people in town ain't getting service. I got about a dozen little jobs piled up for folks, and they're getting sore about it." I didn't say anything for some minutes, while I finished my eggs. He gulped his coffee and looked out the window.

"Tell you what, Mr. Diehl, I'll work on your jobs for a week, then we'll both decide on how it's working out and what the salary will be. Trial period for both of us."

"Sounds fair, Mr.—"

"Emmett," I interjected.

"And I'm Elmer," he countered. "9 to 5 suit you, half day Saturday usually, but we can talk about that if it works out."

So next morning I started my second career. He had a stack of odd jobs that had piled up. Several more window replacements, torn screens, locks and dead bolts to install. Easy enough for one mechanically inclined. But Keonah was a dying town. Most of the young had gone to the cities after school, and major items like furniture and rugs were bought in the big stores in Cedar Rapids.

After that first week, Elmer and I found we could get along pretty well. He didn't seem quite as cranky as I first thought when I bought Mrs. Fashlich's glass, and he seemed relieved when his customers paid for the repair jobs I did with no complaints. We had settled on a dollar above minimum wage with half-day Saturday work, unless an emergency, and car expenses for when I had to go to the customer's site. I didn't really need the money. I had my own investments and pension income, and I could see Elmer's business was not a big moneymaker. Still, things seemed to be picking up a bit, and it felt good to have a reason to get up in the morning, and be a benefit to someone as well.

Chapter V
Rodde's Left Foot

I had been at Diehl's for about two months when he got a call from an antique shop just off US 30. They needed a new set of locks on front and back doors. Some kids had tried to break in and screwed up the old locks. The woman who owned the shop was scared and wanted new ones right away. Elmer got the locksets she wanted and I drove up to her place. It was in a small shopping center catering to the highway traffic. I could see the locks on both doors were simple ones and easily forced. The break-in was from the backdoor, and part of the jamb was gouged out. I called the woman over to look at it and suggested a steel corner plate would be the cheapest repair, and would give the locks added protection. She was obviously shaken by the break-in, though apparently the thieves had been scared off before they could take anything.

I had to drive back to Keonah to get the two corner plates and a hacksaw, but by 3 o'clock the job was done and she seemed pleased about that. She offered me a cup of coffee, which I accepted after packing up my tools and writing out an invoice. Sipping from the mug, I wandered around looking at her antiques—though they probably would have been called collectibles by Francis. I wasn't really into glassware, china, and knickknacks that were barely old enough to vote. Suddenly I spotted something really out of the ordinary. I couldn't believe it. There, on the floor, with several old walking canes and an umbrella stuck in it, was an elephant's foot. A brass can lined the inside, just like the one at the Elkton Lodge. A price sticker was on the brass rim. I could see some engraving just showing from under a corner of the sticker. Crouching down, I lifted the corner of the sticker. "Elkton Lodge" was engraved on the rim under it. The owner was still checking the invoice and hadn't seen me fussing with it. She finally signed the invoice, I took my copy, got one of her business cards and headed for a telegraph office in Cedar Rapids. I was excited, what a piece of luck! I was sure Mrs. Adamson would be interested in knowing about it as soon as possible. I wired:

"Elephant's left foot found.
New owner asking $150. What
should I do? Call or wire
319-533-6102. 506 E. Elm,
Keonah, Iowa, 52244."

I signed it "Emmett" and addressed it to Edie Adamson, c/o Elkton Lodge, Elkton, Ind. and marked "personal". It tickled me to return the confidence she revealed to me in her goodbye cake by using our first names. Driving back to the hardware store, the happy mood stayed with me.

I expected to hear from her that evening, but no call came. My mood turned gloomy by 10 o'clock. Perhaps she was gone for the weekend; it was Friday. No, I argued with myself, the weekend would be a busy time for the Lodge, she wouldn't leave then. So it must be she didn't care or was offended by my familiarity. That was probably it. I regretted using her nickname, but then again, she had given it to me freely. But more to the point, why was I excited at first to have an excuse to contact her, and now to be so depressed by her not responding. After all, I could have written or called or even driven back to Elkton anytime in these past few months.

Why couldn't I clearly understand my motives? Why did that woman affect me this way? Certainly she was no longer young, older than me, I believed, and probably not really considered very beautiful even when she was young. Our conversation gave no hint that we had much in common except widowhood—not a pleasant experience to share with someone, I thought.

The night wore on. I was restless but there was no place to go at 11:00 in Keonah. Finally I went to bed, got a heavy book, "The Life of Vertebrates" I had picked up at an overstocked book sale at the university bookstore, and read. Holding up a heavy book was one way I found that was sure-fire to put me to sleep. It was still on my chest when Mrs. Fashlich woke me by banging on the door.

It was after 9:00 the next morning. "What is it?" I growled. "The house on fire, or what?"

"Wake up, Mr. Borden, I have a message for you. The call came an hour ago. I told her you were asleep. She didn't want to wake you, but said to give you this message by 9."

I sat up at once, it could only be from her. "What is it?" I asked hurriedly, putting on a robe and opening the door.

"It was long distance, from someplace called the Elkton Lodge in Indiana. Do you know it?" Mrs. Fashlich could be annoyingly slow.

"Yes I know it, what did she say?"

"I wrote it down, had to tell her to stop talking so fast. My lord some people think God meant us to go speeding through life. She said the Lodge would send someone to inspect the spittoon—now ain't that something to make a long distance call for!—and you were to meet them at the Airport Motel in Cedar Rapids at 11:30 today."

"Meet who?" I asked.

"She didn't say, just said 'them'."

"Well who called?" I asked again, exasperated.

"Said her name was Clarissa, I think. Talked too fast to be clear. She ought to be better trained for the phone if she works at a hotel. You'd think they'd seen to it when she was hired."

I was a little disappointed. Nothing from Edie herself. I had better think of her as Mrs. Adamson from now on, I scolded myself. And here my attempt at familiarity by making the wire 'personal' was clearly rebuffed. Probably was sending a desk clerk and letting a waitress give me the message. "Mr. Borden," I told myself, "you were an impetuous ass and deserved the slap you're getting."

I showered and dressed carefully. A conservative suit and tie might let the emissaries return a more favorable report of their meeting a serious and respectable Emmett Borden.

Arriving at the Airport Motel about 15 minutes late, I looked around the lobby for someone I might recognize, when I heard a voice behind me: "Hello Mr. Borden." Edie was smiling at me.

"Hello Mrs. Adamson," I replied. We both laughed. "I'm glad to see you again, but I certainly didn't expect you or anyone to come. In fact the telephone message led me to expect the desk clerk, or even Clarissa, though there would hardly have been time for her to call and then fly here," I stopped—"Oh, I hope I didn't cause you embarrassment by addressing my wire too familiarly?"

"Not at all, Emmett, the wire was delivered to me sealed. Clarissa is young but perfectly respects any confidences I give her. Let's have coffee in the lounge and you can tell me about the foot. Also, Emmett, I want to know what you're doing in Keonah. I've heard of Cedar Rapids and Iowa City and the Amanas but not Keonah."

I followed her into the lounge. She was wearing a pale blue dress and navy jacket. I thought blue was a good color for her. I really was glad to see her again, and relieved that I hadn't goofed with my message. We sat at a booth next to the window and ordered. "I may call you Edie?" I asked. She said that after an early morning drive to South Bend, a plane to Chicago, and another to Cedar Rapids she certainly hoped she was meeting with a friend! I explained about seeing the spittoon at an antique shop out at a highway shopping mall, and thought she would like to know about it.

"But is it the missing left foot, Emmett?"

"First of all," I replied, "I re-checked my "Life of Vertebrates" book and verified that the toes have the left front foot configuration, and the way I remembered the one at the Lodge was as a right foot. But more importantly, Edie, 'Elkton Lodge' was engraved on the rim of the brass insert, under a price tag." She seemed relieved.

"Well now, tell me what you've been up to and then we'll go retrieve Rodde's trophy." She lit a cigarette. I had never suspected she smoked, but declined her offer of one. "Do you object?" she asked. I assured her I didn't, that I was a pipe smoker as befits an engineer, but reduced my dependency to one bowlful a day, usually in the evening. The rest of my story didn't take long in telling. She seemed interested in the fact that I wasn't committed to Keonah and that the hardware job was simply a way to pass time more purposefully until I got a better feeling for what I wanted to do.

"But Emmett," she asked after reflecting for a moment, "the woman at the antique shop, is she a regular customer at Mr. Diehl's?" I told her I thought so, since Diehl told me to give her an invoice for the lock service, so I assume she would be on Diehl's monthly billing system.

"Then I think it would be best," she added, "that I see her alone. She should not associate you or Mr. Diehl's store with my visit."

I looked at her, "I guess I'm a little slow Edie, wouldn't it benefit Diehl to have brought her a customer?"

She looked at me and smiled but her voice took on a hardened tone, "I'm not a customer. She has stolen property, Emmett. I have copies of the police report I filed immediately after the theft. It is her responsibility to ensure items she acquires are from the legitimate owners." I guess I looked stunned because she added, "Look, Emmett, I'm sorry if you're disappointed in me, but Rodde taught me some business law, and I will certainly use it."

I'm not disappointed in you Edie, it's just that you are the most complicated woman I've ever met. It will give me many more hours to ponder about you."

"I like your doing that Emmett, but perhaps we'd better go. We're probably taking up space during the motel's lunch hour." Only a lodge keeper would be concerned about that, I thought.

I parked at the far end of the shopping center and told Edie where the antique shop was and where she would find the spittoon. Watching her move quickly down the line of storefronts, I noticed with pleasure that she walked well in heels, no wobbling. There weren't too many shoppers around except at the supermarket. Rather quite, I thought, for a pleasant Saturday. After about a half hour Edie came out of the shop with a large shopping bag. She shook her head at me as I started to get out of the car and walked toward the supermarket. I glanced back towards the antique shop and saw the owner watching Edie enter the store. Fortunately, I had parked between two vans so I was probably not easily visible to her. Edie must have been watching from just inside the door, because after a few minutes two women entered the antique store and the owner, hesitating a moment, had to go back inside. I started the car and Edit came on the run.

"Get out of here quick, Emmett, I don't want her to see you with me," she laughed.

"What happened?" My voice didn't conceal the nervousness I felt at this almost criminal-like escape.

"Don't be afraid, Emmett, it was all above-board, but I don't want you to be saddled with any resentment she may feel. Let's get a quick lunch at a McDonald's or whatever that's not close by and I'll tell you all about it. I'm glad I came, Emmett, it was wonderful! Rodde would have been proud of me."

I decided someplace down towards Iowa City would be safest, and after about 20 minutes we stopped at a Hardy's. Edie got a booth while I picked up two cheeseburgers, milk for her, and a coke for me. After a bite, she told me what happened. At first she played the part of a fussy woman, examining and rejecting objects from the shelves. Then seeming to suddenly see the foot, she told the woman it was a grotesque abuse of a noble animal and at an outrageous price. The woman was offended and told Edie she needn't buy it, that there were surely others that would consider it a rare find. "I'm sure they would, dearie," Edie told her, and taking out the canes and umbrella, picked it up and inspected it. Edie was having some difficulty in holding down her excitement.

"I pulled-off the price sticker, Emmett, and said especially the Elkton Lodge. Oh, the woman said, that place was closed up and the contents sold off several years ago. I bought this from some couple passing through here in a moving van, about a year ago. They needed money and were selling some of their belongings to pay for gas. When I told her who I was and showed her copies of the police file identifying the items stolen she started to panic. I told her to show me her books to verify she was not the thief. Well, she wasn't, thank goodness, I don't know really what I would have done if she were. I'm not vindictive Emmett, I want you to know that. She had paid $20 for it. So I told her I'd reimburse her for what she paid in return for the identification of the thieves when they're caught, which of course isn't likely to happen since the van has probably been re-licensed by now in another state. She was so absolutely terrified that I would press charges for fencing stolen property that she accepted my offer at once. I'm sure she was only duped and I didn't want her to lose money, but she wasn't going to make any off me!"

Edie was very pleased with herself, and I got a fresh insight into Mrs. Adamson's ambivalent nature: clever, role player, aggressive when she felt right about it, but not vengeful, as she had said.

Chapter VI
Dinner With Edie

After lunch she said she'd like to walk around the University campus if I had no objection. It was a pleasant day, and I didn't mind being with her at all. She asked me if I had gone to school here, but I told her no, I had gone to what was then the State College in the central part of the state. "There was a rivalry between the schools, though when I was a student it wasn't in sports since they were in different leagues. The University students would say I went to the Cow College because it was also the state agricultural school, as well as a top engineering college." It was natural then for me to ask her if she had gone to a college in Indiana. She told me no, she was born in California, but grew up for the most part in Cleveland. Her father was an accountant, but both her parents died in a car accident when she was nineteen and a student at Bryn Mawr near Philadelphia. She met her husband at the Lodge during a Christmas break in her junior year, and they were married the following spring, so she never completed college, and, she said with a smirk, that she hadn't learned much that could be useful the time she was there. She didn't seem to want to reveal anymore, so we just enjoyed walking about and touring the Fine Arts Building and its exhibits.

It was getting on to 5 o'clock and I asked about her return reservation. It was at 9 the next morning. "Then we can have dinner tonight, Edie? I owe you one, since you refused to have me billed for Chef Sou's dinner and dessert."

"I'd love to, Emmett. I'm pleased you remembered my chef. But would you pick me up later, say 7, at the motel, I want to freshen-up first? I had to get up very early to catch the Chicago flight from South Bend."

That would give me time to change too, so it was agreed, and I drove her back to her motel. Back at my room, while showering and shaving again, I wondered where to have dinner. For the months I had been in Keonah,

31

I'd never bothered to investigate the more elegant restaurant scene in either Cedar Rapids or Iowa City. Mrs. Fashlich was out, so I couldn't ask her, and anyway, I doubted that she could have given me much advice. Dressing hurriedly, I scanned the newspapers and the Yellow Pages hoping to spot something that wouldn't disgrace me. Finally I decided on suggesting two places: a Japanese restaurant and a supper club. I cut out the descriptions to show her and drove back to the motel. Edie had wanted to buy something in the motel shop when I dropped her off, so I had stopped at the main entrance and didn't know her room location. I parked by the lobby, got the room number from the desk clerk, and called. Edie asked for ten more minutes and said to meet her at the room. The clerk told me it was near the end of a one-story wing. I drove around to it and knocked at the door. In a moment she came out. She had changed to a black dress with a full skirt and a short red bolero style jacket with a glistening black pin of floral design on the left side. No hat, I had never seen her with one, but she carried a small black patent leather purse. I held the door for her. She hadn't let me earlier, by getting to it before I could, but by staying with me as we walked to the car, I was permitted to do so this time.

I apologized for being unfamiliar with restaurants in the area outside of my diner in Keonah, then showed her the clippings.

"No Japanese, Mr. Sou would never forgive me," she laughed. "Let's try the supper club, I feel relaxed now and would welcome the entertainment."

I had made sure beforehand that I knew how to get to both places, so we had no trouble finding the club. It was only a short distance, maybe 3 miles, from the motel.

I had no reservation, but we were in luck. A table was promised in 20 minutes. We went to the bar for a cocktail. Scotch again for me. Edie had a dry sherry. It was not a random choice, she knew what she wanted and asked specifically for Dry Sack. We chatted a bit with the bartender, on the entertainment for tonight—a folk singer on an acoustic guitar who was an instructor in the music department at the University. Edie asked if that meant a lot of college kids would be there. A few, he said, but their clientele came mostly from the business people in town and the professionals at the manufacturing plants in the area. "We like to keep a more mature clientele," he added. "Helps us avoid police problems, so no rock and roll or rap singers." The maitre d' caught my eye and signaled that our table was ready. We ordered another drink and studied the menu. I felt a little nervous, and it must have shown.

"You seem to be concerned about something, Emmett, do you mind telling me what it is? I hope my handling of the antique shop affair didn't irritate you?"

"No, of course not," I replied. "But the fact is, you are the first woman I've taken to dinner since Francis. I'm not sure I've prepared myself very well for this evening; I haven't stored up a lot of small talk to entertain you with."

"My goodness," she laughed, "am I on a date? It's pleasant just to be here, away from the Lodge for a day, and dining with a thoughtful person who did me a great favor in finding Rodde's foot. I felt badly about it being stolen, it seemed carelessness on my part not to have taken even ordinary precautions. I guess having seen them everyday for years made me forget how the unusual might seem valuable to others. But you know, there's lots for us to talk about. First, tell me, I really want to know, are you planning on staying in Keonah installing locks and repairing screens? Can you actually make a living doing this?"

She had broached a question I had asked myself before. Perhaps I should talk about it with her. Maybe putting my feelings into words would help me resolve them. "I really don't know, Edie. I told you this morning that this is just killing time for me. At first I thought being close to the culture a university area offered would be all I was looking for, but it wasn't. Then I sort of fell into helping out at the hardware store. It was something I could do immediately, and I felt good about having a reason to get up each morning. But it's not what I can be content with for long. As for making a living, I have my pension, income from savings, and royalties on several patents I hold. I'm not dependent on that job, but I like to be paid for work that I do. Elmer, that's Mr. Diehl, the owner, couldn't really afford to pay me more. He had let the business sort of slip away. Actually, my odd job work has increased his business a little. There is a whole area around Keonah that needs repair work done. Many older people can't do it themselves anymore, widows, or like Elmer, half crippled by arthritis. The hardware stores in Cedar Rapids won't come out to the small town and farm area for that kind of work."

The waitress was hovering by, so we made our selections and gave her the orders. We both ordered walleyed pike after Edie was assured it was brought in fresh daily from Minnesota. The dining room was filling up. I could see the bar man was right, a mature-looking group who could pay these dinner prices were not likely to cause police problems.

We chatted idly about the kinds of businesses in Cedar Rapids, and the exhibits we saw on our campus tour that afternoon. I was feeling more relaxed now. Edie was self-assured enough not to need constant attention; rather, she seemed to enjoy commenting about the people at other tables. She would ask me what I thought of a woman's dress, whether her hairstyle went with her face, what I thought she saw in her partner, and vice-versa.

"Edie, you are a snoop!", I finally blurted.

"Yes I know," she laughed. "I've always been interested in people, how they dress, how they act, and what I can deduce about their relations with each other. Some, once in a while, suggest they might be worth knowing, but most, I confess, appear too shallow or self-centered for my taste."

"I suppose you were majoring in fashion design or maybe psychology at Bryn Mawr; which was it?", I asked.

"Neither, it was mathematics." I was flabbergasted! "But don't you dare ask me anything about it. My father urged it on me and I didn't want to disappoint him. I became a lot more independent in my views shortly after marriage."

Our dishes arrived and that conversation stopped while we sampled the fish. It was fresh and was served with a piquant mustard and mayonnaise sauce. I would have liked to explore her own piquant comment on marriage, but Edie seemed absorbed in her dinner. We both ate salad last, it was not quite up to the one I had at the Lodge. She looked pleased when I mentioned that. Edie decided against dessert, but we both ordered coffee and I asked for the cherry pie, marked special on the menu. Edie had another cigarette with her coffee, continuing to scan the room while I ate—the pie wasn't bad. The crust had been glazed which is not my favorite way to treat pie dough, but there were plenty of tart cherries.

I noticed that a young foursome had entered and caught Edie's attention. Her eyes followed them to a nearby table. "Do you know them?", I asked.

"That blond girl," she replied, still looking at them, "that could have been me years ago."

The girl was tall, slim, and saucy. Her hair was bobbed, but longer than Edie's. "I don't think so, Edie, you were probably much better looking."

"You're sweet, Emmett," she patted my hand, "but you need much more practice in lying." I thought we were getting along well. Ignoring our fellow diners at last, she returned her thoughts to our table. "Is there a Mrs. Diehl, Emmett?" I shook my head. "Why doesn't he sell the store and go south then? Florida or Arizona would be good for his arthritis. Better than being found dead in the store someday." I said he probably couldn't get much, just what the building and land would bring. I doubted that the business itself, you know the name, established customer base, etc., the so-called 'good will' would be of any value.

"But you could change that if you wanted to. Maybe within a year, promoting you know 'old fashion service and quality' as the ads would say, might raise the value for him, if not to retire, then to take you in as a partner. You could do that for him. I know you're smart and healthy enough to be successful at it. What do you think?" I mulled it over for a bit. Frankly, I wasn't too enthusiastic about it. Elmer might resent my trying to run his business for him, and even if he suddenly became very generous, which I doubted, and offered me a partnership, was that something I wanted?

"Think about it, Emmett. Oh, here's our folk singer." I was glad for the interruption. I owed it to Edie to give her suggestions some more thought, but not tonight. Things have to roll around in my head awhile before they get acted on."

Billed as Merle Jonathon, the singer, with guitar, came in through the lobby, stopped by the table of the young foursome, chatted a moment, then moved to the stage area of the room. Introducing himself briefly, his first piece was the well-known 'E-R-I-E Canal' followed by 'Spanish

Is The Lovin' Tongue'. I caught Edie glancing, wistfully I thought, at the young blond girl. Was she reminiscing of her own youth, or was the girl someone she thought she knew? A friend of her daughter, or perhaps a daughter of one of her younger bridge club members? Edie seemed too satisfied with life, as I knew it from the little she confided to me, to be nostalgic about the past. After several more songs, our entertainer invited the audience to sing along with his next number: 'Foggy, Foggy Dew'. I knew some of the verses, but not enough to join in, but Edie did. Not only did she know the words (I could tell because she didn't hesitate at any point), but her voice was clear and mellow. Now in the lower range, probably what is called a mezzo soprano, though I'm not well-versed about musical terms. The foursome also were singing, and a few other diners; some with hesitation over the later verses. I did join in on the next one: 'On Top Of Old Smoky', forgetting only a few words. Edie looked at me, amused, I suspect, at my voice, somewhere between a rumble and a cackle.

Jonathon's next number, he announced, would be a duet, if some lady would join him. He must have noticed Edie's singing, because after no one volunteered, he looked at her and asked her to do it. Edie protested that she might not know the song, but he said he had the words written out for the partner and that the melody was simple. I was surprised when she agreed to do it and joined him at the microphone. He strummed a few bars to acquaint her with the tune, and then they began, slightly apart in timing on the first few words of 'The Big Rock Candy Mountain', but harmonizing well after that. We all applauded; actually, they went well together. Edie was not a bit shy or nervous, and seemed to really enjoy what must have been a rare public performance. Jonathon also seemed pleased with her performance, asking if she had a favorite. She looked at me, started to laugh, then whispered something to her partner. Jonathan nodded and then started strumming the simple chords of 'Go Tell Aunt Rhoddy, The Old Grey Goose Is Dead'. That performance was still another unexpected side of Edie revealed, as she broadly pantomimed the crying goslings and gander. Edie bowed to the audience, then to Jonathon, and returned to our table. "That was the closest I could get to Grandfather Rodde. Did you like it?" She was clearly enjoying the applause.

"Is there anything you can't do, Edie?" I was enjoying her performance too.

"Some things, Emmett, I didn't do well once, but look, it's after 10, do you think we should leave—while I'm ahead?"

I signaled for the bill. Edie decided to go to the powder room. I noticed that the young blond girl had left her table also. I waited for my date in the lobby. The girl came out of the powder room first, Edie was behind her. When we got in the car I asked her if she knew the girl, but she said "No, she just reminded me of how I was at that age, at least I thought so." Her voice seemed subdued, countering my earlier impression that Edie wasn't subject to rapid mood changes.

The drive back to the motel took only a few minutes. We were both silent. She seemed to be wrapped up in her thoughts and I was regretting that we would be saying goodbye. I parked but didn't move to get out. We sat silently for a few more minutes. Finally she said "I think you find me interesting, Emmett."

Was this a question or a statement? I wasn't sure. She seemed so cool and self-contained before, but tonight, she had shown a different side of herself. Assertive at the antique store, gleefully hamming up a song before an audience, and then nostalgic over, I suppose, some old memory. But I knew what my answer had to be: "Yes I do, you know that," I finally stammered.

"Well then?" she murmured, turning towards me. I kissed her. She was warm and receptive. Years of repression and denial seemed to wash away from me in big waves. We kissed again, longer and more intimate still. My hand thrilled to the silky feel of her dress and the firm body beneath it as I clasped her waist. "Has it been a long time for you?" she murmured. I could only nod.

"Emmett", she whispered, finally pulling back from me, "don't ever buy another car with the shift lever on the floor. That contraption is going to snag my pantyhose and I won't be able to get another pair before my flight."

My whole being, freed at last of the denial my sorrow had imposed on it, ached for her. I reached out for her again. "I've always hated pantyhose, they feel coarse and they look coarse."

"I suppose so, but they are more comfortable than stockings when I travel. No garters needed, you know." Then whispering in my ear, "but why don't you take them off, then we can both be satisfied?"

I woke to a dim morning light and groped for my watch on the nightstand. "It's early yet, Emmett." Edie was already awake. I started to lay back on the pillow, but she drew me towards her.

I woke again with a start. Bright daylight streamed through the blinds. It was after 10 and Edie was gone Probably in Chicago already, I thought. I saw a note on the dresser:

> 'Dear Emmett- I don't like long goodbyes at airports, so I didn't wake you. Leave the key in the door. I've arranged things with the maid so there will be no problem, but you must leave before noon. This was a wonderful weekend for me, Emmett, I hope it was for you also. Please let me know what you decide about Diehl's---Edie'

Chapter VII
A Deal With Snyder

Mrs. Fashlich's disapproving look greeted me on my return. "Well, Mr. Borden, I was about to call the police and report you missing. I guess it was foolish to worry you'd been hit on the head and robbed by those Indiana people. Mobsters were they?"

"What an imagination ma'am"—I was about to explain when I remembered Edie's caution about being associated with the event at the antique shop. "But you've hit it right, Mrs. Fashlich. They tracked me down and I knew I had to meet them and pay up or they'd kill me." What a lie, and, I thought, said with a straight face too.

But Mrs. Fashlich looked skeptical. "Well, what was that spittoon inspection about? I never heard of such a thing?"

I had to scramble for that one. "It's a mob expression for a guy who doesn't pay up. You know, they mean he's someone they're going to spit on. Look Mrs. Fashlich, you've got to keep all this just between us. It's dangerous. The mob doesn't like being talked about."

"Humph! Mr. Borden, I could maybe believed such a thing when you first came here, but now I just don't believe you could have anything to do with gangsters or even that you'd fail to pay a debt, gambling or otherwise. But I spec that where a man goes at night and what he's doing is none of a good woman's business, I'm sure. I'm just glad you weren't in danger."

I went upstairs to my room and lay down on the bed, relieved. The events of Saturday were occupying all of my thoughts, reliving each moment. I knew I must write her a note, but what was I to say? 'Thank you for a wonderful evening'? 'Making love was—' what? Edie would probably consider it boorish of me to mention that. It was strange, I thought, that I felt no sense of betrayal to Francis. No, I had made love but I wasn't in love, surely. Fascinated by Edie? True, she was a definite personality, impossible for one, at least me, to ignore. I sensed a faint hint of her scent still on my sleeve. Perhaps Mrs. Fashlich had noticed it too, and stopped her inquiry about what I had been doing. No, it would take more than a Saturday night for me to be in love again, if ever I could be, but Edie was a woman that was a pleasure to be with. I guess a friend, at least for now. I felt satisfied with resolving it that way, but I also decided not to shower. I would enjoy her presence a little while longer.

That evening, after treating myself to a steak dinner at the diner, I stopped at the drugstore for a box of good stationary, picking carefully over their rather meager stock for something that seemed appropriate for a reserved man. I saw no reason why I shouldn't address her as 'Dear Edie' now. In fact, I felt good about doing so. It was both satisfying and relaxing to be sharing good feelings with someone again. I wrote that I was sorry I missed saying goodbye, but that I hoped I would see her again, and that Rodde's foot was undoubtedly happy to be reunited with its mate. The idea suddenly occurred to me to write a parody of 'Go Tell Aunt Rhody'. I wrote that she could use it in case she decided to join Jonathon for another duet. After some false starts, I concocted this bit of doggerel, not very good, but it amused me, and I hoped it would amuse her too.

> Go tell ole Rodde
> "   "   "   "
> "   "   "   "
>
> We found the el'phant's foot
> The one that was stolen,
> "   "   "   "   "
> "   "   "   "   "
>
> From its Elkton nook.
> Twas hid in a junk shop
> "   "   "   "   "   "
> "   "   "   "   "   "
>
> A sittin on the floor.
> No more a cryin
> "   "   " sighin
> "   "   " pinen
> for 'tis home forever more.
> Go tell ole Rodde

"   "   "   "

"   "   "   "

peace is back once more.

Not quite the original rhyme scheme, but good enough, I thought. I signed the note 'Emmett', addressed it formally to "Mrs. Adamson", discreet enough, and mailed it on my way to Diehl's next morning.

The next month was uneventful. No problems surfaced from the antique shop, which was a relief, though I hadn't seen the owner. I repaired some removable screens for a woman operating a small grocery store in Shopesville. They had been dropped off earlier in the week, and I promised her to repair and deliver them by the following Saturday. Shopesville was just one of many small towns, villages really, in the Midwest. I had never been there, but her directions were clear and I had no trouble finding the store. Fifteen minutes later the job was done and the bill paid. She was grateful for the service; no one else would have driven down to install the screens, and the price was very reasonable. Of course, we could do that because I didn't have to live on what Elmer could afford to pay me, it was just pin money to me, but it was a principle with me to be paid for any work that brought in money for someone else. Actually the work was more important than the pay. It gave me the goad I needed to be active again until I could settle on what I really wanted to do, though I confessed I hadn't been giving that much thought lately.

A little cafe was just down the block, so I decided to stop in and get a cup of coffee. It was still only mid-morning and there was only one other man sitting at the counter. Young, and with a tan that wasn't acquired in Iowa at this time of year. I couldn't help but overhear his conversation with the young waitress, who evidently knew him. The gist of it was that he was going to sell his dad's machine shop and was preparing an inventory for the sale, but was undecided on whether he should hold an auction or advertise and sell it directly. I was mildly interested in seeing what tools he had, maybe there might be something we could use for Diehl's repair shop business. I didn't want to butt in on his talk with the waitress, but after he left I asked her where this machine shop was. Two blocks east on the street in front of the cafe, Main Street, and left on Pine for one block would bring me to Snyder's Machine Shop. She also volunteered that the young man was Carl Snyder's son, up from Texas for his father's funeral, and staying on to close up his estate. I had a second cup of coffee while she rattled on about young Tom Snyder, who had been a school classmate of hers.

Leaving the cafe, I walked to Snyder's and found Tom inside the wooden garage-like shop. Telling him I had overheard his conversation at the cafe, I thought he wouldn't mind if I looked over the tools to see if there was anything I might be able to use. It was a mixed bag of relatively new machines and some old ones, but all seemed well cared for. Lots of hand tools as well as a good metal cutting lathe, a milling machine, two drill presses, a grinder, spot and acetylene welders, a small and a medium sized sheet metal brake, a power hacksaw, and a large bandsaw. Far more than we could use at Diehl's, but a reckless impulse seized me to buy the whole lot and sell it myself. I would need someplace to store the tools, maybe the shed back of Diehl's would do, or Mrs. Fashlich's garage, which was pretty empty now that she had given up driving and sold her car. Also I would need some help in moving the stuff to Keonah.

Snyder asked if I was interested in anything, as he had finished the inventory and wanted to lockup. He was surprised when I told him I might be interested in the whole lot, if we could agree on a price. He asked for $7500, but I reminded him that if he went to auction he would have to advertise pretty widely, as well as pay a hefty percent to the auctioneer, and with no guarantee that he could sell most of it. I also counted on his wanting to get back to Texas as soon as possible, so I added that he would certainly have to wait a week after posting notice of the sale before the auction could start. We finally agreed on $4000 and that he would help me move the tools to Keonah.

Snyder would want to go to Keonah anyway to cash my check. The bank would be open until 2:00 on Saturday, so I suggested he call them and verify the check was good. Before we settled though, I also called Diehl about using the shed and his pickup truck. Elmer didn't sound too pleased with the idea, I suspected because he thought I'd spend all of my time selling the tools and the repair business, while still small, was a profitable sideline, and would suffer. However, I won him over by promising a split on any profits if he helped. I suppose if you analyzed it, you would say I probably felt I owed Elmer something for sending me to the antique shop which brought Edie and me together for a delightful Saturday. I didn't think of it that way though. Anyway, I made sure I got a copy of the inventory from Snyder before I left. I promised to be back next morning to start clearing out the shop.

Fortunately, Elmer's shed was in pretty good shape. The roof didn't leak and the floor and doors were sound. My luck was even better than I expected because it had 220 volt electric service, power I would need to demonstrate the mill and lathe. A few hours work that afternoon cleared out a space for the bigger items; the hand tools could probably be kept in the store itself.

As it turned out, Elmer had known Tom's father and, in fact, had sold him some of the hand tools that were now coming back. The next day, Sunday, we drove his old pickup truck down to Shopesville and Tom and I started loading the smaller tools of my big buy. We made four trips in all that day, moving everything but the lathe and mill. I wouldn't let Elmer do any of the heavy lifting because of his back, so Tom rode back with us on each trip to help me unload. For some items, like the big drill press and the bigger sheet metal brake, which were too heavy for the two of us to lift onto the truck, we partially disassembled them. It was a long day for all of us, and returning to Shopesville after out last load, mainly to bring Tom back, I picked up some coffee and donuts at the cafe. We drank it at the shop so we could consider how we were going to move the mill and lathe. Tom got the operating manuals from the file box (which I would take back to Keonah) to check the weights. The mill was 2400 lbs and the lathe was 800. Definitely not a 2-man job to move. Old man Snyder had casters on some of the tools—the power hacksaw, the welding units and bandsaw—so that he could position them in the limited space of his shop as the work required. That helped us considerably in moving, and I wanted the mill and lathe on casters also so they could be moved more easily for display and inspection by prospective buyers.

Elmer said he had about a dozen heavy duty casters in stock. "Had 'em for years, but can't remember why I stocked them, there's no call for such hardware now, anywise not in Keonah. Probably won't be able to bolt them onto the base of the mill or lathe. The mill has feet for stem type casters, mine has four holes for bolt or screw mounting. As for the lathe, there's no place to attach casters." After mulling over the situation a bit further, and another bite on his second donut, he suggested I cobble up dollies for both machines from 2X4's, attach the casters to the dollies, and lift the machines onto the dollies.

"That's fine Elmer, real fine thinking," I replied a bit testily, because I was really tired. "But how are we going to get these elephants onto the dollies, and furthermore, how are we going to get them up the 4' onto the bed of your truck and back down again?"

"Now Emmett, don't get all het up. I ain't finished yet. Maybe we can lever one end of the mill up on the dolly, block the casters from rolling, and then lever the other end up and slide the danged thing until it sits square on the dolly. Maybe if we oil the top of the dolly it'll slide along pretty easy like."

"Now son, that's the second step solved", he continued. "You make a long ramp from 2X4's and we use that come-along we took back to Keonah on that last load to help haul it onto the truck. The two of you should be able to do it if you make the ramp long enough. Better double up on the 2X4's for the ramp if it's a long one." Elmer looked pleased with himself, but I could see Tom was a little leery about the two of us winching 2400 pounds up the ramp, much less holding it back so it could be rolled back down safely when we unloaded it. The problem reminded me of an article I read long ago by some archeologists discussing how the Egyptians built the pyramids.

"I think it's too risky Mr. Diehl, the two of us aren't going to be able to control it, and if it tips over it'll probably be ruined." Tom stopped for a moment, then suddenly got up, announced he'd be back in a few minutes and left the shop.

I decided to take measurements of the mill and lathe bases that I would need to build the dollies. In about 20 minutes Tom returned.

"I think I've solved all the problems. I was trying to remember how Dad got these things into the shop in the first place. Of course they were delivered by a truck fitted out for this purpose, but we can get the same effect right here. My friend, Bud Eisner, at the Phillip's 66 gas station and garage will bring his wrecker over when we're ready with the dollies. We make a sling from two pieces of heavy chain, slide them under the mill base, between the feet, then connect the ends to the hook on the wrecker's hoist. Bud will power up the hoist and lift the mill onto the dolly. Then we can reposition the chains to go under the dolly and hoist again to get it onto the truck bed. We'll probably need some guide ropes around the mill head so Emmett and I can steady the thing during the lift, and Mr. Diehl can back the truck up under it."

"That sounds pretty good to me," Elmer admitted. "I should have thought of it myself. Now for getting it off the truck when we get to Keonah, we can get a couple of guys from the lumberyard to help on the come-along. Four of you ought to be able to handle it."

So that seemed to solve the problem. I told Tom I'd probably be back with the dollies and ramp by Tuesday morning. Elmer would have to stay at the hardware store, but I thought Eisner could back his wrecker, which would do just as well as backing up the truck. Monday I built the dollies and ramp. Fortunately there was no pressing repair work to do, but even so, I didn't finish until nearly 8 o'clock.

Tuesday morning I was back in Shopesville. Tom and Bud Eisner were waiting for me, and after about 2 hours work we had both the mill and the lathe safely on the truck. I gave Bud $50 for the use of his wrecker, which seemed fair to me and started off for Keonah, Tom following in his car. I took it slow to avoid bouncing the load around. We had tied both machines down so they wouldn't roll around, since they were on casters, but better safe than sorry.

I hadn't seen Elmer that morning as I had taken the truck and dollies to Mrs. Fashlich's Monday night so I could get an early start. Elmer came out to the shed as I backed up to the door. "Emmett, we're going to make the unloading very easy." He was grinning and clearly pleased with himself. I could sense he was actually enjoying working on this whole engineering problem. Maybe it was a practical challenge he had missed out on for years, as he let his lumbago constrict himself to shuffling about behind the register.

"I was talking to Sam Voss last night," Sam was one of Elmer's Monday night pinochle group; he owned the lumberyard a few blocks down from the hardware store. "He offered to loan us his forklift to unload the truck. So we won't have any problem with ramps and come-alongs. I'll just give him a call and he'll be up in a few minutes." Both Tom and I were relieved at this easy solution. I had been worried all night about safely unloading the truck. Tom and I untied the ropes holding the mill and lathe steady on the truck bed, and in about 15 minutes one of Sam's men rode up on the forklift. It was an easy job. The lift moved the machines right into the shed with no sweat, and it occurred to me that Sam's forklift might be borrowed again—at a small fee—if we had to load either of the machines again for a buyer.

With such a happy ending I offered to treat Tom and Elmer to the Tuesday lunch special at the Keonah diner—fried chicken with milk gravy.

Elmer and Tom did most of the talking, reminiscing about Tom's dad and the decline in opportunities for the small shop owner in small farm towns. Later, Elmer asked me how I expected to sell the big items in Keonah when old Mr. Snyder couldn't make much of a living doing machine shop work these past few years.

I hadn't really thought that out. I had jumped into this deal impulsively. Not characteristic of me to do things that way. Was I subconsciously forcing myself into unfamiliar situations just to see what happens? If so, it certainly didn't start at Snyder's shop. I could see that the change had already happened when I left New York, not quite knowing what I would do. By simply taking events as they occurred: the stop at the Lodge, Edie's invitation, the repair job at Diehl's, and the elephant's foot affair, I had been pushed further along that way, a drifter. Maybe my brain, numbed by Francis' death, was finally crying for problems to be worked on again, a purpose for getting up each day. Very small accomplishments certainly, not in the same class as my work as an engineer, but at least I felt I was living again.

Later that night I thought about it some more. Clearly I would have to advertise. That would mean ads in Cedar Rapids, Davenport, and the twin cities of Rock Island and Moline, across the river in Illinois. Thinking back on my college days, I realized a visit to the mechanical engineering department at the University might also prove worthwhile. The next morning Elmer and I skimmed through some of the more recent machine tool catalogs I had picked up at Snyder's. From them we could set tentative prices and get what key specifications were needed for the ads.

By the end of the following week we had gotten several phone inquiries from some of the small manufacturing plants and machine shops in both Cedar Rapids and Moline. We sold the band saw and lathe to a plant in Moline.

Happily they had the foresight to arrive with a flat bed truck equipped with a large hoist so we had no trouble loading both items. We kept the dolly. They didn't need it, and it might come in handy later as it was about 6 feet long. Big enough for moving a lot of things. The acetylene welding unit and some hand tools went to a shop in Cedar Rapids. I could see these sales were perking up Elmer's interest. A little early success always helps, me, as well as Elmer.

I decided to follow up on my thoughts about the University. The school year would end in a few weeks and I should make my contact right away if I expected to make my pitch before the engineering administrators left for the summer break. Elmer agreed to spare me for a day—it was after all 'store business', so I soon found myself in the mechanical engineering office at the University. Unfortunately, the head of the machine shop wasn't interested, but suggested the art department might be. At first I thought he was spoofing me, but seeing my incredulous look, he explained that they were getting interested in metal sculpture, not casting bronze figurines, but pieces fabricated from sheet metal, bars, rods, whatever. He suggested I see a Mr. Ridetti, who had talked to him earlier about whether they could share in using his machine shop equipment for sculpture work, but the size of some of the pieces they might be working on would take up too much space in the shop, especially when the work might take weeks to complete.

I wasn't sure what kind of equipment the art department could be interested in; art was not my field. I'm not a cretin, I do visit a gallery now and then, and Francis and I did have reproductions, mostly impressionists, but I never considered the mechanics of how you do painting or sculpture work.

I was surprised to see the young blond girl that Edie was interested in at the supper club manning the reception desk at the art department office. She told me Mr. Ridetti was teaching at the moment, but would be free at 3 o'clock. I decided to wait there for him, and picked up a course catalog to read, hoping I might find other departments that could use some power tools. After a few minutes, I became aware that the girl was studying me. I put the catalog down and smiled at her. "Do you recognize me?" I asked.

"I think I've seen you before, Mr. Borden, but I'm not sure where."

"A month or so ago at the supper club in Cedar Rapids," I prompted. "You were with Mr. Jonathon."

"Oh yes" she exclaimed, "and you were with that woman that Jonathon coaxed up to the stage for a duet. Now I remember. She was pretty good. Professional I suppose."

"Not to my knowledge," I replied. "Actually, she manages a hotel in Indiana, and her performance was certainly impromptu and a surprise to me." She said nothing further so I returned to browsing through the catalog.

Ridetti arrived a little after 3 and the girl told him I was waiting to see him. I explained that the engineering machine shop manager suggested that his department might be interested in several machine tools for their metal sculpture courses. I had taken the precaution of making some Polaroid shots of the major tools before coming, and showed them to Ridetti. He was interested, thank goodness, and we discussed prices and when he could inspect the machines. I gave him directions to Diehl's, and we agreed to meet there Sunday morning.

Making my way back to the reception room from Ridetti's office, the blond girl called to me, "Mr. Borden, I wonder if you could tell me a little more about your friend? Well, actually, I don't mean that. What I mean is do you think the hotel might be interested in summer help?"

"I really don't know," I replied, "what kind of work were you thinking of? Are you a student here?"

"Anything, actually. I'm a music major, but I need part-time and summer work to help pay my school costs. The school year is ending in a few weeks, and my work here will end then too. Unfortunately, I haven't found a summer job yet and I'd like to get one lined-up as soon as possible. I've worked at summer resorts—waitressing mostly—but competition for those positions has been pretty heavy this year, and I was a little late in getting my applications in." She searched through the desk drawer and handed me a resume'. Her name was Kitty Adair. I handed the resume' back and suggested she send it to Edie and gave her the address of the Lodge.

Driving back to Keonah, I couldn't help thinking about the unexpected coincidences that happened to me since my chance stop at the Lodge. Were I at all mystical minded, I could well feel some invisible hand was pushing me toward some important future event. But I'm not mystical, just an old engineer, not so superstitious as to believe that chance encounters are anything but chance encounters. If they turn out to be important, its because of what you make of them. I did decide to write to Edie though, and alert her that the application for Kitty Adair she was about to receive would be from the saucy blond that reminded her of her youth. Perhaps that would do them both a favor.

Ridetti did show up on Sunday, and after trying out some of the tools, settled on a bending brake, the power hacksaw, and the arc welder. I promised to deliver the items to his studio at the University as soon as he called that the bursar had prepared the check for me.

The next few days were busy ones. Several calls came in—responses to my ads—wanting to arrange for inspection visits. I had written to Edie about Miss Adair, and she wrote back that she was interested, but I thought I detected a curiosity about my relations with the girl. I decided not to refer to Miss Adair again in my letters. Edie was complex enough to resent my reading between the lines, truly or not. Thinking about this made me want to see her again. Couldn't I just drive up to the Lodge some weekend, or would I need some other excuse? Ordinarily, just telling her I'd like to see her again should be reason enough, and welcomed, but Edie was not ordinary and I really knew almost nothing about her private life. She could well resent my uninvited intrusion, perhaps embarrassing her relations with employees of the Lodge. Even, perhaps, with another male friend in Elkton. It suddenly hit me that she needn't have been a hermit from life, as I had been after Francis died. For all I knew, our brief affair may have been only a lark for her, a safe adventure away from home. No, I decided, I would need some other excuse for seeing her again. The excuse came several weeks later. But first I need to conclude the Kitty Adair story, since it would have future consequences on Edie and the Lodge.

Ridetti phoned me the following Wednesday that the bursar had approved the purchase, and the check was waiting for me. Elmer and I loaded his truck with the welder, brake and saw—with help from a couple of high school boys lounging in the diner at only $5 apiece—and I drove down to the University.

Ridetti was waiting for me, also with a couple of hefty students, and it was a quick job to get the truck unloaded, and the machines set up in the studio area set aside for metal sculpture. On our way back to his office, I expressed my appreciation for his commandeering some of the football squad to help us unload. At first he looked surprised, then offended, and finally, seeing my honest face, laughed hilariously. "Borden, you've been out of touch. Those boys are students in my sculpture course! There's nothing wimpy about metal sculpture, let me tell you!"

Another blow to my engineering ego, but he gave me the check and we parted on friendly terms. I decided to stop by the reception desk in case Miss Adair was there. She was.

"Did you hear from Mrs. Adamson at the Elkton Lodge?", I asked.

"Oh, ah, Mr. Borden", she stammered. "I didn't write. I guess I didn't think they would really be interested."

That exasperated me. Had I risked Edie's suspicion for nothing? "For god's sake girl, I wrote to her to expect a letter from you. She said she might be interested. She remembered seeing you from my description. I wouldn't have bothered her if I had known you weren't serious." My irritated tone clearly flustered her.

"Oh, I'm so sorry, Mr. Borden. I just didn't think you would have taken the trouble to mention me, few people really do that kind of a favor. If she remembered who I am, I'll write at once. I really am sorry to have caused you any trouble." I nodded and left.

What is it with young people, I asked myself? They ask for help, and then ignore what you do for them. I'm not happy getting old and grey, but I certainly wouldn't want to be young again if I had to be like that! But by the time I got back to the truck, I had cooled off. Maybe, I thought, she had just gotten disheartened by too many 'No thank you, we're all filled up'! Miss Kitty apparently wasn't as saucy as my first impression of her. More mayonnaise than mustard, I muttered. Perhaps, though, my irritation was more likely because of having caused Edie to have any suspicion there was anything going on between me and that girl. At least I read such suspicion in her letter. I must somehow find a subtle way to assure her there was nothing there.

Chapter VIII
The Rockford Opportunity

Bit by bit, Elmer and I were selling off old Mr. Snyder's tools and machinery. We kept a separate book on the sales and expenses so we could compute the net and each one's share. I'm sure Elmer could see that we had more than recouped the initial cost and advertising expense already, so anticipating the profit, I suggested to Elmer that he might want to use some of it to expand the service side of the business. The easiest and cheapest thing to do would be getting a grinder and a stock of blanks for duplicating keys. Later, maybe, he could consider a sharpening service. Knives and scissors at first, then maybe adding saws, axes, and hedge shears. These are obvious steps to take, and he should have started long ago. Somehow he had lost initiative, even interest, in maintaining his business, but now he seemed more energetic and receptive to my suggestions. Still, I could sense an occasional concern about the future. It was not clear to me why he might be worrying, until I took a call from a small manufacturing plant in Rockford, Illinois. They had heard about our ad and were interested in the milling machine. I couldn't expect them to buy it sight unseen, it was our most expensive item, and photos would hardly be satisfactory proof of its real condition, so I wasn't surprised when they asked if a machine shop operator they knew in Cedar Rapids could stop by and inspect it. If his report was satisfactory, they would call back and we could arrange for delivery. Later that afternoon, a Mr. Farnsworth called, identifying himself as the man Rockford Stamp and Die Works wanted to examine the mill. I agreed to have the machine set up for a test operation that Sunday, and gave him directions to Diehl's.

Farnsworth arrived early Sunday, just as I got there with a pot of coffee and donuts from the diner. He spent an hour looking the machine over, taking measurements between sips of coffee and a munch on the donut. He was a dunker. Something I hadn't seen for years, and never understood why people would like a mouthful of soggy dough. I just sat and watched, drinking my own coffee, as he tested for backlash in the gearing, spindle play, and squinted all around for rust spots. Finally he clamped a piece of steel he had brought with him, I presume of the grade Rockford would be using, sorted through the box of end mills that came with the machine, selected one, chucked it up, and made a few trial cuts, measured the slots with a precision caliper, moved the carriage back and forth a few times, cut some more slots and measured again. Thanking me for the coffee, he packed up his steel sample and instruments and said he'd report directly to Rockford. Not a word on what his conclusion was. I cleaned up the steel chips, locked up the shed, and decided to take in a movie in Iowa City.

Late Tuesday afternoon Fred Aubitz, the Rockford production manager, called. They had gotten Farnsworth's report and were ready to negotiate for the milling machine. I was asking $5000, but Aubitz offered $4500 claiming the shipping costs would make it too expensive for them. We dickered for a few minutes when I suddenly realized here was an excuse for seeing Edie. I told Aubitz if they would pay for the trailer rental I would haul it to them for free. We finally agreed on $4800, they pay the trailer rental. He wanted Farnsworth to come back and make sure the machine was safely loaded and secured on the trailer so there would be no damage. He was to call me back on when he could arrange for Farnsworth to come, and meanwhile I could check on availability of the trailer. Elmer thought I should take the truck instead, but I couldn't see driving to meet Edie in an old truck, so I insisted on towing a trailer with my own car. That meant renting a trailer hitch also, but what was money when seeing Edie again was concerned.

By the time Aubitz called back, I had checked on the availability of a flat bed trailer and hitch, and was assured it could be rented for one-way use to Rockford. I gave Aubitz the rental charge, which was acceptable, and he told me Farnsworth would come down Friday morning. That would give me time to get Voss's forklift, hoist the iron elephant onto the trailer, and still be ready for an early start to Rockford.

There wasn't quite enough time to write Edie, so I sent her a wire asking if I could stop at the Lodge late Friday. I told Elmer I wanted to take Saturday and Monday off to look around the Chicago area. I needed Monday to drive back to Keonah. He agreed but seemed apprehensive about it. It then dawned on me that maybe he thought I was looking for a new job, so I tried to reassure him by saying I planned to visit with some old friends that had recently moved to Chicago.

Mrs. Fashlich had a message for me when I got back to my room after a diner dinner. Someone had called and left a phone number for me to call back after 10 o'clock that evening. From the area code and exchange I recognized it had to be from the Lodge. I waited impatiently for 10 o'clock. After half an hour, which seemed like half a day, I decided to invest my time a bit more profitably by considering what further action I could take to sell off the remaining Snyder tools.

I waited nervously until a quarter after 10 to compensate for any difference in clocks when it suddenly dawned on me that Elkton was on eastern time, an hour later. I hurriedly ran to the phone and dialed long distance.

"I'd just about given you up for tonight, Emmett." I apologized, mumbling something about forgetting the time zone difference, and asked if I could stop by for the weekend after making my delivery. My heart fell when she said she'd rather I didn't. "Not a good idea Emmett," she said, but then added "Why don't I meet you in Chicago, Saturday? We'll be much freer away from the interruptions from the Lodge, and perhaps we can take in a show. I haven't had a free weekend since we last met. Can we do that Emmett?"

With relief, I assured her that would be fine, but how will we meet? Should I pick her up at the airport, or what? She surprised me by saying she was going to drive in, and that we should meet at the Chicago Carillon hotel, probably around 11 A.M. Saturday. She told me to remember the phone number, it was a direct line to her suite, in case any problems came up.

Afterwards I thought that meeting away from the Lodge really was a better idea for both of us. I was sure Edie wanted to avoid any gossip about an affair in such a public place as the Lodge, and further, there was more we could do in Chicago than just sharing a bed—however wonderful that would be again. Tomorrow would be a busy day, not only reserving the trailer and hitch for Thursday afternoon and arranging with Voss for use of the forklift, but also checking on where the hotel was and making reservations.

Shortly after 5:00 Thursday Farnsworth called, telling me he hoped we hadn't moved the milling machine yet. Oh, oh I thought, the deal had fallen through. I was becoming very anxious when an opportunity to see

Edie was involved, but he was only concerned that he supervise the loading to assure Aubitz that no damage had occurred. He seemed nervous about it, so I told him about the availability of the forklift and that we were awaiting his presence before starting, but I hoped he would come before 9 A.M. since I was going to drive to Rockford very slowly.

Farnsworth arrived at 8:30 the next morning, just as Voss whirred up with the forklift. I scurried off to the diner for a jug of coffee and donuts again This time I got some jelly ones just to see what Farnsworth would do with them. It was a disappointment. He ate 3 without dunking a single one, and expressed pleasure in my having discerned he preferred the jelly kind. I had discerned no such thing, but it put him in a more affable frame of mind. So we had no trouble loading the trailer. Voss worked the forklift. The trailer groaned a bit, but Farnsworth just munched away, nodding approval as we completed the loading. I had gotten several mover's blankets from U-Haul when I picked up the trailer, and a cheap plastic drop cloth from the store to wrap the machine so it would be protected against rain or any wind blown debris or stones kicked up by traffic during the trip. But Farnsworth insisted first on personally blocking the pallet casters and roping the machine and pallet securely to the trailer. He clearly knew what he was doing, and I could see that unless I wrecked the trailer, the machine would arrive in Rockford in perfect working order.

I got underway by 10 A.M. My car had no trouble pulling the trailer, and the weather was cool enough so there was no concern about its overheating. I took US 30 to Rock Falls, then 2 to Rockford, about 150 miles, not too much traffic and only 4½ hours.

I found the factory with no trouble. Aubitz was waiting for me. We got the mill unloaded by rolling it off the trailer via my ramp, which I had the foresight to bring along, so I hadn't wasted my time building it. Aubitz had two huskies to help hold back on the ropes, and the monster rolled off slow and easy. Aubitz asked me if I wanted the pallet, which I did, since I had borrowed the casters from Elmer's stock. He asked me if I could wait until about 4 o'clock, his shop foreman would have the machine positioned in the desired location and we could leverage the pallet free. I was anxious to get going since Chicago was still 100 miles away. Seeing my concern, Aubitz suggested I drop off the trailer and then come back. The U-Haul office was not too far away, so I agreed and left. I got back at 4:30. Aubitz had an older man busy checking over the mill, which was still on the pallet. Protesting that it should be O.K. because his representative, Farnsworth, had supervised the loading and securing, I was a little annoyed.

"Just checking," the man muttered, giving me a sour look, "that my son did his job right."

"Ah, I wondered why you had picked up a man in Cedar Rapids for the checkout," I exclaimed. "And I suppose he's the one that let you know about it, 'cause I hadn't advertised in Rockford papers."

"Young Farnsworth did his apprenticeship here, under his dad. A couple of years later he decided to set up his own shop in Cedar Rapids—his wife wanted to be closer to her parents," Aubitz explained. It seemed to me, however, that young Farnsworth probably wanted to escape his dad's supervision even more than his wife wanted to be near home. I was getting itchy to get away, but old (he worked slow enough for me to think he was old) Farnsworth was still taking his time, checking this and that, looking in the gearbox and measuring squareness and parallelism. I walked to the front of the shop where I had seen a vending machine and bought some coffee. Aubitz joined me. I asked him about the best rout to Chicago and the Carillon Hotel on Michigan Boulevrd. He suggested Interstate 90 east, then 290 south just before Des Plaines. But also advised me to wait awhile because the commuter traffic in all the cities around metropolitan Chicago would be pretty heavy until 7:00. Finally Farnsworth called Aubitz over and I could see them engaged in a short discussion and inspection. My anxiety to get away made me suspect they had uncovered a problem, and that I would be faced with a bigger headache than traffic jams if I had to haul that damn contraption back to Keonah. But it wasn't so. Aubitz said they had decided it would be more convenient for them if they left the mill on the pallet so they could reposition it as needed in the shop. I was immensely relieved that I wouldn't have to tow it back to Diehl's. However, the casters were not mine to give away, so I told Aubitz I would have to charge for the casters as they came from Elmer's stock. Aubitz looked at Farnsworth and Farnsworth allowed as how they were good heavy duty swiveling casters with locking brakes. "$30 apiece," I said, "but I'll throw in the pallet and ramp for free." Farnsworth thought that was too much, and after further muttering between him and Aubitz, they offered $25 apiece. I accepted, feeling that Elmer would still make a profit on them, considering that since he had them in stock for 5 or 6 years, he had paid a lot less for them. Aubitz bought us some more coffee while he wrote out the check for the mill, trailer rental, and casters. By 6:30 I got out onto the Interstate and headed east. By the time I passed Elgin, traffic was beginning to thin out a little, and by 8:30 I had parked at the hotel garage.

CHAPTER IX
CHICAGO WEEKEND 1

I registered as Mr. and Mrs. E. Borden of Keonah, Iowa. Edie hadn't said I should do so, but surely she would expect me to. Again I felt somewhat unsure of myself. Why did I feel that way at my age? My relation with co-workers, men and women, over more than 20 years seemed to me to show reasonable self-confidence. I was never timid or unsure with Francis during all of our marriage. Why am I different with Edie? Mulling it over while unpacking, I realized again that I knew very little about her. While she seemed to have said much when we first met and toured Rodde's titillating collection of cultural obscenities, and when we walked along the campus at Iowa City, and later, talked at the supper club, I couldn't help but feel these glimpses she offered of herself were not all of a consistent whole. Perhaps there had been too much of an early sexual ambience to our meeting to give me enough distance to see her true character. Perhaps, also, I was thinking too much like an engineer, expecting her to be as regular and predictable as a machine. Maybe this was so, conditioned as I must have been by Francis' complete dependence on me in those last few years. I was unused to the confident assurance and independence of an Edie. Could I rein in my long denied need enough to let us know each other better?

Keeping that last thought uppermost in my mind, and telling my stomach to wait a little longer for its dinner, I went down to the lobby desk to see what amusement I could find for Edie on Saturday. Looking over a list of theater offerings the clerk handed me, my eye caught a matinee performance by the Chicago Opera of Der Rosencavalier. I asked the clerk if she could check if orchestra seats were still available. I was in luck, she reserved a pair for me. I marveled at myself for such assurance that Edie would arrive in time, and that she would want to see an opera, after my earlier musing on self-confidence.

Remembering that I was caught unprepared for dining in C.R., I got several suggestions from the desk clerk on nightclubs and restaurants, including a strong plug for their own. Planning Sunday seemed to be a problem until I looked at a flier the clerk had given me about the Chicago zoo. Pandas and white tigers were featured. That seemed like a good idea, an afternoon stroll would give me a better chance to learn more about my Elkton friend.

The phone interrupted my Saturday morning shave. It was only a little after 8:00, hardly likely that Edie could have arrived from Elkton unless she started very early, which also seemed most unlikely. But it was Edie.

"Have you had breakfast yet, Emmett? This is Edie" she added unnecessarily. Her voice was distinctive, low in pitch, soft, but not particularly feminine, that is, not sweet sounding. I told her I was still shaving and asked where she was calling from. "I'm in the lobby, can you meet me in the coffee shop?" Thinking she had just driven up, I asked if she wanted to freshen-up first. Laughing, she said some people thought she was fresh enough already. I said I'd be right down and we hung up. I finished shaving, dressed quickly, glanced around the room to see that it would be reasonably presentable when we came back, and scooted for the elevator.

She was facing the door, in a booth at the far corner. "Hello Emmett." I bent down and kissed her cheek.

"I didn't expect you until 11:00 or noon, Edie. It must be a 4 hour drive from Elkton and you had the morning rush hour traffic too."

"I drive faster than you Emmett," she laughed.

"Still, you had to get up awfully early," I replied, sitting down opposite her.

"Oh no, I came in last night."

"But then why didn't you come up to the room?" Then I realized I had assumed too much. "I registered as Mr. and Mrs. Borden, Edie, I guess I was too presumptuous."

"Don't be so negative Emmett, I'm going to sleep with you. Why do you think I'm here?" Smiling at me she added "I felt a little discretion was warranted. Registering in my name, at my usual place, would take care of any emergency calls from the Lodge, though that's not likely, we haven't any specials booked for this weekend, fortunately."

The waitress interrupted any further explanation and we ordered. Edie had already gotten her coffee while waiting for me. "But where are you staying? You said your usual place, where's that?"

"It's the Chicago Woman's Club, Emmett, just a few blocks from here. They have only a few rooms, catering mostly to professional woman on business trips to Chicago. I've stayed there many times when I was housekeeper, ordering supplies and later when attending the Midwest Innkeepers Association meetings. Men are not permitted beyond the lobby, so Mrs. Adamson's reputation is never compromised—yet!", she added with another laugh. "My excuse this weekend is shopping for summer clothes and the theater, so I hope you have some legitimate entertainment planned for me." The word 'legitimate' seemed to amuse her.

Her playful mood cheered me up and I no longer felt at loose ends, fretful about our plans and expectations being at cross purposes. Putting on a superior look (at least I thought so) I replied "certainly, I thought a little high culture was appropriate to compensate for your having to travel so far. And now that I know you're well rested, not having driven in this morning, I feel even better about my choice." I stopped, taking several bites of my corned beef hash and poached egg, which had arrived just a moment before.

"Well goodness, what is it?" Edie's breakfast was not as robust as mine: one soft boiled egg and dry toast. Apparently coffee was her most urgent morning need, not food. "Well, Emmett?"

"I have opera tickets for the matinee today. Der Rosencavalier. Do you know it?"

"That's wonderful. I haven't been to an opera in years. The Red Soldier? No, no that's not right, The Gentleman of the Rose—very loosely translated by way of the very little left of my college German. But beyond that, I'm not sure of the story."

"It's by Richard Strauss, Edie, and the music is really wonderful. I think they have staged it well. I saw it, oh maybe 10 years ago at the Met in

New York. It's been a favorite. I brought the program booklet for you so you can get the gist of the story. As for your German, I don't think it will matter how much is left. In opera, I can barely understand the words even if its sung in English. In fact, I confess, for most operas, I feel the music is much better if you don't know every word. The librettos are often really silly and the emotional impact of the music seems to be diluted—at least that's my feeling, but Der Rosy is an appealing story."

We chatted on about operas and music for a little while longer, finally finishing breakfast about 9:30. It was a very pleasant hour, relaxing, even when Edie asked about Francis, what she liked about music, where we went on vacations, her hobbies and interests, and how we met. I no longer felt uptight telling her about my married life, she seemed like an old friend, taking pleasure in my pleasurable memories, thoughtfully avoiding the period of Francis' illness. Had she sensed my desire for more companionship, something to share with her besides a bed? Perhaps so, for after I paid the bill she announced that she wanted to do some shopping before the opera, and would I mind being alone for a while. "Please Emmett, I'd rather you not come with me. Can we meet at the club at 1:30? That should give us enough time to get to the theater."

I acquiesced, not sure why she didn't want me along, but since I hadn't expected to see her until 11:00 or 12:00 I hadn't thought of what we would do earlier. I confess, I didn't want to be alone with her in my room—our room. I might not resist the temptation to be intimate and I was still unsure of her reaction if I didn't, or even if I did, for that matter.

I'm sure she enjoyed the opera. I could see her foot beat time softly during the waltz, and did I see a slight tear when the Marschallin bid farewell to Octavian? Afterwards we stopped for coffee and a sweet roll. "That was a most pleasant afternoon Emmett. I could feel the sweet melancholy of the Marschallin giving up her lover to the young Sophie. Could it be happening to me do you think?"

I was startled at her question. "Do you have a young Octavian?", I blurted.

"Well not exactly a young one," she smiled, "but does he have a Sophie?"

This seemed like a confidence I hadn't wanted from Edie. "I haven't the slightest idea Edie. This is a part of your life I know nothing about. I'm not even sure I want to know about it." She must have sensed my sudden coolness. Reaching across the table, she touched my arm.

"Have I upset you? I'm sorry, I shouldn't have alluded to Kitty, it's just that—".

"Kitty!", I interrupted. "Are you imagining that I'm involved with that snip? Oh Edie, how could you think I would have an affair with someone and then send her to you? Dear Mrs. Adamson, would you please hire this girl I'm screwing for the summer!"

For the first time I saw consternation in her eyes, she blushed, stammering "Forgive me Emmett, it was a catty thing to say, I'm ashamed of myself for being a suspicious old woman."

I was still upset. "Did that girl say anything to you that implied I had a relation with her?" I demanded. "Did she?"

Edie was crying. "Please Emmett. Oh please forgive me. I've been foolish in a way I never thought I'd be foolish in again. No, no, she never implied anything. She only said you suggested she write me. You told me that too. I hadn't meant to let my fears surface like this, blame it on the opera if you must."

As usual, my temper, quick to explode, evaporated away just as quickly. "I've hurt you Edie, it's you who must forgive me. I've looked for an excuse to see you again because I thought you'd resent my just coming to the Lodge. Don't let's spoil this time together. It's probably just a result of not eating lunch. Low blood sugar you know," I added, trying to be reassuring.

"Yes, let's say it's due to that." She wiped her eyes and tried a smile. As we walked out she asked me if we were still having dinner together. I told her I had made a reservation at a club not far from the Carillon for 7:00, and that if she stood me up I'd commit suicide at the Woman's Club by cutting my throat and leaving a note blaming it on the hard-hearted Mrs. Adamson.

"Save your life for me, Emmett, I'll meet you at the hotel, say a quarter to. Let me off at my club to freshen up a bit and get an overnight bag packed." I kissed her on the cheek, hailed a cab for her, said a quarter to was fine, and said I also had wanted to shop, so I'd walk back to the hotel.

CHAPTER X
CHICAGO WEEKEND 2

A cab took us to the Rive Rouge Club. I was glad I had made reservations as there was a crowd waiting to be seated even though 7:00 seemed an early dinner hour for a big city. I checked Edie's light evening wrap. Though it was June, the evening was cool from a gentle lake breeze. Waiting in line for the maitre d' to seat us, Edie told me to go ahead and she would join me at our table after combing her hair and, I suppose, the other innumerable things women find necessary to do in the powder room before they are willing to display themselves in public.

I had ordered Scotch on the rocks for me and, as a guess, remembering our last dinner at C.R., a Dry Sack sherry for Edie. The drinks arrived just a moment before she was shown to our table. Aware that I had glanced at her legs as she approached, she leaned across to me and whispered "No pantyhose tonight, Emmett, silky stockings and very feminine lingerie to add to your pleasure in undressing me—you're blushing, how sweet! Now you make me feel young and deliciously wicked again!"

"Since I always seem to be so obvious, Edie, I'm surprised that I could make you feel deliciously anything."

"It wasn't quite that obvious, just a faint flush around the ears. Except for that unpardonable slip this afternoon, I've schooled myself to be perceptive."

After we had given the drinks a sip, I nodded to the maitre d' who was hovering by. "Are you Edie, madam?", he asked, placing a richly wrapped small box by her plate.

"What's this, shall I unwrap it here?", she asked with surprise and perhaps a little confusion mixed with pleasure in her voice.

"Go ahead, Edie, it won't explode or embarrass you." She unwrapped it carefully. It was a fine orchid corsage I had ordered when I left her that afternoon. "A peace offering, but I shan't pin it on, I'm not good at that." She looked pleased as she fastened it on her left shoulder. By luck the colors went well with her dress, a shimmering blue satin with a full skirt.

"I should be the one making the peace offering, Emmett, but let's let it be past us."

We ordered a second drink, the conversation centering on my current activity as a secondhand machine salesman. She was surprised that I had netted nearly $3000 for my share, but thought I had been a little too generous splitting 50/50 with Elmer. I reminded her that my pension, patent royalties, and investments were adequate for my modest needs, and that taking these small risks was insurance against vegetating again.

Our waitress was hovering nearby so we studied the menu. Edie selected salade nicoise, veal marsala with boiled new potatoes, while I chose mushrooms stuffed with crabmeat, shashlik with lentil and rice pilaf. Edie approved, "You really are more cosmopolitan. Lamb kebabs, I wouldn't have suspected that, or that lentil and rice pilaf would have appealed to you. Perhaps I don't know you as well as I thought—or do I?"

"No," I replied, deciding to amuse her with a story, "it's my Slavic nature coming out."

"Slavic?" She looked surprised. "But I thought your name was Borden. That's certainly not Slavic."

"Actually Edie, it's Bordonovna, Emmettsov Bordonovna. My father was Count Bordonovna. He escaped from the Soviets as a young man in 1921. I Anglicized it after he died."

Edie stared at me for a full minute and then laughed. "Emmett, you really are a terrible liar. Although I don't actually know Russian, I've read enough Russian novels to know that your father's name would have to be Bordonovitch, son of Bordon, not Bordonovna, daughter of Bordon."

She had me for just a moment, but I recovered quickly. "No, he had to make a living on the stage as a female impersonator, so that is why—"

"No, no," she interrupted, convulsing with laughter. "Your face gives you away every time. You're Emmett Borden and you've always been Emmett Borden, the gentle man who, happily, stopped at my Lodge 6 months ago, and is now entertaining me at dinner in this pseudo French Rive Rouge restaurant with that crazy story."

Edie didn't let me try another fib, but started telling me about dining experiences during the occasional trips abroad she made with Rodde. "We were in London, at Simpson's-on-the-Strand. Grandfather ordered fresh oysters as an appetizer. The waiter brought mine, a small slice of smoked salmon on toast points, and an egg cup for Rodde.

You know, the kind that have a large and small bowl joined at their bottoms. The egg cup was on a saucer, large end down, while the small end was filled with cocktail sauce. Granddad waited for him to bring the oysters, expecting them to be on the half shell, as usual in this country, but they didn't come. Rodde began to fume—he had a short temper—and looked around for the waiter. I caught the maitre d's eye, and he came to our table. 'Yes, madam, you wish something?' He was most polite, but very remote. That irritated granddad even more. 'Where's my oysters my man?', waving a fork at his plate. 'What is your kitchen doing, dredging them out of the Channel?' The maitre d', giving him a supercilious look just said 'Your pardon, sir', and lifted up the egg cup letting the half-dozen shelled oysters roll out of the bottom end onto the saucer. Grandfather was crushed."

"I was delighted," she continued. "Rodde's ego, as an experienced world traveler, took a hard knock. He had to admit though that the oysters were excellent. Whenever he got into a snit about something missing at the Lodge, I always asked him if he had looked under the egg cup. It never failed to calm him down.

"We can't get really good oysters in Elkton at a decent price, or I'd serve them that way. It would be another novelty for the Lodge. I'm a bit worried we may need some such novelty."

"Of course, you could offer other oyster novelties," I jested. "Sauted oyster plant maybe, or even Rocky Mountain oysters."

"But that's sweetbreads, Emmett, we have served it on occasion, but it doesn't seem to appeal to most Midwestern palates."

"Who told you they were sweetbreads?" I could hardly keep from laughing at her innocent look.

"Why Rodde had them once, I think, when we took a trip west. He was looking for some Indian crafts to put in the display cases, and invited me to join him. It was in western Nebraska, near Chadron, I think. We had stopped at a diner there. I asked him what he had ordered and he gave me a bite to taste, and that's what he told me they were, cut into chunks and fried with a batter coating. What's the matter?" she asked as I couldn't hold it back anymore, and burst out laughing.

"Oh Edie, Edie, what a delight," I gasped, and whispered in her ear "they're calves testicles!" It was a pleasure to see her startled blush, then she laughed too.

"Why that damned Rodde! You're right, Emmett, that would be a novelty menu item, but it would probably ruin my reputation among the better cliental at the Lodge. I don't think I'll risk it."

By now we were both very relaxed, and afternoon's accusations forgotten as we talked lightly about other food experiences. I described a rather greasy bear steak at a lodge in the Bad Lands National Park, and whale steak in New Bedford. She mentioned a roast rack of wild hare in Munich, complete with a few buckshot pellets undiscovered by the chef, and a Moroccan dinner in Tangiers where she committed a faux pas by reaching into the communal plate for a piece of barbecued lamb with her left hand. Our food had arrived, and the evening was going very smoothly. A small band began playing, and couples from other tables started dancing.

"Ah, at last, music of our era," Edie exclaimed, and added "I think we can dance to that. You do dance don't you, Emmett?"

I was embarrassed to say that I hadn't danced in years, but if she wasn't too critical I'd give it a try. The floor was pretty crowded so the best we could do was sway a little to the beat, but Edie didn't seem to mind, though it was evident she was a good dancer and deserved better than I could offer. "I'd better take some lessons," I murmured, "if we get a chance to do this again." Edie smiled but said nothing.

After the slow medley, we ordered liqueurs with our coffee and watched a more energetic group move onto the floor. "Perhaps I should arrange for regular weekend dinner dances at the Lodge. That might be a way to keep our competition at bay. What do you think, Emmett?"

"But you don't have competition," I objected. "I stopped at the Lodge because, fortunately, there were no motels off the Interstate."

"There may be now. An electronics company has moved to Elkton, and a zoning change has been requested for building a motel just at the edge of town, near their plant."

So that was the reason for her remark earlier that afternoon. "Maybe, Edie. It probably depends on how big this electronics company is. It would have to draw a sizeable number of overnight business visitors, I would think, in order to make a new motel profitable, considering that most would fly into South Bend, then drive a rental car to Elkton. That's room business, not weekend dinner dance customers. Now if the company is moving new employees to Elkton, they would be possible customers."

"I'd like to have both." She thought for a moment, then turned to look at the dance floor.

Taking the hint, I invited her to try me again. "I may be less rusty, second time around, madam." I think I was.

The bright June sun, filtering through the partially drawn Venetian blinds, woke me from one of the most restful night's sleep I'd had for months. Edie was facing the bureau mirror brushing her hair. She was wearing a pale blue summer robe. Edie was right, her lingerie was very feminine, lacy, but elegant and probably quite expensive. But then, I thought, she would never be seen in anything cheap or tacky. The robe seemed to be made of very fine cotton, it lent an air of crispness that was more flattering to her mature figure than a clinging silken one. Still it was thin enough to confirm that she was wearing nothing underneath. The bra and panties were partially visible, draped over the shower curtain bar in the bathroom. I was used to this female practice of partial dressing from the early years when Francis and I traveled. Last night I had fumbled for several minutes trying to unhook that bra, until Edie told me, impatiently, that this model fastened in front. Did I need more lessons about female attire at my late age?

"You're awake, Emmett," she said, and turned towards me. "I hope my washing didn't disturb your sleep." She looked at me for a long moment, hesitated, then sat on the edge of the bed next to me, slipping her hand under the sheet. "I thought you were," she murmured. "Is it the lingerie I bought for you yesterday, or is it me?"

Her directness still surprised me a little, but I managed to conceal it. "The lingerie was certainly exciting, Edie, but mostly because of the way you fill it."

"Nicely put, my sweet." She bent down to kiss me, pushing the sheet aside. "I probably should save this for tonight," she whispered, "but I don't really want to. Mornings seem so luxurious to me. Do you mind?" She moved on top of me. Edie was not really asking for my permission, but I responded by undoing the sash of her robe.

Later I called down for room service, ordering ham and eggs for both of us. "You know I never eat that much," she protested, but I told her she would need it for we were going to spend the rest of the morning at the zoo. "You're taking me to see the other wild animals?" she laughed, and disappeared into the bathroom. By the time breakfast had arrived she had showered and dressed.

Discussing the mechanics of getting to the zoo over our meal, which contrary to her professed light appetite, she finished with relish, I accepted her offer to drive us there. This would give her, she said, an opportunity to change to a more appropriate dress at her club and check that no messages had come for her, when she picked up her car.

I waited for her in front of the Carillon after getting directions and a map from the bell captain. Again, I enjoyed the opportunity of a relaxing stroll with her through the zoo grounds, not quite the same as at the university campus some months before. Then we were essentially strangers sharing a serendipitous elephant hunt. Now we were friends, I thought, not platonic, but yet too infrequently met to be considered lovers. I did not attach great significance to her accusation—no, that's not the right word, Edie had not expressed the degree of bitterness an accusation required. Her tears were most likely due to chagrin over misreading my character. I could not assume that Edie regarded me as other than an unattached male, pleasant to be with, undemanding of her time, and discreet enough to dally with on occasion with no risk to her health or reputation. My own feelings were perhaps becoming more serious, though I was as yet unable to see clearly where I was going or how Edie would fit into that yet-to-be-found future. I did know that my stay at Keonah was not going to be my ending-up point. To think of Edie leaving the satisfaction of managing the Lodge, her friends at Elkton, her position among the business community there, to say nothing about telling her children, adults though they were, that she was going to live with a screen and window repairman in the village of Keonah was ludicrous. Nor, on the other hand, could I see what life I could lead by joining her in Elkton. I would have to do something significant there, and clearly something apart from the Lodge, to avoid being perceived as a kept man. I shuddered at such a thought, no, never, never could I reduce myself to that perception. It would be a sin on my memory of Francis. My dear Francis, would she understand my seeking an end to the loneliness of the years since she left me? Wake up Emmett! Francis is dead. She can't be appealed to for approval. Act like the rational engineer you once were and you must continue to be. Are you feeling guilt for enjoying a new female relationship? Such romantic nonsense! Yet there is a need for romance in me. I had that need filled with Francis, but it did not leave with her, only repressed until now.

Leaving the Lincoln Park Zoo by mid-afternoon, we headed back to the city on the North Shore Drive. Edie parked at a garage near her club. Too late for lunch and yet too early for dinner, we stopped at a small tea room nearby. Edie asked if I had any plans for the evening. Again I was fully prepared with reservations at a dinner theatre in the Loop area. "Not a Strindberg play I hope," she teased. "It would end this nice day on a sad note, I'm sure."

"No fear" I assured her, "the food is continental and the performance is a small scale version of 'The Fantastics', a happy Romeo and Juliet. We eat at 8:00, so you may safely order some of these 'lovely little tea sandwiches'", quoting the menu description.

Again Edie returned to her club to change for the evening and check for any messages. There were none. We met in the Carillon lobby at 7:30. She had changed into a tailored pantsuit. Black slacks of lined satin, cut somewhat full in the leg and a jacquard jacket, predominately green, but with complementary lighter colors in the patterned figures. Beneath was a silvery grey silk blouse. One of the pleasures she gave me was the elegance of her dress. Even though I was sure she chose her clothes mostly for her own pleasure, I felt she was fully alert to my own appreciation. Even as I complimented her on her dress, I couldn't help being reminded how inappropriate my life in Keonah would be to this fashionable lady. I also reminded myself to get a few new suits before I saw her again.

Dinner, fortunately, matched the elegance of my date. I splurged on champagne instead of cocktails. We skipped the appetizers and went directly to the main course. She ordered rolled veal scallops stuffed with chicken livers and prosciutto, accompanied with saffron rice. I had boned breast of chicken, stuffed with prosciutto and cheese, with a side dish of polenta dressed with a few mushrooms in a delicate cream sauce. We had a light green salad last to freshen the palate before coffee and liqueurs. No other sweet seemed appropriate.

The musical was done without intermission and truncated somewhat from what I had remembered many years earlier, but the singers were good, especially El Gallo. Edie said she had not seen it before, which surprised me. It had been very popular and toured extensively. Perhaps she had been more secluded in Elkton than her wardrobe suggested.

We returned to the hotel directly after the performance. I could see she was beginning to tire. It had been a long day, and even I was beginning to droop. "In the morning, Edie?", I asked.

"In the morning, Emmett, and a luxurious end to a wonderful weekend," she replied.

It was a luxurious morning, Edie made it so. We ate a light breakfast in the coffee shop and then she was gone. I did not try to delay her, remembering her dislike of long good-byes.

The weekend had been expensive, nearly a thousand dollars for me alone. I had no idea what Edie had paid for having what amounted to a telephone message center at the Women's Club. My share of the profits from the milling machine were nearly spent, but I decided to spend a little more. Before leaving the hotel, I consulted the Yellow Pages and selected from among the display ads

---

WARD INVESTIGATIONS

DISCREET   -   REASONABLE

325 Harlem   Oak Park

312-699-2431

Fortunately I found a parking spot in front of the building. Ward was on the third floor. There was no Mr. Ward, and the office was about as large as the ad, but the man inside, Matt Elkins, seemed honest enough. I explained that I wanted to get the birth date of a person driving an Indiana car. I gave him the license number and make and model of the car, but that I didn't want the driver to be aware that an inquiry was being made. Elkins told me it would be easy enough to find out who owned the car from the state auto registration office, but that may not tell me who was driving. I should have realized that Edie may have listed the Lodge as owner; it would make more business sense for tax purposes to do so. Elkins said if I had the name of the driver he might be able to get the data from the driver registration file. He assured me the inquiry would not get back to Edie, so I gave him her name and address. It was a hundred dollars more for my weekend, but I wanted a reason on tap to send her a gift I had in mind. I couldn't just ask her when her birthday was, I wanted to surprise her. Elkins said he'd get the information in a week or two and mail it to me, but I think he really wanted to be sure my check cleared first.

Chapter XI
A New Activity

Mrs. Adamson was on my mind a lot during the drive back to Keonah, and for days afterwards. I had a better feeling for Edie than before Chicago, but not for her role as Mrs. Adamson, owner of the Elkton Lodge. I relived my intimacy with Edie many times, as I guess lonely men usually do. Warm and playful as a younger woman might be, yet mature enough to cherish, as I did, the ability to give pleasure as much as receiving it. But as Mrs. Adamson she appeared cool, contained, a businesswoman careful of her public image to Elkton associates and whomever they might likely encounter. Why hadn't she remarried? I was certain that she must have had opportunities to do so during the more than 10 years of widowhood. Surely her Edie side would have welcomed it. I decided I needed more exposure to Mrs. Adamson before I could really understand her. She was worth the effort, and as a sensible first step I would give more thought to her concern about the future of the Lodge.

Elmer was glad to collect on the casters, which, as I had suspected, had been a constant reminder to him that he hadn't been careful enough in his inventory investments. A few more screens had been brought in for repair over the weekend and were waiting for me, also he had sold a few more items from the Snyder pile, which was pretty nearly gone by now, at least of the good stuff. I asked him if he had given any further thought about my suggestions for expanding the services we could offer, but he hadn't. I told him we really needed a key duplicator to go with our lock business, and that it wouldn't be too big an outlay to get started. Elmer agreed that we probably should, but clearly he needed pushing to do it. Meanwhile, I decided to talk with Herb Macklinberg who owned the Keonah Pharmacy about setting up a copier service. I was surprised after my first few weeks in Keonah about the lack of some facilities that I thought were ubiquitous in America. Keonah was very slow, leaden you might say, or maybe its merchants felt suppressed by the bigger cities of C.R. and Iowa City, so close by. Of course, the bank and local lawyer had their own copiers, but that didn't help the rest of us. Anyway, I asked Herb if he wanted to join me in setting up a copy service. He seemed interested, especially when it was an added reason to get people into his store, and maybe make other sales too. He had space for it, I could service it, being only half a block away, and we'd split the profits and expense. While in Chicago I had gotten the address of a copier agent, so I wrote off for details. In a few weeks we were in business and the dimes started trickling in. Somehow, that cool Mrs. Adamson had wound up my clock again, and I was busily ticking away. Elmer must have heard the tick-tock because he soon agreed to get the key duplicator.

Saturday, the first week back from Chicago, was a half-day at Diehl's for me. My landlady was busy preparing a tea for her lady friends as I entered. "A letter for you Mr. Borden," she told me, raising her eyebrows. "From Ward Investigations. I hope it's not those Indiana gamblers after you again." Did she have a snicker in her voice? No matter, I smoothed it away by telling her it was merely a credit report I had requested on a Chicago business interested in buying some of Snyder's tools on time payment. As I started upstairs to my room, she invited me to have tea with her ladies. "On the porch, Mr. Borden, at 2:00."

"Yes ma'am" I responded after I was halfway up. I hurried on up, anxious to read Elkin's report. He had gotten what I asked for all right, but it surprised me to see that Edie was not 5 years older than I as I had first judged her to be, but actually 2 years older. Her birthday was August 10, fortunately, which gave me a little time to find a suitable present.

I joined my landlady and her guests, who had arrived while I was changing clothes and washing up. The weather was pleasant on the porch, not too hot for mid-June, or buggy yet. The tea was also pleasant, with an assortment of homemade cookies offered as well. A Midwestern mix of oatmeal crisps, nut brownies, and sugar cookies with dried apricot chunks on top. The cookies were very good, but I tried to be polite and not eat too many. Mrs. Fashlich insisted, however, that there were plenty, so I munched away during the conversation. Mostly it was on the weather, gardening, and gossip about town. Mrs. Voss, wife of Sam Voss of the lumberyard, had brought her garden book along and was explaining to Mrs. Fashlich about the way to properly trim the lilac bush in the backyard—which was pretty badly overgrown. "See," she exclaimed, pointing to a diagram, I suppose, "you leave the second year stems because they bloom next year. Cut the older ones back, down close to the root. Oh! Here's that nice gazebo I've been wanting Sam to build for our backyard. Our house doesn't have a nice front porch like this, and it would be so nice to be able to sit outside, shaded from the sun and screened from the bugs." She sighed again, "but Sam's always saying he's too busy."

"Well why don't you hire someone to build it for you? Goodness knows, Mina, by July you'll be eaten alive sitting in that backyard. I told you putting in that garden pool would just make a breeding ground for mosquitoes." Mrs. Fashlich had an exasperated tone. Apparently it was Mrs. Voss' favorite topic, complaining about Sam's failure to do this or that for her. I had some sympathy for Sam.

"Why, I bet Mr. Borden could build that for you, he's pretty handy with tools—that is if he's staying on."

I was startled by Mrs. Faslich's comment, almost dropping my third oatmeal crisp.

Mrs. Voss pressed the garden book on me, "Do you think you could build that for me, Mr. Borden?" I looked at the picture. It was an octagonal structure, one step up from the ground, with lattice work rising perhaps 3' from the floor to a railing and scalloped lattices at the roof edge, which was an eight-sided peaked affair of wood shingles topped by a rooster weather vane. Nothing too complicated, I thought, except possibly for the shingled roof. The weather vane would have to be bought.

"I suppose so, Mrs. Voss, are there plans available?" I asked, assuming they would have to be sent for and so, relying on the inertia that kept Mrs. Voss from having it built long ago, nothing would come of it.

"Unfortunately no," she replied, "but surely you could do it from the picture. Dotty (she meant Mrs. Fashlich, though I could never imagine calling her that) says you're very handy."

It was a fact that things were pretty slow at Diehl's the past few weeks, which was why I was taking Saturday afternoons off. Still, the roof might be a problem. "Really, Mrs. Voss, your husband would have to approve of such a project first, it's not a trivial expense."

"Call me Mina, please," she cooed. Mrs. Voss was certainly in her mid-forties, but it still sounded like a coo to me. "I'm sure Sam will approve, and anyway, it will be from my own money. I'll talk to him tonight." She seemed so excited about getting on to a gazebo at last that it must have been her dearest dream wish for years. I was sure Sam would scotch the whole idea so I'd be safe from any further concern about it. I was wrong about that, however, as it turned out.

After the ladies had left, I helped Mrs. Fashlich carry in the dishes, helping myself to the last nut brownie. "What did you mean, ma'am, about my staying on? If you want your room back you have only to tell me. I'd be sorry to move, but I certainly wouldn't want to stay where I'm not wanted."

Mrs. Fashlich protested. "Goodness no, Mr. Borden, it's just a comment I heard. Elmer had mentioned to Sam Voss during his card night he thought you were looking for a new job in Chicago. Sam told Minerva and she told me."

"Minerva is Mina Voss," I asked?

"Mina is Minerva, and let me tell you, Mr. Borden, if you do any work for her be sure you spell out in advance what it is. She's flighty about sticking to a plan—always was big on changing her mind. Wants it this way, then that way. Why it's no wonder Sam Voss never built the gazebo, or much of anything else for her after her garden shed fiasco years ago."

Later I drove into C.R., looking for a gift for Edie. Jewelry, I thought, would be appropriate, not as risky as clothing in sizing, not too crudely intrusive on her sensibility as lingerie. I was still unsure what our relationship meant, both to me and to her. Except for our first meeting at the Lodge, she had never talked in any detail about her children, or even her grandchildren. No pictures to press on me, no amusing stories about their growing up. Very much different from the friends Francis and I had. They always had some boringly pleasant or proud event to chatter about, often oblivious to the pain and frustration this caused Fran, wanting so desperately to have her own stories to tell.

By late afternoon, I had canvassed half-a-dozen jewelry and department stores without seeing anything I really liked. Plenty of rings, necklaces, earrings and pins, but none I felt unique enough to be a gift from me that she would be pleased to remember. I wasn't particularly hungry after all of Mrs. Fashlich's oatmeal crisps, but I decided one more shop would be it for today, before I headed back for the Keonah diner. I was browsing around the counters, finally deciding that a pin was probably my best bet, when Ridetti walked out of the little office room at the back of the store. "Hello, Borden," he boomed at me. "Afraid you won't sell any tools here. This is a store for more delicate things than bending brakes." He was evidently pleased with his quip and laughed. I didn't resent it, Ridetti was O.K., but he had his own weak spots to poke at.

"I was hoping," I told him, "to see if you'd done anything with those tools yet. Maybe an angle iron pin, or an anchor chain bracelet. But I guess your work is for exhibits, not something one would actually pay money for to wear."

"Wrong again, Borden, I do occasionally make something to sell, and people have bought them to wear. Not angle iron or sheet metal! I do do jewelry you know."

Now that was interesting. "Sorry, Ridetti, you've too many talents for me to be up on. But I'd like to see some of your work, maybe I'd find a pin I'd like. Have you got anything here I could see?"

"Aha! now you're the buyer! Nothing of mine here on display. I don't work that way, I do jewelry by commission, but I can show you some pictures of some of my pieces. Drop down to my office, Tuesday afternoon if you can make it, and I'll show you what I can do. But listen, Borden, commission work is not a $50 pin kind of thing."

A unique designer pin might be just the right thing, I thought. But if Ridetti's expensive I'd better reconsider my own opportunity for earning a commission on the Mina gazebo. Especially after what I'd blown on the Chicago weekend!

Monday, I had to reassure Elmer, in some subtle way, that I hadn't been looking for a job in Chicago. I was still trying to figure out how to do this when Sam Voss walked in.

"The misses says you might be willing to build that damned gazebo she wants. Is that true?" I might, I told him, if he approved and we could agree on the plans and money.

Elmer was nearby and piped in "'spect you and Sam might agree on the plan but that won't mean anything to Mina. Sam ought to warn you that Mina will have you building a dozen gazebos before you finish one, eh Sam?"

"Elmer, you don't know what you're talking about." Voss drew himself up importantly. "If Borden here and I agree on the plan, that's what will be built." But Elmer wasn't going to let him off so easily.

"Sure, it'll be built Sam, just like the garden shed. First a simple lean-to, then she changes her mind and wants it enclosed, and when that change is halfway done decides she needs a sink, so you had to run 50' of water line from the house and dig a French drain to boot. A $100 lean-to turned into $1000 and a three month job."

I decided Elmer must be ragging Sam because he lost money in their last pinochle game. It must have been a nice piece of change, maybe even $10, since Elmer wasn't done yet. "You were always a softy with women. You should have laid down the law with Mina, that's the way to do it."

"Now be careful, Elmer," Sam bridled. He wasn't going to lay down and play dead for Elmer, however he might be twisted about by Mrs. Voss. "So you know all about handling women, you damned old bachelor. You did a great job with your niece, laying down the law; got you a long way with her didn't it! Haven't heard from her for years, have you Elmer! If Borden and I agree, that will be it, I tell you!"

77

I decided to end this bickering before it escalated to the point where they broke up the pinochle club. "Well, Sam, let me draw up some plans to show you and the misses. I'm sure we can agree on something, since she seems to be set on one like the picture." Before he left, though, I did get agreement on how the gazebo would be placed. It would sit on concrete blocks, no dug foundation, so we wouldn't have to fuss with a building permit.

"No need to squabble with Voss over this gazebo," I told Elmer after Voss left. "Things are slow here for now, and you won't have to pay me for any time I spend on Voss's project. I'll always be available should the need arise, and after all, it can't be more than a few weekends to complete the job, no matter what ideas Mrs. Voss gets, because the terms of the job will be clearly spelled out at the beginning. Also, you know, you'll be selling some hardware items to Sam for this job. Not much, screening and door latches and hinges, certainly, but it's still good business for us." Elmer seemed mollified, and I told myself to find some excuse to ask his opinion about building the gazebo. He likes that.

That evening I studied the picture Mina gave me. The thing seemed to be about 8' across, and slightly less from the floor to the start of the roofline. Sketching out the octagon gave me a little less than 3' wide for the doorway, accounting for the width of the 2x4 studs. That seemed adequate, but to make sure, I decided it would be safest to chalk out the floor outline on Voss's driveway and have Mina set her lawn chairs inside it to be certain that it was big enough. Four chairs and a small table seemed about right to me, but god knows what Mina expected. The picture didn't show any furniture inside.

My biggest immediate concern was deciding on how the floor joists were to be laid out. After trying several schemes, I decided on placing 8 concrete blocks at the points of the octagon, and 2 butted together at the center. The 2x4's that formed the perimeter would rest on the 8 blocks, and another 8 pieces would run from the points to sit on the center blocks. The scheme is simple if you're into building, but if construction is not exactly your box of candy, I've sketched a diagram of the floor plan. Exterior plywood gussets inlaid into the ends of the 2x4's would be nailed into each joining end of the perimeter pieces and their included radial joist. The center of the radial joists would be nailed to an octagon shaped piece of plywood, also inlaid into the joists. With this scheme, the flooring could be standard 5/4 x 6 deck planking laid parallel to the door opening and extending to the perimeter. There would be plenty of support and nailing points for the floorboards. That was enough for the moment, I thought, pleased with myself.

I took Tuesday afternoon off and drove down to Ridetti's office at the University. He had Polaroid snaps of rings, pins, and bracelets he had made. Mostly they were based on geometric figures, not exactly what I was looking for. Sensing my disappointment, he asked me what in the hell (his word) I was looking for. Since he was so blunt about it—this seemed to be Ridetti's standard operating procedure—I told him I wanted a pin, but one of more traditional (Ridetti snorted at this) design, floral perhaps, silver with either a blue stone or blue enamel somewhere on it. "Can you do flowers?", I asked.

"Of course I can do flowers; butterflies, birds, whatever, if that's what you want." He pulled out another drawer in his desk and got a small photo album from it. "Here, Borden, look through this. What kind of an engineer are you to want messy flowers instead of nice regular triangles and spirals?" This was more like it. One piece seemed close to what I wanted. It was circular in shape, formed by intertwined vine-like plants with tiny leaves sprouting on alternate sides.

"How about this one," I asked him, "except I'd like a bouquet of long stemmed flowers lying diagonally over the intertwined vines? Maybe a mixture of blue and yellow enameled petals."

"Um" was Ridetti's only response.

"How much will that cost?" I asked him again.

"Well, what size Borden, that's like asking you engineers how much does a bridge cost?" I hadn't thought about the size, but picking up a ruler from his desk, I decided about 1½" diameter would seem to be right. Ridetti thought for a minute, then said about $400. "Too much for you, Borden?" It was a lot, more than I had originally thought of spending, but it would be one-of-a-kind and made especially for her, so I told him I could afford it, but like a good engineer I

79

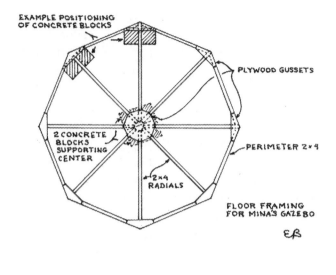

EXAMPLE POSITIONING
OF CONCRETE BLOCKS

PLYWOOD GUSSETS

2 CONCRETE
BLOCKS
SUPPORTING
CENTER

PERIMETER 2×4

2×4
RADIALS

FLOOR FRAMING
FOR MINA'S GAZEBO

ℰℬ

XI-7A

wanted some prior assurance that I'd like the design. "Borden, you're a pain in the ass, but I'll accommodate you this time in the hope my art will reform your cretinish nature. Give me your address and I'll mail you a sketch in a few days." Ridetti certainly did not conform to my apparently faulty image of the effete artist type.

That evening, after supper, I drove over to the Voss house. It was a modest sized frame house placed on a nicely landscaped front yard. The driveway led to a separate garage in back, and next to that was the infamous garden shed. Further back was a clump of trees, mostly maple and oak, a small pond, whose kidney shape clearly identified it as Mina-made. Sam answered my knock and called Mina to join us. I chalked the floor plan on the driveway and suggested they arrange the lawn chairs inside to see if that size was satisfactory. Sam thought it was O.K. but Mina felt it was a little crowded for four. We haggled a bit when Mina suggested 12'. I could see Sam wasn't happy about something that large, so I told her "I can't handle something that large by myself, Mrs. Voss. Let's settle on 10', that's the most I will commit to. We have to also consider where it's to be placed and then agree to the height." There was a flat open space on the opposite side of the backyard from the garage, which seemed suitable. Mina's picture suggested a height about half again its width. That would be about 15'. Luckily, that seemed too high to fit comfortably near the clump of trees, so we agreed to 12', excluding the rooster weather vane. I promised Sam I'd make a scaled sketch of the gazebo and estimate the lumber requirements.

In a way I was excited about the project. I'd never built anything as big as this glorified outhouse, and it would be a challenge and a learning experience. But on the other hand, making the sketches was a chore since I had no drafting tools. Working out how the 8 studs were to be fastened to the sills and braced without compromising the airy look of the gazebo in Mina's picture caused me a lot of agony. They had to be made secure not only because they supported a large and heavy roof which would be even heavier when the winter snows of Iowa pile on, but also because there was no sheathing or cross-bracing possible that normally stabilizes wall studs in a house.

Mina wanted screens on the gazebo because of the biting bugs from her backyard pond. The picture she gave me didn't show screens and I had never seen a gazebo with them. Come to think about it, I'm not sure I ever saw a real gazebo up close either. I didn't realize at that point what a pain those screens were going to be, or I might not have been so enthused about the project. I decided to consult Elmer about the screen construction. My first thought was some simple wooden frames with screening nailed on, but since I felt they should be removable, I realized that their size would make them pretty heavy to mount and dismount, and further, they would be quite likely to warp after one or two seasons and become useless at keeping out mosquitoes. He suggested making them out of the same aluminum screen frames we were used to in our repair work. I didn't know we could order strips of that stuff along with right angle joiners that could be easily hand riveted to the strips to form the frame. Now I realized I could make a much stronger doorframe that would resist warping but still keep it light with an aluminum frame screen insert.

By the following Monday I had completed the sketches and material estimates for Voss. Elmer had priced the screens for me. I noted that he wasn't giving his friend Voss any discount, and, in fact, was charging him for the time I would have to spend making them. Was he getting even with him for his pinochle losses, or for Voss's jibe about his niece?

Mrs. Fashlich had a letter for me from Ridetti when I got back to my room late that afternoon. I was relieved to find his sketch was expertly done.

It gave me more confidence that the workmanship would be first class. I was even more pleased and excited to see that Ridetti had chosen a spray of orchids for the flowers. Would Edie remember her orchid corsage? The orchid petals were to be enameled in pink and yellow and the tiny leaves of the entwining vines were pale blue. It was very handsome and Ridetti wanted a handsome price--$600. Would Voss be willing to pay that for building the gazebo? I would soon find out, as he called me to stop over to his house that evening after supper. My own supper was fairly good that evening at the diner. Chicken pot pie and warm apple pie. Mrs. Olsen who supplied pastries and cakes for the diner from her home, had a nice light touch with dough, one reason why I continued to eat there regularly.

So I was in a pleasant state of mind when I arrived. Mina was not there, she was attending a meeting of the local garden club, Sam told me with some relief. I was relieved, too, when he said she had approved the general plan.

"However, Borden," he said, "I think you should change the 8 posts. I don't really like your idea of paired 2x4's, I think single 4x4's would be a sturdier and neater choice. Doubling the 2x4 sole plate between posts will add more support against sidewise movement. There's a fair amount of

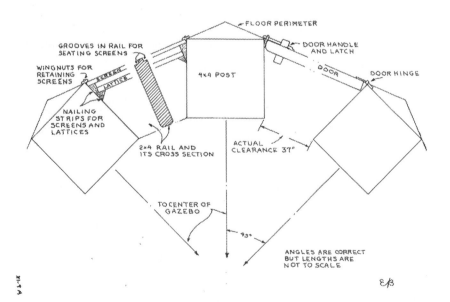

wind load during the spring squalls we get here." I agreed but told him I was concerned about my ability to make square cuts with my handsaw on such a big piece as a 4x4. "We'll do it at the lumberyard on our radial arm saw," he assured me, and then added that if I worked on the weekend, I could use their portable chop saw for the rest of the work. That was a relief, since I hadn't thought I'd have any power tools available except a drill and saber saw I could borrow from Diehl's. He also suggested using white plastic latticework, rather than wood, for the decorative parts. He was clearly concerned about cutting down on any maintenance work he'd have to do later on. I thought it best to point out to Sam the problem with screens and lattices that I had in working out the plans. I had decided to mount the screens on the outside of the gazebo for ease in putting them up and taking them down and for giving room on the railings inside the gazebo for resting elbows and teacups. But this meant the latticework would be behind the screens (again see sketch if you can't visualize the situation). "It'll darken the white a little, Sam. Do you think Mrs. Voss will mind?" I asked him.

Sam decided she probably wouldn't and I promised to look for the palest or most transparent screening material I could find. He'd priced out the wood and cedar shingles at about $1500, obviously using his costs, not retail. The metal screening seemed expensive and he wanted to know if he was getting a price break as a fellow merchant.

"Elmer priced that for me," I told him. "I can't give you wholesale prices for that, I only work for Elmer, you know. However, you might dicker with him if you want. You might remind him you helped him out with the forklift when we were loading Snyder's milling machine. I don't have to tell you how to deal with Elmer, you've known him much longer than I have, but I can offer you some advice, don't bring up his niece again, he was pretty upset about that. Apparently he's very unhappy about it, but why, I don't know, it must have occurred some years back.

"Well he shouldn't have needled me about the garden shed, the damned old goat. Anyway I'll talk to him about it. Now you didn't indicate what your fee was going to be. I understand you're going to work on this on weekends. Are you going to charge by the hour on the job?"

"I don't like charging by the hour, Mr. Voss, it leads to bad feelings, in my experience. Is he padding his bill? Should I have to pay for any mistakes—

you know in advance that I haven't built a gazebo before, so while I suppose 3 or 4 weekends should do it, I don't really have any experience on this kind of job, and frankly I'm not a professional builder. It's your wife that wants it done and she could have hired a carpenter anytime to do it for her. I think I'd like to do it, but I don't do things for free. Let's start with a charge of half your material cost, $750. Is that acceptable?"

I must have given too low a figure, Voss agreed right away, subject to regular inspection of the progress. So there it was. I'd paid for the pin and gained another project which would further bolster my recovery from the deep melancholy of Fran's death, still with me despite Edie, but no longer so debilitating.

I called Ridetti the next morning and told him I was pleased with the design and although he had bumped his estimate by 50% which was unconscionable, he should go ahead. I also told him, interrupting his protests, that I was mailing him a check for $300 as an advance to seal the bargain and pay for the silver.

Chapter XII

Charlie Voss

On Thursday I stopped at the lumberyard, telling Voss to deliver the concrete blocks and 2x4's for the foundation perimeter, as I planned to start that Saturday. I could see there was something bothering him. "You know, Borden," he mumbled, "I have some second thoughts about this." Here it goes, I thought. If Mina was indecisive, it must have rubbed off on her husband too.

"You want to cancel the job," I said with a sour expression? "After all my work on the plans and estimates!"

"No, no," he interjected. "No, I want you to go ahead, but I think we should talk a bit more about the foundation. Since it's setting on blocks above the ground by only a few inches, I'm concerned about rain run-off collecting in any low spots which won't dry out very well, since it's shaded from the sun. It might get pretty damp in the gazebo, and unhealthy. Mina is susceptible to dampness you know. Also, it could be a breeding ground for bugs. So what I thought was to dome about 6" of sand inside the perimeter, and lay some black polyethylene sheeting over it. What do you think?"

I thought it was a good idea, agreed enthusiastically, and was relieved that I would be starting, and even that I might expect useful advice from him during the construction. It has always been important to my self-esteem to do a good job on any project I undertake. It earned me respect when I worked as an engineer and made Fran proud of me. I wouldn't want to feel I would be letting her down. It seems I would always be judging myself by what Fran would think of me. Neurotic perhaps, to feel her looking down on me, but that's the way I still felt. No one would replace her as my conscience. I was sure of that.

Getting the foundation set, level, and secure was the first and most important step. I had thought a lot about how to do the job right. An octagon is not like a rectangular barn or shed. Wood and concrete blocks are made with 90 degree corners, but there are no such corners in an octagon, which can be divided into 8 isosceles triangles, I had finally decided on first making a jig of two adjacent triangles—just the 2 edge beams of the perimeter and their three connecting radial beams, the floor joists. This would be a quarter of the support for the floor. You can see what I mean if you look back at my floor plan sketch. I would set the two concrete blocks at the center of the octagon, drive an iron rod between them, marking the center of the floor. Then by drilling a hole in the center of the radial beam gusset and setting it and its attached beams on the rod, I could set the first perimeter block at the correct distance and orientation so that the two perimeter beams and the radial beam between them rested on the block. Thus no part of the block would project on the outside to interfere with the 1x6 skirting that I would later add to hide the foundation blocks and perimeter beams. The next block could be set by just rotating my jig 1/8th of a circle so that the same radial and perimeter beams rested on the next block, repeating this process for each of the remaining 6 blocks. I could then remove my jig, level the blocks, and grade the sand Voss wanted to a nice low mound between the circle of blocks. Then lay the polyethylene over the sand, spade a narrow slot in the ground between the perimeter blocks so I could bury the edges of the poly, sealing the sand inside and securing the edges of the plastic cover.

It took all of Saturday morning to make the jig and temporarily set the perimeter blocks in their approximate locations. I had bought sandwiches and a can of soda at the diner during breakfast, and was taking my lunch alfresco, so to speak, when I noticed a skinny little kid sitting on the back steps of the Voss house watching me. "Who are you?" I challenged with a grin. "The building inspector?" He grinned back and said he was Charlie Voss and he lived there. Sam's youngest son, apparently. I finished my brief lunch and got back to the hard part of the work, lifting the jig onto the iron pivot rod and fussing the first perimeter block in its approximate position. I had to be careful in turning the jig to the next block so as not to bend the pivot rod. It was going to be hard on my back, I realized. I had to stay bent over to hold up the outside edge of the jig and at the same time sort of shuffle sideways to get to the next block. I had to rest a minute after orienting that block before repeating. My back was going to be sore, I was sure of that. By the fourth block I had to take a longer break, and stretched out flat on the grass. I noticed Charlie had left. Bored I supposed.

What had I done on summer vacation when I was his age, 13 or 14, I guessed? Bicycling around town, hiking in the woods, and generally goofing off. It was my last carefree summer, I remembered. Next year I was doing whatever summer jobs I could find that earned me money for dates and buying meters and stuff for my radio hobby. I was orienting the sixth block when I heard a voice saying "that's the dangest idea I've ever seen, Borden." It was Sam Voss, with Charlie along side. "Charlie called me to come out and see what you were doing."

"Well, it seemed to me to be the best way one man alone could get the foundation set properly. How would you have done it?", I challenged.

"I don't know," he responded, "I guess I never gave it a thought before, but now that I see the thing laid out here, I can see that an octagonal shape poses some unique problems. I can also see why you sided with me on not going over a 10' span." He and Charlie sat down on the steps to watch as I set the last two blocks, and then carefully lifted the center gusset of the jig off the pivot and slid the whole thing off the blocks. String and a line level (borrowed from Diehl's of course) trued the top of the blocks level, being careful not to alter the orientation of the blocks. The sand fill and ply cover were next, and last, for that day. I knew I was going to be stiff, but the hardest part of the job was over. Sam said it would be safe to leave the chop saw and hand tools in the garden shed for the night. I washed most of the dirt off me with the garden hose and wearily climbed into my car and headed home. A soak in a hot tub for an hour helped some. Meatloaf supper at the diner, followed by Mrs. Olsen's peach pie and two cups of coffee helped some more and an early bedtime would, I hoped, heal the rest. Next morning I got ready to go again, not in A1 shape. After all, I'm getting old and working at Diehl's hasn't actually been strenuous exercise. The Voss's had apparently gone to church, as no one seemed to be at home when I got there. I don't go to church, there's too much mysticism in religion for me. You might say I am an unbeliever, but that's not really so. I believe there is order in the universe, but not much purpose that man can understand. No, I'm more of an agnostic, there may be a god, but I haven't been convinced there's any proof of it. I can say one thing, if man was made in the image of God, does God ever get back pains from looking down on us? No sir, if man is made in the image of God, then God is an image of man, and so he must be an engineer—clever, an exceedingly clever engineer, but fallible for all that. He needs to perfect the design more so we don't have these aches and pains and sores and disease. God knows he's had enough time to have gotten it right. But then, maybe this world is just his prototype of the final model to come. If so, he's got a few bugs to fix before setting out the final design. Swatting mosquitoes from Mina's pond, I felt he was spending too much time perfecting the insects.

I had gotten the rest of the perimeter and radial floor joists cut and screwed in place and was starting to measure, cut, and screw down the floorboards, starting at the door side of the octagon and parallel to that edge beam. I was on my third piece, selecting a plank, laying it in place, then scribing the two ends where it met the perimeter beams, then carrying it to the chop saw to cut on the scribed lines. More bending and lifting work, when I noticed the Vosses must have come back because my young overseer was sitting on the back steps watching me again.

"Hello Charlie Voss," I said. "Checking on me, are you?" He just grinned. Stopping a minute for a rest, I asked him, if he was so interested in building work, why he didn't work at the lumberyard.

"I would" he replied, "but mom won't let me."

"Afraid you'll get hurt, Charlie?", I asked, seeing as how he was rather slightly built. "I would think your dad could find some safe work for you to do."

"Well, I guess he could. Sweeping up sawdust and sitting at the desk. I didn't want that," Charlie replied, "but mostly mom doesn't want me to hear all the cussin' and swearin' she says the men down there do."

"I heard a lot of that too when I was your age, but it had more the effect of convincing me not to imitate them," I told him. It suddenly occurred to me I could cut out a lot of this bending and stooping I was doing, and maybe give Charlie something to do that he might like better than sweeping sawdust.

"Well," I said, "you can't spend your summer just sitting there and ending up with nothing to show for it. Now I could use an apprentice for this job. $5 a day on Saturday and Sunday if you want to work, and your mom agrees. Ask her."

I couldn't tell whether it was the chance to earn money or the chance to build something big that moved him, but he was gone in a flash. In a few minutes Sam appeared. "Charlie says you want to hire him, is that right?" I told him it was, that he could help me in marking up the floorboards and maybe some other light jobs where four hands would be a help.

"Well I'm agreeable, but he's not to use the chop saw, or any power tools, he's still just a little boy." And over-protected I thought.

So I got a helper, and Charlie turned out to be an eager one. Except for the long boards at the middle of the floor, he could lift the shorter cutoff pieces, lay and mark them at both ends while I did the cutting and nailing. With his help we got the floor laid and the first layer sole plates on the perimeter installed by late afternoon. I paid my helper and called it quits until the next weekend.

During the week, when I couldn't work on the gazebo, I gave more thought to Mrs. Adamson's concern about the Lodge. I recognized that I thought of her as Mrs. Adamson in that role, but as Edie in our more intimate and private relationship. I wasn't, I was sure, becoming schizophrenic, it was just that she seemed to me to exhibit two aspects of her personality in those different roles. Anyway, I finally wrote her about some of the ideas that occurred to me. It wasn't necessary to go into great detail about them since I had no idea of her financial status, town ordinances, or the feasibility of making additions or major alterations to the building. It did seem to me that the Lodge had room for some expansion into the parking lot in back. I suggested a health spa, with a small pool, sauna or hot tub and an exercise room. That would be expensive, I knew. Quite expensive, but if there was no equivalent facility in Elkton, no YMCA or YWCA, then she should consider it, as the new motel might well be planning one. It would draw some room guests I thought, but by selling memberships it could pay for itself by drawing local people. The health craze must have touched the hinterland of Indiana by now. Years ago, Fran and I had joined just such a facility and found it very enjoyable, especially during the fall and winter months. Remembering our experience at the C.R. supper club, another thought was that she might arrange for weekend entertainment in the dining room. In fact, something ala Jonathon's folk songfest. I even suggested she could feature herself, on occasion, but that was more tongue-in-cheek. She might be Edie in C.R. on a lark, but in Elkton she would be the upright Mrs. Adamson. I thought she might find local talent that would be suitable at reasonable rates, and would itself draw local fans. My best idea, though, one that tickled my fancy, was to partition-off the rather large lobby and set up a small bar. The "Black Hand Cafe" I called it, if she moved those two chairs from the lobby into it, along with the spittoons, and find, maybe, some pictures and posters to decorate the walls; ones a little more discreet than Rodde's saloon art. Maybe he already had them stashed away, feeling they were too tame for his poker room.

On the next weekend, Charlie and I got the eight 4x4 posts installed, the second layer sole plates that Sam had suggested, and the top sill that would tie the posts to the roof. Charlie was a big help to me, holding a level against the posts while I temporarily braced and then toenailed them.

It was now the beginning of July and starting to get that hot and muggy Iowa summer weather I dimly remembered from my youth. In New York we lived closer to the shore and could get frequent relief with the sea breezes, but here in the midlands there were no such breezes. Still, the countryside was pleasant to see with neat rows of corn and wheat. Mrs. Fashlich spent a good bit of time on her shaded porch, occasionally entertaining her garden club ladies and listening to Mina talk about the progress on her "folly," as Mrs. Fashlich liked to call it, and how much her Charlie seemed to be taking to his new job.

Diehl's would be closed for the Fourth so I would have an extra day off. It was now time to worry about how I was going to do the roof on the gazebo. I said I had drawn plans for Voss's approval and made lumber estimates, but I hadn't actually worked out in detail how I was going to connect the roof rafters together at the center of the roof and to the top sill. Octagons were turning out to be a messy construction shape to deal with, and I had no experience with them, or ready access to any books on how to build them, so I was pretty much on my own. But I was, after all, a trained engineer and supposed to be able to solve problems myself. I toyed with several ideas, all involving complicated wood shapes that could provide good solid nailing surfaces, but none of them seemed really adequate for any heavy snow load or strong winds.

Finally, I decided that steel brackets, bolted to each rafter and then welded to a short steel pipe would be both strong enough, and even better, make it feasible for Charlie and me to get the whole affair assembled, rafter by rafter, atop the 8' high 4x4 posts. What I needed first was to arrange the eight brackets radiating out from the central pipe at 45 degrees to each other. I would need some kind of jig to hold them in place at that angle so they could be welded to the pipe (see sketch).

Business was rather brisk on the day before the Fourth. Elmer was selling charcoal and lighter fluid for backyard barbecuing, fireworks, small American flags, and cans of mosquito and bug spray, but things quieted down a bit after lunch, so I had a chance to go out to the shed in back and grub around the scrap iron junk we had carted back from Snyder's machine shop. Luckily I found some flat strips of 12 gauge steel, enough for the brackets, and a short piece of piping. While I was cutting the brackets from the flat stock with a hacksaw, Voss sauntered in. "Elmer

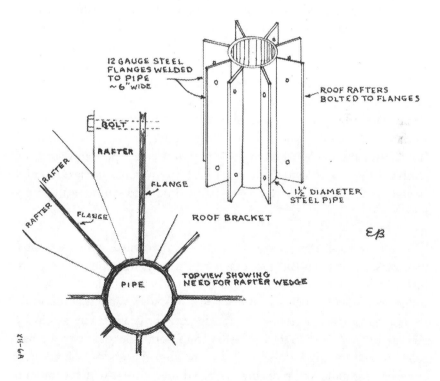

said I'd find you here, Borden." I nodded, continuing to saw, as it was slow going. "Mina asked me to invite you over to our barbecue tomorrow; if you're not otherwise engaged." I was pleasantly surprised, and grateful for an excuse to have an extra day of rest and an escape from still another diner dinner. I also realized that I shouldn't have thought I could work on the gazebo while the Vosses might want to use the backyard. This would be my first invitation out since coming to Keonah, what was it, 6 or 7 months ago? I told him I would be happy to come over. "About 4 o'clock, Borden" he said, "and don't get all dressed up."

After he had left, I scooted over to the state store before it closed and bought two bottles of sparkling burgundy to offer my hostess. While I didn't know what Mina thought about liquor, I was sure that she would accept, if not acquiesce in, something between champagne and Coca Cola.

Elmer let me lock up so I could finish making the jig. Cutting the brackets and drilling the bolt holes was a tedious job, but slow and steady was the way to do it properly. I filed and smoothed the cut edges so there was no risk of getting scraped while bolting the rafters to the brackets. It took another two hours to cut the eight grooves in two pieces of plywood that would hold the brackets upright between them, 45 degrees apart, and a circular groove for the end of the pipe. Standing the short piece of pipe in the round grooves between them, passing a bolt through them and the pipe to hold the jig together, it was an easy final step to align the slots in the plywood so that the steel brackets could be slid upright in the grooves till they met the pipe. There was sufficient room between the brackets, I thought, for the welder to reach the junction between pipe and brackets. I finished by 7 o'clock, too late to get back to my room to clean up and then go to the diner, so I washed up at the diner and sank wearily into a booth to eat.

There was no letter from Elkton for me when I returned to my room, so I guess Mrs. Adamson wasn't too impressed with my suggestions. Excepting for my bank statements and quarterly investment reports, letters from the Lodge were the only items I usually got. Mrs. Adamson always enclosed her notes in plain envelopes, at my suggestion, to avoid any gossip by Mrs. Fashlich. She thought they were from South Bend since Edie had also arranged for them to be mailed away from the Lodge, she got that from the postmark, and probably suspected they were from my gambling friends. Just as well. I might be able to use that as an excuse to get away for a weekend to see Edie sometime soon. I fell asleep thinking about when I might see her again.

I was not the only guest at the Voss barbecue. Mina's sister, Phyllis, and her husband were there. They lived in Davenport. Charlie was proudly explaining to their young daughter the work he had done on the gazebo. Phyllis was a few years younger than Mina, but a lot more sophisticated. Her husband was George Mercer, of Mercer Motors, as gregarious and talkative as you'd expect a car salesman to be. He must have been fairly successful at it, judging by the jewelry Phyllis wore. Sam said to dress casual and Phyllis did, slacks and a silk blouse, but that didn't prevent her from including several heavy gold bracelets and a jeweled pin holding a bright scarf, draped loosely around her neck and pinned to her left shoulder. She wore her dark brown hair pulled back from her temples and coiled into a bun at the back of her head. She was a very attractive woman. An asset to George that I'm sure he enjoyed displaying.

Charlie pointed at me and told his Aunt Phyl that he and I were building this big 'zebo. She looked curiously at me. Later, sitting on the lawn chairs sipping the burgundy, she asked me the usual questions of a stranger. Where was I from, what did I do, and where my wife was, noting again my wedding ring. I avoided extensive explanations, simply stating I was widowed and had recently moved to Keonah for my health. Later I saw her talking to Mina and looking in my direction, but I knew Mina had no further information to give her. A single man always seems to be a source of curiosity to a woman, happily married or not.

The barbecue went well, I thought. Voss supervised the grilling of the steaks, with Charlie standing by to squirt water on any flare-ups. Unfortunately we had no sweet corn, it had been a little too cool in late spring for quick growing. I was disappointed, but Mina had made a good potato salad, and Phyllis, to my surprise, had brought blueberry and southern peach pies. Her own make, and she didn't look like the domestic type.

While I was congratulating Phyllis on her pies, and sipping my second cup of coffee, Mercer and Voss were over at the gazebo. Sam called to Mina to bring him the picture of the gazebo which he showed to Mercer. They had a long discussion before eventually calling me over.

"George was wondering if this could be pre-fabricated, Borden," he asked me. "You know, pre-built sections that could be transported by truck and then quickly assembled on site in a day?" I hadn't thought about that, it wasn't necessary for Mina's job.

"I suppose it could be engineered that way," I told him after a few moments thought. "Probably would need more metal fittings for bolting the sections together, so the labor savings would be reduced by the cost of the bracket and bolt hardware. The big obstacle, though, might be preparing the site. You know, setting and leveling the blocks supporting the floor. I would have to think some more about how that might be expedited, but why would you want to know?"

"George thought there might be a market for selling them," Sam replied.

"Possibly," I said, "but are you sure Mrs. Voss would appreciate having copies of her gazebo sprouting up among her neighbor's yards?" George had a good gaffaw at that and slapped Sam on the back. I could see Sam was embarrassed, but the idea had some appeal to me. More as an engineering problem to solve than as a business venture. I suggested that perhaps George could get a reading on Mina's feelings by having Phyllis ask her if she would mind having copies made.

I sauntered back to the patio table. Mina wasn't there but Phyllis was just pouring herself the last of the burgundy. "Have another piece of pie, Mr. Borden," she said. "I can see you liked the peach one."

"I did indeed," I replied, sitting down on a chair next to her. "This has an unusually good peach flavor. How did you do it?"

"Just a little trick of mine, Mr. Borden. I use good ripe peaches with no skin blemishes so I can mince the peach skins and add them to the filling."

I cut myself a good wedge and asked "may I cut you a slice also?"

"A very small slice then." She smiled at me, adding "I never eat much pastry, it works against the fit of my clothes," while smoothing an imaginary wrinkle along her hip line lightly with her free hand.

"Your mother must have taught you well then," I said, handing her a plate with a small wedge of blueberry. "This is even better than Mrs. Olsen's. She makes the pastry for the diner here, but she must sample her work a lot. She'd make two of you."

"Oh, you mean Lottie. Yes, I know her. You must not have tried Mina's pies or you wouldn't have supposed mother taught me. She buys frozen ones at the store," she added with just a little smirk. "I thought I'd give Sam a treat by bringing them myself. Pastry actually was one of my best courses at school—I found I liked handling dough." She smiled broadly. "Mr.—now I can't keep saying Mr. Borden, it's much too formal at a barbecue. I'm afraid I didn't catch your first name. You do have a first name don't you?"

"My parents were very poor, but they did manage to save enough money to get a Christian name for me: Emmett," I replied between bites. "Do you mean you actually learned this in high school?"

"Hardly, Emmett, my pastry making is more polished than that. No, I majored in home economics at the State University before I married George."

"You mean at Ames? I went to Ames, when were you there?"

She opened her eyes as wide as she could. "Some years after you," she replied archly, and then softened it with a smile. I shouldn't have asked. "Tell me, is Charlie really helping you on the gazebo?"

"Certainly," I replied. "I pay him $5 a day on the weekend, and I think he's enjoying having a real job. Why?"

"Mina's always been afraid he'd get hurt working at the lumberyard, I'm surprised she let him get close to heavy boards and saws."

"I offered him the job, as long as he got permission. Of course, Sam said he's not to use the power tools, though I think he can handle the drill with no danger. It could be good for him, to build a little more self-confidence and muscle."

"Yes, I think so. Mina's overly protective. Too much so for a young boy; they grow up too timid. Looking straight at me, she handed me her plate and, getting up, added "I don't think a man should be too timid either. What do you think Mr. Borden?" Without waiting for a reply she turned around and walked into the house

I decided it would be prudent to thank my host and escape

CHAPTER XIII
RAISING THE ROOF

The next day, a note from Ridetti said the pin was ready. I asked Elmer for the afternoon off, there was nothing going on at the store after the Fourth, so I could drive down to the University. I suspected that Ridetti was anxious for the balance due for his work. The pin was even better looking than the sketch he had sent me, probably because the colors were more brilliant next to the sheen of the silver. He was clearly pleased with his handiwork and had fitted it in an elegant little leather-covered box. I wrote out a check for the remaining $300. Handing it to him, I suggested he might give me a free half-hour of his time to weld a small project for me. "Free?" he barked, "artists don't create for others for free, Borden."

"But this isn't art," I countered. "I just want you to use the welder you bought to fasten some metal pieces into a bracket for me." I showed him the pieces and the jig. "After all, I didn't squawk when you upped the price on the pin by 50%." I fitted the eight brackets, butted against the pipe, into the jig and handed it to him. After another scowl and a grump, he switched on the arc welder, put on a leather apron and gloves, adjusted a facemask and proceeded to weld. It took about 15 minutes—he was good, and I had my roof bracket. I thanked him and smoothed his ego a little by telling him if the lady liked the pin I might commission something else from him next year. That evening I used the shed back of Diehl's to cut a slight slope in the planks for the rafters in preparation for Saturday's "roof raising." The eight rafters would be paired 5/4 x 6 planks, one on each side of a bracket, held together by two bolts through the planks and their enclosed bracket. Sturdy enough, I was certain.

I still had not heard from Edie. Had my suggestions appeared too shallow for her? Rather than mope over the awkwardness of a long distance relationship with a woman about whom my own feelings were not fully clear, I sat down later that evening to write her a note on my activities and the barbecue. I did not mention my conversation with Phyllis, except to pass on the peach pie recipe which she might ask Mr. Sou to try. While I had concluded that Mrs. Mercer enjoyed playing the flirt on occasion, I remembered too well Edie's suspicions about Kitty Adair to risk her being hurt again, however unwarranted.

Early Saturday morning I drove over to the Voss home. Charlie came out the backdoor as soon as he heard me drive up. I told him we were going to try and get the rafters up and asked him if he had a bicycle helmet. He nodded and went inside for it while I unloaded the rafters from the trunk. I explained to Charlie that he would need some kind of a support to hold the metal bracket at the correct height and centered until we could get at least three rafter pairs bolted in place. Charlie nodded again, he was not a great talker, I decided, but I asked him if he had any suggestions. After squinting at the bracket and the eight posts for a few minutes he surprised me with an idea I had myself considered in just a little more detail the previous evening. It was simple, but effective. Two 2x4's, crossed and supported at their ends on opposite posts, with some scrap 2x4 pieces clamped to them near the crossing point, and the bracket set on top of them, would do the trick. I congratulated him and we set about doing it. I insisted on his wearing the helmet for protection in case something fell while he was underneath the bracket and I was on the ladder securing the rafters to it. It took a lot of shifting of the supporting 2x4's until we got the crossing point centered over the floor. I dropped a plumb bob from the crossing point while Charlie measured its distance from the supporting posts. When they were all equally spaced I nailed the supports temporarily to the 4x4 posts. I had anticipated this approach, so I had brought along a half-dozen large C-clamps to fasten the short pieces that were to hold the bracket at the correct height to the crossed 2x4's. A bit more fussing about with the clamps, and we finally had the bracket in place.

The next step was to trim the bracket end of the rafters at an angle so they would butt tightly against the pipe part of the bracket. I needed a straight piece of thin wood I could lay against the pipe while the other end rested on a 4x4 post. This would define the angle to cut the bracket end of a rafter and also by subtracting from 90 degrees, the angle to notch the other end which would rest on the post. I asked Charlie to see if he could find something that would fit the bill. After a few minutes he came out of the garage with two wooden yardsticks stamped "Voss For All Your Lumber Needs." "We could clamp these together to give us about 5', couldn't we, Mr. Borden?"

"We certainly could, Charlie," I replied. Charlie showed me he was more capable than his mother gave him credit for. He also told me there was another step ladder in the garage, so he could get up to hold the other end of the yardstick on the post while I used a sliding bevel to get the angle at the bracket end. I cut the bracket end of a rafter on the chop saw and used a handsaw to cut the notch at the post end. It was also necessary to trim the thickness of the rafters where they met the pipe to a wedge shape in order for them to butt against the pipe. There is just not enough space between the flanges on the small circumference of the pipe to accommodate the full thickness of the paired rafters. I had made a jig that held the rafters securely upright at the chop saw so I could cut the wedges quickly and with no risk of losing a finger or two. That would put a permanent halt on any further construction.

Then, with Charlie holding one of the rafters at the post end and me at the bracket end, I marked the location of the bolt holes. Since the rafters were to be paired, one on each side of a bracket, I cut the second one using the first as a template, and carefully drilled the bolt holes in both.

I suggested a short break before we fastened the first pair of rafters in place. Mina brought out two cokes while we were sitting on the kitchen steps. "I can see you're thinking about something Charlie, what is it?" I asked.

"We were so careful in centering the bracket, I was wondering if we could use the first rafter as a template to cut all the others. It would sure save a lot of work." Mina patted him on the head and said he should let Mr. Borden decide how the work should be done. I could see Charlie shrink a little. A little re-inflation was needed I thought, so I assured Mina that I valued Charlie's suggestions, that he had a good grasp of how the construction was going, and was already a great help. Mina gave a resigned sigh and went back inside. I told Charlie we'd give his suggestion a try, but cautioned him that working on such a large structure, even standard-sized wood will actually vary slightly in size so adjustments in length might be needed, and it would be best to test fit a rafter on the other brackets and see which ones could be cut to that pattern and which would need a slightly different length. As it turned out, four of the remaining brackets could accept the same rafter pair, while the remaining three needed an extra quarter inch adjustment in cutting the notch to fit the 4x4 posts. The bolt holes in any case had to be individually marked and drilled. We finished installing the rafters by late afternoon and called it quits for the day.

Sunday morning I started cutting the triangular plywood pieces for the roof sheathing. The Vosses were at church, as usual, so my helper wasn't available. I was getting a little achy in the legs from so much up-and-down-the-ladder work, marking the piece for cutting and then test fitting on the rafters. Since I had cut the rafters with a shallow curve on the top edge, I decided the sheathing should be screwed to them rather than nailed in order to securely hold the stiff plywood snugly to the curve. Unfortunately, the deck screws I had been using were threaded the whole length of the shaft, making it more difficult to snug the sheathing to the rafter. I was about to go to Mrs. Fashlich's to phone Elmer and see if he could open the hardware store and get a box of partially threaded screws, when the Vosses returned. Sam saw me at the gazebo and came over. I explained my problem to him and he said he thought they had that type of screw at the lumberyard. I rode down with him.

"You know, Borden, Charlie sits out in back nearly everyday looking at and talking about the construction, it seems to have completely absorbed his interest. I hope he's really helping."

Another Voss needing reassurance. "Of course he is," I replied. "You don't think I'm paying him for nothing, do you? But as a matter of fact, I think you could relent a little on his using power tools, Sam. Not the chop saw of course, but the drill and jigsaw are quite safe, and would be a big help. Charlie seems to me to be a careful and sensible young man. Give him a little more work experience this summer, I'm sure he'll eat it up."

"He's already eating it up, Borden. Mina says he's eating twice as much as usual!"

Charlie had changed his Sunday clothes to blue jeans and was waiting for me when we got back from the lumberyard. I explained what we had to do, and that his dad had agreed to let him use the drill. He liked that, but could he be trusted up on the roof? I decided not for today. Best to let him practice drilling holes in some scrap first, but I needed the drill myself, so Charlie's practice would have to wait. Fixing a screwdriver bit into the drill, and with my assistant handing up the sheathing pieces, we got all the sheathing in place in a few hours. Being somewhat over cautious, I decided to calk the seams where the triangular sheathing pieces met. Next weekend we'd lay the shingles. And maybe the railings too.

I was tired from crouching on top of the rafters and sheathing. It was becoming very clear to me that I had significantly underestimated how long this job was going to take, and mulled over the idea of asking Elmer for a week off to wrap it up.

I spent the last hour of the afternoon watching Charlie practice with the drill and jigsaw. He was O.K. with the saw, it was pretty light and he had a good eye and quick reflexes to cut right on the line I scribed for him. The drill was another matter, it was a ½" heavy duty model and Charlie really didn't have the muscle for it. I could see the struggle to hold the drill had depressed his ego. He must have been taunted a lot for being so skinny. I tried to cheer him up by telling him I'd get a lighter drill for next week, and that before we were done he'd put on enough muscle to get on the football team. He gave me a wan smile, but was still in the dumps when we quit.

Chapter XIV

A Date With Edie

Mrs. Fashlich had a telegram for me when I got home. "From California, Mr. Borden." Trust Mrs. Fashlich to checkup on my mail. I should never have given her that line about the Indiana gamblers. I'm sure she was on constant alert to make certain they weren't lurking outside to waylay me, or worse, to break into her house and murder us all. My smile set her at ease, it was from Edie. But in San Francisco? It was short, telling me she could make a layover in Minneapolis during her flight back if I was interested in meeting her there. Of course I was interested! It would be next Friday, and I should wire her on Wednesday, care of the Western Union office where she had sent it. It would be about a 5 hour drive, some 250 miles. She had given me the expected arrival time, about 7:30 in the evening, so I could leave at a reasonable hour. No other details were supplied, except the flight number, so I didn't know how long we would be together. I decided to just let the planning wait until we met. Rather than let the gazebo wait for an extra weekend, the next day, Monday, I decided to ask Elmer for time off for at least part of the week as a part of my two week vacation. He was grumpy about it, but since things were slow after the Fourth, he agreed. I would take off from Tuesday through possibly Monday. I was sure Edie would want to be back at the Lodge by Monday, so she'd continue her flight on Sunday, but why risk cutting short our meeting, which was already infrequent enough. During my lunch break I walked down to the lumberyard to tell Voss I'd be working on the gazebo starting tomorrow through noon Friday. When I asked him to get the shingles delivered and another batch of 2x4's for the railings, he seemed to be wrestling with some objection.

"What's bothering you, Sam? I thought you'd be happy to get most of the mess in your backyard cleaned up."

"It's about the cedar shingles, Borden. I don't carry them, they're expensive and I'd have to send a truck into C.R. or Davenport for them." I told him

I wasn't happy about them either. The problem of ensuring against water leaks along the eight ridges of the octagon wasn't fully solved in my own mind. You just don't bend wood shingles like you can asphalt ones to cover the gap where the shingles meet at the ridgeline. But I reminded Sam that Mina especially liked the rustic look they gave the gazebo, so I had no choice but to agree.

"However, if you can change her mind, do so," I told him. "Show her some of the asphalt shingles you have in a similar color. But if you can't, see if there's any calk compatible with cedar that we can use. And also, if it has to be cedar, be sure to get plenty of copper or stainless steel roofing nails. Remember the sheathing is ½" and we don't want any nails protruding inside the roof, so size the nails according to the thickness of the shingles you get, you know at the thick nailing end. I'll need them first thing Wednesday, but get the roofing paper and 2x4's and several boxes of 2½" deck screws for tomorrow. And oh yes, tell Charlie I'd like him to help tomorrow if he's free." Poor Sam, he'd have to try and sell Mina on asphalt shingles. And poor me, I knew he 'd lose and I'd better figure out what to do about the seams where the shingles meet at the ridges.

Charlie, bless his skinny little self, was waiting for me the next morning. I had him practicing with the 3/8" drill while I used a router to round the top and bottom of one side of the 2x4's and cut grooves for seating the screens on the other side. I also made some jigs for holding the 2x4 railings in place. When I finished, he helped me measure each of the 7 railings (no rail at the opening for the door of course). They were cut with a 67½ degree miter on each end—such is the geometrical pain in the neck with an octagon. I also made 2 drill guides for drilling the pocket holes for the screws in the rails and 14 brackets from 2x2's to add support to each end of the rails where they joined the 4x4 posts, all of which had to have a compound bevel at the post end.

Charlie used the 3/8" drill to make the pocket holes in the brackets while I clamped the jigs on adjacent posts, clamped a rail to the jigs, and scrunched down between the posts and under the rail to screw the rail in place. While I moved over to the next pair of posts, Charlie screwed the brackets to the rail and posts I had just finished. I kept a check on him to be sure he spaced the brackets on both rail and post properly to leave room to attach the screens and lattice decorations, but the was doing fine.

Of course his wrist got pretty tired seating those long screws, so I finally suggested he use the drill fitted with a screwdriver bit and to get a can of paste wax from his mother to lubricate the screws. He still had to lean into the drill to keep the bit seated in the screw head, but by the third rail he learned how to do it without stripping the screw heads. When the rails were in place, we took our lunch break. Not at Mina's, though. We drove down to the drugstore and had ham sandwiches and hot fudge sundaes. We had just finished when Herb Macklinburg called me from behind the rows of cans and bottles covering the prescription counter. Seems he had tried to get me at Diehl's to clear a paper jam in the copier. Charlie joined me as I opened the machine, dropped the toner pan, and after poking around fished out a mangled sheet of paper. I decided to add some toner while I was at it. Charlie had crouched down to peer into the paper path and asked me questions about the feed mechanism. "Charlie," I told him, "you're going to make a fine engineer someday, you've got the curiosity and good mechanical sense that's needed. I hope your mom lets you use them more." He said nothing, but looked pleased at the compliment.

Back at the gazebo, Charlie got to work finishing the bracket installation. For my part, I was up on the roof laying and stapling the roofing felt. I finished before Charlie, who was getting tired arms pushing on the heavy drill, and helped him with the few remaining brackets. We finished up about 4 o'clock. I drove down to the lumberyard to see what luck Sam had with the shingles, and also to rip a number of triangular strips from a batch of 2x2's. We needed these as nailing strips for the screens. The ripping had to be done on a table saw kept at the yard, and required some fussing around with wood scraps and clamps to make cutting the long lengths accurate and safe. It was becoming increasingly clear why octagonal floor plans were rarely found anymore. The amount of special cutting and trimming needed was just too labor intensive.

Sam had the shingles and would bring them over in the truck when he closed up. "No colored calk, Borden," he told me, "and anyway it probably wouldn't stick well on such a resinous wood as cedar." He also gave me a little 'how-to' pamphlet that his wholesaler in C.R. had. I gave it a read while at the diner that evening. Most of the shingling instructions were what I had expected from my experience with asphalt shingles, but the part on hip roofs, which the gazebo roof resembled, interested me. I decided to give the "true Boston hip" approach it described for roof ridges a try.

It looked neat and I thought lightened the heavy look of wood shingles meeting in 8 ridges.

The true Boston hip called for aluminum flashing pieces under the ridge shingles, so after a two-egg and sausage breakfast at the diner—I would need this for ballast on the roof—I stopped at Diehl's to borrow some tin snips and at the lumberyard for a roll of flashing, and the telegraph office to wire Edie an O.K. for Minneapolis.

My eager helper was waiting for me again. "Didn't you eat breakfast Charlie?" I asked. Mina was on the back porch and answered for him.

"He had his cereal, Emmett, and I must say, his appetite has certainly improved. He used to be such a finicky eater I worried about him being so thin." Charlie made a face for me, fortunately Mina couldn't see it. Charlie was at that pre-puberty age when many boys resent solicitous female concern, especially from their mothers.

After explaining to Charlie how the nailing strips were to be attached, cautioning him about making sure they were nailed in straight and plumb on the posts and that the triangular pieces were to go on the outside of the 4x4 posts, and the 2x2's on the underside of the top sill and underside of the rails, he was eager to get started at once. But first I had him try out the jigsaw again on the piece of scrap so I'd be sure he could handle it safely in cutting the ends on the nailing strips for the top sill and rail.

An hour later we were both busily banging away with hammers, occasionally stopped the racket to cut wood or chalk a line on the roofing paper. By noon I had half the shingles nailed. Mina called out that she had fixed lunch for us, so I saved some diner money. It was hot working on the roof, so I was glad she had made cold chicken sandwiches, lemonade and fresh peaches. I took the opportunity to discuss paint with her while eating. I thought an oil-based semi-transparent or opaque stain would be best for water-proofing the wood and suggested she ask her husband to bring some color samples home with him. "Are we that close to finishing, Emmett?" she asked.

"Well," I responded, patting Charlie on the back, "my partner here has been pushing me pretty hard to keep up with him. We'll need to paint before the screens and latticework are installed. You know of course that Sam wants the white plastic lattice, so there will be less maintenance work, so a nice choice would be some darker color, perhaps a mossy green or even a dull red, but you decide." A shade of green would be my choice. Mina wasn't flamboyant enough for red, but if the gazebo was Phyllis' that might be a different story, I thought.

I worked later that day, deciding to get all of the shingling done. There was plenty of light until 8, but I finished by 7:30. I was very tired, and getting sort of tired with the gazebo too. It was turning out to be a much bigger job than I had anticipated. I told Charlie to quit at 6 when his father came home, though he would have liked to continue.

I struggled out the next morning, took a little more time over my coffee at the diner, and finally got to the Voss house by 9:00. Charlie was already banging away at the last few nailing strips. I must admit that in the morning light the shingled roof looked pretty neat. I had cut the roof sheathing and rafters flush with the outside edge of the top sill, but extended the first double row of shingles out several inches further to form a narrow eave that seemed to make the whole structure blend better into the grounds.

Expecting that a perfect seal between the sheathing and top sill couldn't be made, I was prepared to calk the joints on the inside to close any access point for mosquitoes. By the time I had finished that, Charlie was finished with the nailing strips. We checked them over carefully with the straight edge of a board. He had gone a good job, only minor paring with a chisel on a couple of corners was necessary.

I set him to work to carefully measure and record the length and width of openings between the posts and top of the rails and the top sill, and on the underside of the rails and floor sill for each section of the octagon, except for where the door was to go. These were needed to build the screens, which I would do later at Diehl's. While he was doing that I started cutting pieces for the door. The door would open outward and close tight against the posts and a quarter-round piece nailed onto the top sill. To avoid the possibility of the wood swelling and sticking at the bottom against the floor, I left about a ¼" opening at the bottom of the door. I certainly wasn't going to nail a back-stop on the floor for people to trip over. But by grooving the bottom of the door and fitting a T-shaped rubber molding into it—the leg of the T pointing towards the floor, and just slightly flexing when the door was closed—I could get a good seal. It didn't need to be weather-tight, just bug-proof. Charlie watched me as I chiseled out the mortises and cut the tenons for the door pieces. We told Mina we'd have lunch at the drugstore since I 'd need the table saw at the lumberyard to cut rabbets for the door screens, and stop at Diehl's for T-molding, door hinges and a simple door latch.

By the end of the day, Charlie and I had completed assembly of the door, had it hung and the latch attached. I asked Mina if she had chosen the color, as painting would start tomorrow. She had after much arguing with Sam, according to Charlie, agreed to a medium shade of green. "Good choice, Mina," I flattered her. "It will blend well with the house color and create a cool look to the gazebo. Just what you want in the summer."

Friday morning we started painting. I had brought some disposable plastic gloves along and made Charlie wear them, as well as myself. I wasn't going to meet Edie speckled with green. Of course we each wore painters caps, courtesy of Voss Lumberyard, and a couple of good brushes, courtesy of Diehl's, but which would still be on the bill. I laid out the schedule for Charlie. I would be on the ladder painting the underside of the roof sheathing, rafters, top sill and upper parts of the posts, while Charlie would do the lower parts of the posts and rails. He seemed a little disappointed that I would be gone at noon until probably Tuesday evening, but I told him I expected him to give the floor two coats over the weekend, and that he could help me, if he wished, in making the screens and lattice. That cheered him up, plus the $30 for his work through Sunday. My last words at 11:00 were to be sure and put the lids down tight on the paint cans and make sure the brushes were cleaned in the jar of paint thinner and then washed in hot soapy water before he quit for the day. I was just about to leave, when I suddenly decided a postscript might be needed. "Charlie, when you paint the floor, which is the last thing of course, remember to start at the back of the gazebo and work towards the door."

"Very funny, Mr. Borden. You can't get trapped in a gazebo, they don't have any walls!"

CHAPTER XV
<u>MINNEAPOLIS</u>

Returning to my room, I showered, shaved extra close, and dressed. I had packed a small bag earlier, so I was already to go by noon. Meeting Mrs. Fashlich on my way out, I told her I would be gone for the weekend, and probably return Sunday night or Monday, and not to notify the police this time. Looking me up and down, from my shined shoes to my freshly pressed summer suit, she cackled "I don't think you're dressed to see your gambling friends this time, Mr. Borden, but be careful anyway, Mina will be anxious about your finishing her gazebo. I don't think Sam Voss or Charlie will do it for her if you can't." And with that admonition I took off. I drove at a comfortable speed, making several stops for lunch, etc., so I would be reasonably rested when I got to the Minneapolis airport. I made it by 6:30 with no trouble. The plane from San Francisco was on time and I met Edie at the arrival gate. She gave me her cheek to kiss, a nice change from the handshake at C.R., evidence of her pleasure, I hoped, in seeing me.

"What have you been doing, Emmett, you're as brown as a nut? You look thinner too."

"I'll tell you all about it, Edie, as soon as we get your baggage and find a place to stay. I'm afraid I didn't make any arrangements yet. I didn't know how long your layover would be, or what plans you might have. Your wire was remarkably non-informative. Were you saving money, or just being mysterious?"

"Maybe a little mysterious," she laughed. "I made reservations for us myself, at the Nakomis Hotel. We're Mr. and Mrs. Adamson. It will be a change for you, Emmett, your new identity through Monday morning. I hope you don't mind."

"Is this a women's lib marriage, Edie, where the man changes his name?"

"Not lib, just a convenience in using my Visa card number to guarantee the reservation. I called them from San Francisco when I got your wire. You see, you're my date this weekend, so the treat is mine."

While she waited at the baggage ramp I picked up a Nakomis brochure from a wall rack nearby, for directions. I had been in Minneapolis some years ago for my company, so I had some familiarity with the major routes. The brochure gave me directions from the airport and a few minutes later we were on our way, down the 35W expressway into the city, and left on 7th Street to the hotel. I let Edie out at the lobby entrance while I drove down to the garage. By the time I rejoined her she had registered and commandeered a porter for the bags. Our room was high up and spacious, with a good view of the downtown. Edie started to unpack while I was tipping the porter. I caught her from behind while she was hanging a dress in the closet. Encircling her waist, I pulled her close to me, nuzzling her neck and ear, but she twisted away. "Whoa there. Aren't you hungry, Emmett?" she laughed.

"Man does not live on meat and potatoes alone, Edie."

"I certainly hope not, but entree first, dessert later, Mr. Adamson. Just look at you. You must have lost 10 pounds since Chicago. Were you sick or on a diet?"

"I never diet, Edie, I've just been working too hard. But you're right, let's go eat, but where? It's been some years since I was in Minneapolis, and restaurants come and go quickly. In fact, I don't believe this hotel was here when I last visited. How did you find it?"

Edie ignored my last question, but taking another look at me said "It is steak and potatoes for you, Mr. Adamson. I simply won't be seen with a man people might think lighter than me. Murray's is just a few blocks away and their steaks are quite good. Now you unpack while I freshen-up a bit and we'll be off."

She was still Mrs. Adamson as far as making decisions were concerned. But I didn't mind letting her lead tonight. After all, she said I was her date.

Murray's advertises itself as the home of the butter knife steak. I had eaten there once and found their steaks very good. We had no trouble getting a good table at that rather late dinner hour. Over our cocktails, Edie insisted on hearing about my activities first. I had brought along Mina's picture of the gazebo to show her. She thought it was a large project to tackle by myself, so I told her about hiring my helper, Charlie. She seemed amused about it. "I have the impression you like him, Emmett, but you're not paying him enough, perhaps you ought to give him a bonus when it's finished."

"Yes, I thought of that. But actually I'm only getting $750 for the whole job and I've already put in over 10 days, excluding making the plans and estimates. I badly underestimated the amount of work involved, but building it intrigued me. It's strange you know, how reckless I've been since I met you, taking a flier on Snyder's machine tools, and then this job. You seem to have catalyzed me back to life." Edie smiled at my remark but said nothing. "Now tell me what you were doing in California, it couldn't have been a meeting of the Midwest Hotel Association."

"I have a new grandson, Emmett." She selected a few photos from her purse to show me. "It's my daughter Sharon's third child, and a rather difficult delivery, but all is well thank goodness." I studied the pictures, curious as to what Edie might have looked like at her daughter's age, about 25 I guessed. There was some resemblance, but hairstyles have large effects on women's looks. Her daughter was a brunette and wore her hair in a more bouffant style. She seemed to be about as tall as Edie, but thinner. A handsome young woman, I told her. Edie took the pictures back before I could give them more than a quick glance, and started to study the menu.

"You don't seem to want to talk much about your family. Is that true, or just a wrong impression?"

"I suppose it's true—but not because I'm hiding my family from you. There are no secrets to hide, but they're grown-up and have their own lives, and now I have my own life too. You noticed that I arranged that Sharon would not be aware of your wire to me. I want some of my life to be apart from my children, my own privacy to live and enjoy without the need to explain to them, or answer their questions or concerns. Rodde's will gave me an independence and position of my own, and I like it well enough to guard and preserve it."

"Well enough, Edie, then you may tell me as much or as little as you wish. However, you asked for, and I sent you, some suggestions on the future of the Lodge, not all of which, I'm afraid, were new to you. But I had no idea of what was financially feasible for you, or what building or zoning restrictions might apply. So, Mrs. Adamson, what's happening?"

Before she could respond, our steaks arrived, their rich aroma sharpened my hunger, and Edie's too, I was sure. "But let that wait a bit," I added, "this must be enjoyed hot." We ate in silence, except for approving comments on the steaks and au gratin potatoes. Edie enjoyed good food but was careful about the amount, so after finishing half her steak she offered me the rest.

Our conversation resumed over coffee. Edie offered me a cigarette, but I declined, mumbling something about preferring my pipe, which I had left behind in my hurry to get started. There was a sensuality about the way she smoked. I had only seen her smoke perhaps three or four times, and then only when she was relaxed, sitting down, and with coffee. Her pleasure seemed to be from the smell of the tobacco smoke, not from the taste. It was much like my enjoyment of pipe smoking, but without the fuss of loading and lightning and measured puffing so as to keep the bowl cool and the mouth dry. If her habits were different when she was alone or busy at the Lodge I didn't know. I did know that she seemed satisfied with the one cigarette and didn't light another.

"There are some problems about extending the building, Emmett," she began. "The city is anxious to cut down on on-street parking, so any extension that materially reduces the parking spaces available on the lot may have considerable opposition. I did arrange for an architect to consider your 'Black Hand' bar suggestion. I liked that one, I'm even sure Rodde would have liked it. I also considered weekend entertainment, even before your suggestion. That's still a possibility but it would require enlarging the dining area for a stage and I'm not sure cutting into the public rooms would be good. I don't want to lose my club and community meeting business or private parties. However, music in the present dining area is quite feasible and I've had some discussions with local artists. Oh, by the way, Emmett, did you know that Kitty Adair plays the harp? Now that would add class to Mr. Sou's cuisine. That appeals to me, though she could

111

only be there for the summer, but perhaps an early start next year might be possible."

By now the dining room was nearly empty. I signaled for the check, but Edie insisted on paying, giving the waiter her credit card. I still felt funny about that, old fashioned I guess, but when Edie reminded me again that she had called me for the date and was entitled, if not obligated, to pay, I had to acquiesce. "After all, Emmett," she laughed, "I'm still leaving you with the most important male prerogatives. You can open doors for me, light my cigarette, and make love." I had to accept her reasoning, what else could I do, start a fight after waiting so long to see her again?

We walked back to the Nakomis. Most of the stores were closed and the streets pretty well deserted by then, nearly 10 o'clock.

I exercised one of my prerogatives almost at once, caressing and undressing her as soon as we were in the room. I did not fumble this time with her bra. It fastened in back—the most convenient place during a standing embrace. Guided by my gentle nudge, Edie lay on the bed and raised her hips so I could remove her pantyhose. "Sorry about those," she murmured, obviously remembering my comments about that garment, on what seemed a long time ago. On impulse I bent down to kiss the valley formed where her thigh and hip met. I felt her body suddenly tense, and heard her startled question "What are you doing, Emmett?"

I kissed her again, softer but a bit lower. "Making love to you, Mrs. Adamson, a prerogative you left for me." After a moment I felt her muscles relax a bit, but I could sense her unease remained. With no further desire to press an unwelcome embrace, I got undressed, kissed her goodnight and turned off the bedside lamp.

Lying there, I wondered if Rodde's exotic collecting had misled me about Edie's sophistication. I had made love to Francis many times that way when her illness left her too weak for more active participation, so I hadn't thought of it as an unusual thing. But of course it is unusual, perhaps the most intimate caress a man can give a woman.

I rose early next morning, washed, shaved, and dressed while Edie was still asleep. Or so I thought. I had just slipped my wallet into my jacket pocket when I heard Edie's good morning greeting. I responded with a kiss on the top of her head, about all that was showing outside the sheet. I was about to sit next to her, but she suggested I wait for her in the coffee shop. Quizzical, but obedient, I left, telling her not to be too long.

I was finishing my third cup of coffee, drinking slowly, when she arrived. "You're looking much better, Emmett, steak and potatoes were clearly what you needed, and now I think a western omelet will round out the cure." Was Edie's uncharacteristic heartiness an attempt to hide embarrassment?

"What was my illness that these eggs are going to cure, doctor?" She looked away without answering, fussing with her napkin. I waited a bit for a response, but she pretended she hadn't heard me. "Are you embarrassed, Edie?" I asked.

"Of course I am," she blurted, seeming undecided about whether to laugh or cry. "You caught me unaware last night, damn you, and I reacted like a naive schoolgirl! I spoiled the evening for you and I hate myself for that."

"But Edie, you didn't spoil anything. I merely offered a closer intimacy which you didn't happen to want."

"Well, you couldn't get much closer," she countered. Suddenly she started to laugh. "After nearly 20 years of marriage, two children, and 10 years at the Lodge with Rodde's erotica—and even letting it stay in my card room, I have to admit that there were some gaps in my experience with men."

"But surely your husband--." But she interrupted me.

"No, Frank didn't. His approach was more taking than giving. So you see, though I had read about—about last night, I hadn't actually experienced it. But enough of this, the room is filling up. We'll order, and it's still an omelet for you, Mr. Adamson; then we'll decide on the activity for today."

Back in our room, we looked through the brochures I had picked up at the lobby desk. The Guthrie Theater was doing a revival of Ibsen's 'Enemy of the People'. A little heavy going I thought for a summer weekend. Anyway, my call to the box office disclosed they were sold out, but we were in luck when I called the Old Log Theater. Matinee tickets for 'The Importance of Being Earnest' were available. I started to give my credit card number to reserve the tickets when Edie stopped me. "My treat remember, Mr. Adamson," and handed me her card.

"Let's try Gustino's for dinner, Emmett. They have waiters and waitresses singing opera arias. It should be fun." I made reservations for 7, again as Mr. and Mrs. Adamson. That left us a couple of hours free until theater time.

I asked if she wanted to go shopping. "The Mall of America, Edie? Or we could take in The Sculpture Gardens. There seems to be a lot to see." I was scanning the Twin Cities event brochure when I felt her arms around me.

"No shopping, Emmett, would you let me redeem myself with a second chance instead?"

Edie's libido always seemed higher in the mornings, but then I noticed she had showered before coming down to breakfast. Perhaps I had been too impetuous last night.

We lost track of the time and had to rush to make the theater.

Chapter XVI
<u>Minneapolis 2</u>

"How's your blood sugar, Edie?" I asked as we left the theater. It was 4:30 and we had missed lunch by spending so much time working on her redemption. We were nearing the St. Olaf Hotel.

"Are you asking in earnest," she quipped, "or are you hungry?"

"Hungry," I replied, and turned into the hotel. We started toward the coffee shop just off the lobby when I saw a placard announcing a tea dance in a small reception room. Intrigued, I guided Edie towards the hostess at the entrance. She led us to a small table near a miniscule clearing that was masquerading as a dance floor.

"The band is taking a short break," she said, placing a single sheet menu on the table. After waiting a very long time for a waitress to take our order—actually only about 10 minutes—I was about to signal the hostess when Edie stopped me with "she approaches, she is nigh." Carrying on with the Oscar Wilde theme, she asked the waitress if cucumbers were included in the tea sandwich assortment.

"Oh you've been to the play," our waitress replied, smiling after a puzzled moment. "Yes they are, but for ready money only."

"Don't mind us," Edie laughed, "we're suffering from a wild fever. We'll have the assortment. Oolong for me, and Black Russian tea for my theater companion, Mr. Bordonovitch."

The girl looked at me doubtfully. "He doesn't look very Russian."

"First generation immigrant," Edie lied. "His mother was a French actress. Her company had an engagement in Moscow where she met Count Bordonovitch. They narrowly escaped the KGB during the Stalin purge and emigrated to America. He's gathering material for a book on regional theaters, so I brought him here. We're doing the Guthrie later."

"How did I do?" Edie asked after the girl, seemingly impressed, left to put in our order.

"Too good, Mrs. Adamson," I replied. "She may want my autograph when she comes back, and I can't write Russian. Anyway, I told you it was Bordonova."

"You know I had to change that, Emmett, she may know that's the wrong ending. Being so near the theater, she probably knows some of the actors and directors."

Our tea and sandwiches arrived along with a second, more careful scrutiny of my face. Mumbling a few 'das' and 'nyets' in a sufficiently guttural voice, I busied myself with the food to avoid any questions from our waitress. Edie however seemed to relish her little charade and carried on a conversation with the girl about the theater, the clientele that came to the tea dance, how long ago it had been started, etc. I was glad to see the hostess wildly waving for our waitress to tend to a new couple she had seated.

The band, actually only a little trio, had returned and started a fox trot medley, not that the younger couples on the floor gave much concern about that. They had all their own steps, though the floor was too small for really flamboyant figures.

"Aren't you going to ask me to dance, Comrade Bordonovitch?" Edie smirked.

"Da," I replied, and rose to pull her chair back. Mostly our dancing consisted of one or two steps forward, then the same backward. The floor was very crowded, fortunately, so my skill wasn't challenged too much, and also, fortunately, it gave me an innocent excuse for holding Edie close to me.

"Are you simply being pressed by the crowded conditions, or is my magnetic presence drawing you to me?" she murmured, tilting her head back to look up at me.

"Of course," I replied, leaving her to supply her own reason, which she did.

"I'm glad, Emmett, I was afraid St. Olaf might be violating the fire code maximum occupancy rating. I'll turn the magnet down a bit at the end of this medley."

After a few more minutes the trio abandoned the fox trot for a faster disco beat. Even if I had wanted to, there just wasn't enough room for all of us to do it right. We returned to our table. Edie searched her purse for cigarettes, but came up empty. I got up to get her a new pack. "Templeton Filter Kings?" I asked. She nodded, surprised that I had observed her brand.

Passing the waitress on my way to the lobby, I asked her to bring more tea. "Da," she replied with a smile.

"Spas-i-bah," I responded with a grin—my garbled Russian 'thank you'. Since our Chicago exchange at the Rive Gauche I had tried learning a little Russian hoping to tease Edie some more, but finally I had to give it up. I couldn't get my tongue around all the variations on vowel sounds and the unreasonable running together of so many consonants.

"Nyhzahshtah pah zhalstah," she responded. Then, seeing my blank look, translated for me with a wink "You're welcome."

Back at our table I warned Edie "no more make believe Russian with the waitresses. She's on to us."

Giving Edie the cigarettes was a good opportunity to give her the pin also. I handed her the pack and placed the matches over the jewel box, setting it by the side of her cup. Feigning preoccupation by tying a shoelace, I left Edie to light the cigarette herself.

"What is this, Emmett?" I straightened up to see her holding the box.

"A birthday present," I responded, "for whenever your birthday is, but you may open it now if you like."

"I will, thank you. You're a couple of weeks early, but you wouldn't have known would you, or would you?" Her quizzical look turned to wide-eyed surprise as she saw Ridetti's handiwork. "Wherever did you find this? It's an almost perfect copy of the orchid you gave me."

I confessed that I had it made special for her. Turning it over she saw Ridetti's name engraved on the back. "The name seems familiar somehow."

"He's an art instructor at the University. I sold him some of Snyder's tools, remember, and when I found he did jewelry, I commissioned the piece. Oh, by the way, Kitty Adair worked in that department, so don't mention his name if you wish to keep our relation private."

"I'll wear it tonight, Emmett. Thank you, it's very handsome." I was pleased that she seemed pleased. Well worth the price.

It was almost 6:00 by the time we finished our second cup of tea, and the crowd was beginning to thin out. Edie signaled the waitress and gave her credit card for the bill. I noticed on the receipt the waitress had scribbled something in Cyrillic and signed it 'Natasha'. I was embarrassed, but Edie just laughed. "Let me copy the note," I asked, "I'll get it translated by someone at the University when I get back."

Leaving, we passed our waitress, and letting Edie go ahead, I slipped a $10 bill in her hand to ease my embarrassment and mumbled "spahseebah, Natasha," hoping my accent conveyed my intended 'thank you' and not some inane word.

A message was waiting for Edie when we arrived back at our hotel. "I'm sorry, Emmett," she told me, "it's from Clarissa. She's relaying a call from my attorney. The zoning board has scheduled a Monday hearing on my proposal for certain alterations on the Lodge. He wants to discuss how we might counter some board opposition before the meeting. I'll have to leave sometime early tomorrow."

I raised my hands in a gesture of despair and reached for the phonebook for airline reservations numbers. The best bet seemed to switch her Monday reservations to Sunday on the same flights in order to simplify the interconnection from Chicago to the South Bend airport where she had parked her car. Her luck held out, both flights were underbooked, and the change was made. She would have to be at the airport by 3:00. I had no desire to remain in Minneapolis after Edie left, so I thought I might as well head back to Keonah after taking Edie to the airport. I decided to give Charlie a call and let him know I'd be back a day early and find out how his paint job on the gazebo was progressing.

A surprised Mrs. Voss answered my call wondering what I was doing in Minneapolis. Visiting a favorite relative was my current excuse, and after a brief exchange of greetings she called Charlie to the phone. My partner seemed excited over my calling him long distance. His first long distance call he said. He reported that the second coat of paint would be done Sunday and should be dry enough by Monday noon for us to walk on it. He had made more progress than I had expected. I thought maybe he might have worked too fast to do a good job, but he told me his dad had checked it over when he finished about 4:00 this afternoon and seemed satisfied. Charlie was very proud of having been given sole responsibility for a big job and doing it well. Sam was pleased also, as I found out Monday.

"I think my partner has been doing O.K. in my absence," I told Edie. "I owe you $2.75 for the call, it had to go on the room bill of course." She had been freshening-up in the john while I placed the call.

"You like Charlie, don't you?" she said, smiling at me. I told her I did, naturally enough. After a moment she added, startling me: "You are still fertile aren't you, Emmett?"

My stunned mind blurted out without really thinking, "You're pregnant!"

"Hardly," she laughed. "That would be a miracle. Not a virgin birth for sure, but a miracle anyway. No, that's not been possible for some years. What I meant was you could still have a son, you know—or daughter. I suspect you'd make a good father. Why waste the potential? Your own if possible, or adopt."

"Single men would not be an acceptable adoption prospect, Edie, and my sex doesn't give birth."

"Don't be naive, Emmett. Both objections have the same solution. But we'd better hurry if we're to keep our dinner reservation."

Five minutes in the bathroom were sufficient for a touch-up shave with the electric razor and we were on our way. I was still too surprised by Edie's question and comment to give it any really serious thought.

Gustino's was crowded and bubbling with chatter from a mixture of young and old. Edie suggested a sparkling wine would fit the atmosphere better than cocktails, and ordered Asti Spumonte. My hostess was leading again, but that was appropriate since it was still her treat. We decided to share an appetizer due to the rather late tea, and munched on a rice and cheese mixture rolled into tiny balls and deep fat fried. They were quite good with a pleasant contrast of crunchy outside and soft inside. I was almost sorry we hadn't ordered two helpings.

"I like this, Emmett. The dining room at the Lodge is really a little too old fashioned." But then she mused, "but how far could I go without offending Chang Sou? He has strong opinions on dining decor—probably too much experience with officers' clubs. But no matter, Elkton isn't large enough to attract this many diners. Still I think adding some entertainment will give us a bigger draw. That issue is one of the things my lawyer is bringing up to the zoning board hearing Monday."

Edie scanned the menu while I poured another Spumonte. "Will you let me order for you," she asked? Nonplused by her request, I could only stare at her for a moment. Then regaining my composure, I told her I would enjoy that, hoping that was the response she wanted. "That just burst out of me, Em, honestly, and for the most ridiculous of reasons. I suddenly felt domestic and wanted to cook you a dinner, which of course is impossible right now, but at least I can select the menu."

What had come over my date? I thought at first it was the wine, but then she was already in a quirky state at the tea dance.

I told myself 'no matter', she is enjoying the day. Perhaps it is a delayed final release of tension over her daughter's difficult delivery.

The noise level suddenly dropped as a phonograph began the instrumental music lead-in for the tenor aria drinking song from Cavalleria Rusticana. I had heard it often enough on WQXR New York to remember it. One of the waiters, young and rather handsome, sang. I thought he did well considering the poor acoustics of the room and the rattle of dishes. At the very least, he looked the part of young Turridici, which few top rank opera singers do. Amid the general clapping, our waitress brought our dishes.

Edie had ordered in Italian and had commandeered my copy of the menu, so I didn't know what we were getting. I knew no Italian, in fact I didn't have fluency with any foreign language. I didn't need it as an engineer and avoided the subject, except for my abortive effort to learn enough Russian to discombobulate Edie. As it was, I was unsure Edie's Italian was really so good. She seemed to have stumbled over some words, stubbornly refusing to point to the item on the menu, so I wondered if the dishes were what she had expected. They must have been as she expressed no surprise at their appearance.

As I somehow expected, Edie had ordered fish for herself: a small whole baked trout with mushrooms, very attractively served. For me, boned breast of chicken stuffed with prosciuto and cheese. Chicken Bolognese. I had made it myself a few times, but with Smithfield ham. The vegetables were served separately—that is, to be shared. An excellent spinach mold with the ubiquitous Parmesan cheese, and fresh asparagus dressed with lemon and olive oil.

There is a certain skill required in eating fish served whole, and Edie had learned it well. When I commented on how efficiently and neatly she peeled back the skin and lifted the top half of the filet (she had waved the waitress away) from the backbone, she told me her housemother at Bryn Mawr taught all her girls proper table manners. "I got an A+," she said laughing, "but it was a non-credit course."

Our salad, Edie advised me, was a house specialty: radicchio, chopped cucumber, celery leaves, and pimento dressed in olive oil, of course, and a touch of tarragon vinegar. I ate it with a crisp Italian roll. Edie omitted the bread, clearly continuing her struggle against gravity. I have had no such problem, and find good breads a delicious treat not to be passed by, though I don't slobber it with butter. Butter is best, in my opinion, when it is in an amount just to be noticed, but not enough to intrude on the taste buds. I had to stop munching however. A pretty young waitress, accompanied by phonograph, began a Puccini aria.

"You are a sentimental romantic, Emmett," Edie murmured. "I could see it in your eyes, that far away look of longing for something when her voice swelled."

"Not sentimental or romantic anymore, Edie. Just a maudlin old engineer showing a bit of melancholy. It reminded me of better times."

"That was Ko Ko San's farewell to life. You thought of Francis again?"

"The opera was a favorite of hers. I try to avoid hearing it. I miss her, Edie, I'll always miss her."

I resumed with my salad and roll, crunching down on it with a hard bite, meant to discourage further discussion on this subject. Edie must have sensed my mood, saying nothing further.

Our waitress arrived just then and Edie gave her the dessert order as she cleared the dinner and salad plates. I noticed a man waiting behind her as the plates were gathered. Edie looked up, surprise all over her face, as he said hello.

"What in the world! Robby!"

"How are you, Edie?" he asked, and turned to nod at me.

I could see she was embarrassed for a moment, but regaining her composure and giving me a straight look, boring right into my eyes, introduced me as her cousin, Mr. Borden, and him as Robert Carlton. We exchanged hellos. I thought Edie would be more at ease if I left for a bit, so I asked them to excuse me while I went to the men's room, and offered Carlton my chair. I waited in the lobby for a while until he left the table and then came back. Edie had regained her composure.

"I hope you didn't mind the divorce, cousin Borden?"

"I didn't mind, Edie, but aren't you going through a lot of complications just to hide a date? He's not from Elkton is he, this Mr. Robby?" She flushed at my mention of his familiar. Edie looked around the dining room.

"He's gone" I told her, surmising that's who she was looking for. "I waited until he left before coming back so you'd be free to talk. By the way, he was with another couple, husband and wife, I presume."

"Not anymore," Edie answered. "He was assistant manager under Rodde. When Rodde died and left me to manage the Lodge he thought our relationship entitled him to a share of the Lodge too. I told him I didn't think so, so he left. He was not aware of the circumstances behind Rodde's giving me the Lodge and I saw no reason for him to know. No, that's not right, I saw reasons for him not to know. Anyway, it became clear to me his interest in me was not all in my mature charm." She said that with a sour tone, and then vehemently "Men can be such bastards."

"Me too, Edie?" I asked. "Am I a bastard?"

She reached over to touch my hand. "Not you, Emmett. You're the gentle lover I woke from a long sleep."

"And then there was your husband," I added.

"Oh yes, there's Frank. Not exactly a bastard, Emmett, but not a faithful husband either. I knew it early. It was easy for him to play around, a handsome military man, often away from home. I learned to live with it for the sake of the children. I had to share him with other women, but I insisted he be discreet and to stay away from my friends. He was scrupulous about that, having his flings when he was at some other base during a mission."

The waitress interrupted us with dessert. Zabaglione with a dish of small almond cookies.

"I hope to god you didn't describe me to Robby as your lover, Edie, or did he ask?"

"He asked. I simply told him I stopped on my way back from San Francisco to get your views about enhancing the Lodge's appeal. I identified you as an investment counselor who suggested I look at this place as one possible idea."

I told her it was probably a lame excuse. "If he's really a bastard he'll try to find me listed in the telephone book and not finding me, check at the hotels under your name or mine and find a Mr. and Mrs. Adamson registered at the Nakomis."

"I suppose so." She seemed resigned to it.

I decided to change the subject by following up on the singing waiter theme, suggesting how she might try a mix of opera, some Gilbert and Sullivan for lightness and humor, and some popular classics; where she might find performers at a reasonable rate, not yet professionals, but music students who'd wait tables for the benefit of adding some experience to their resumes along with money. We lingered over Strega for a few more songs and then left.

Chapter XVII
Funning With Phyllis

The drive back to Keonah was a leisurely one that late Sunday afternoon. I felt relaxed and drove accordingly. Edie and I had a late morning breakfast after packing, and decided we had time before her flight to drive over to St. Paul and take the two hour riverboat cruise on the 'Josiah Snelling'. I insisted on its being my treat. I bought her a gaudy straw hat to shield the hot sun reflecting off the Mississippi. We ate hot dogs and sauerkraut, drank beer and strolled happily along the deck. Edie was delighted at my suggestion we have our pictures taken by the shipboard photographer. He took several shots for each of us.

The distinction between Edie and Mrs. Adamson was fading from my thoughts. I would have her picture now to remind me they were one, but I was beginning to realize there never was a distinction. Mrs. Adamson was just Edie wearing a protective cover after two disappointing relations. I had concluded that her affair with Carlton was emotionally much deeper than our own. For one thing, it happened a few years ago, how many I wasn't sure, but probably while Rodde was still alive, and that was more than five years ago. She would have been about 40 I guessed, and still susceptible to a romance. That burst of bitterness, after Carlton left our table, couldn't have been caused by just a casual affair breaking up long ago.

I suddenly realized I'd missed my turn from US 35 to US 218. "What am I doing?" I asked myself. "Is Edie Adamson a clock I'm trying to take apart to see what makes her tick? It ought to be enough for you, Borden, to enjoy her company on these rare occasions without trying to psychoanalyze her." Finally finding a place where I could safely turn around, I decided to concentrate on my driving, leave Edie Adamson her mysteries, and to just be grateful for the pleasure her friendship has given me. I did think of Edie as a friend, a friend and occasional lover that's true, but it would require zero separation to become much more. Would she give up the Lodge for me, or could I find an acceptable function in Elkton? The first couldn't even be considered. Married to a hardware clerk at near minimum wage? Whatever I was before, now I was simply a drifter. I had no purpose before me anymore, and certainly I could see none in Keonah. As for Elkton, I would again need some purpose in being there, adequate to support us both—I would not humiliate either of us by letting her friends think of me as being kept. That is not man's function, not ever mine. No solution presented itself.

It was late evening by the time I got back to Keonah. I decided to stop along the way for dinner. After Italian the night before, I chose prime ribs at a steakhouse just outside of Waterloo, baked Idaho with sour cream and chives, tossed green salad with avocado dressing, and a hot fudge sundae with maple walnut ice cream. An indulgence after a blissful weekend. Cut short, unfortunately, but then Edie had called me her gentle lover. I liked that.

Monday morning I stopped at Voss's to check the gazebo status. Charlie spotted me and came out to join me. The painting was finished and dry. He had done a good job. I told him so. Only the screens and latticework remained. Seven of each for the upper sections, above the rails and ditto for the lower, plus one screen for the door. It would be a fair amount of work which fortunately could be done at Diehl's. I realized now that I could have saved work and cost by arranging the design so that a single screen replaced each top and bottom pair, but it was too late.

"I guess the painting was the last job for me," Charlie said disappointedly. Thinking about fussing with those 15 screens alone, I decided to ask Charlie to help. He was delighted, but I cautioned him he would have to get his mother's approval since he would have to work at Diehl's.

Minerva had mellowed a bit after seeing how her Charlie had worked on a project long on her wish list, with enthusiasm, and without incident, except for lots of paint spatters on his hair and clothes, so she came out and gave me her consent. I told Charlie to come down right after lunch and to be sure his measurements were correct.

Elmer hadn't expected me 'til Tuesday, so no outside work was scheduled. I started making an adjustable jig from a carefully selected straight and flat length of 5/4 x 6 plank and some 1 x 2 sticks. I had worked out the design some weeks earlier so it was just a matter of drilling holes and routing a long narrow slot down the length of the plank, in the center of its width. The purpose of the jig of course, was to hold the aluminum frame pieces for the screens securely in place and square while the corner connectors were screwed in place to join them. Also with the frames clamped in the jig, it would be easier to stretch and spline the screening cloth.

Imagine the outline of a square, about 18" on a side, and its 2 diagonal lines. Extend one end of one diagonal about 5', slightly shorter than my plank, and cut the outline of the square at both ends of the other diagonal. Now imagine that you separate the two parts of the severed square by pulling the part on the extended diagonal some distance away from the other part, but keeping its corner on the line of the extended diagonal. You now have two L-shaped figures on that extended diagonal, but one is the upside down mirror image of the other. Pin the corners of the L's onto the diagonal so they may swivel. Finally, let the pin of one L be fixed on the diagonal so the L can still turn on the pin, but can't move along the diagonal. Let the pin on the other L be free to move along the diagonal, but be able to be clamped at any particular distance that you wish.

Having cut the four aluminum frame pieces for one screen (call them 2 long and 2 short pieces for convenience, since a screen will in general be a rectangle) to proper length (miter cuts of course at each end), clamp a long and short piece onto the legs of one L, butting the mitered ends snugly together at the corner of the L. Do the same at the other L, however, making sure that the long piece is clamped to the leg sticking out of the opposite side of the diagonal. Ditto again for the short piece. Now the movable L with its clamped frame pieces can be moved and turned along the diagonal until the free ends of the frame pieces meet, short butted to long. Clamp the movable L to the diagonal and the frame pieces will be rigidly held in a true rectangle, ready for the corner connectors to be screwed onto the frame pieces and the screening cloth to be splined into grooves in the frame.

The slot I routed in the long plank corresponds to the extended diagonal. The pin for the movable L, actually just a bolt, would pass through the slot and could be locked in place by tightening with a wing nut. A hole drilled near one end of the plank would allow the other to be fixed in place by a similar bolt, but still free to turn. Both L's have to swivel of course because the slot in the plank defines the diagonal of the rectangular frame, and the angle that diagonal makes with the sides of the rectangle depends upon the length of its sides. Thus the jig could accommodate any size frame, limited only by the length of the plank chosen.

Each L was formed by lap-joining at right angles a pair of the 1 x 2's and carefully drilling the pivot bolt hole midway along the diagonal going from the outside to the inside corner of the L.

I was more pleased with the design than Elmer, who thought it was a little overkill, but I countered that he wouldn't think so after making 15 screens without it. Thinking back, I could have used the jig to make the wood frame for the gazebo door if I had only made the jig earlier.

Charlie and I set to work making the first screen. The actual doing of it would explain how it worked to my young but bright helper. I selected one of the smaller sizes for a starter, the ones under the railing. Fortunately Elmer had a good miter box so we could cut the ends of each frame side at 45 degrees accurately with a hacksaw. I clamped a pair of frame pieces to one L while Charlie did the same on the other L. I slid the movable L until the free ends of a long and short piece met, then tightened the wing nut to lock it in place. I had Charlie measure the two diagonals of the frame to check that it was square. It was. We screwed the corner connectors onto the frame pieces and started applying the fiberglass screen material. I explained to Charlie how the rubber spline tubing was applied and how to notch the corners of the fiberglass so it would fit neatly in the frame grooves without wrinkles. Charlie pulled the screening flat while I applied the spline. The first screen took a little time to finish, but that was a learning period for Charlie. By the end of the afternoon we had completed two more screens and I decided to call it quits for the day, and invited my helper to join me at Macklinburg's soda fountain for a coke.

"Gee, Mr. Borden," Charlie talked between sips, "I didn't realize how much work had to be done making all those jigs. I somehow thought we'd just be sawing and nailing on the 'zebo itself."

"Well of course," I replied, "we could have done it without making all those jigs, but it would have been harder I'm sure, and not really as professional a job. You know, some people characterize us humans—you and me

Charlie—as the tool using animal, but that's not the true description. Many animals use tools of one kind or another. Almost always a stick or rock they pick up. What distinguishes man is the fact that he has the foresight to make a tool that is appropriate to the job he is doing, and a jig is just a tool made for a specific job. That is one of the most important things a good engineer does." I admit I was puffing myself up a little, but for a good cause, and the cause materialized at once when Charlie said he thought he'd like to be an engineer too. I gave him a pat on the back and told him I thought he'd make a good one.

The next morning we completed another 5 screens. I had decided to skip to the larger ones to see how well the jig worked on them. Just before noon a call came for an emergency window replacement. A softball had gone askew and broken a window, out on West Cedar Street, so I had to abandon the screens for awhile. Charlie thought he could go ahead on making the smaller screens while I was gone. I agreed, but asked Elmer to give him a hand if necessary. I was prepared for an objection, but apparently he had taken a liking to Charlie too.

The window took longer than expected. Elmer had neglected to tell me it was a second floor job and the stepladder we carried in the truck wouldn't reach that high. I had to put the ladder on top of a patio table in order to get to the window. A risky makeshift arrangement, only slightly improved by our customer commandeering the ballplayers to steady the ladder. I got back to Diehl's about 4 o'clock to find Charlie and Elmer wrapping up the last of the small screens. When I handed Elmer a copy of the window bill he mumbled something about my jig working out better than he had thought. A small triumph for me. Elmer was not much given to praise. I had thought his lumbago and declining business had soured his outlook on life, but he hadn't been complaining about his aches lately and business had picked up since I started working for him. Maybe he had some other disappointment nagging him. Perhaps Mrs. Fashlich or Sam Voss might explain it. They had known him for a long time and might oblige my curiosity, if I got up nerve enough to ask.

By Thursday noon we completed all the screens. I stacked them in the truck and Charlie and I drove over to his house and stored them inside the gazebo. I told Charlie he might as well have lunch at home, but if he wanted to do some more work he could stop back at Diehl's later and we'd discuss making the lattice decorations. Before returning to Diehl's, I grabbed a quick lunch at the diner and then picked up a bundle of white plastic lattice pieces from the lumberyard.

Cutting the decorative lattice pieces and attaching them and the screens was the final step in finishing the gazebo. I was anxious to finish the job. It had been a rather exhausting summer for me so far. I certainly wasn't used to all the stooping and lifting and crawling on my knees on the roof. I didn't let Charlie know how I felt though, it might spoil his pleasure in a summer of real accomplishment; maybe it was his first, and maybe it started him thinking seriously about what he wanted to do with his life.

Using the cardboard container from one of the bundles, we drew the pattern for cutting the upper lattices, the ones attached to the top sill. It wasn't complicated, just scalloped bottom edges former by arcs of a big circle. I showed Charlie how to draw them using string and a pencil for a compass. Tomorrow we would cut them so that by the weekend we could do the installation and be finished.

The next day, at Diehl's, I marked the first lattice using our cardboard pattern and cut the scallops using a sabre saw while Charlie watched. I let him mark and cut the next one while I watched. He was doing a good job, so my supervision was needed only to ensure he was handling the saw safely. We finished the 7 top lattices—there was none for the door—and the next day the 7 bottom ones, which were only simple rectangles cut to size.

Friday afternoon I had to go back to the antique shop. The owner had called Elmer about replacing a broken window. Not another attempted break-in, she told me. Just an unfortunate accident while re-arranging some shelves. While she was checking my bill I looked through her collection of collectable junk. I didn't expect to find another of Rodde's treasures, but I did find a large rooster weather vane sitting in a corner on the floor. It was copper, partly shiny and partly still coated with a green patina from corrosion, but on the whole in good shape. The price tag said $175, which seemed a little much to me, but it might look nice on top of the gazebo. Since I had told Mrs. Voss my work would not include making one, she might be interested in buying it. But first I examined the base to see how it might be attached to the roof. The compass points were fixed on thin rods attached to a larger central one on which the wind vane with the rooster on top rotated. The central rod looked as though it would fit into the pipe of my roof bracket. I thought I could orient the thing with a pocket compass and then secure it with self-tapping metal screws through the pipe, near the bottom end underneath the roof. A little more work would be necessary to cut a circle out of sheet copper, form it into a cone shape and solder it to the rod. This would be a flashing to direct rain away from the opening of the pipe. I decided to give Mrs. Voss a call so she could decide if she wanted it.

Saturday and Sunday we installed the latticework and the screens. The latticework went easier than I had expected. First because the fit was good. Secondly because Charlie could hold them in position while I used the screwdriver attachment to the drill to fasten them in place. The gazebo was done at last—or almost because Mina had bought the weather vane and I had to install it. I took it home with me after work Sunday so I could make the copper fitting at Diehl's during the week.

My young friend was both pleased and unhappy about the end of our job. He had learned a lot that summer, impressed his parents—and me—and had something really big to show off to his friends. He also had earned some money! The gazebo had occupied his thoughts so much that now that it was done he was sort of at loose ends. I told him he should be glad he had a few weeks left of his summer to recover before school. I certainly felt in need of a rest.

Work had started to pick up again at Diehl's. People were checking out storm door and window inserts and we had a few more glass replacements to do—probably a result of careless storage. I didn't get a chance to finish the fittings to Mina's rooster until Wednesday. That afternoon, after work, I drove over to the Voss house to install it. Charlie came out to watch, fortunately, as he could tighten the screw from inside the gazebo while I was on the roof holding the thing aligned with the compass.

Mina and Sam came out to inspect the final result. I thought it looked pretty good. Mina decided to celebrate with another barbecue on Sunday and insisted I had to attend. I didn't object.

I said the gazebo was finished, but that was not actually true. I had one job yet to do and arranged for a long lunch hour for the next day. My errand took me to a jeweler I had visited in C.R. while shopping for Edie's pin.

By the time I arrived Sunday afternoon, an hour late because I was supposed to bring Elmer and Mrs. Fashlich along, and Elmer was slow. The party was in full swing. Mina had invited the members of her garden club, all seven of them and their spouses, and the Mercers too. Sam was busy at two grills getting the coals started. A laundry tub was nearby, loaded with ice, beer, and soda for the kids and teetotalers. I added two bottles of sparkling rose' I had bought. Mina had spread herself for this day, final fulfillment of her dream house, by planting masses of bright flowers in beds on each side of the gazebo door and blue rug juniper along the two adjacent sides that could be seen from her kitchen door. Charlie was showing his cousin, the Mercer daughter, and several other kids details of his share of the job. I was about to join in on his job description when Phyllis sauntered up to me.

"I'm sorry, Mr. Borden, but Mina asked me not to bring pies today. She said she had arranged with Lottie Olsen for a special dessert treat."

"In that case," I replied, "I might just as well go home, the party's ruined for me. But surely you haven't forgotten my Christian name already, and after I brought some Lancers' Sparkling Rose' just for you?"

"Of course I remember your name. How could I forget after you told me how your poor parents scrimped and saved for it. It's Emmett, isn't it? I suppose the baptism costs are very high for such a name. I looked it up, it means industrious, old English or German I believe. Or is it Latin for ant? But I think I will have some of your wine, if you really brought it for me. Beer and coke are not really to my taste." Her shoulders gave a refined shudder. "Would you mind getting some for me? Anyway you can't leave yet, I believe Mina wants to take pictures."

I went searching for a corkscrew. I felt perfectly at ease with Phyllis this time, having decided to bat her banter back at her and see how she reacted. I poured her a glass and opened a beer for myself. "Mrs. Voss has her garden club here, and in fact she did a nice job of planting around the gazebo. Do you garden also?"

"Not hardly, Emmett." She showed me her hands, smooth with moderately long, carefully lacquered nails. "George hires a gardener to do the lawn and flowerbeds. He doesn't like to see me scratched and dirty. My talents lie more in arranging flowers than in potting sheds."

I had just poured her second glass and opened a second beer for myself when Mina called me over to the gazebo. She wanted to take pictures with me standing by the door. I called to Charlie to get a hammer and saw from the garage and join me. "You want both of us, Mrs. Voss, Charlie was my partner in building it. But you must wait another minute, we aren't quite finished yet." She seemed a little perplexed, but waited until Charlie arrived with the tools. I took a small shiny brass plaque out of my pocket along with four brass escutcheon pins and nailed the plaque to the doorpost at eye level on the latch side. Charlie peered up at it and let out a scream of pure pleasure. "Do you like it, Charlie?" I asked. He ran over to his dad and pulled him to the gazebo to see it. It was a plate I had engraved by the C.R. jeweler: 'Built by C.E. Voss and E. Borden" with this day's date underneath. Finally Charlie's excitement cooled down enough for Mina to snap her pictures of us in front of the gazebo holding our tools. Me with the saw, Charlie with the hammer, and wearing a grin almost as wide as his face.

Leaving Charlie to put the tools back in the garage, I lit my pipe, figuring that outdoors no one should complain. Phyllis was apparently curious about the commotion Charlie had made over the piece of shine by the door and moved up for a closer look. Several members of the garden club were near her, inspecting Mina's flowerbeds. Phyllis looked like a racehorse among a trio of Clydesdales. She still wore her hair pulled back from the temples. Its dark shine complemented a lilac colored linen suit. I couldn't figure out how she kept it from creasing, remembering the problem Fran had with linen.

"She's not like her sister, is she, Mr. Borden?" It was Mrs. F. who must have seen me watching Phyllis.

"Well," I replied between puffs, "She is a few years younger and has had only one child."

"George Mercer likes to show her off, so he spends too much money on her clothes, but you watch yourself, Mr. Borden. She may like to play games, but she won't take a chance on losing her bread and butter."

"Certainly, ma'am, but you needn't worry. I can appreciate her looks, but she's not really my type. Now that you mention games, I wonder if she likes gambling. I could introduce her to some of my Indiana friends. What do you think?"

"You don't fool me, mister." Mrs. Fashlich surprised me with a poke in my ribs. "Phyllis wouldn't go for the perfume they wear!" Laughing at her own joke, she moved off to join the ladies at the flowerbeds.

I decided to sample my own wine and picked an empty chair to sit. Elmer, Sam, and Mercer were inside the gazebo inspecting the roof beams, I suppose, and crowding some of the ladies sitting by a table Mina had placed inside.

As expected, Phyllis soon joined me. I poured her another glass, warning her it was the last one.

"That was a nice thing you did for Charlie," eyeing me over the rim of her wineglass.

"Oh he earned it right enough," I replied. "Saved me from an awful lot of scrunching down to put in the rails and lower lattices. I think he enjoyed working on it. His first big job I suspect, and it'll be here for years to remind him of this summer. Charlie Voss is a very likeable kid."

"I think, Emmett, you should call him a young man now. Working with you seems to have given him a lot more assurance, and my goodness, he seems to have filled out and grown up more since I saw him at the 4th of July picnic. Some men can be hard on their sons, but I think you might make a good father. You had no children, Mina told me. You should give it another try. I might be able to arrange it for you, you're not too old yet. Would you like that?"

"Who and where?" I asked politely.

"I would have to think, but probably Davenport or nearby. You could get away to meet there couldn't you?"

" A tempting offer, Phyllis, but George might object, don't you think," deliberately misinterpreting her.

"Fresh!"

"Flirt" I responded. She thought she should be offended and started to get up, but seeing my grin she stopped, looked at me for a minute, and settled back in her chair, probably to prepare a better put-down.

"I suppose you think you're funny. That was a crass thing to say, and cruel. And what are you doing but laughing. How could you say such a thing? I thought you were a nice man."

"I am a nice man and you're a very pretty women, but that was a patronizing offer to make to me. You know very little about me. For all you know that could have touched a tragic part of my life I was trying to forget. But confess, Phyllis, you're not really hurt because I meant no meanness. If I made you flush with anger for a moment, it only added radiance to your beauty."

"Well, if you put it that way, but in the future just ask me to pinch my cheeks, then you won't have to be so rude." That little exchange seemed to put us on more or less equal terms.

"You won't mind if I light up?" I asked, tamping a fresh load of tobacco in my pipe.

"George likes cigars," finally breaking her silence, "but no matter how expensive, they seem to have an acrid smell, which your pipe doesn't. Would I seem to be prying again if I asked what brand that is? It has a somewhat musky odor. Reminds me of a cow barn or the lawn fertilizer our gardener uses."

I put the best interpretation on her rather ambivalent description to keep the atmosphere friendly. "I've smoked it for years. I have it blended especially for me by Dunhill's. Since moving here they have to send it to me from New York. Expensive to do that, but it's one of the few pleasures of my past I can still enjoy." I was about to banter with her further by expounding on how the different ways of blending and cutting tobacco affect pipe smoking when Elmer came over.

He gave Phyllis a nod, to which she responded with a very cool "How are you, Mr. Diehl?" in a tone that implied she didn't really care. He ignored her question anyway.

"Nice job you did, Borden, but Mina's up to her old tricks. She's talking about wanting electricity out there, god knows why. It'll only draw more bugs. Anyway, Sam said to tell you he's about ready at the grill so you two better get in line."

"You old goat," Phyllis muttered at Elmer's back as he puttered off to the grill himself.

"I didn't know you knew him well enough to call him that," I said as we got up to join the others.

"Oh I know him all right. Nan was a friend of mine. We went to school together though she was a year behind me. Nan was his niece," she added noting my blank look. "She went to live with him after her parents died. Her mother was supposed to be his favorite sister, but he sure didn't treat Nan as though she was."

Mrs. F. brought her plate over to our table. "I want to be sure you're getting enough to eat," she told me. "Phyllis eats like a bird. I don't want her to set a bad example for you." I could see that my landlady's plate had little more on it than Phyllis', so I knew she was concerned about something other than my stomach being filled.

"Oh I always encourage a man's appetite," Phyllis retorted.

To which Mrs. F. responded, "But you don't give them much to eat deary." Before anymore such pleasantries could be exchanged I volunteered that Phyllis told me she was a friend of Elmer's niece.

"I understand they had some kind of disagreement and wonder if that accounts for Elmer's sour disposition?"

Mrs. F. decided to sit and offer her opinion about it, to Phyllis' dismay. "Well they did have a squabble all right, over a boy from the University. Elmer disapproved, thought he was a bad choice and insisted she stop seeing him. Nancy took off with the fellow. Elmer finally tracked them down, Omaha I think, but by then they had gotten married. It lasted about a year or so. Elmer was right, the boy was no good, beat her as I recall from the divorce papers, but Nancy wouldn't come back and refused to have anything to do with her uncle."

"Probably didn't want to put up with his 'I told you so,'" Phyllis added. "He could have handled it better, but the more he ordered, the stubborner she got."

I asked what happened to her, but neither seemed to know. "Nan just broke off contact with everyone in Keonah," Phyllis replied.

Further comments about Elmer's niece were interrupted by Mina's call to Phyllis to help serve the dessert. I started to get up, telling Mrs. F. I was going to get another ear of corn, but she stopped me by offering hers, with the excuse that she couldn't really eat anymore. I think she lied.

"You don't seem to like Phyllis" I told her. "She seems harmless, just enjoys teasing I suspect."

"A married woman ought to know her place," Mrs. F. snorted. "It's all very well to get men interested when you're single and looking for the right one, but she ought to get over that business after marriage and being a mother. Doesn't set a good example for her daughter. But finish your corn, Mr. Borden, it's best eaten before it gets cold." I was halfway through, my third ear as a matter of fact, when Charlie came running up telling me to come and see what his mother had for dessert. Mrs. F. joined me as Charlie led us to the gazebo. I expected a cake since Phyllis had said Mrs. Olsen had made something special, but not that cake!

"I want you to see this before Phyllis starts cutting," Mina said excitedly. "Isn't it just the cutest thing!" I don't talk about food being cute. That's not the way I approach things going into my stomach, but I wasn't prepared for that item. I didn't know how it was going to taste, but I guess cute was an appropriate description. A decorator's delight, it was an eight-sided cake, covered on the sides with pale green icing and some narrow criss-crosses of white icing piped into a simple suggestion of the upper lattices of the gazebo. The shingled roof was imitated by what I suppose was another layer of cake cut into eight wedges and coated with chocolate icing. I was impressed, and even Mrs. F. and Phyllis, who once said she loved handling dough, seemed impressed. Mina called everyone to come see Lotty Olsen's masterpiece, so things got pretty crowded inside the gazebo. I worked my way back outside, after congratulating Mina on her inspired dessert.

There were still a few ears of corn sitting on the side of the grill so I grabbed one. I love corn-on-the-cob, if its really fresh picked. Something you can never really get in a restaurant. My mother used to husk and boil them, but Sam roasted them on the grill with the husks on. A little messier to eat, but an exceptionally sweet taste. I was partway through when my flirty friend arrived with two slices of cake, a thin one for her and a fatter one for me. "Don't let that old biddy say I didn't feed you, Emmett Borden," she whispered. "I'll wait until you've finished your corn. Now I notice you eat typewriter style."

Pausing my work on the corn, I questioned "typewriter style?"

"An engineer and you haven't noticed? I'm disappointed in you, Emmett. You eat straight down the ear from one end to the other, turn the cob to a new row and start over again, left-to-right just the way a typewriter works, well the old manual ones at least. Others start at one end and eat clear around the ear before moving to the right." I admitted I hadn't really noticed and asked which way she ate.

"Oh I'm a typewriter type too, but George is a rotator. I've often wondered whether there is some personality characteristic revealed by how people eat corn-on-the-cob. Maybe the typewriter kind are in a hurry to get to something new while rotators are more meticulous about finishing things up before moving on. What are you going to do, hurry on to another gazebo, Mr. Typewriter?"

"I don't really know, Phyllis," I replied. "I hadn't given it much thought. Rest for a bit I guess. I haven't been this active for what seems a long time. But of course, if personality can be analyzed by how one eats corn, then there are really more than just two types." I was going to show Phyllis how an engineer would examine her personality deductions. "Take the typewriter style eater, is left-to-right or right-to-left affected by being right or left handed? And maybe we ought to consider whether it would be more accurate to define the direction in terms of whether one eats from the large end of the cob to the smaller end, or vice-versa." Phyllis started to speak but I cut her off by continuing. "Then, of course, one might be very efficient and reverse direction at the end of a row. And still another characteristic should be considered. Is he acquisitive if he turns the ear towards himself to get to the next row, or more inclined to giving by turning the ear away from himself? Of course that applies to rotators too, and also which end of the cob they start at. Which way does your husband turn the ear?" I would have continued my analysis but I could see she was getting bored and might leave so I changed the subject by asking if the cake was any good and whether Mrs. Olsen had an octagonal cake pan or used a round one and simply sliced off edges to make it octagonal.

"Did you ever see an octagonal cake pan, Emmett?" she replied in an exasperated tone. "Anyway it's a four layer lemon chiffon. It's good but rather heavy on the icing. Men usually like excessively sweet things, probably to counteract their natural tendency to sourness. But you didn't answer my question."

"You mean about another gazebo? Your husband and Sam had suggested the possibility of making and selling them, but I haven't really given a lot of thought to that yet." I stopped as I saw Mercer coming to our table.

"What have you two been talking about so much?" he asked Phyllis somewhat petulantly. I answered for her seeing she was a little irritated by the tone of his question.

"We were discussing the various ways people eat corn-on-the-cob. I can give you a briefing on the different styles if you're interested. I find it a fascinating subject and wondered if your wife knew of any historical references on the subject, being a home economics graduate, I understand."

"No thanks, Borden." I had apparently set his mind at ease. "Business is my interest. And speaking about business, have you given any further thought about the proposal Sam and I suggested last time?"

I told him I hadn't had a chance to sketch any plans for estimating, wanting to finish this job for Mina before the summer was nearly over, but maybe I could do something within the next few weeks. He seemed satisfied and left to tell Sam.

Phyllis was amused. "Thank you, Emmett, for opening his safety value. George gets jealous about my friends sometimes. Without any reason of course," she added carefully.

"But don't you deliberately encourage it? I notice you don't seem to spend much time with the other ladies, or their husbands. Not that I have a complaint about your company. Far from it, look at how much I've learned about corn and cake pans in just one afternoon."

"I have women friends, but not these garden clubbers, and as for their husbands, well they wouldn't bother George much, and George needs to be made to worry just a little now and then. It keeps his interest up." Rising and stacking our dishes, she tossed me her last tease as she left, "Anyway I know how to calm him down, after we get home."

By now the afternoon was wearing down as well. Mrs. F. was also, and leaving the ladies, came over to ask me to take her home. Deciding I had batted wits with Phyllis enough for one day, I agreed but went to check with Elmer. He told me not to bother, he'd get a lift back with the Kirby's. Joe Kirby being one of his pinochle buddies who lived near his place. I said goodbye to my hostess, thanked her for inviting me, wished her well with her garden structure, told Sam I'd get in touch later about Mercer's proposal, and catching Charlie, handed him an envelope, warning him not to open it until the guests had left, and waved an inclusive goodbye to the remaining guests, including Phyllis.

Mrs. F. allowed me to open the car door for her and waiting till I got in, asked me what I had given Charlie Voss that couldn't be opened in front of the guests. "Just a check for $200, Mrs. Fashlich. A bonus for good work."

"Land sakes, Mr. Borden, you're a softie. I only hope you made enough on that job to pay your rent too. It'll be cold this winter if you have to sleep in that gazebo!" She had a good laugh at her little bit of fun. I laughed too, but in truth, I thought with Edie's pin and Charlie I might even have lost money on that job.

CHAPTER XVIII

BARKING DOGS

What a relief, the gazebo was done and if I never saw another it would be too soon, but that was not meant to be. I had promised Mercer, sort of, I'd sketch some plans for estimating. Why did I allow myself to get drawn into this business again? A convincing explanation just didn't present itself to me. I suppose it might be just another manifestation of drifting along, or maybe it was having a fear of retreating into a cocoon again, as I had for those few years after Fran's death, if I didn't grasp at any excuse for something to nag me into continued motion. I had let myself become infected with the 'no' function after Fran. It is the simplest way for one to retreat from life's bruises, saying no to every overture. You don't get involved that way. You avoid many future frustrations and disappointments by saying no. So why, after my expert cultivation of it, had I flipped over to the 'yes' function, accepting Mercer's proposal my latest yes? Psychological introspection is not one of my skills, not even one of my interests, but it did dawn on me after a few moments, that the problem was maybe a classic engineering one. I was like an engine without a governor, racing ahead in one direction or another because I had no one dependent on me. No one whose interests and well being must be considered in every decision. Edie, and even Phyllis, had an answer for me, get married again. Perhaps I should. Certainly I had already thought of Edie, but I could see no solution to the problem of where and how we could live together. Certainly not to one like Phyllis. A handsome ornament for George Mercer, but too calculating and, I was sure, too cold, in spite of her fondness for innuendos, for me. Fran had spoiled me. She was my light in a dark world and my light had gone out. The prospects in Keonah seemed limited in career and companionship. Well, tomorrow, or maybe the next day! Meanwhile, I'd better give some thought to commercial gazeboing.

Elmer was busy at the daybook when I arrived at the store, making out the monthly bills, except he closed his books on the 15th. I had taken care to identify each item I had gotten from stock that was for the gazebo so

Voss would have an accurate material cost. The screens were separately identified, since I didn't know what price he might have finagled out of Elmer. For the other items, I used Elmer's posted retail price.

A few days later Voss called and asked me to stop by the lumberyard during my lunch break. I assumed he wanted to know how I was coming on Mercer's project, but that wasn't it. Honestly, I had forgotten, believe it or not, about getting paid for my work! So when I told him I hadn't worked out some of the sticky details on how to set the gazebo up, he said that wasn't it.

Voss had totaled the material bills, the amount coming to about $1900, not including the screens. Well above his original estimate, but then he had added items I hadn't included in the initial plans, the doubled sills, the heavier posts, and paint, which I hadn't included at all, as well as an under estimated cost for the cedar shingles. He had the screen costs shown below the material subtotal, but I told him not to include them in calculating my share, only my labor installing them, say $50. He looked surprised, but I reminded him that Elmer had already stuck him for my labor in building them and I wasn't going to collect twice for the same work. After all, I have to live with myself, and who wants to live with a cheat.

"Well at least let me reimburse you for that bonus you gave Charlie. You didn't need to do that, Borden, it's a lot of money for a 14 year old even today."

Fortunately the phone rang and Voss had to answer it. Fortunately, because it gave me a few more moments to reflect after my initial reaction, which was to say O.K. Voss had pinned on the wall behind him the picture Mina had taken of Charlie and me by the gazebo, Charlie holding the hammer and wearing a proud and pleased-as-punch grin. Something inside me didn't feel right.

"I can't accept that either," I told him after he hung up. "Charlie earned that money, Mr. Voss, he helped me a lot and did a good job. I don't think he'd feel he really earned his pay if he found out the money didn't actually come from me. I have too high a regard for your son to risk undermining his self-confidence over a few dollars, so no reimbursement. I hired him and I'll pay him."

So it was finally settled, and Voss wrote me a check for $900, we rounded off the cents but included the $50 screen installation. And so my summer of aches and pains was a net loss if I added in the pin for Edie. No matter, I'd made the summer a memorable experience for a young man and I still had a chance to recoup by doing the plans for Mercer. I'd fix that deal so I'd profit without having to build another damned gazebo.

That weekend I started seriously considering the Voss-Mercer operation. Clearly the structure would be built at Voss' yard and trucked to the buyer's site. Mercer was to promote the sales and take the orders—if any. So my principal concern was to design the structure for easy transport and assembly, preferably by two men only, and in one day if the travel time was not too great. Overnight stay for a longer set-up time would be expensive. Justifiable only if the customer was at a considerable distance from Keonah. I divided the job into four phases: setting the concrete blocks, placing the floor and posts, attaching the roof, and finally adding the rails and latticework.

Now that I had actually built one, the first and second phases were easy. An octagonal form of the correct size, light in weight and cheap, could be made from lengths of 1" PVC pipe bolted to eight plywood pieces that were cut and drilled for the bolt holes to produce the required 135 degree angle. Laying this form on the prepared ground defined the position for the concrete corner blocks. Further, by adding other holes in the pipes, the same form could be reassembled for 8' and 6' models.

The floor and supporting beams would be prefabricated in two halves. The halves would be laid on the positioned concrete blocks and bolted together. A rough calculation showed that two men could unload the floor halves from the truck and move them into position without too much strain. The final floorboard covering the opening needed to provide access to the bolt holes in the floor joists would then be screwed into place. As for the 4x4 posts, hanger screws would be inserted at each end during fabrication at Voss's. The machine threaded end of the screw at the bottom end of the post would be fitted into holes drilled into the floor and into a metal bracket attached to the outside end of the floor joist. This required the boards covering the outside perimeter and concealing the concrete blocks to be left off until the nuts could be attached to the hanger screw protruding through the bracket. But I figured that with an electric drill-driver to attach the screws this would be a quick job. The posts would fit into a fish-tail cut on the bottom sill to prevent any twisting of the post. The floor sills, of course, would have been prefabricated and nailed to the floor.

So far, so good, but the roof posed the real problem. I wanted it to be prefabricated as two halves, just like the floor. Completely finished except for adding the ridge shingles to cover the joint between the two halves. The halves would be bolted together from the inside where ready access to the roof rafters existed. The problem was how to get each roof-half raised to sit securely on top of the posts until they could be bolted together. Clearly the steel pipe with its welded-on brackets to which the high end of the rafters were bolted on Mina's gazebo wouldn't work here. Also it was clear that the modification needed would be to split the pipe with each half and its attached brackets bolted to the rafters of each roof-half. Then after lifting one half-roof, bolting its outside edge to the hanger screws on its posts, and temporarily propping it up at the other end so that it wouldn't fall, the other half-roof would be lifted, bolted to its posts and then the two pipe halves bolted together and the roof would become a single rigid structure again, supported by the eight posts. No problem if we had a big derrick sitting outside the gazebo with a long boom to hoist the roof-halves. Voss didn't have one. He had a forklift of course since we used that to unload Snyder's milling machine. But that would require a separate truck to haul it to the site. Not a very practical idea I thought. Each roof-half would be too heavy for two men to lift it the 7 or 8 feet needed to set it on its posts. Probably four men could do it, three to lift and hold it while the fourth set the prop and fastened the rafters to the hanger screws at the top end of the posts. Too many men, and yet not enough to lift and steady the half roof comfortably and safely. Asphalt shingles are heavy!

I thought about the problem for the next several days, off and on, while working at the hardware store. What I needed was a tall temporary pole that could be set on the gazebo floor, at its center, with a block and tackle mounted on top to hoist each half-roof. So, good! Except that the pole would have to be maybe 12' to 15' long and small enough in diameter to fit inside the split pipe. What could I find that would be rigid enough for that job? Maybe a 4" diameter heavy-walled steel pipe might do it. Bolt the bottom onto a flat steel plate with steel braces welded to the plate and bolted 4' up on the pipe to stabilize it and help resist bending. The split pipe on the roof would have to be 6" diameter to allow the pole to fit easily inside. That's about as big as I'd want that, since I would have to cover the open end with something watertight and decorative.

I decided to talk to Farnsworth in C.R. and see what he thought about it and also to sound him out on whether he'd be interested in making the thing as well as the metal fittings for the gazebo itself. I couldn't ask Ridetti, he'd probably kick me out of his workshop for demeaning a true artist with triviality, even if I countered that I had assumed he had to worry about such practical matters in building his large scrap iron monstrosities.

I called Farnsworth and arranged a meeting at his shop after work the following day. He remembered me, so no long explanation on the phone was needed. I found him munching on doughnuts and coffee in a little cubicle partitioned off from the workshop to form an office. Accepting his offer of a gooey doughnut and some vile coffee that must have been brewed that morning and kept hot all day, I briefly described my problem, showing him my sketches and weight estimates.

He had what I didn't have, a reference book on steel fabrication with tables on elastic bending load limits for pipes, I-beams, and U-channels. My hopeful guess that a 4" pipe would be adequate was confirmed. In fact we could go to 16' length and still be perfectly safe. My proposal for bolting a flanged plate at the bottom of the pipe enabling it to stand upright didn't meet with much enthusiasm however. Instead, he sketched a more complicated scheme involving a set of four U-channel pieces 3' long, their bottom ends welded to the corners of the plate and their top ends welded to a short steel ring slightly larger in diameter than the pipe. Directly below this ring a second ring would be welded to the plate. The whole scheme could be erected by slipping one end of the pipe through both rings. Two men could then tip the pipe upright, turning on the edge of the plate as a fulcrum so that it rested on the floor of the gazebo. Done! I asked him to quote me a price for making the hoist, including a hook at the top of the pipe for attaching the block and tackle. Satisfied with his solution to my major worry, I showed him sketches of the other metal fittings I would need fabricated. They were all simple except for the split pipe and brackets connecting the roof rafters, and for that, I would provide the jig. He agreed to give me a call on the price in a couple of days.

By the end of the following week I had completed sketches of the basic gazebo, details of the joints to be cut and how the floor-halves were to be joined, how the posts and rails were to be attached, and a complete size listing of the lumber required. Along with Farnsworth's pricing for the metal fittings and hoist, I was ready to talk to Voss again. We arranged to meet at the lumberyard Sunday after lunch. Voss looked over the sketches, asked a lot of questions over the necessity of the hoist, but finally agreed that keeping the installation down to one day and two men justified Farnsworth's figure of $400. We left it that Sam would price the materials, the expense for the two-man erection crew, and my suggested labor time to cut the wood and assemble the gazebo at the yard before disassembly and loading onto the truck, and then he and Mercer would make a final decision. As for my charges, I told Voss I'd want a royalty of $200 per unit sold, and a one-time charge of $500 for constructing the jigs and supervising the construction and assembly of the first unit. I got no comment from him about that.

The week passed uneventfully at Diehl's. No major repair or installation jobs. It was probably a little early for people to get the storm windows out and find them broken. The newer windows with self-contained storm and screens were not very plentiful in Keonah, which had mostly older homes. It seemed cheaper to hassle with separate storms and screen installation and repair than to invest thousands of dollars for new windows. Still a hardware store finds customers everyday for all the little items it carries, though you couldn't say business was a booming success. The daily grind was occasionally altered by a call from Macklinburg to clear bad jams in the copier and add toner. That venture seemed to be booming. It was surprising how Keonah residents had been unknowingly deprived for years because they couldn't copy letters, bills, cancelled checks, newspaper clippings and recipes to send to Aunt Jane and Uncle Joe, or favorite poems from library books to son Bob or daughter Jean and whatever. I wondered if any office machine manufacturer had tried to make a reasonably simple home copier for a hundred dollars? Maybe in my next life I should give it a try. It could be my way to becoming a millionaire, which gazebo building could never do.

Voss called on Saturday to see if I could go to Davenport with him on Sunday to go over the arrangements with Mercer. He would drive, and pick me up at Fashlich's at 10:00. I agreed. About an hour later he called again. It seems George told Phyllis and she decided to cook Sunday dinner for me and the Vosses. I asked him if Sunday dinner at the Mercers was at noon or six. It was at noon so we wouldn't be driving back too late. Mina didn't enjoy night driving he explained. Sam had a big Oldsmobile so the 60 mile drive was quick and comfortable. Mina offered me the front seat, but I chose the back where Charlie sat. Sam took the Interstate so there wasn't much to see along the way but late summer fields, so my erstwhile partner and I talked mostly about his school program for his sophomore year. Sam joined in with the comment that Charlie had changed his subjects from earlier plans, undoubtedly because of his summer's work. Mechanical drawing, shop, and geometry were now on his schedule of electives. Charlie was enthused about it, and Sam was pleased, but Mina still worried about the dangers of shop and the effect close work on the drawing board would have on his eyes. I had the distinct feeling my presence this summer had liberated Charlie from some of the smother his mother laid on him.

The Mercer home was of moderate size on a rather small lot. Brick construction and attractively landscaped, in a quiet, refined neighborhood befitting Mrs. Mercer's sensibilities in dress. That is, good quality, well-fitted, tasteful, not flashy. Charlie disappeared with Carrie, the Mercer daughter, and a young girl, Lisa Albena, whose mother Phyllis introduced as her friend Rosalin. George mixed drinks which we had in the office/den he had converted from one of the extra bedrooms. The ladies had wine and chatted in the living room. Dinner would be at 1:00, Phyllis warned George as we headed to the den. That gave us about an hour to go over the plans and cost estimates. Most of the discussion concerned the mechanics of how the gazebos would be transported and assembled at the customer site. It was agreed that a completed model would be needed to show prospects, and that it would be set up in a corner of the Mercer car lot. We adjourned to the dining room when Mina called us that Phyllis was ready.

I was interested in how Phyllis' cooking would compare with her pie baking. She had told me she liked working with dough, for which I had proof she did well, whatever other implications her comment had. It was a typical Iowa Sunday dinner, centered on roast chicken, but with a delicious cranberry and orange sauce instead of the usual gravy. The potatoes were new to me, apparently done as boat-shaped slices about 1/8" thick that were, she explained when I asked, deep fat fried twice so that they puffed up like a crisp fat cigar. The vegetable was fresh peas and carrots sprinkled with toasted almonds and chopped parsley. The salad, a melange of various greens, sliced mushrooms, black olives, and minced red peppers, dressed with olive oil and a herb vinegar that I couldn't identify and which Phyllis wouldn't reveal, claiming it was of her own making and she was going to keep it her own. Dessert was not pie, instead a double chocolate torte that begged for second helpings. Phyllis had extended herself, I was sure. Everyday meals like that would have led to a George much bigger even than he was. But whether it was to impress me, give another taste of the sinful pleasure of gluttony to her brother-in-law or to tweak her older sister, I didn't know. The children didn't eat with us. They wouldn't have appreciated the nuances of Chef Phyllis' food. They were confined to the kitchen to feast on hamburgers, French fries and cokes and seemed happy for it, ending with a special treat of raspberry ice cream parfaits.

Phyllis had seated me next to Mrs. Albena, who corrected me, politely, when I called her Rosalin. "It's pronounced Ro-sah Lynn, Mr. Borden (the 'o' was long), not run together. Unusual perhaps, like yours. Emmett, I believe, if Phyllis pronounced it right." I apologized for my ears, agreed it was one I had not encountered before, but melodious.

She seemed pleased with my characterization and went on to talk about herself without any urging on my part. She had met Phyllis some several years ago, after advertising her services as a seamstress and dressmaker. "It was a small talent I had that I could use to earn a living and be at home to raise my daughter. Phyllis said you are widowed, Emmett?"

Naturally I assumed she was also a widow, but before I could ask she told me she was separated from her husband. "He was an accountant. We lived in Chicago then, a nice home in the Brentwood section. But things went somehow wrong. He embezzled money from his firm and just disappeared when it was discovered during an audit. That was five years ago. After three years of not hearing from him I filed for separation and moved here. I couldn't keep our nice home, Lisa was only 8 then, and I couldn't find work that would meet the mortgage payments and daycare for Lisa too." She wiped away a tear. "Anyway, I wouldn't have stayed, it was too humiliating." I was embarrassed by this unexpected personal revelation and mumbled a few words of sympathy, and was grateful when George suggested we finish our discussions in the den.

The excellent dinner did nothing for George's disposition. We immediately got down to pricing, and my fees. George claimed my $500 initial fee was much too high and thought $200 was more than enough with $150 for the royalty, claiming he and Sam had the biggest investment to make on the project and took all the risk. I got no support from Sam who seemed somewhat cowed by his brother-in-law and wouldn't even offer a comment. Mercer didn't bully me, I react immediately to an attack like that. I simply pointed out that since no gazebo would be built, excepting for the sample, before an order was received, the biggest investor was Sam and me for the sample material and my labor for the design and supervision. "Your investment, Mercer, is a vacant area of your car lot to hold the sample and bill of sale forms. Well maybe a few hundred dollars for advertising, though a sign on your lot will probably be sufficient, and half the cost of the hoist."

The discussion got a little heated about our relative contributions to the project, when I decided to break it off. "Look, Mercer, I appreciate the excellent dinner you served, but I've been a professional engineer and I won't sell my design services for what you offer. If I want to pursue this business, I can do it without you. Diehl and I can build the damn things in the back of the hardware store in our spare time and sell them. Diehl's make money, I'll make money, and Sam'll make money supplying the wood. You won't make anything." I walked out, leaving a stunned Voss to confer with his overbearing brother-in-law.

The argument had apparently overwhelmed whatever sound proofing the Mercer house contained, because Phyllis pulled me aside to find out what happened. For some reason she seemed relieved when I told her.

"That's George's way," she said. "He thinks he can bully anyone to get his way. Try a little Phyllisism on him. Offer a compromise, say knock a hundred off the one-time charge, but add fifty to the royalty after the first five are sold, and let any special orders to be priced later. I found that kind of an approach often works with him."

"But do I want this job anyway?" I asked. "Am I just asking for more arguments later?"

"Why not, Emmett? Just think, as a business partner you'll be able to enjoy my cooking again on occasion." It was a dumb reason, but she said it with such a coy smile I had to laugh.

"It's a reason," I said, "and anyway I've already done work on it." Just then Sam came into the living room to coax me back. A quick calculation showed me if we sold 5 units, Phyllis' suggestion would only be $100 less than my own, and after 7, I would be ahead. I offered her proposal, not mentioning that it was hers since Mercer was so touchy, as a compromise, but Mercer was adamant. Things got a little noisy again when suddenly Sam broke in.

"Will you two dogs stop barking at each other! You forget I've got the most at stake here. The sample's going to cost me about $3000, figuring only my own costs for the materials and the hoist and the labor and the use of the truck. Borden has dropped his initial charge to $400 for the design and supervision, and George wants something for advertising and sales work. Let's say that's $400 also—now wait a minute goddamn it George! That's not what you get, that's what you spend. So that's about $3800 invested in the sample. Now what do we do with it? If we sell the sample first we'll need another one and also it may cause a paint problem if the customer doesn't want green. Also my cost will go up since I'll have two truck trips to make and two takedowns and erections to each unit. And if we don't sell it, what happens to it?"

Sam had a point neither I nor Mercer had considered. I thought about it for a bit but Mercer offered a workable solution first. He suggested we sell the sample after the first 5 units. His reasoning being that prospects could go to some of our installations to see the units if they needed to. He could work just as well with photos of some of the sold units, especially if they were landscaped as Mina had done hers. It seemed like a reasonable solution to me—if we managed to sell 6, but of course if sales dropped off we could sell the sample sooner, and if not--?

"George will sell 'em," Sam insisted. "He's good at that." So it was settled. I agreed to the lower initial fee and to wait until the sample was sold for my design fee, but higher royalty after 5 units, and with Sam's support, insisted on a formal contract agreement to be written by George's accountant.

Sam suggested we start back to Kenoah, as he didn't want to drive after dark, but accepted our hostess' offer of coffee before leaving. Mrs. Albena declined the coffee, pleading she had a customer scheduled for a fitting at 5 o'clock, got her daughter into her summer jacket and said her goodbyes and 'pleased to meet you' to me and Mina. Phyllis offered to give me an extra slice of torte to take home, which my sweet tooth was glad to accept, and asked me if I'd bring the cups and saucers into the kitchen while she cut the torte. That was her excuse to give me Rosa Lynn's phone number and address. "Give her a call, Emmett, I think you'd like her."

"She's married, Phyllis, would that really be proper?"

"Separated, Emmett. Desertion for five years is good grounds for divorce. I think she'd accept a date with you. Why continue to waste your life. It's no credit to your Francis."

I took the slip of paper she offered me with Rosa Lynn's address, but said nothing further. Perhaps I was wasting a life. Anyway Sam and Mina teased me on the drive back to Keonah by pointedly wondering why Phyllis had invited Mrs. Albena.

CHAPTER XIX

THE WEATHER VANE

Voss' response to the Mercer/Borden argument gave me a little more respect for his character. Since I had expected to get my design fee paid up front, I hadn't given any thought to how much money he'd have tied up in the sample, or when he'd get it back. It must have become clear to Mercer that while we could do without him, he'd have trouble trying to do without us. He'd have to search for a partner to design, build and install and in all probability he'd have to fund at least half the cost of the sample himself.

I'm not sure why Voss had pressed his advantage to get Mercer to agree. Maybe he saw this as an extra source of lumber sales or a way of getting some return on the idle time his employees had when business was slow. Anyway, he wanted to proceed immediately.

The next day, Monday, he stopped in at Diehl's to discuss how we were to start on the sample. Elmer decided to sit in on the discussion, though unless a customer wanted screens there wasn't anything in it for him. Still he offered his 2¢, particularly about the $400 hoist. But besides objecting to its cost, he had no workable alternative to offer. Anyway, Sam agreed to start cutting lumber according to my plan, keeping good records on the quantity and time involved. I agreed to start on the jigs and give Farnsworth the O.K. on making the hoist and various fittings.

"Oh, by the way, Borden," Sam called back as he was about to open the door, "Mina has agreed to let Charlie help on the assembly phase. He persuaded her after his summer apprenticeship. Thought you might be pleased." I was.

I bought the PVC pipe and an assortment of bolts and screws from Elmer's stock and planned to work on the jigs and form that evening after we closed the store. At noon I called Farnsworth and gave him the

O.K. to start on the hoist and whatever metal brackets he could form without my jigs. By Wednesday the jigs were finished so I drove them up to his shop. No doughnuts this time, he was staying open a little later, waiting for me, so I guess it was too close to dinner for a snack. The plate, rings, and U-channel braces were assembled and welded. Only the pipe was missing. "I'm having that trucked in," he explained. "Should be here by Friday when you can pick up the brackets, but make it late afternoon since I've got to weld the attachment for hanging the block and tackle."

I was about to leave when I spotted a trade calendar hanging on a wall of the little partitioned space he used as an office. You know the type I'm talking about. The kind companies print and give to their customers as advertising reminders. Usually in shops, like his, where mostly men work, the calendars are nudes, or slightly more discreetly, bathing beauties, but this one sported a classic roadster car, something from the 30's, with a girl at the wheel, in profile, a bright red scarf streaming out behind her to give the impression of a carefree ride in the sunny country air. I guess there was a vague resemblance to Phyllis in her slim figure, judging by the arms showing from a short-sleeved blouse, her neck, and profiled face. It all looked trim and healthy and it struck me that if I could mount something like that on a weather vane it would be a perfect top to a gazebo sitting at Mercer's Motors. Farnsworth had several wall calendars hanging about so I had no qualms about asking him to give me that one and a piece of aluminum sheet about number 8 gauge (nearly 1/8" thick if you're not into metals) and around 12" by 20".

That evening, after a so-so meal at the diner, I cut out the outline of the car and girl and rubber-cemented it to the aluminum sheet. The next day, things still being slow at the store, I carefully cut the aluminum around the picture. Using a carbide scriber, I marked the center of the wheels, the headlight and radiator outline, letting the scribe cut through the picture. Again, being careful, I peeled the picture off and pasted it on the other side. Following the cut marks made by my scribe, I scribed the same features on the obverse side of the aluminum. Fixing the scribe into the pencil side of a compass, I scribed small hubcap circles on both sides of the wheel outlines. Finally, I penciled outlines for the letters N,E,W,S in block capitals on the remaining pieces of aluminum, along with a small arrowhead. Cutting the letters was easier than the car, there being no inside cuts to make. Still,

I broke a couple of saw blades on the whole job. Working with a file and a sheet of emery cloth, I cleaned up the cut edges and wiped all surfaces with paint thinner.

"Hey, Mr. Borden!" I heard the shout about the same time as the whir and rattle of a contraption close behind caused me to flatten myself against the bay window of Macklinburg's drugstore to avoid whatever it was hurtling down on me. It was Charlie.

"I thought we were friends, and here you are trying to run me down," but I said it with a grin.

"Sorry if I scared you," he apologized, "but it looked like you were going to your car, and dad asked me to see you right away about when Mr. Farnsworth would have the floor brackets ready." I told him they were promised for late Friday and I'd drop them off Saturday morning. I was coming back to Diehl's after my lunch at the diner when my gazebo partner spotted me.

Crossing to my car at the curb, I took the weather vane parts out of the trunk. We walked together the short distance to the store. That is, I walked while Charlie wheeled his bike. I asked him how he was doing on his second job. He was pretty glum about it, not having much to do until it reached the lattice and rail stage.

"In that case, you can help me on the weather vane, if you want. But you have to keep it a secret," I told him. "I want to surprise your dad and uncle Mercer."

I asked Elmer if any work had come in while I was at lunch, but he said no, things were pretty slow. I called Voss and relayed the schedule about the floor fittings. Elmer decided to get a bite to eat after all. Usually he has lunch first, then I go, but not today. "Not hungry, Emmett," was his excuse. I didn't believe him, but I learned early not to press him on personal matters. He just ignored those questions, or snapped a 'none of your business' at me.

So Charlie and I were free to fuss with the vane for a while. Last night I had considered the problem of mounting the letters and car onto rods that formed the rest of the vane. At first I thought of aluminum rods, they would do for the compass points—the direction letters, but the stick holding the car and arrowhead would have to be balanced about the pivot point, and I hadn't come up with a neat way of adding weights on the arrowhead end to compensate for the greater weight of the car. I mentioned my dilemma to Charlie, but he didn't see what the problem was. "Isn't it just a matter of drilling a hole in the stick for a small nail that can be pounded part way into the vertical stick, you know, like a toy propeller?"

"I don't think so, Charlie. If the stick holding the arrowhead and car isn't balanced around the pivot point—your nail—it's going to tip down at the heavy end and drag along the vertical rod so it will take a stronger breeze to move it. Besides, tipped that way it's going to look sort of cheesy. I don't think your uncle would like that. Not at the price he's going to set on the gazebo. It might give a sort of slapdash impression of the workmanship on the whole business."

Charlie still looked a bit skeptical, so I thought a little lesson on dynamics would be a good post-graduate course, so to speak, on my theory of commercial gazeboing.

"You understand, Charlie, that you can't balance the combination by just moving the pivot point until you get the car end to balance the arrowhead end." He looked a little blank. "I'll explain it a little more. In order for the vane to point into the wind, the turning force of the wind, we engineers call it torque, on the car end must be greater than that on the arrowhead end. The torque is proportional to the product of the area of the car and the distance of its center of pressure from the pivot point. The location of the center of pressure will be the point where the car balances, since the thickness of the aluminum is constant. Ditto for the arrowhead. But for balancing the vane, the torque due to gravity on each end must be equal. If they are not, the vane will try to tip down at the greater end and increase the friction at the pivot so it won't turn freely in light winds. Since that torque is the product of the weight of the car or the arrowhead and the distance of its center of gravity from the pivot point, it will be the same as the wind torque. So if you balance against gravity by moving the pivot point you also balance against the wind torque and the vane won't reliably point into the wind.

"The solution of course is to balance against gravity by adding more weight at the arrowhead end that won't add to its wind area. But adding weight to a round rod so that it won't spoil its clean silhouette and obscure the arrowhead doesn't seem easy."

"Oh, now I get it. It seems so obvious after you explained it, I should have seen it myself."

"Look, my young friend, you can't expect to know everything all at once," I reassured him. "Vanes probably started just the way you said: turning loosely on a nail, and not too accurately. Years of analysis and refinement, with many false starts, were needed before man had a clear understanding of the design principles. We really understand very little about how the world actually works, so much of our progress has to start with a cut and try approach.

"As a matter of fact, the weather vane problem is very similar to one I encountered when I was a young engineer, maybe twice your age." Such a long time ago I thought. He could have been my own Charlie, working together on a weather vane for my Francis. Damn these reveries! I scolded myself. I can't keep reminding myself of what might have been. Recovering, I gave my partner a pat on the head and asked him how we were going to solve this problem, now that he understood it.

"We could make the arrowhead out of lead. Wouldn't that add balancing weight?"

"Too soft," I objected, it would probably get bent after a few twigs got blown against it, or even gravel kicked up by passing cars."

"Well, how about mounting the arrowhead and car on a U-channel? You know, like the aluminum frame we used for the screens on mom's g, instead of a round rod. Then we could hide the lead weight inside the channel."

"Just the thing, Charlie. Let's see what we can find that might do". Scrounging around the junk box of metal scraps we still had left from the Snyder deal, and Elmer's own stock, we found some ½" round aluminum rods and a 1" heavy U-channel.

While Charlie watched, I cut a narrow slot on one end of a rod and fitted a direction letter part way into the slot. That way most of the letter would stand out clearly. Charlie thought he could cut the slots on the other three ends with the hacksaw. I agreed, but cautioned him that he must keep the slots on each rod parallel so the direction letters would all be standing upright.

"How're you going to do that?" I challenged. He thought for several minutes, then clamped the rod to the bench so that the letter I had affixed lay flat. Finding a ¼" thick piece of flat stock in the scrap box, he placed it at the other end of the rod, and using a sharp nail laid on the flat piece, scribed a line on the end of the rod, and a short line along both sides of the rod.

"I can use these lines to guide the hacksaw while I make the cut. The slots should then be parallel. How's that?"

"How's that?" I echoed. "That's great! Charlie, I'm really proud of you."

With Charlie's solution, we soon had the slots cut, including one on the end of the U-channel to hold the arrowhead. I scrounged up some aluminum flux and solder and we soon had the letters, arrowhead and car fixed in place. A good afternoon's work, and for me, an additional pleasure in seeing again how the summer's work on the gazebo had stirred up Charlie's brain and bolstered his self-confidence. So far, so good, but more work was needed. I began to feel that the $175 Mina paid for her rooster weather vane wasn't such a bad deal after all.

How to mount the contraption on top of the gazebo was still to be worked out. I realized that the compass points could not be permanently fixed on the roof, since the gazebo would eventually be sold and its final location would in all probability not be oriented the same as on the Mercer parking lot. Also the simple cone I used to cover the pipe opening of the roof bracket on Minas' g might not look good on this one, because of the much larger pipe diameter I had to use to permit the hoist to pass through. The solution came to me that evening at the diner. I had been sketching some possible designs while eating, none of which seemed to fit the car silhouette in style. When I gave him the plans Sam had questioned me about how I was going to cap the roof opening and I had told him I'd get something on paper before he started construction, so I was a little late.

Seeing I was finished with the lamb stew, Sally, the waitress, brought me a coffee refill and asked how I liked the stew. "Pretty good," I told her. "And especially the dumplings, light as little clouds."

"Mrs. Olsen's," she laughed. "There were so many complaints about the package mix we were using that the cook persuaded her to mix up a batch along with the cake and pie assortment she brought in this morning."

That did it, reminding me of the gazebo cake she made for Mina's dedication party. I suddenly realized the perfect roof cap would be a miniature gazebo of my own. Not made of cake however. Back in my own room, still savoring a double slice of Mrs. Olsen's raisin pie, I set to work on making a scaled plan for my gazebo on top of a gazebo. Of course, it wasn't a miniature of the big one exactly. For one thing, I couldn't have openings like the real one, that might let water run under the roof shingles. I toyed for a minute with the idea of little plexiglass windows, but discarded that in favor of simulating the windows with white paint. No need to turn this into a doll house project, I had to keep Sam's labor costs in mind, though I decided to make this first one myself. Using cardboard that the laundry packaged my shirts in, I cut out a full-size pattern for the roof section. These 8 sections would not meet at a peak—another departure from the big one—since I wanted a flat area for mounting the compass points and vane. I cut another pattern for the small octagon that would serve as the flat of the roof, and a rectangle for the sides.

Saturday afternoon, my half day off from Diehl's, I cut all the pieces from wood scraps at the lumber yard, and Sunday, in Mrs. Fashlich's basement, I glued and nailed the thing together, using epoxy for the glue to ensure water proofing. Then Monday, at Diehl's, I drilled a hole through the flat top for the mounting bolt. I had already fixed how the compass points would be mounted. I had cut two circular pieces of 5/4" wood, about 6" in diameter. A little rubber cement temporarily held them together, one on top of the other like an Oreo cookie. Clamping my wooden cookie in a vise I drilled two holes at right angles to each other, centered on the seam, and another hole through the center of the circles. A long bolt passes through that hole and through the hole in my flat roof, and extends through the roof bracket pipe. Another round piece of wood, a little bigger than the pipe diameter, and serving as a big washer on the end of the bolt could be snugged against the bottom of the pipe with a wing nut to hold the whole thing tight against the real roof, yet it could be loosened just enough to re-orient the compass points if needed.

The compass point rods were cut in two and laid in the half-round holes of one of the halves of my wooden cookie. I drilled a small hole near the end of each rod, and using small screws, secured the rods in place. Making sure of course that the slots for the letters were vertical. A tapered block of 4x4 wood about 6" long would hold a short piece of aluminum rod on which my vane would be pivoted. The block was then screwed onto the top half of the second cookie half, and that half then screwed to the bottom half. And there it was, all done, except for adding the balance weight and painting, which I did on Tuesday and Wednesday. I spray painted the compass and vane with several coats of flat black, and when that was dry, a small jar of red gloss enamel did the scarf, and a little silver paint did the hubcaps and radiator shell. I thought it looked great. Elmer even agreed. Mellowed a bit, I thought. I'd paint the miniature g later when Sam was ready to paint the real one.

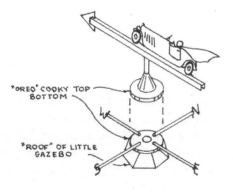

"OREO" COOKY TOP
BOTTOM

"ROOF" OF LITTLE
GAZEBO

THE MERCER WEATHERVANE

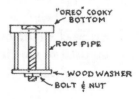

"OREO" COOKY
BOTTOM

ROOF PIPE

WOOD WASHER
BOLT & NUT

EB

CHAPTER XX
CHARLIE SOLVES A PROBLEM

Voss had sent his truck to Farnsworth's that Friday to pick up the hoist and remaining metal brackets, so assembly of the gazebo started on Saturday. My plans were pretty clear, and Charlie was there to help (already an experienced builder) so I only needed to stop by on occasion during the following week to check on progress. The critical erection task was hoisting the roof-halves, and Voss agreed to wait until that Saturday afternoon when I could be there to help.

Elmer decided he'd like to watch the roof raising as well, so we posted a notice on the hardware shop door that we'd be closed Saturday at noon. We weren't going to lose any business, things being as slow as they were.

Joe Nichols and Ezra Boggs were the men Voss had assigned to the g job. Nichols was the youngest, maybe around his mid-twenties, shorter than me by a few inches, but much huskier. Boggs was Voss's foreman, a lanky man in his forties with some carpentry skills. The floor halves were joined and the posts and rails erected by the time we arrived, with the hoist just being set in place in the center of the floor. Charlie and Elmer were checking out the roof-halves when Farnsworth drove up. I was surprised to see him there, but he said he wanted to see how well the hoist worked.

Sam, Ezra, and I had a short discussion on whether both roof-halves should be carted inside the gazebo prior to hoisting, or just one at a time. Since Ezra was to handle the hoisting, we let him make the decision. One at a time, at least for this first try. It would give him more room around the hoist. So Ezra and Joe carried the first half inside the g. It was a very awkward piece of construction to handle, and I was already beginning to worry about their ability to lift and set it in place on top of the four adjacent posts. The lift rope on the block and tackle was fitted with a sturdy hook that slipped into a hole near the bottom of the split pipe roof bracket. Another rope, running through a pulley mounted on top of the hoist, and with a hook at its end also, was slipped into an eyebolt temporarily attached to the midpoint of the top sill plank, equidistant between the single center rafters. Ezra began hoisting the roof while Joe kept a little tension on the rope attached to the sill plank. He was positioned on the same side of the gazebo where this half of the roof was to be placed. The rope of course was passed around the pulley wheel from the bottom and then out over the top. This tension kept the sill edge of the roof from banging against the hoist as it was raised.

When the roof was lifted high enough so that the plate was just above post height, Joe could draw the sill plate over the posts by pulling on the rope, while Ezra lowered the top of the roof slightly by slacking off the lift rope. Anyway, that was the theory. The trouble was it didn't quite work that way. In fact, it didn't work at all. The roof was just too heavy for Joe to pull the sill plate out over the posts, since the angle of the rope reduced the effective leverage he could exert. Finally, I stepped inside the gazebo, and mounting a small ladder, lifted and pushed the plate over the posts. Ezra eased off slowly on the lift rope while I guided the plate onto the hanger screws atop the posts. Just as I had done on Mina's g, the rafters were paired planks (An exception was the rafters at the straight edge of the half-roof. These were single rafters, since the other half-roof section contained their mates.) bolted to both sides of the split pipe roof bracket, except that a short piece of plank was inserted between each rafter and its side of the bracket. This simply spread the separation between the paired rafters so that enough room was created to fix a nut onto the post screw. The sill plates spanned this gap. A metal plate was screwed onto the bottom side of the sill pieces and the post screw passed through a hole in this plate.

With the first roof-half in place, the nuts tightened on the post screws and a wood prop placed to support the center portion of the roof when the lifting rope was unhooked, another conference took place.

Both Farnsworth and Elmer joined in this time and several suggestions were offered: a second block and tackle to replace the top pulley, giving Joe more leverage with the sill rope; a prop with its own pulley, stuck in the ground outside the gazebo, so that Joe's rope passed through it in such a way as to give him more leverage; a box-like contraption mounted on four wheels with a slanted top, placed inside the gazebo that could be pushed against a rafter, wedging it up and onto the post—that one from Elmer. None seemed particularly good. As for me, I was both embarrassed and depressed that my original scheme was unworkable. Finally Sam decided the best scheme was simply to do what I did, have another man on the erection crew. It meant another $100 a day for the erection costs, but as he said, it was probably safer, with an extra back to lift the floor and roof halves out of the truck, and also helped ensure the job could be completed in one day.

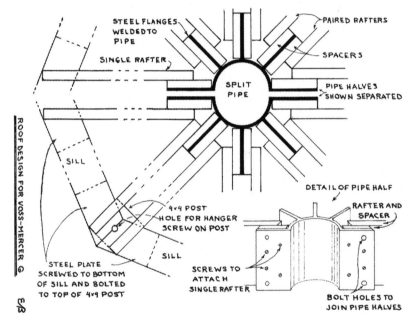

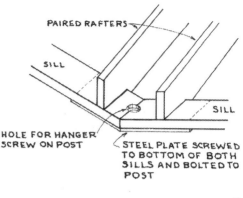

PAIRED RAFTERS

SILL

SILL

HOLE FOR HANGER
SCREW ON POST

STEEL PLATE SCREWED
TO BOTTOM OF BOTH
SILLS AND BOLTED TO
POST

EB

XX-28

No one blamed me, and after all, none of us had prior experience at this job, so it was reasonable to expect some problems to arise. Still, I should have given the procedure more thought since I had recognized early that the roof would be the biggest problem.

Planning now on a 3-man crew, with me as number 3 for today, we carried in the second half of the roof, connected the ropes, and hoisted away. With Joe pulling on the sill rope and me pushing from the inside, the roof-half went in place fairly quickly. We didn't tighten the sill nuts on this half though. Leaving them loose gave us a little play so that Joe, on the ladder, could align the bolt holes on the two split pipe roof brackets, slip the four bolts, two on each side, into place and snug them up. I called the roof brackets split pipes, but actually they were more of a U-shape, with two flat strips welded on each side. These strips were the flanges for attaching each single plank and its spacer of the roof half. The rafter and spacer were temporarily screwed to the flange with flathead screws, recessed so the flanges on the two pipe halves would have flat surfaces for mating. The bolt holes were drilled into these strips. Finally the sill nuts were tightened and the roof was in place.

I breathed a sigh of relief, but I was a bit too soon. The next step was to remove the hoist by pulling up on the pipe until its bottom cleared the top of the roof. It was just too heavy for one man on the roof, even with another inside the gazebo helping lift the pipe. The slope on the roof made for a very unsure footing. Finally Ezra and I had to help Joe out on the roof while Farnsworth and Sam waited on the ground to grab the pipe ends after we pulled it free from the roof bracket.

This time Farnsworth offered the solution, saying he had worried about this while fabricating the hoist, having decided on his own to use the whole 18' length of pipe that his supplier had provided. He went to his car and got an electric hacksaw and cut the pole into three 6' pieces, explaining that he'd weld short pieces of pipe on the ends of two of the hoist pieces. The inside diameters of the short pieces would be just slightly larger than the outside diameter of the hoist pipe. They'd be a sort of collar into which the three hoist pieces could be slid. Each 6' piece would be light enough for two men, one on the roof and one inside, to dismantle easily. Putting the bottom and middle pieces in his van he promised to have them back before next Saturday.

That ended our work for the day. By next Saturday the gazebo would be painted and the lattices cut. Then when Farnsworth brought the hoist pieces back, we could dismantle the g, load it into a truck and be ready to haul it to Mercer's and put it together again. Before leaving Sam asked me about how I was going to close the hole in the roof, but I said I had that all worked out and would show him at Mercer's.

I said no one blamed me for the roof lifting fiasco, but I did. This was an inexcusable engineering mistake that a little more careful thought and less unwarranted extension of my experience on Mina's g would have avoided. True, engineering is not a mathematically exact science, since there are so many variables you can't always be certain you haven't overlooked any critical ones. Still, I should have recognized the inherent problem Joe's lack of leverage on the rope would cause, and worked out an alternative method. I felt the humiliation no one else expressed.

So I considered the problem again that night, finally deciding to give Elmer's suggestion a try. I discarded Elmer's box and slanted top idea, but kept the four wheels and added a roller on top of an 8' piece of 5/4 x 6" plank, all well braced. The wheels would be swiveling casters from Elmer's stock. Only the roller would have to be found elsewhere. I had a key to the store now, but thought it best to give Elmer a call and tell him I wanted to work on his scheme Sunday. He stopped by Sunday afternoon, ostensibly, he said, to see how I was making out, but more, I suspected, for the satisfaction of seeing his ideas take fruit. I had it all done except for the roller, which I assumed would require a trip to a woodworker's supply store in C.R. sometime before Saturday. What I had in mind was a roller like the ones on Voss's table saw extension: metal, turning on ball bearings, with the axle projecting from the ends so I could fashion brackets to attach it to my plank.

Monday was a busy day. It often is with the weekend giving men time to fuss around the house and yard, either breaking things for us to repair, or finding they're short on lawn or garden fertilizers or seed, so I didn't get a chance to locate a source for my roller. By Wednesday things had slacked off a bit letting me have a few minutes to consult the C.R. Yellow Pages. Charlie stopped by late that afternoon. Mina had given him the job of installing some hooks on the garden shed. After Elmer rang up the sale, Charlie stopped by my worktable at the back of the shop to say hello. We chatted for a bit about his plans for school, geometry and mechanical drawing were his favorites. He said he'd probably find shop a little boring after his summer on the g job. "The projects we would get are so simple, Mr. Borden."

I told him there would probably be several more 'zebos this year and he'd soon get plenty of work on them. He was about to leave when he saw my strange looking contraption in a corner of the shop. It wasn't easy to miss, with its nearly 8' tall post rising in close proximity to the ceiling.

"I call it 'Diehl's wheeled wonder'," in response to his question. "You remember the struggle we had getting the half-roof up onto the posts Saturday? Well, Mr. Diehl had suggested a sort of ramp-like contraption we could push under the center rafter, wedging the roof up. I decided to build one and try it out this weekend when we reassemble the gazebo on your uncle Mercer's car lot. I'm just hung-up for the moment on finding a roller to set on top. I changed Elmer's slanted top to a roller to make it easier to wedge up the roof—less friction you know. I was looking for something like the extension table rollers on your dad's table saw, though it doesn't really have to be that fancy, any round roller would do I guess, so long as it wasn't breakable."

Charlie asked me why I couldn't make one using a short piece of pipe, but I explained that fitting an axle in the pipe would probably require some welding of end caps on the pipe to support the axle. "I don't think I could arrange for that before Saturday. Now if I had a lathe I could turn a roller from wood and simply drill a hole for the axle, but we don't have a lathe, so I'm looking for something I can buy that'll do the job."

After a few moments thought my young friend said he might have something that would do. Promising he'd be right back, he scooted out the door and dashed off on his bike. A half-hour later he came running in waving a big wooden rolling pin.

"Will this do, Mr. Borden?" The pin was a well made heavy piece of hard maple that turned easily on its handles, probably on nylon bearings.

"By god Charlie, I think that'll do just fine. I should have thought of a rolling pin myself, and saved all the searching with just a trip to the grocery store. But this is your mother's isn't it? I'll have to get another one."

"Mom gave it to me years ago when I was playing with modeler's clay," he explained. "She uses a glass one filled with ice water. Aunt Phyllis gave it to her to try to improve her pie dough. Aunt Phyl said it would help keep the dough chilled, but mom doesn't do much about pies anymore."

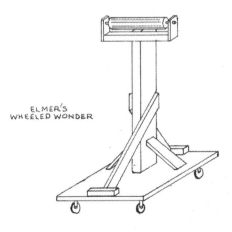

ELMER'S
WHEELED WONDER

EB

XX-SA

166

Mounting the rolling pin on the stand was easy. Just a couple of end blocks, drilled out to slip over the handles and screwed to a crossbar at the end of the post. The whole thing was done in an hour. Charlie went home pleased with himself for solving my problem so easily. At least I surmised so from the happy look on his face as he waved goodbye. Farnsworth delivered the modified pipe sections that Friday, so all was set for trucking the dismantled g to Davenport and another try at erecting it on the Mercer lot. Elmer decided to go along again. I guess he wanted to see how well his wheeled wonder worked. We went in my car, following the truck. Sam drove ahead in his own car to guide us to the car lot. Mina wouldn't let Charlie go with him, much to his disappointment. Seems he had promised to help her with some fall planting and neither Sam nor Mina would let him off the hook. We arrived around 9:30. I had put on some coveralls over my good clothes, I didn't plan on doing anything more than fastening the cupola on the g, but it was just possible that Phyllis might offer us dinner and I wasn't going to show up in work clothes.

The second assembly went smoothly. Nichols and Boggs were more adept this time and by noon we were ready to attach the roof, when Phyllis arrived with a lunch hamper. Chicken sandwiches, hot coffee, and individual blueberry tarts. She hadn't expected Elmer so she was one tart short, but Boggs was mildly diabetic so sweets were out for him. Elmer got one anyway, so I didn't get two.

The first half-roof was hooked onto the block and tackle and hoisted just about 8'. Snugging the lift rope around one of the hoist braces, Boggs was free to push the roller under the center rafter while Nichols pulled the roof away from the hoist to give him the necessary clearance. Then Nichols dropped his line and replaced Boggs at the roller. Working together, with Boggs directing, Nichols slowly pushed the cart forward, its roller raising the edge of the roof to just above the height of the posts. It wobbled a bit, but Nichols found he could push the cart with one hand and steady the roof with the other. Boggs inched the lift rope down until the roof sill plank was pretty horizontal and just above the post the center rafter was to be bolted onto. Snugging the lift rope to a hoist brace again, Boggs was free to guide the mounting plate on the sill onto the hanger screw atop the post and loosely secure it with a nut. Nichols could now roll the cart out of the way and help Boggs guide the sill plate on the remaining posts.

It all went easily and fairly quickly. Elmer was pleased as punch that his suggestion worked. A pleasure that probably more than compensated for having to close the store on a Saturday.

The other half-roof went up just as easily, except that a little more maneuvering was required to get the unpaired rafters (the ones where the roof-halves joined) above the mounting plates. These plates were screwed to the sill on the unpaired rafters of the first half-roof section. After both halves were in place and secured, the plates would be screwed onto the sills of the single rafters of the second half-roof, completing the paired rafter.

Bolting the pipe halves together at the center of the roof and pulling the hoist sections out, now that they were cut into more manageable 6' sections, also went easily. In another hour the two men had attached the decorative lattice and the perimeter boards at the outside edges of the floor, concealing the concrete blocks, and ridge shingles where the half-roofs met.

Since everything was pre-painted, the job was done, except, as Sam reminded me, for the covering over the opening at the center of the roof. "Did you come up with something for that?" he asked me.

I didn't reply, instead, opening the trunk of my car, I brought out my cupola. Painted green with white windows, it matched the color of the gazebo quite well. I asked Boggs to hand the thing up to me after I used the ladder to get on the roof. Using my pocket compass, I oriented the compass points and held them in position while Boggs slipped my wood washer on the end of the bolt protruding through the bottom end of the joined pipe halves and screwed on the nut.

The last step was getting the weather vane from the trunk, getting back up on the roof and screwing it on top of the cupola.

"Done," I announced. "How do you like it, Mercer? Seems appropriate for the location doesn't it?" Sam couldn't help himself, and nearly doubled over with laughter at his brother-in-law's surprised look as the roadster swung in the breeze.

"Very nice, Emmett. Wherever did you find it?" Phyllis asked.

"I made it, Mrs. Mercer. Don't you recognize the driver? I patterned it after you."

"It might look like a girl from down here, but hardly me. I would never wear a scarf of that garish color. I always prefer subtlety in everything. Anyway, that car is clearly from before my time!" Still I could see from her smile that my handiwork amused her. "By the way, have you called Rosa yet?" she asked. Telling her I hadn't had any free time, and that she probably wouldn't be interested in seeing me, Phyllis opened a purse slung over her shoulder, fished inside, and handed me a quarter.

"Call her! Why waste your time sitting around Dottie Fashlich's or having a diner meal with Diehl instead of a pleasant evening with Rosa Lynn? Why do you think I brought her to meet you? I didn't think you were that slow!"

She was right, what was I waiting for, another rare visit with Edie? I asked Phyllis for her phone number, and getting it, walked to a corner of the lot to a pay phone.

Reminding Rosa of who I was, which she said wasn't necessary, she remembered me, and explaining how I happened to find myself in Davenport, I asked if she would care to have dinner.

"I'd love to, Mr. Borden, but I don't think I can get a sitter for Lisa on such short notice."

"But that won't be necessary, Mrs. Albena, ah Rosa Lynn, we can all have dinner together, if you like." She agreed, thought Lisa would like that, and gave me her address. I set the time for 5:30 so Miss Albena wouldn't be kept up late, and headed back looking for a suggestion from Phyllis for a suitable restaurant. Coming closer, I could see her attention was focused on a young man standing by a car a little way further down the lot. A couple were walking around the car, the male kicking the tires—a meaningless display of assumed automobile expertise. Clearly the young man had to be one of Mercer's salesmen, ready with his sales book in his hand. I watched as he took a quick look around, then nodded in Phyllis' direction. She responded with a smile. Unaware I was next to her, I whispered, "Do you think a handsome salesman helps with women buyers?" Startled for a moment, she turned, but seeing it was only me, regained her composure.

"I'm sure, Emmett, looks aren't everything to a woman."

"Not unless she has the other things already. But I need a recommendation. Mrs. Albena and her daughter will have dinner with me and I don't know a suitable restaurant. What do you suggest?"

"You're taking Lisa too," she laughed. "Does Rosa Lynn feel she needs protection?"

"It's simply a problem in finding a sitter on short notice, Phyllis. I suggested it, so maybe I need protection." She gave me directions to a place and hurried off to her husband who was looking at us. I didn't particularly like Mercer, he had too much ego with no apparent qualities to support it. At least to me. I thought he was pretty dull, no interests outside of his business, and going to fat rather quickly, considering his age. Not that it was all his fault. It might be hard even for me to keep trim on Phyllis' desserts. I wondered what she had seen in him. She seemed too smart to dally with an employee. Risky business, especially since the guy probably had only his looks to recommend him, and chances are, might not be too discreet about his affairs.

Nichols and Boggs were loading the truck with the hoist, the disassembled octagonal piping used to set the foundation blocks, their tools, and the wheeled wonder. Voss seemed pleased that the second assembly had gone smoothly. Perhaps changing his mind about needing a third man on the crew. "You'll give Ezra your plans for the cupola?" he asked. I assured him I would, but thought he ought to exclude the weather vane. I told him he could probably find sources for a whole series of weather vanes of different designs that customers could select from. "Making your own would probably be a headache, and customers will undoubtedly have their own preferences for what they want on top. Probably making unworkable scribbles on what it should look like. Anyway, it will be more profitable for you to sell it separately. I'm sure you can get a picture catalog from the suppliers and order as needed. By the way, if you're going straight back to Keonah would you mind giving Elmer a lift. I've arranged for a date for this evening?"

"I'm glad to hear it, Borden," he laughed. "With Mrs. Albena?" I nodded, a little embarrassed that my date would be so expected. "Mina told me

Phyllis had planned that lunch to introduce you two. Enjoy yourself, Borden, I'll take Elmer off your hands for this evening."

He walked over to the truck to tell Elmer he would be riding back with him. For my part, I went looking for a washroom in Mercer's garage to clean up, shed my coveralls, and check my shaving condition. I was relieved to see I could get by without making a trip to a barber. There is something about me that prefers to avoid barbers. I can't avoid haircuts, not being able to do it myself, but shaving is another matter entirely. I guess it's the impersonal touching and patting and pushing of your head here and there that gets me. I have to sit passively, for safety's sake, with all my blemishes under close inspection. You lose dignity—and have to tip for it besides.

Chapter XXI

Rosa Lynn

I timed myself to arrive at Mrs. Albena's promptly at 5:30 by parking a block away and waiting until one minute beforehand. The address revealed a small wood-frame house of uncertain age, but well past eligibility for voting. The young Miss Albena answered my knock, accompanied by a barking dog.

"Mr. Borden?" she asked, and when I nodded and replied "Miss Albena?" she curtsied and motioned me in.

"Mother will be down shortly, Mr. Borden." Remarkably grown-up manners, I thought, for an 11 year old. The dog looked at me suspiciously. I was invited in all right, but he wasn't sure if I was to be trusted. I asked if he had a name, holding out an open hand for his inspection.

"Rags," my young hostess replied. I told her it was a very appropriate name for a dog that looked like miscegenation between a wire-haired terrier and a small collie, and maybe other ancestors of unknown heritage. I didn't say 'miscegenation', I only thought it. Sensing it was probably safe to approach and take a sniff, he came up close. After several sniffs he allowed me to give him a pat on the head and a scratch behind his ears. We were now friends.

"Do you have a dog, Mr. Borden?"

"No, I had one once when I was about your age," I replied, and then in response to her next question, I told her his name was Woof.

"Woof? That's weird. What happened to Woof?"

"Regrettably, I couldn't keep him from chasing cars. He got run over one day. I cried for days and days, but later got a cat."

"And I suppose you called it Meow." Miss Albena seemed skeptical of my story so I told her, "No, her name was Splotch."

My soon-to-be dinner companion invited me to sit. I took a straight chair, she sat on the couch, Rags lying on his paws at her feet, keeping his eye on me just in case he had misjudged me. Miss Albena was very well trained, never failing to keep an inconsequential conversation going to avoid any embarrassing silence.

"I would like a cat too, but mother says Rags is enough trouble as it is. I don't think he's any trouble. I take him out for a walk everyday. Do you like cats better than dogs, Mr. Borden?"

"Well I have strong opinions about that Lisa. I may call you Lisa?" She accepted my familiarity with a nod and waited for me to continue. "I really feel, after Woof, that most people don't deserve to have a dog. A dog is honest, brave, faithful, and uncritical of man—or woman. Pleased to be a friendly companion, asking only to be properly fed, given a suitable spot to rest, and a kind touch. Most people do not have the moral character or kindness to match their dog. What most people deserve is a cat. He—or she, a cat's gender is irrelevant—is selfish, opinionated, totally concerned with its own pleasure and comfort, indifferent to your convenience and continuously demanding attention. A cat is never really your friend, he— or she, as the case may be—simply tolerates your presence. In fact, once you take it in, it considers the house its own and you its servant. So most people, at best, deserve a cat."

Lisa listened politely, clearly skeptical of my philosophy on pets. "Didn't you like Splotch, Mr. Borden?"

"Oh yes, Lisa, she stayed with me for years before dying peacefully of old age in her sleep. I was too broken up to ever attach myself to another pet." I stopped as Rosa Lynn entered from upstairs. After an exchange of greetings, she asked if Lisa had kept me entertained, but before I could reply my young companion volunteered that Mr. Borden had a dog and a cat once and that people really deserved to have a cat. Lisa had extracted those parts of my lesson on pets that suited her, showing a natural good sense to discard, if not forget, the rest of my monologue.

I have not described Rosa Lynn before, so I'd better do it now. Edie was fairly tall with a mature figure. Phyllis was just slightly shorter, and sleeker. Quite good looking. I do not need to describe Kitty Adair as my contact with her was minimal. Rosa Lynn was just under average height, maybe 5' 3" or 4", and perhaps about 135 pounds. Comfortable looking rather than heavy, and having, as any man could not help but notice, a rather full bust. A blond, but not naturally so. Hair of medium length, softly waved, complemented her soft, smooth complexion. Not beautiful, but good looking with small but regular features. I often miss noticing the color of eyes, that must be an inconsequential feature for me, but Rosa's were green. Her clothes fit very well. To be expected of a seamstress. The dress of soft cotton was full-skirted, brown paisley print, with a wide green belt at her waist. She did not wear a jacket, probably to better display a long double-strand pearl necklace. I guessed she was about 30, but I later learned she was closer to 35.

I was glad I had worn a suit under my coveralls. My ordinary daily clothes would have been disgraceful next to them both. We left almost at once, though I took a few more seconds to give Rags a farewell pat.

Dinner was at a stylish restaurant called Le Bon Gout. I'm afraid I gave Phyllis a demerit for picking a place with such a name, but the service and food were more than pleasant. The bill reflected this, but then it was only money spent to extend my tiny social circle. We were dining early so there were not many other tables filled, which helped keep the noise level down. A sound system played semi-classical music softly, and the lighting was kept low. A romantic atmosphere that I sensed Rosa Lynn liked.

The first serious decision was on drinks. For Rosa Lynn it was Chablis, available by the glass, and for me, my usual Scotch-on-the-rocks, so there was no problem there. Miss Albena was the problem. Did she want a coke? No, too ordinary. A Shirley Temple? At 11, would we be encouraging her to glamorize drinking? Nothing? She would feel we were treating her like a child, which of course she was, but why rub it in. The waitress, sensing our indecision, suggested a rose' mimosa. "What is it?" I asked, never having heard of it before.

"Pineapple and orange juice, grenadine syrup, and a touch of orange bitters, club soda, and served in a tulip glass with a maraschino cherry and silver straw." She rattled it off in quick tempo, adding at the end "Most kids love it."

I told her it sounded horrible, but we'd let Lisa try it. She did like it, and it looked elegant in the tulip glass. The straw wasn't really silver, a plastic look-alike, but Lisa saved it.

Rosa Lynn ordered a salad appetizer and chicken marsala. I went for the salad also and a T-bone, while Lisa, with her mother's approval had a shrimp cocktail and a small portion of Rosa's chicken. Our dinner conversation rotated among Lisa's ballet lessons, Rosa's seamstress business, and my job at Diehl's and the gazebo sideline. I sensed that Rosa Lynn avoided questions about my marriage, probably because of Lisa's presence.

All in all it was a pleasant evening out. By the time we arrived back at the Albenas', sprinkles were falling with distant thunder threatening a more serious downpour to come. The ladies waited until I got the tricky car umbrella unfolded, and we then made a dash for the porch. Rags was barking as Rosa Lynn unlocked the door, but I was prepared for him, having my steak bone in a doggy bag. "Is it all right" I asked Lisa, holding the bone at knee height, arm outstretched.

"Of course," Rosa laughed. "Take him into the kitchen, Lisa," she added as Rags tentatively sniffed at it, decided it was USDA Prime, carefully grabbed it, avoiding my fingers which were clearly ungraded and hence of suspect quality.

I was invited in for coffee, but declined with thanks, pleading I wanted to start back to Keonah before the storm broke. Rosa, possibly unsure about the sincerity of my excuse, thanked me for the dinner, adding, "If you had given me a little more notice, Emmett, I could have gotten a sitter."

It was necessary to reply: "But I enjoyed the evening. Two charming dinner companions at the same time. It was my good fortune to finish work at Mercer's early enough to give you a call and find you free." Promising to give more advance notice next time, we said our goodbyes and I drove off just as the storm broke. I had to concentrate on the road, visibility being very poor heading into the rain. But I did have a moment, during a brief let-up before the next heavy cloud swept over, to consider whether I should let Edie know. I decided to sleep on the question until tomorrow.

Chapter XXII

<u>Sins</u>

"There are two types of sins, Emmett, don't make them." This was my mother's advice, long ago, as I prepared to leave for college. "The sins of commission are acts you do that you shouldn't. They are the easiest to avoid because they are overt, not easily hidden, and there are moral and civil laws to guide your behavior. The sins of omission are harder to avoid. These are the sins from failing to act when your conscience tells you what should be done. Often you will be the only one aware of this failure. It will be that conscience alone that must guide you. Don't disappoint your father or me." I hope I never gave her cause for distress; she never accused me of either sin, though it sometimes was difficult to avoid the latter.

This was not a religious thing. My mother did go to church on a semi-regular basis, but was not fanatical about it. After I reached my teens she did not insist I attend. Frankly I thought, as I got into my early teens, that she did it because she enjoyed the social opportunities it provided. My father was a religious skeptic. He almost never went to church, he simply couldn't bring himself to sit and listen to the words without squirming with the suppressed desire to cite counter examples, or to extend religious maxims to an often absurd or clearly immoral conclusion. He especially was fond of asking believers where Cain's wife came from, since Eve was described as the mother of all mankind, other than Adam of course, or did he marry an un-named sister? And if so, does that mean God approved of incestuous relations? "I like to start from the beginning," he once complained with an innocent face, to the minister of mother's church, "but I can't seem to get past that part." Mother dragged him away before anymore badgering could occur.

Still, he left me with a healthy dose of skepticism, but not a lack of conscience. So I debated with myself as to whether I should let Edie know about my date with Rosa Lynn. I finally decided a dinner date was just an innocent social event and I needn't say anything about it yet. No real need to cause Edie any concern, I thought, but I still felt vaguely uneasy about it.

176

I was surprised to hear from Voss, later in the week, that Mercer had sold two gazebos already. I began to think that maybe George Mercer had qualities I hadn't fully appreciated. Elmer was disappointed that neither sale had involved screens, which were a big ticket item, while hanger screws and deck screws were not. Still, as I told him, screens might seem more desirable when sales are made in late spring. I had some concern about Elmer. He seemed to be even more gloomy than usual, and often arrived well after I had opened the store. "Lumbago is acting up again" was his only explanation when I asked him if anything was bothering him.

He should have been a little more cheerful as grass seed and fertilizer sales were holding up well and for some unknown reason paint was also doing well. I was not especially pleased with things either, and the minor boom in hardware business didn't do anything to overcome it. Frankly, I began missing feminine contact. Edie was so far away, and she seemed to require special occasions for us to meet, that I wondered what future our relationship could have. Rosa Lynn was much closer and certainly an occasional date with her wouldn't dent my bank account the way another Chicago weekend with Edie would. I even threw into my rationalization Edie's suggestion that I marry again. So I skirted a little closer to committing a sin of omission by calling Rosa Lynn for another date, but still not telling Edie.

So I called Rosa Lynn and made a dinner date for Saturday. Earlier I had stopped at an AAA office in C.R. to see what the Davenport area offered for dining other than Le Bon Gout. Looking over the many advertising folders and fliers they kept on a display rack, I selected several for the quad cities area that included Davenport. One immediately grabbed my attention: a dinner cruise ship. Rosa hadn't dined there but said Phyllis had, and apparently enjoyed it. I hoped I'd enjoy it too, remembering the very pleasant hour I had spent with Edie, several months ago and miles further north on this same river.

The sitter was already there when I arrived at the Albena home. I greeted Lisa, patted Rags and promised I'd save a dinner bone for his letting me borrow his mistress for the evening.

Evidently Rosa had felt the need to be a little more decorous on our first date by ordering a small glass of wine. Tonight though, her choice was a gimlet. I had to give gin a pass some years ago. It seemed to find a hole in my stomach that led directly to my head. Scotch didn't do that, so I stuck with my usual. If Rosa's living came from sewing, she must have done well for herself, judging by her clothes. Being on the river in early September, she had dressed for cooler weather, wearing a dark green pants suit. A wedge of silver silk blouse peeked out from the V-shaped open collar of the jacket. No necklace, but dangling silver earrings of moderate length hung from pierced ears. A rather ornate enamel and silver ring where her wedding ring would have been surprised me. She had worn a gold band on our previous date, and at the Mercers.

"I left Joe's ring at home for tonight," she said, observing my glance at her hand. "It wouldn't have been appropriate, do you think?"

"I guess it depends on how you feel about your husband, Rosa Lynn, but you won't mind I hope, if I still wear mine. I remember my marriage with fondness, though the end was painful for us both." Perhaps the healing process was at last starting. I found I could talk a little about Fran, in response to Rosa's questions, without dwelling morbidly on her death. Rosa seemed to have a knack for drawing me out without seeming to pry. For herself, by the time we ordered a third cocktail, she was quite unemotional about her own marriage.

"Joe just left one day. He wrote a note, telling me about the money he took, apologized for leaving Lisa and me, but didn't want prison. Fortunately the house and car had been put in my name earlier—I guess he had been thinking about theft well before doing it—so they couldn't be attached by his firm. I should have had sense enough to secure a civil separation order immediately to protect myself financially, but a judge decided anyway to let me keep the house and car when Joe's firm claimed they were paid for by the embezzled money. I haven't heard from him since," she added after a moment's pause.

I asked as politely as I could, why she hadn't remarried. "You're quite good-looking, you know."

"I know," Rosa interrupted with a giggle, expanding her chest with an exaggerated deep breath, "what men find attractive." The gin must have found a hole through her stomach too.

"There's more to a woman than her body," I objected. I dimly recalled I was echoing a comment Edie made to me long ago.

"I know that. You say you know that, but how many men know it? Anyway, I'm Catholic, Emmett, a church divorce would be difficult, though I might try for an annulment—if the man was a good Catholic with a really good job. To ensure Lisa's future" she added, trying to soften the mercenary sound.

Did that put me in my place? A hardware clerk. But her tone didn't suggest she was putting me down. Maybe I was too self-conscious about clerking at Diehl's. I decided we were getting on thin ice and had better order.

The menu was not quite as elegant as the Bon Gout, but with 3 drinks it didn't much matter.

A small combo was making noise in the cocktail lounge. Rosa asked our waitress if she could serve our after-dinner coffee there. Several couples were dancing on a postage stamp size open space in front of the band. My date clearly wanted to dance. She swayed slightly to the music and her eyes followed the dancers. The beat was a little fast, the dance steps mod, and I wasn't too keen about the floor, which rocked slightly with the waves. Still, I felt I should invite her onto the floor, apologizing at the same time that all Bordens were born with deformed feet.

Fortunately my partner was skilled at making a tangled knot look like a neat beau, so I didn't feel too ludicrous doing the more contemporary dance steps. An hour of this brought us to 10 o'clock, and time for Rosa to relieve Lisa's sitter. I paid the bill, ransomed the car from valet parking, and we headed back to the Albena house.

"You may park, if you like, Emmett." I wasn't quite prepared for such an invitation so soon, but to avoid any possible misinterpretation, I asked, smiling broadly, "Does that mean I have your permission to kiss you?"

"A man deserves some small reward for giving me a very pleasant evening, don't you think?" Rosa Lynn moved closer as she spoke. I did not overstep the invitation, we kissed, she murmured something I couldn't make out, and with a laugh, broke away.

"I don't want to risk having to make too lurid a confession tomorrow. We have a new priest in our church. He's very young and it might shock him. Goodnight, Emmett, and thanks again."

Rosa was out of the car almost before I knew it. I hurried after her. "My present for Rags," I said, handing her the doggy bag. "And thanks for the kiss."

I decided on the drive home, that now I had better write to Edie.

By next morning, I changed my mind, deciding instead to call. Waiting until early afternoon, when I could be reasonably sure Edie would be in her apartment, I dialed her private line number. A woman answered, not Edie, a much younger voice, probably Clarissa. She said Mrs. Adamson was not in, and when I asked if she would be in later in the day, my party asked who was calling. I told her, and she confirmed my guess.

"This is Clarissa, Mr. Borden. Mrs. Adamson is out of town. We don't expect her back until Tuesday. I asked if she was with her daughter, remembering that Edie had said she had a difficult birth, but the answer was no, and after a moment's hesitation, Clarissa said Edie was on a business trip, in Minneapolis. I left no message. I was sure Clarissa would tell Edie I had called.

Edie in Minneapolis, and she hadn't invited me to join her. Even a business meeting leaves evenings free. And a business meeting over a weekend? No, Mrs. Adamson, I think you're visiting Mr. Carlton.

I wasn't really jealous. Edie didn't owe me anything, rather I owed her. She had pulled me out of an emotional ditch I had dug for myself over several years. And after all, she had known Carlton much longer than me, and by her own admission, it had not been the casual affair that I was sure our relationship was. Even from the beginning, I had felt Edie was enjoying the opportunity for a fling that could be safely done away from Elkton with little risk of compromising her reputation.

Still, my conscience told me I should be honest with her. It really didn't matter if she was seeing someone else, I had no claims on her, nor had I even thought she would want me to. I could even be mistaken in thinking she was seeing Carlton. So I followed mother's advice and wrote her that same evening. Not a confession, just a review of the events of the past weeks, the gazebo deal with Voss and Mercer, and that I had taken Mrs. Albena and her daughter to dinner once, and Mrs. Albena once again. I finished the short note with questions about how her plans for changes in the Lodge were progressing and hopes that her new grandchild and daughter were in good health. A friendly note between friends.

Chapter XXIII

A Stalker?

Edie wrote me toward the end of the week, though I didn't receive her letter until the following Tuesday. Clarissa had told her I had called, and expressed her 'sorrow' at missing my call. Her reasons for being in Minneapolis were to meet with the builders of the new motel and try to work out an arrangement that would minimize the potential impact on the Lodge. It seemed a reasonable thing to do. She made no mention of seeing Carlton, nor offered any excuse for not extending an invitation for me to join her, just that negotiations were lengthy and complicated. As for Rosa Lynn, she had very little to say, only that she trusted my dates were a pleasant relief from the tedium of Diehl's and Mr. Mercer's lack of appreciation for my design efforts.

Perhaps this sounds as though her letter was cool, maybe even a bit chilly, but the tone was actually not much different from her previous letters. Neither of us put mush in our correspondence. I was, frankly, a little relieved that Rosa Lynn would not come between our friendship.

But my relation with Rosa Lynn turned out to be rather short-lived anyway. We did a Sunday matinee school ballet featuring Lisa in the 'corps de ballet', followed by a pizzeria supper, at her request, followed by coffee and dessert at the Albena's. No doggy bag for Rags, but I stopped at a deli on the way to their home and bought two hot dogs for him. Rags and I were now good friends, and so was Lisa. I thought Rosa Lynn appreciated my including her on an occasional date. Rags was sprawled next to my chair, probably waiting for me to put down the cake plate and give him another head pat; his tail wagging slowly across the rug.

"Rags doesn't do that with Mr. Kelso," Lisa remarked. "I think he likes you better."

"You shouldn't say things like that, Lisa. It's not polite and anyway you don't know how Rags feels. Now say goodnight and go to your room," Rosa admonished, flushing a little and clearly flustered. "Mr. Kelso is a member of our parish, Emmett," she added for my benefit. "His wife was one of my first customers shortly after Lisa and I moved here. She was a good friend."

"Isn't Mrs. Kelso still a friend?", I asked. "You used the past tense." Rosa seemed reluctant to answer my question, which I thought was innocent enough, but perhaps there was a falling out over a sewing matter.

"Janice Kelso died two years ago. She hemorrhaged during childbirth." Rosa's tone implied an end to this subject.

"But you're still friends with Mr. Kelso?" I continued. "It wouldn't be right to drop him after her death, as though he didn't matter anymore."

"On occasion," she replied reluctantly. I decided not to pursue it, Rosa was clearly uncomfortable, so I thought it best to say my goodbyes.

Driving back to Keonah, I thought about broken marriages. Mine and Kelso's from death. Edie's from death too, but it had probably died before then from the roving-husband disease. And Rosa's abandonment, which was worse than a death, since it left her entangled with a ghost her religion wouldn't let her banish. Then there was Phyllis of course. But that was only my suspicion. George could continue in ignorance and they might survive as a pair. I wondered if Kelso had children, then I wondered why I wondered that.

During the week, I succumbed to curiosity and consulted a telephone directory for the Davenport area. I found several Kelsos listed, but only one, a Robert Kelso, whose address seemed reasonably close to the Albena home. I was going on the basis that Rosa had said he was in her parish, so, looking at a map of the town and addresses of Catholic churches made it seem likely he was the one. The next entry in the directory below his, listed a Robert Kelso Insurance Agency, so I knew a little more, and enough to satisfy my snooping sin.

Mrs. Carter, Diehl's housekeeper, called Friday that Elmer wouldn't be in Saturday. I told her I'd stay at the store all day, though that was normally my half-day only. I supposed his lumbago was bothering him again, but she said he had a bad chest cold and Doc Jensen had ordered him to stay in bed. My boss was beginning to worry me. Lumbago was an acceptable complaint, even if it wasn't a medically recognized diagnosis. There's nothing lethal about a backache I was sure. But Elmer's age and weakened condition, so obvious to me during the past several weeks, was reason enough to worry about a cold turning into pneumonia or flu.

I had thought of calling Rosa Lynn for another date Saturday, but decided to put it off since by the time I got the store closed it would be too late to see her for dinner.

Elmer was back at work by the middle of the week, though he still didn't look too good. I told him he should have stayed in bed for the rest of the week and gotten fully recovered, but he just waved me away, saying he'd recover faster on his feet. "So be it then," I told him, "Can you handle Saturday, 'cause I could use the afternoon off?" I got his grumpy O.K. and called Rosa Lynn that evening. I had a dinner theater event in mind, a little too mature for Lisa I thought, but I told Rosa I didn't want to cause her problems with too frequent calls on her sitter. She assured me she had several sitters available. She reciprocated sitting with some, and paid with mending work with others, so it wasn't a burden on her finances. I was relieved about that.

I had gotten to like the dinner theater arrangement for a date, especially when I had to travel to get there. No ticket problems, just a call for reservations, and no worry about rushing the dinner to make sure we got to a theater in time. True enough, it generally was not gourmet dining, but except for Mrs. Olsen's pastry, better than the Keonah diner.

The show was an abbreviated production of Nunsense. A good choice for the small stage since the scenery requirements were almost non-existent. My date was not carried away by the fun. She thought it was almost sacrilegious to portray the good sisters in an almost ribald way.

I told her she took her religion too seriously, the world itself was evidence that God too had a sense of humor. Why else would he allow so many fools to be born. "You're not very religious, Emmett," my companion retorted, to which I had to plead guilty. But Rosa wouldn't let it go at that.

"You're very nice, Emmett," she continued. "Lisa likes you, and you've been good to include her with us on occasion. I know it meant a lot to her to have a man pay attention to her. Joe left at a critical stage for a young girl. She was just about 4 years old then, and needed the confidence a loving father could give. But my religion is very important to me."

Had this been Phyllis talking to me, I could have enjoyed a verbal bout, but Rosa Lynn seemed too sincere in her beliefs to engage in even a light-hearted challenge.

I thought it best not to risk offending her sensibilities further by parking, but as I was about to stop in front of her house, she told me to drive on past. As I did so, I noticed a car parked on the opposite curb, a faint glow from a cigarette indicated a man was sitting inside. "If you're afraid, Rosa," I said, "I'll walk you to the door."

"I'm not afraid, Emmett, drive on a few blocks then turn down a side street and park." There was just a faint hint of a laugh in her voice. I parked in front of several other cars in the middle of the block, away from the streetlights, and sat for a moment, completely at a loss as to what had suddenly happened.

"I said you were nice, Emmett," Rosa murmured, moving closer to me, "but you're so slow." She put my hand on her breast. "I know you want to do this. All men do. Just stay above the waist and it will only be a minor sin."

Even through the thin fabric of her blouse and slip, and the heavier nylon of her bra, it felt delicious. Neither Fran nor Edie was so well developed. It seemed much too soon when Rosa murmured "I think you had better take me home now."

The man was still sitting in the car when I drove up. I opened the door for Rosa, but she said I needn't escort her to the door. I remembered to hand her the little paper bag for Rags, thanked her for a very pleasant evening and got back in my car. I waited until she had opened the front door before driving off. Just at the edge of town I found a pay phone at a mini-mart. Rosa answered my call, assuring me that she was all right. "I was concerned about the man in the parked car," I explained, "and wanted to be sure you were safe."

"Perfectly all right, Emmett," she laughed, "just an insurance matter that needed immediate attention. Oh, and by the way, Rags appreciated the goody. I hope you did too."

Did I collide with another Robert, I wondered? No matter, there was no commitment spoken or implied between Rosa Lynn and me, and I'm not the jealous type in such a situation. Mrs. Albena had every reason to see other men if she wished. She had Lisa's future as well as her own to provide for, though her hanging on to an absentee husband was going to be a serious obstacle in finding such security.

As for me, I felt like a man who had gone out for a sandwich and had somehow been given a feast instead. Not that I had a fetish for one part of anatomy over another. Frankly, they can all be delightful, and though face and hair claim my first attention, it's compatibility of character, or personality if you prefer to call it, that matters most.

CHAPTER XXIV

KELSO

Sam Voss called me at Diehl's Monday afternoon. Mercer had sold another gazebo, this time with screens. I had to admire his salesmanship. He was a go-getter, and that, probably, in his younger and slimmer days, was what had attracted Phyllis. It's not what you may be thinking, Phyllis Mercer would not have seen herself in the role of a submissive wife, content to follow a masterful George. Nor would she stomach a timid, dependent, mate. I think she liked the challenge of holding her own against pressure, not collapsing or being herself overwhelmed. I believe I had taken her number correctly at our first meeting at Voss's Fourth of July picnic. In contrast, I did not feel I understood Rosa Lynn that well. Was I thinking too much about women? Possibly, but then I would feel strange if it were men I thought about.

Getting back to Voss's call, I thought I'd better check our stock of aluminum screen channels and screening cloth. We would need more for this job. I told Elmer the good news and asked him to order the materials. I started on the screens with what we had on hand the next day. This screen design was to be somewhat simpler than the one I used on Mina's. One large screen instead of two, for each section of the octagon, but with added bracing at the corners to minimize racking the screens during installation or removal.

I was working at the back of the shop along towards noon when I heard someone asking Elmer for me. In a moment a well-dressed man, younger than me, about my height, but stockier, came striding up to me, Elmer behind.

"You're Borden?" he demanded, his tone immediately irritating me. I put my tools down and nodded, asking who he was.

"Kelso," he blurted.

"Ah, Mrs. Albena's stalker," I threw back at him. This Robert's face flushed with anger, his hands clenched into fists. I stepped back a foot or two, just out of his reach and readied myself, but Elmer suddenly stepped in front of Kelso, a hastily grasped sickle in his raised hand, advising the visitor to cool down.

"It's all right, Elmer, nothing is going to happen. I'm sure Mr. Kelso just has some questions to ask me." Elmer, seeing Kelso's fists unfold, went part way back to the front of the shop, but prudently took the sickle with him. Kelso took a few deep breaths, to get a hold of his temper I suppose, giving me a chance to look him over a bit more carefully. His clothes, as I had noticed at first, suggested he wasn't short of money. He wasn't bad looking either, not exactly handsome, but a long way from ugly. He had a full head of dark brown hair cut fuller than I would wear, and a well-trimmed moustache, which I also wouldn't wear.

Still struggling to keep control, he asked what my intentions were with Rosa. His pronunciation was not quite like mine, no accent on the a, but there was no question about who he was referring to.

I told him the truth, as plainly and quietly as I could that I had formed no intentions about anything with Rosa, adding that our relation so far was confined to dinner, an occasional theater, with Lisa accompanying us several times, and that I was very fond of Rags.

"I've told you, Mr. Kelso, now tell me what your intentions are besides spying," I said grinning. That was nasty, but I thought his actions deserved it. I'm not without a mean streak when provoked. Kelso bristled again. I reached for a small hammer, but it wasn't necessary, he got his temper down enough to tell me he intended to marry her.

That really surprised me, "Rosa had never mentioned a proposal to me, besides she's not divorced!"

"I'm investigating that. With the Bishop. I think it can be arranged," he muttered, not happy having to answer my query.

"You've talked to the Bishop," I echoed. "Was Rosa with you?" He admitted she wasn't.

"You like sneaking around, don't you. How can you do that without her permission? How do you even know she'd want to marry you, have you asked her?"

"No, I haven't yet, Borden, have you?"

"Why don't you ask Rosa. Maybe she'd save you a lot of work." That seemed to finish our exchange, except for Kelso's parting shot as he turned to leave.

"I hope Rosa knows what kind of living she'd have with you, a dirty clerk in a rundown store in a rundown town." He stomped out and that was the last I saw of Mr. Robert Kelso.

Unfortunately, Elmer heard his last comments. Shaking with anger himself, he called him a stuck-up bastard and asked me what the guy did that gave him airs. I told him he sells insurance in Davenport. "Yah, takes peoples' money for protection and then tries to cheat 'em on their claims." I didn't share Elmer's views on insurance. I told him not to get upset, that if Mrs. Albena wants him, she can have him. Still Kelso read my condition exactly. I had no future at Diehl's, and no income to properly support a wife, much less a young girl with a hungry dog.

Lunch at the diner did little to raise my spirits. Even Mrs. Olsen's sour cherry pie tasted a little too sour. I decided to wait several weeks before calling Rosa again. It would give Kelso a chance to find out where he stood. I was myself unsure whether my religious indifference would be very compatible with Rosa's apparently strong beliefs. Not that it seemed of major important at the moment, as long as she stayed committed to a marriage bond with the absconding Albena. Now there was an interesting question. If Rosa didn't benefit from the embezzlement, what did he use the money for? Gambling, drugs, women? Rosa gave no hint that she had asked herself these questions, though it seemed incredible that a wife wouldn't know, or want to know. Too many years had gone by for her to still be waiting to join him, wherever he ran to. And where did he go? He didn't embezzle enough to live well in the States that long without working, and to secure a good paying job as an accountant without revealing clues to his past employers would be difficult. A valid social security number would need to be provided, references established that would give a satisfactory response to any new employer's inquires. It seemed too complex and risky to me, but then the whole idea of embezzlement seemed stupid. Even more incredible that he could abandon a wife and child, neither of whom showed signs of being difficult to live with. So, had he left the country—perhaps for Mexico where he could easily enter without a passport, and then hide away. The money would last much longer. Or was he already dead, more likely if he was involved with drugs or gambling. Without further investigation this was just idle speculation. I certainly wasn't going to call my Chicago detective—what was his name? Oh yes, Ward, Ward Investigations I think. Later, working on the gazebo screens, the thought popped into my head of an even more bizarre explanation. There was no embezzlement and no Joe Albena. Rosa wasn't married. Lisa was illegitimate and the whole story was made up to provide a more respectable background. That explained the missing husband, but an embezzler hardly provided Rosa with respectability. Even I could think up a better story than that one. Also, I continued, arguing with myself, evidence for a marriage, childbirth, and separation could be easily checked. Anyway, Phyllis seemed too shrewd to fall for that story, and that included Kelso who could initiate investigations easily as part of his insurance business.

It was all over my head. My whole orientation and training as an engineer and loving husband left me unable to fathom the motivation of Albena. I probably should have read more detective stories to find an explanation.

CHAPTER XXV

LISA

Since starting to date Rosa Lynn, I began the practice of picking up a weekend copy of the Davenport newspaper, just to be alert to any events suitable for dating. I found one a week later, a magic show at the college in Rock Island. A Sunday matinee performance, good for both Albenas I thought, and then a leisurely dinner to follow, and an early drive back to Keonah. I felt a need to let Rosa Lynn know sex was not uppermost in my mind. Frankly, despite the lusciousness of our last meeting, I felt uncomfortable about her marital status. If I accepted at face value the fact that she was only separated, and that even the mild intimacy she offered was tinged with her concern about sinning, too rapid a progress along those lines could cause us both a headache.

Edie was a different situation entirely. She was free, independent, and had initiated and encouraged an intimacy that I was sure she thoroughly enjoyed for her own pleasure. Anyway, I called Rosa early that Saturday. She thanked me for the invitation, but since she had a commitment for Sunday evening she didn't think she could accept. "Lisa would have loved the magic show, Emmett, but I can't go." She was surprised when I offered to take Lisa alone, and after asking me to hold for a moment while she called her, returned to say Lisa would be delighted. A few more minutes were taken up in settling the time and being assured a sitter was already arranged for.

The show began at 3:00 so I arrived at 2:15, assuming Lisa was just like her mother and would not be quite ready. But she was, and after a few pleasantries with Rosa we were off across the river to Rock Island. We got fairly good seats, up close to the stage, a plus for a magic show. Actually there was more, three jugglers, throwing balls, bottles, Indian clubs, and sticks in all kinds of patterns between them. This was the warm-up act, I guess, for 'Mr. Marvello'. My young date's attention never left the stage, her eyes large as saucers as rabbits and pigeons appeared and disappeared

191

accompanied by Marvello's unceasing patter, intended to distract attention from his hands, and quite successfully.

At intermission we fought the crowds out to the lobby where coffee and sodas were on sale. I splurged on a 'gourmet' cappuccino and treated Lisa to a cream soda. We were sipping away in a corner, away from the jostling throng of kids of all sizes more or less herded along by half as many adults. Lisa spied a friend, then another, and soon was busy chattering away with half a dozen young girls. For my part, I exchanged comments with the other shepherding adults about the weather, the possible ways the quart of water Marvello poured into his top hat disappeared, etc. One, somewhat older than Rosa I gauged, who knew Lisa and Rosa, was not so subtly curious about who I was, and my relation to Lisa's mother. I thought I was fairly good in fending her off by explaining I was simply Lisa's sitter, obtained on short notice, and for this afternoon only. Fortunately the bell sounded for the second act before she could press me for further gossip.

I herded Lisa back to our seats and settled in for the disappearing assistant trick, the selection of a kid from the audience to show how Marvello pulled money from his left ear and a red scarf from the right one. I had seen it all before, but still it was nice to see how ecstatic my young date was over the magic. I found myself musing a bit about how my little girl, if I had had one, would have reacted. She would have been some years older than Lisa I guessed, with red hair like her mother, not dark brown as Lisa's was, but just as lively. But thinking of her at Lisa's age, I would certainly have given her both a dog and a cat. And what would her name be I wondered. Probably Mary Amelia after our mothers, both gone by the time of our marriage.

The end of the show shook me out of that sad reverie, thank goodness. Pointless musing over a past that never was. We followed the crowd out to the parking lot and sped across the bridge to Davenport. It was 5:30 and getting dark now. I suggested we stop for supper on the way home and Lisa agreed. Hamburgers and ice cream seemed appropriate. The 'Cow Barn' Lisa told me was her favorite place and more or less directed me to this glorified kid's eatery, done in psychedelic splashes of non-complementary colors having no discernible resemblance to any animate or inanimate object.

It was crowded and noisy, but we were lucky and found a tiny table in a corner, somehow unclaimed by the several dozen customers of mixed ages and genders milling about. I was the only adult, lost in a sea of torn blue jeans, dirty sneakers, immature beards, and mis-applied make-up. A few, like Lisa, looked like Dresden dolls, but only by comparison. We ordered the featured 'burgeroos' to be followed by sundaes, banana split for me, hot fudge for my date. Conversation was a little sketchy due to the constant chatter of the other Barn inhabitants, and Lisa's scanning the newcomers to see if any of her friends came in.

Suddenly she popped out of the chair and fought her way to the front. I was doomed, squeezing through the crowd, she returned with a friend and the inquisitive mother of the magic show intermission. I stood to be introduced by Lisa to her friend, Sharon Healy and Mrs. Healy. Lisa's protocol for introductions needed fixing, both for precedence and completeness. I supplied the latter by giving Mrs. Healy my name and hand, which she returned with thanks for sharing our table, all 4 square feet of it. Seeing the addition, the waitress returned for their order. I asked that we all be served together, if possible.

"This table is too crowded for last names, don't you think?" And before I could give her my views, Mrs. Healy volunteered her first name, Meagan, and asked if I spelled my first name with one or two m's.

"'Two m's and two t's," I responded. "The extra letters came free with the christening. Waste not, want not, was my parents' motto." Meagan Healy gave me a polite smile to show she got my wit, but not so generous that she would be suspected of awarding me more than an E for effort.

"Rosa and I attend the same church," continuing with my interrogation, "but I don't believe I've seen you there. You're not Catholic I presume?"

A direct attack I thought, might repel this snoop. "No, I'm not even religious. God wounded me without cause, so I chose to get even by ignoring him."

I was mistaken. Mrs. Healy was not shocked silent. "God cannot be ignored, Emmett," she replied. "But Rosa would not have entrusted her Lisa to a really bad person. She is very devout. But you're just teasing,

193

Emmett, your wife has undoubtedly made Rosa aware of your brand of humor."

"Not very likely, Mrs. Healy—Meagan, I've been a widower for many years, and anyway, Mrs. Albena and I never discuss religion. As you say, she is devout. Only a crude heathen would try to shake her faith. I am neither, and would derive no pleasure in forcing my views on another."

Before she could think up another question, I put one myself to Lisa. "What are you girls giggling about?"

"I told Sharon about your dog. She thought 'Woof' was a peachy name. Would you mind if she used it when she gets a dog?" Looking at the young Miss Healy with a mock serious expression, I told her she could, but only if she got a well-mannered one and treated it well. From the corner of my eye I caught Mrs. Healy looking at me, puzzled at first, then quickly changing to a satisfied smile. By then our burgeroos had arrived. That is, three burgeroos and one tuna on toast for Meagan. Not really Cow Barn appropriate, I thought, but only a crude heathen would force his opinions on others. Further conversation was devoted exclusively as to why Lisa removed the pickles from her burgeroo and Sharon added them to hers, but discarded the onion slice. I enjoyed mine, as served, with an exaggerated display of smacking lips; congratulating Lisa between bites that the Cow Barn was an excellent choice.

With the delivery of the sundaes, butterscotch for Sharon, but coffee for her, Meagan relaxed a little as we both laughed at the gooey mess the girls made around their mouths. I offered, but Meagan rejected, to pay the whole bill. So I let her compute her share.

On the way to the car I asked Lisa if she thought her sitter had arrived, it now being a little after 7 o'clock. "Didn't mother tell you?" she said in surprise. "I'm to stay overnight at Kate Molina's house. I always do when Mr. Kelso takes her to the casino. Mom says she gets back too late to have a sitter wait up." With me in tow, my navigator got us to the Molinas. Kate's mother took charge of my date, we bid goodnight, and I left for Keonah and Mrs. Fashlich's.

I couldn't help but wonder if Lisa's overnight stay was because of a late date, or simply for Rosa to have an empty house for dalliance. No matter, I couldn't think of a more boring way to spend an evening than long hours at a card table or roulette wheel, so maybe a little sex would flavor it up. But I was not a Kelso, I was not going to park by her house to see what happened when they returned. I did think I had been a little too free trying to shock Meagan Healy with my religious views. She was sure to mention it to Rosa as a means of finding out just what our relationship was.

Chapter XXVI
A Song Of The Auvergne

My next date with Rosa Lynn was our last time together. Several weeks had gone by since Lisa and I had attended Mr. Marvello's magic show. We were very busy with late fall clean-up and winter prep work at Diehl's and I couldn't get away for a Saturday date. Also, I was just too tired for a Sunday evening drive to Davenport and back. I suppose the Cow Barn exposure to a crowd of noisy teens and pre-teens made me feel older even than I was.

When Elmer agreed to my half-Saturday off arrangement, it was predicated on the amount of business, or rather, lack of business. So finally, when things slowed down a bit on a Friday, mostly because of a two-day rain that stopped outdoor work, I was free to call. Rosa was also free for that Saturday, so by 5:30 I was on the road, arriving at 6:45 because I just loped along. Rags was glad to see me after a long absence. I could tell by his enthusiastic tail wagging and sniffing. A scratch behind the ear, and a promise of a treat when I returned later assured him we were still the best of friends. Lisa, I was informed, was next door, Mrs. Polanski having agreed to take care of her under the promise that Rosa would be back before midnight to relieve her. That was all right with me, I had nothing special planned, just dinner and, hopefully, another lesson on disco style dancing from my date. Rosa had suggested an Italian restaurant just outside of Bettendorf. Excellent calimari she said. I didn't tell her I hadn't tried squid before, or that my natural inclination would be to pass it up. But why he a prisoner of ignorant prejudices, I'll let Rosa choose the menu and maybe I'll find something new and good.

Fortunately, for me, the squid were cut into rings, losing any suggestion of a squiggly creature with too many arms, all with suckers. It was served as a salad appetizer with tomato wedges and a slightly spicy sauce. Actually it was quite tasty, even to the tomatoes which for that late fall date were still ripe and sweet. Definitely not the deceptive abomination usually found in restaurants. You know the kind, they look ripe, being a nice rich red all over, but having absolutely no taste. I had asked Rosa to order for me, and unlike Edie, her Italian was sure and evidently competent enough for a detailed discussion with the waiter on the composition of the dishes. We stuck to a simple Chianti to go with the pasta and a complicated main dish of rolled and stuffed beefsteak. Conversation was mostly about how much Lisa had enjoyed the magic show and Rosa's appreciation for my willingness to include her occasionally on our dates. But over coffee, after a few minutes of silence, she said that Mrs. Healy had mentioned meeting us at the Cow Barn.

"Yes, Lisa spotted her friend Sharon, and since we had taken the last open table, offered to share it," I explained quickly, wanting to get to the more important item of where we might find a place to dance. But Rosa Lynn didn't let go.

"So Lisa told me. Meagan Healy told me other things too, Emmett. She seemed to think you were hired as a sitter for Lisa. Did you tell her that?"

I confessed I had. "Your friend Mrs. Healy seemed too interested in our relation and since I knew nothing about her or how you felt about her, I thought that would be sufficiently innocuous. She should really have asked you about me."

Rosa responded by saying Mrs. Healy's daughter was a friend of Lisa's, but that she was not particularly friendly with the woman. "That was all right, Emmett, but it wasn't so good to tell her you didn't believe in God. She spread it all over the parish that I entrusted my daughter to an atheist."

So Meagan Healy had lost no time in confronting Rosa with my unfortunate remark. "Not atheistic, Rosa, more agnostic. I'm sorry if my comment to Mrs. Healy, which was only intended to shock her into stopping her prying, is causing you embarrassment." A perfect defense for her suddenly flashed into my mind. "After all, Rosa, you can't be expected—it might even be against the law—to require passing a religious test before hiring someone."

Rosa looked unconvinced. "Some people will know I didn't hire you. Meagan Healy will wheedle it out of Lisa that we've dated. At least one person knows that already."

"Mr. Kelso, I suppose."

"Yes. I guess you know about him from Lisa." Poor Lisa, she'll be in the middle of this mess.

"No, it wasn't Lisa. Your friend Kelso paid me a visit a couple of weeks ago. It wasn't a friendly one." I could see my chances for a pleasant evening were going down the drain rapidly.

Rosa looked vexed. "He had no right to do that, Emmett. What a mess the men in my life have made. I couldn't believe Joe would steal, and then to run off and leave me and Lisa to face the shame alone. Why couldn't he have been man enough to take his punishment. At least he could have let me know where he was. I could have joined him and we could have started all over again."

"I'm not going to defend him, Rosa, but he probably did the best he could for you. He's gone. If he'd stayed he'd be imprisoned—maybe for twenty years and you'd be where you are now, alone. If he told you where he went you'd be an accessory and jailed yourself if you didn't tell the police. Surely they were watching you in case he did try to contact you. It's probably a Federal offense and the FBI would have made a tap on your phone, and even intercepted your mail. This way, after 5-7 years you could have the marriage dissolved by having him declared legally dead, or as Kelso implied, you have a chance of getting it annulled by the Church. He's working on it."

"Robert is trying to get an annulment?" Rosa seemed surprised. "And without asking me first! You see what I mean: a crook, an arrogant Irish hot-head, a non-Catholic—and even worse—an atheist, and several lechers besides!"

I thought Rosa was very unfair to include me in her list of male disasters. After all I corrected her calling me an atheist though I had to admit my opinions might be a little stronger than agnostic. Anyway, an atheist by definition is non-Catholic, so her grammar or semantics was off. But I especially resented being included with lechers. Rosa had invited the little intimacy we shared. Even accusing me of being slow. "I guess you don't feel like dancing?" I finally asked. Rosa shook her head and suggested I take her home.

I started to pull into the curb in front of her house, when she broke the silence that had begun when we left the restaurant. I had tried to start a conversation several times along the way on what I thought were innocuous subjects, but she hadn't responded.

Drive around the corner please, you know, where we parked before." I did so, not sure what she had in mind.

"I'm sorry I've been sulking, Emmett, it's very unfair to you. It's just a mess and not really your fault, but I don't see any future for us, together, I mean. You've been one of the nicest dates I've had, and very good with Lisa, but even if I managed an annulment, I couldn't marry someone outside the Church."

"Anyone can become Catholic, Rosa." I really didn't know why I said that. It was the first time marriage had come up.

"Yes, that's true, but it would be a terrible sin to convert and not really mean it. Anyway, could you manage a family, does your job pay enough for that?" Sneaky Kelso must have found out what I got at Diehl's and put it up to Rosa. Easy enough I guess for an insurance agency to get a financial report from my bank.

"I have other sources of income Rosa," I replied with some heat, "and anyway I could go back to my engineering career if necessary."

"Perhaps," she sounded unconvinced. "I'm sorry I mentioned money. It was unkind of me. Anyway, an annulment, even if I could get one, would take time and all the while we'd be playing these little sex games after each date, and I'd fall into sin."

I was stunned and immediately resentful. "Why didn't you tell me how you felt at the beginning? I don't consider a kiss sinful."

"But it wouldn't stop there. Do you think I'm made of stone?"

"I wouldn't have thought so Rosa, but good god you've been separated for 5 years, if you haven't gone beyond kissing in that time, what would you expect me to think!"

"I hope you will still think well of me, Emmett. Yes, 5 years, but I didn't date until I moved here. Phyllis Mercer thought I should, she introduced me to some single men. A salesman at George's business, her landscaper, and I don't know where she met the others. Most of those I didn't date, and for the rest, it was easy to keep control. They pushed, and that's the wrong way to interest me. Of course, I told you about Robert Kelso. You didn't push so I wondered about you. Now I'm all confused. I know what men want and it's unfair to be a temptation and still stay out of reach. Anyway, I'm not old enough to be put on the shelf. At least I don't feel like being a nun despite my faith. Damn it!, after 5 years this do-it-yourself kit is hardly enough, that's why I'm afraid."

Baffled, I asked "What do-it-yourself kit are you talking about Rosa?" She looked at me in surprise.

"Haven't you used one?" She held her hand in front of my face, fingers spread apart. I was so embarrassed by my naiveté I could only mumble. "Oh."

Rosa suddenly kissed my cheek, opened the door on her side and gave me her parting words. "Goodbye, Emmett, please don't call me again. I need to resolve my problem without having to fight temptation at the same time."

I started to protest, saying I'd drive her home, but she just shut the door and walked off. And that was it! No more Rosa Lynn, no Lisa, and no more Rags. Poor me, and poor Rags, I hadn't even the doggie bag I had promised him.

This sudden breakup, so unexpected and so complete, demanded an explanation, but I was too upset to think about it very clearly until I was nearly half-way back to Keonah. It just seemed unreal to credit all Rosa had said as truth. Oh I certainly believed the Phyllis story. It was right in tune with my own observations. Probably the salesman and landscaper were beginning to bore her, or were getting too hard to put off, so she sent them on to Rosa. As for me, I didn't have any illusion I was that irresistible. No woman had shown interest in me back East even when I was still at work, after Fran's death, and no wives of my friends tried to introduce me to any. Maybe they sensed I wouldn't have been interested then. Edie, of course, was a different matter. First, she was a widow, not encumbered like Rosa; second, she was financially secure with a business to run; further, not immersed in the concept of sex as sin, perhaps even wanting to enjoy having the occasional affair her husband had practiced on her—so long as it was discreetly done; and finally, we were more closely matched in age.

So maybe that had something to do with it. Maybe my friend Kelso had hammered at Rosa about my being older—too old—for her, nearly 15 years, as best as I could guess. Yes, and that on top of my dirty, no-future job at Diehl's could have convinced her I was not a suitable replacement for her missing Joe. Still we could have seen each other occasionally until she found some more serious interest. Why drop me now when nothing she dreaded was even threatening? Had Kelso given her an ultimatum, him or me? Very possible. He sure acted the jealous possessive type. I could see Rosa weighing the pros and cons. On age, looks, income and position, and religion he had all the pluses. The only negative I saw was that he was a creep, but that was only my opinion—well, Elmer's too. Now it wasn't any longer necessary to tell Edie. No real sins of commission had occurred.

After a bit I turned the radio on, good music from the University station at Iowa City. A lilting soprano was singing a hauntingly beautiful melody. I didn't understand the words, they sounded somewhat French. Just as well, I let her voice bring out my own feelings at that moment, loneliness, and again, somehow, a sense of loss. I remembered an old print my mother had framed, called 'Sweet Melancholy'. This melancholy didn't seem so sweet. At the end of the song the announcer repeated the name of the piece. 'The Shepherd's Song' from 'Songs of the Auvergne'. I thought I'd look up the words, maybe get it on cassette for my radio.

CHAPTER XXVII

ELMER DIEHL

Business was picking up again, the week following my meeting with Rosa Lynn. Bags of fall fertilizer and grass seed; bulbs to plant for next spring's showing, hopefully; leaf rakes and new mower blades.

Towards the end of the week Mrs. Fashlich stopped by to hand me a letter. Not her main reason, just on her way to the store for a selection of daffodil bulbs. The letter was important, but not terribly important, just the quarterly account summary by my investment broker, a stock advisory, and the only immediately useful thing, a check for interest on bonds held in street account name. I like to get that money sent directly to me, rather than leave it in the brokerage account, especially since my bank account needed a boost after dates with Edie and the Albenas, mother and daughter. But that was nothing to worry about. What was a worry came with Mrs. F.'s scream for help.

I rushed to the front of the store to find her trying to keep Elmer from falling off the ladder we use to get items from the upper storage shelves lining the left wall. "I can't hold him, Mr. Borden," she screamed. I could see that. He was slumped on the ladder, several rungs up. Her thin body was pressed against his back, her arms around his waist and grasping the ladder. I eased him down and laid him on the floor. His face was very pale, breathing shallow. He was barely conscious. I tried to keep calm, but I guess my voice sounded shrill when I hollered at Mrs. F. to run to the corner and get Macklinburg at once. I grabbed a coat and whatever else I could find close-by to wrap him up for warmth.

Mrs. F. returned on the run with Macklinburg, and so out of breath I was afraid she'd be our next patient. Herb Macklinburg was a pharmacist, not a doctor, but I knew he had practical medical knowledge for this situation. Elmer was regaining consciousness, helped by the added warmth of the coat and worn old blanket I found under the glass-cutting table. Thank goodness he seemed to have suffered no mental damage.

"I just felt faint," he protested, trying weakly to push Herb aside and get up. I told him to shut up and lie still.

"I've told you a dozen times, Elmer, to let me get up the ladder, damn it!" I was shaken and upset, so I guess I wasn't much good for soothing words. Herb asked me to call Doc Jensen, giving me the number from memory.

After hearing me describe Elmer's condition, Jensen said we'd better drive him to the hospital in C.R. and meet him there. Herb, thank goodness, said he'd ride with me, just in case of a relapse, if I'd drive his car.

I closed the store, asked Mrs. Fashlick to let Elmer's housekeeper, Mrs. Carter, know what happened, and waited for Herb to drive up.

Doc Jensen arrived at the Lutheran Hospital Emergency Ward shortly after we did. I had driven as carefully as I could to ensure jolting Elmer as little as possible. We had laid him out on the back seat, well covered up to keep him warm and reasonably comfortable. Herb was not comfortable, deciding he'd better sit on the floor in back, to keep an eye on Elmer in case he had another attack. The ER attendants had responded at once to my hoarse holler for help, wheeling a gurney out to the car. The four of us got Elmer out of the car and onto the cart, just as Jensen drove up. There was nothing more Herb and I could do but wait.

"It's happened before you know," Herb explained to me in the waiting room. I didn't know that.

"All he ever complained about to me was his lumbago. That's why I told him to stay off the ladder. But the stubborn old bastard did whatever he wanted to." Herb sensed my distress, but couldn't have known why I was so shaken. Those memories of Fran's last few hours of pain the drugs could no longer suppress had flashed into my consciousness, as if it were yesterday. I suddenly realized Herb had brought us coffee. Maybe to calm me down and stop my pacing back and forth; maybe calm himself too.

"Another cup?" he asked. I nodded glumly, wondering when we'd get some kind of word from Jensen. Herb got up to go to the little coffee shop off the lobby when I realized it was nearly 4:00 and neither of us had eaten lunch. Pulling out my wallet I handed him a five and asked if he'd bring us both some sandwiches.

"Any kind, Herb, it doesn't really matter." He nodded and was gone.

I felt a little better after the sandwich and second coffee. "Elmer's in his 80's, Emmett, it's not really unexpected you know."

"I suppose not. It just caught me by surprise, Herb. I wasn't prepared for something like this happening." And then I just let it tumble out about Fran. "I thought I'd put that behind me by now, but I guess I hadn't." There was really nothing Herb could say after that. We sat, neither of us speaking until Doc Jensen returned.

"Elmer's resting quietly," he told us, adding "You can go back to Keonah, Herb. Somebody's got to run our only drugstore. I'll see that Borden gets home all right. The hardware store can stay shut without the town collapsing, but Elmer wants to talk to him for a bit."

Herb was clearly relieved to get back. His only helper, a young woman, couldn't fill prescriptions, and anyway, probably had to get home herself to fix supper.

As soon as Herb left, Jensen told me he had sent for John Trable at Elmer's request. Trable was Elmer's lawyer. I sensed more bad news was coming. Responding to my questioning look, he said "I told Elmer his heart was very weak, and while I was hopeful he'd recover, it would be wise to make sure he had his affairs in order. For you only, Borden, I'm not that hopeful.

Jensen must have called Trable sometime earlier since the lawyer and his secretary entered after a few more minutes. Jensen and Trable conferred quietly off in a corner of the lobby, and then, signaling to us, led us to the elevator and then to Elmer's room.

"How are you feeling, Boss?" I asked, hoping I had managed a cheerful tone. He looked very weak. Tired, as though he hadn't slept in days. Still, work was on his mind.

"You'll open the shop tomorrow, Borden?" he murmured, almost a whisper. "Doc Jensen's not going to let me up for a few more days." I assured him I'd keep the store open till he returned, and was about to ask if he wanted me to make out the monthly bills, when he raised his hand to stop me. "I asked John," pointing to Trable, "to make some changes in my will, just in case. You brought a copy, John?" he asked. Trable nodded, pulling a folder from his briefcase.

"My niece, Nancy, is listed as a beneficiary on the bonds. That doesn't change, if she is still alive. If not, her children, but under no circumstances to her former husband. If it goes to the children, I want you, Borden, and John, to establish a trust fund for them until they're of age. The store and the bank accounts to you, Borden, except for the gift to Mrs. Carter, already listed in the will."

I was stunned. "That's not right, Elmer!" I protested. "It should go to your niece, or her children, same as for the bonds, or at least to some other relative."

Elmer tried to push himself up, causing Jensen to gently prop a pillow under his shoulders and caution him against unnecessary movement. "Look, Borden, she can't run the business, you'll have to do it, so you might as well have it. Besides, I won't have another fella calling you a dirty clerk like that what's his name that came looking for a fight."

"I won't do it, Elmer, you've put me in a bad position. If your relatives are alive they'll feel I've taken advantage of your illness. You'll be all right in a few days and can think this out more carefully about the store then. No, I won't accept it."

I didn't add that if Elmer died I'd probably leave Keonah. I might well move on before then. My experience with Rosa Lynn had almost convinced me I should find some place and something better for the rest of my life. Even owning a hardware store in a decaying town wouldn't have impressed Rosa.

"Borden has a point, Elmer," Trable said. "But Nancy, or her children can't run the store unless Borden's there to help, and, no offense, Borden, but what's to keep you in Keonah?"

I didn't answer his question, I had no answer, even for myself. "Let's make a compromise," Trable finally suggested. "Make Borden and Nancy equal partners. That should avoid Borden's concern about undue influence, and give your niece—or her children—someone experienced to manage the business." Elmer nodded his assent, but I was still concerned.

"It's asking for trouble. She doesn't know me, I don't know her, and even Elmer apparently couldn't control her, Trable. Half the store is too much. I couldn't buy her out, and she probably couldn't buy me out. Even worse, would she come back to Keonah to help run the place, or would I have long distance communications in order to make business decisions? No, let's do it this way, let Elmer appoint me temporary trustee to advise her, but with no final legal power over business decisions."

Trable considered it for a moment, then suggested that Elmer give me a 10% share to ensure keeping my interest in running the store properly until she could handle it herself. It seemed a reasonable compromise even to Elmer. At 10%, I could get out if we really clashed, yet it gave my non-binding advice some weight as a minority owner.

The secretary took Trable's dictation on the agreement terms, then left for the lobby to type the will. Jensen insisted on quiet for his patient. The typed will was returned for signatures after a half-hour. Elmer signed, and Jensen and a nurse signed as witnesses. With that done, Jensen shooed us out so Elmer could get some rest.

Trable's secretary, a Mrs. Carol Brindly, I found out later, walked out with me. Trable and Doc Jensen hung back in the lobby for, apparently, a private conversation.

"You're a strange one, Mr. Borden," she commented as we waited for Trable to join us. "Giving up thousands of dollars to a woman you don't know and who doesn't know you. I don't know any man who would do that."

"Why am I strange?" I replied after a moment's surprise over a confidential secretary commenting over a matter that shouldn't have concerned her. "I didn't really give up anything actually. I don't have the store, and frankly, probably never will have it. Elmer Diehl will undoubtedly want to change the will when he's back on his feet. This way he can do it without having to explain anything to me, or risk causing my resentment. Anyway, I don't want to have that store anchoring me to Keonah. I'm not sure I'll be staying here much longer. And from all I've heard, Nancy What's-Her-Name is just as stubborn and cantankerous as Elmer!"

She looked back to see where Trable was, then turned to me saying, "Nancy Hoegh may not want the store either, but you're still strange to give it up." By then Trable joined us and we left in his car without much further discussion.

Elmer died two days later, peacefully, in his sleep. I visited him each day, closing the store for a couple of hours at noon. Conversation was mostly a monologue by me about which customer bought what, who asked how he was doing, etc. Just things to pass an hour without needless excitement. Even so, I'm not sure he really heard me, he was very drowsy, not asleep, but not fully conscious, or at least attentive. I was just getting up to leave on the second day, when he mumbled for me to come closer. ""Find Nancy for me, Borden." That was all. I nodded, saying I'd find her and bring her back to see him. He nodded, letting me know he heard that much.

Trable called me at the store the next morning. The hospital had notified Doctor Jensen that Elmer had died, and Jensen called Trable. I closed the store at noon, posting notice of Elmer's death on the door, and that I'd re-open probably tomorrow. I was to meet with Trable to discuss the funeral arrangements, and my role as trustee, but I decided to stop by the lumberyard first to tell Voss and ask him to let Elmer's other friends, his pinochle gang, mostly, know. Voss asked what I was going to do, and what would happen to the store, but I had no ready answers for him, only that his niece was the principal heir. I also called Mrs. Carter, but she said Trable had already told her. Finally I headed for the diner for a rather glum lunch before meeting with the lawyer.

It was too soon to give any serious thought to my own future. I had promised Elmer I'd find his niece, though I no longer felt bound to my promise to bring her back to Keonah. Elmer was gone, so the promise had no meaning to him, or to anyone else I could think of.

Trable had the will, bank account statements, and a listing of the safe deposit box contents laid on his desk when I arrived. Before getting into the financial situation, I asked him about funeral arrangements, was I supposed to do anything? I was relieved to hear that he would arrange that. Elmer had specified what he wanted done in the previous will and Trable had simply asked his secretary to incorporate those details in the new one. The funeral would be in the Lutheran Church in town. I doubt Elmer was a churchgoer, he had never mentioned religion to me, nor had I even noticed him near the church on those Sundays I used to stroll about the town. Still, he was probably keeping his options open, just in case. Anyway, a brief service would be held for the benefit of his friends on Monday. I asked if his relations would be able to get there on such short notice, but apparently, other than his niece, there were none, and neither of us knew where she was.

As executor, Trable had power of attorney, but as trustee of the store for his niece, as well as minor partner, I would continue to operate it, draw checks to pay bills which he would countersign, and deposit income. He was preparing the documents needed for probate, which was fine. I didn't want to go through that business again, but I had to take inventory so we could determine the estate taxes and the income tax due. I agreed to do that. And even though I was a co-owner, Trable felt I should continue to draw my salary. My share of the business profits would come at the end of the fiscal year. These were all legal matters, cut and dried for the most part. The difficult matter was to find his niece, and as quickly as possible, since it was most desirable that she decide on how she intended to pay the estate taxes, and what was to be done with his house and personal effects. I suggested we ask Mrs. Carter to box up Elmer's clothing and whatever other personal items, razors, watch, tie pins, etc., all except letters, photos and any documents that might be helpful in tracing his niece. We agreed to meet at Elmer's house that evening, after supper, and sort through those items for clues. I went back to the store to start the inventory, not a trivial job, since I had to document and estimate current prices for hundreds of hardware items, some of which had been around for years. For nuts and bolts, and screws and nails, I took the shortcut of simply pricing them by weight—no finicky separation by sizes. That will have to do for the IRS and my majority partner.

There wasn't much to guide us in finding Nancy Hoegh. A few pictures, the latest one, apparently, was a high school graduation party showing her, Elmer, and some friends. Mrs. Carter identified who the niece was, but was uncertain about some of the others. I thought I recognized Phyllis Mercer, nee Harlow, then, and Mina Voss, but no one else. There were some letters addressed to Nancy Geiger Hoegh in Omaha, from Elmer, as indicated by the return address, but these had been marked 'Return to Sender' in penciled block letters, and were un-opened. Did she mark that herself, it surely wasn't the way the post office would do? They were post-marked some 10 years previously, so they probably wouldn't be much help, but I'd wire that address anyway. At least we could start with Nebraska. I suggested to Trable that he get the county sheriff to wire a request to the Department of Motor Vehicles in Lincoln to see if the niece had a current driver's license and address. I thought an inquiry from the sheriff would expedite a response. Trable agreed and thought we ought to try the same thing in Des Moines and Sacramento in case she followed an Iowa custom and went to California. I promised to talk to Phyllis Mercer who might have some later correspondence. I took the picture with me.

My first stop was to the Voss home to see Mina. She looked at the picture I showed her. She could identify Nancy Hoegh all right, and of course Elmer and Phyllis, but she was very uncertain about the others. "You understand, Emmett, these kids were much younger than me, I probably knew their names then, but so many years have gone by and I haven't kept in touch. Actually, Nancy only invited me because I was Phyllis's sister. I was married then, with two children, Adrian and Sam Jr., so my friends were from a different circle. Charlie came later," she added unnecessarily. "Phyllis would probably remember. Shall I give her a call?"

I was glad she offered. I didn't want to risk making the call myself and having George Mercer answer the phone. That might create more suspicion in his mind than I'd care for, and probably trouble for Phyllis, who seemed to skate a thin line already with other men.

Phyllis was at home and after Mina explained the situation, said she could probably identify the group. I asked Mina to see if Phyllis could meet me at Mercer's Motors in a couple of hours and to bring any later addresses she might have for Nancy.

She was waiting in the office when I drove up. George was with her. I showed her the picture and thought it best to explain to George why I was there. It seemed to satisfy him and I was glad he left to talk to some prospects. I didn't know what relation Phyllis might have had with some of the boys in that picture. It was before she married him, but I was sure George could be jealous of a mosquito that bit her.

There was nothing wrong with her memory. She identified everyone in the picture. The future Mr. Hoegh was not among them. Unfortunately, Phyllis had not kept any letters from Nancy, so I couldn't get additional addresses.

I thanked her for her help, explaining in a few short words why I had asked her to meet me at the office, and prepared to leave.

"You're not seeing Rosa Lynn?" she asked.

"I'm afraid not, Phyllis. She is a nice woman, she has a very charming young daughter and a friendly dog that I could become attached to, but there's no future between us—her words. She's either still waiting for her husband to come back, rich and vindicated, which seems unlikely, or a good Catholic man of more substantial prospects to replace him, neither of which I can offer."

Phyllis gave an exasperated sigh, and with that I left, preferring to avoid any more detailed discussion on that subject.

Chapter XXVIII

Nan Hoegh

The Nebraska License Bureau finally located a Nancy Hoegh, in the little town of Glenly, 10 or 15 miles southwest of Omaha, depending on where you start measuring. She had retained her married name—if this was the right one. I decided the safest procedure would be to see her unannounced. First to make sure this was Elmer's niece, and if she was, then more importantly in view of her deliberate avoidance of any contact with her uncle and former friends in Keonah, to prevent her taking flight before we could meet.

It would be a long drive, about 300 miles, so I started out early Friday morning. I took the Interstate to Omaha to make the best possible time. The view across the rolling hills of middle Iowa was still pleasant in this later part of Fall. Corn harvest was of course over and the stalks for the most part were pretty much mowed down. The leaves had turned, but compared to the Fall scenery in the forested Northeast, there weren't as many trees to produce the dense riot of color of New England. While Iowa is not a desert by any means, it's a bit too dry and too extensively cultivated for forests.

Arriving in Glenly in the late afternoon, I stopped at a Phillips 66 station for gas and directions to her address. It wasn't hard to find the place, Glenly is only a village of a couple of thousand, and has no complicated street system. Nan Hoegh lived, as I did, in a rented room of a small wooden house. Her landlady responded to my knock, and after assuring her I was respectable and had a legitimate business purpose, gave me directions to the drugstore where Nan worked. I found her making change at the cash register.

Pretending to be looking for something on the patent medicine and nostrums shelves, I compared her face with the graduation picture I had brought along. As she appeared in the picture of 15 or so years ago, she was

211

a pleasant-looking, cheerful girl of maybe 18 or 19. Now she looked a little worn, a little too thin as though she didn't eat enough, about 5'-5" though I couldn't tell if she was in heels or flats, and plainly dressed, a heavy brown cardigan over a greenish colored blouse. Except for a wedding ring there was no other jewelry in evidence. Her straight brown hair, combed back from her face, hung loose at shoulder length in a no-nonsense style. I couldn't help thinking of the contrast she would make next to her old friend Phyllis.

Waiting until her customer had left, I selected a package of cherry cough drops and handed them to her with a dollar bill. She looked at me as she started to ring up the sale without actually seeing me, the usual behavior of a salesperson shielding herself from the boredom of the job and keeping interaction between herself and the customer to the barest polite minimum.

"You are Nancy Hoegh, formerly Nancy Geiger of Keonah, Iowa," I stated as bluntly as possible. Startled, she looked at me, seeing me for the first time.

"Do I know you?" Her tone and expression were instantly defensive. "Who are you?"

"You do not know me, and before I answer your other question, will you please answer mine. I don't want to state my business to the wrong person. It's not really business, probably the opposite, but it's personal to Nancy Geiger Hoegh only," I added reassuringly, seeing a sudden wariness in her face.

She didn't answer me at once, but called to someone in back, at the prescription counter, that she was taking a break for a few minutes. "All right, mister, I'm Nancy Geiger Hoegh. We'll go over to the lunchroom across the street and you will tell me who you are and what you want. I can take 15 minutes off, so make your story short and to the point."

I held the door for her. She marched through with no 'thank you'. I followed her across the street, but let her open the cafe' door herself, she's so independent.

"Coffee, Suzy" she called to the waitress behind the counter, and headed for a booth towards the back.

"Make that two," I added and joined her. She had chosen the side facing the door and the cash register. Probably thinking it better if she wanted to leave or call for help.

"Talk."

Up close, I noticed she was missing an eyetooth and her nose wasn't quite straight. "I'll talk," I told her, "but I need more proof you are who you say you are." Pulling out the graduation party picture, I asked her to identify some of the people.

"Where did you get this?" she blurted. "From Mr. Diehl? Look, you can tell him to leave me alone. I'm not going back there!" She started to get up. I stopped her at once with the blunt retort that Elmer Diehl was dead. She sank back into the booth, stunned for a moment, then asked again, a little more civilly, who I was.

"When you correctly identify these people," I replied, pointing again at the picture.

"That's Phyllis and Min Harlow, Uncle Elmer, me, Joyce Delmar, Peter Adel, Jimmy Smith, and Tina Brown." It checked exactly with the names Phyllis Mercer had given me.

"O.K.," I responded, "you're probably who you say you are." I stopped for a minute as the waitress brought the coffee. Continuing, after she left, I told her who I was, that I worked for Diehl at the hardware store, and that Elmer had appointed me her trustee in his will. I was glad that her immediate responses was when did he die, and how, not what was in the will. "You would have been notified at once," I added, "but we had no address for you, only the vague information that you had gone to Omaha. I put ads in the personal column of *The World Herald*, but that's always a slim chance you would see it, even if you stayed in Omaha. Your uncle was buried in Keonah and as soon as I got a response from The Nebraska Motor Registration Bureau that you were in Glenly I drove down."

She sat quietly, her coffee forgotten. I think she was starting to tear up. I could barely hear her whisper that she was really alone now. "Your husband, former husband, is still alive isn't he?"

"I don't know," she muttered, and pointing to the gap in her teeth and nose, "do you think I feel anything for him but contempt? At least Uncle Elmer never abused me, however much we argued. Did you come all this way just to tell me about my uncle? You could have just written you know."

"Not really, there might be several Nancy Hoeghs in Nebraska, or you might have gone back to your maiden name—I checked on that too. I told you I am the trustee in your uncle's will. Except for a small bequest to his housekeeper you are almost the sole heir. The exception is that I'm to receive 10% of the hardware store for serving as trustee and financial advisor to you. I have no authority over how you decide to use your inheritance," I added hastily, "just a source of opinion should you want it. I made that clear to Elmer in accepting his request to serve."

She said nothing, just sat staring at her coffee that was getting cold. "Don't you want to know what the estate is?" I asked. She seemed lost in some sort of mental desert of dead memories, but I told her anyway. It had to be done.

"There's about $200,000 in municipal bonds with you listed as the beneficiary. They bring in about $10,000 tax free a year. Elmer didn't like paying taxes. About $4500 in his personal checking and savings accounts, $7500 in the business checking account, the house on Pine Street, and the hardware store, both mortgage free. They're being appraised, I have no idea of their value yet. Also of course, I'm still inventorying the store stock, and checking accounts receivable and payable. I don't think that's too much, again Elmer didn't like to carry debts or loan money. As for the hardware business, you know Keonah's not a thriving commercial center, probably wasn't even when you lived there, and your uncle didn't try to compensate by expanding his services, at least until I was hired. Anyway, his last income tax report showed a net profit of about $10,000." Still nothing. "Did you hear me, Mrs. Hoegh?" I sharpened my voice to get through to her.

"Yes I heard you. What am I supposed to do? He's buried already isn't he? Look, Mr. Borden, I've got to get back to work." She fished in her purse for some change and started to get up. She didn't really seem to grasp the situation.

"Look, Mrs. Hoegh, you don't seem to understand. You've got to return to Keonah. You've got to prove you're his heir in probate court, you've got to run the hardware store or do something with it and the house. You've got to sign papers on transferring the bonds and the bank accounts, and you've got to decide how you're going to pay the estate taxes, that'll reduce the estate by about a third. I'm the trustee but I can't do all that for you alone. Better ask for an emergency leave from the drugstore until you can get this estate in order."

She just stared at me. I think she was still in shock, but I really couldn't see why. Here she was suddenly getting as much from the bonds alone as she must have earned clerking in Glenly, and she hadn't been close to Elmer for a dozen years. I took her arm, dropped a bill to Suzy, and steered her across the street. A man in a white lab coat was at the register. I assumed he was the manager. I told him the situation and that Mrs. Hoegh would have to have leave immediately. She nodded when he asked her if that was true. Apologizing for her, I said I hoped this didn't put him in a bind, but I could see he wasn't overwhelmed with business, at least today. I asked for his business card so I could call him if necessary.

"Did you drive to work?" I asked as we left the store. She shook her head so I opened my car door for her and we drove to her rooming house. I noticed an old junker parked in front of the house and asked if that was hers. It was. I told her she'd never make it to Keonah in that thing, probably wouldn't even get safely over the Missouri. "We'll go in my car. First thing in the morning. Now I've got to find a motel for the night, you be packed and ready to go by 7:30. We'll get breakfast on the way."

"Just a minute, mister," she seemed to have got her senses back. "You asked me to prove my identity, but I'm not going anywhere with you until I know you're on the up and up."

"Thank goodness you're finally showing some common sense. Of course you should verify what I've told you." I pulled out my address book and handed it to her. "Go inside and call these people. First John Trable, he was your uncle's lawyer. He will verify your uncle's death and who I am. You probably don't know him, so call your friend Phyllis' sister, Mina Voss, she knows me or call Phyllis Mercer, but she's in Davenport. I think you know Mrs. Fashlich, at least she knows you. She's my landlady, she'll also vouch for me. Here's a ten dollar bill, pay your landlady for the calls, but make the one to the lawyer first before he closes his office. Now get going." She went.

I lit my pipe and waited. About a half-hour later she came out. Handing me my address book, she said "I'm not quite dumb enough to use your numbers for checking. I got the long distance operator to look them up. No one answered at Phyllis', but Mina verified everything. She even said you were nice. The lawyer and Mrs. Fashlich said I could trust you. The phone bill was $8.39," she was opening her purse for change, but I told her to keep it, I would bill the estate for expenses. I hadn't seen a decent motel close to town when I drove in, so I asked her if she knew of any, also a good place to eat—not Suzy's lunch room. I was hungry. It had been a long drive and my back was getting sore from sitting.

"There's a good motel and restaurant near Papillion, Mr. Borden. About 5 or 7 miles from here, east on 370. I can show you if you'd like."

I could sense her attitude had changed, not so contentious now that she knew I had told her the truth. "I'll find it, thanks. You will probably want to take time to pack and say goodbye to your friends for a while."

"There's only one bag to pack and I haven't any friends here, Mr. Borden. At least none that will miss me for a while, so if you'll follow me you won't get lost." She drove carefully so as not to lose me at stop signs and left turns, and after twenty minutes or so she pulled into a reasonably decent looking motel. I walked back to her car and asked if the restaurant we had passed, a mile or so back, was the one she had in mind. It was. I was about to remind her to be ready the next morning when I decided to suggest she might just as well meet me at the restaurant for dinner as it will be easier for me to bring her up to date on the state of Elmer's business so she will have some idea of what she might want to do with it. "Don't worry, Mrs. Hoegh," I added noting her hesitancy, "your expenses will be paid by the estate. The probate judge will give you access to the checking account pretty quickly since there will be people in Keonah to identify you. Do I need to add you'll be perfectly safe with me?"

"I guess not, Mr. Borden. I'll wait for you at the restaurant. I appreciate your concern about expenses. I haven't been able to save much, and anyway, the bank is closed." I watched her drive off and then checked into the motel. After a quick shave and a clean shirt, I drove back along the highway to the restaurant. Nan was waiting for me by the receptionist. It looked O.K., a family place, but quiet and not very crowded. We took a booth and glanced at the menu.

"Could I have a drink?" she asked. "It's been an unsettling afternoon."

I told her of course, and smiling, added "I'm sure it has been. Unexpected, but your prospects are good certainly. Your uncle wasn't exactly a miser, but he was cautious about spending and investing. You are the one that benefits from that."

Her idea of a drink was a glass of red wine. I had my usual Scotch, but dressed up with a lemon twist. We studied the menu without talking until the drinks arrived. I decided quickly enough on today's special, chicken pot pie, and put the menu away. "Having trouble deciding?" I asked after a few minutes.

"I guess so," she said. "Usually I only have a can of soup and crackers for supper. I can only use a hot plate in my room, supposedly for boiling water for tea in the morning, but Mrs. Thomas—that's my landlady—doesn't mind my opening a soup can."

She finally decided on a veal cutlet platter. I hoped that was going to be the start of a better diet. I shuddered at the thought of my going to bed on a pea soup and saltine supper.

"Are you trying to lose weight or do you have ulcers, or what? That sounds awful for a working girl."

"Neither. My job doesn't pay much. I have to economize. I suppose it doesn't seem like much of a life to you, but I'm independent and I've been saving a little so I can stay independent." We sipped our drinks, and then she added "Mina said you were widowed, Mr. Borden, but you're wearing a wedding ring." Women certainly seem to notice that, even though mine was only a plain gold band and didn't seem to me to be that obvious on my finger, darkened from the summer's work on the gazebo.

"For remembrance of my wife, but you don't wear your wedding ring for remembrance do you?" I responded.

"Hardly, I've got this," she pointed at the gap in her teeth and then touched her nose, "to remember him by. I wear it to keep men away. I don't need anymore mementos from them."

"Men don't abuse women," I protested, feeling I ought to defend my sex, "only boys that failed to grow up."

"Well, one or the other ought to be labeled so I can tell them apart," she snapped bitterly. "Anyway, I'm going to make a pretty picture back in Keonah with what my adolescent husband left me."

"You'll probably get a few clucks from the old biddies about the evils of elopement, but most will be sympathetic I'm sure. But you don't have to be quite that truthful. Say you were hit by a drunk driver, that's not too far off the mark. And in fact, I highly recommend you erase those reminders as soon as possible and take a more positive outlook on life. Now that you've got money, get an implant and have a plastic surgeon straighten your nose. Remember, you're a business owner and have property."

"You're right," she replied, smiling suddenly. "Maybe I'll even order some dessert! But what am I getting into as a businesswoman? I only worked at Uncle's store for one summer, keeping his accounts. He didn't feel I should get dirty handling rusty bolts and poking in dusty bins. I'm pretty sure I can't run a hardware store, and I'm almost sure I don't want to. Were you in the hardware business, Mr. Borden?"

I felt it was only right that she should know something about her junior partner in Diehl's, so I gave her a quick biography, omitting of course any reference to Rosa Lynn, Mrs. Adamson, or the Elkton Lodge. That was my business, not hers.

"So you're an escapee too," she murmured thoughtfully. "You from the place that reminded you of a painful end to a happy marriage, and me from an unhappy one."

We had finished our drinks by then and the platters had arrived. I was pleased to note that her appetite wasn't constrained to soup and crackers. She cleaned up everything on her plate, including the parsley garnish and the somewhat tired looking zucchini. Skinnyness distresses me. It's a constant reminder of the precariousness of life, as well as the perverseness of its having created a need and pleasure in food, but requiring us to inflict pain and death to others in order to get it.

Over coffee we talked about the prospects for the store. I told her of my proposals to Elmer to expand his services, but acknowledged that now, if I were the only one there, it would be difficult to continue providing delivery and installation service, which seemed the only way we could compete against the chains in C.R.

"Can the business support still another person, Mr. Borden?"

I smiled at her, "Since we're partners let's start using our first names. Mine is Emmett, an odd one these days, which you may shorten to Em if you wish. And do you wish to be called Nancy or what?"

"Nan will do nicely, but I think I'll call you Emmett. But my question?"

"Frankly, Nan, it doesn't really support two people now. I have my investment income to fill out my salary at Diehl's. I only took the job at the salary Elmer could afford in order to have a reason to get up in the morning. I don't think you'd find an experienced man for that salary. But there are certainly some other options you can consider. But that'll wait until you're back in Keonah and better able to judge your future. Now, about dessert?"

We parted a little before 8:00. Nan assured me she would be ready at 7:30 next morning.

Chapter XXIX
Dinner With The Boss

She was ready on time, and after an hour's drive, I pulled off the interstate at an exit marked 'Food – Gas'. I ordered ham, hash browns, a fried egg and coffee. My rider ordered tea. She watched me cut a bite of ham, mix it with a little egg yolk, chew and swallow. The hash browns looked good and tasted even better. After another helping, she signaled the waitress and asked if she could have a poached egg on toast. "If I watch you eat anymore meals, Emmett, I'll need bigger clothes."

"I hope so," I responded between bites. "A shopkeeper that looks starved isn't going to attract customers. They'll figure business must be bad and the place is about to go under. But I'll have a lighter lunch, so you won't feel tempted. We should be in Keonah before dinner, so you won't have to watch me eat that meal either."

"Oh!" she said as if she suddenly realized something. "Where am I going to stay?"

"Why, I assumed," I told her, "in your uncle's house, your old home. I called Mrs. Carter, your uncle's housekeeper, last night and asked her to turn the heat up, stock the refrigerator, and get some frozen dinners you can heat in the microwave. That will hold you over the weekend. From then on you're on your own. But by the way, Mrs. Carter, you needn't feel obligated to keep her on, she was planning to move to Cedar Rapids and stay with her sister."

We reached Keonah around 4:30 that afternoon. I carried her bag into Elmer's house, now Nan Hoegh's, checked that Mrs. Carter had left everything in order, including clean sheets on the bed, fresh towels, and a note on what was in the freezer. Things I wouldn't have thought of. I told her I'd probably be at the store Sunday continuing to inventory the stock if she needed to see me, but otherwise, we'd meet at Mr. Trable's office at 9:30 Monday.

By the end of the following week Nan had decided she would stay in Keonah. "It's no worse than Glenly, and having a house is better than renting a room," she told me, and added "I probably know as little about the pharmacy as I do about hardware, so they are at my same level of ignorance. I will need to go back however and get the rest of my clothes and the car. I can't continue to impose on you in going to Cedar Rapids." I had loaned her my car to go to a dentist in C.R. for the implant. It would take several more visits and then she would need to see the plastic surgeon in Iowa City to erase the last of her shame.

I was opposed to her plans. I told her I didn't trust her jalopy to go 300 miles on the open highway, and that she could ask her landlady to pack her clothes and send them here. And as for the car, have a local garage buy it for whatever they'll give. "You can buy a good one here to replace it." But she was adamant and there was no point in further argument. I did ask her to have the local garage check it over before starting back. "A lone woman in a disabled car on a lonely highway can be a temptation to a creep, and there are a lot of creeps around. Try to stay alert and aware of what's going on around you," I warned her.

"I always do, Emmett." She pulled a small can of Mace from her pocket. "I know how to use this and I'm not afraid to use it. I have my former husband to thank for making me aware of creeps."

She took the bus early next morning and I was relieved to get a call that evening that she had arrived in Glenly. Two days later the jalopy pulled up in front of Diehl's just before closing time.

"I followed your advice, Emmett," she announced. The mechanic had it tuned up and replaced the fan belt. I had him put on four new tires after we took a good look at the old ones. There was no trouble on the road."

Now that she was committed to stay in Keonah, Nan began coming down to the hardware store everyday. "I've got to work" she told me, "at least until we figure out how to get the estate taxes settled." She ran the cash register, kept the books and handled some of the customer needs. Technical questions came to me along with key duplication and replacement work.

Storm-door business was starting up again. People were getting them out of summer storage and finding they had been careless about where they put them, so I had cracked glass to replace. After Elmer's death, I had made a deal with Farnsworth in C.R. for weekly delivery and pickup of tools and knives for the sharpening service I had asked Elmer to start. It wasn't a big item for us, but it enforced our service motto and we got peripheral sales from it. It helped Farnsworth too. He told me he started soliciting sharpening in C.R. itself. Mostly from meat markets, so it wasn't impacting our farm and household business. We had a butcher client too, who got too tired of doing his own honing.

After a few more weeks, Nan began pestering me to let her do more in the store. "I don't feel like I'm pulling my weight, Emmett. At least show me how to run the key duplicator and cut glass."

"O.K. on the duplicator, nix on the glass, at least for a while. If we get a glass-cutting table someday I'll reconsider, but many window pieces are too heavy for a skinny girl and if a pane slips you'd get a bad gash. I'll show you how to do plexiglass replacement though for those who want to go the more expensive route."

She didn't like my comment on her weight. "I may look skinny, but I'm not a softy," she barked. "After all, whose the majority owner here, you or me?"

"You are, but you're still skinny. We'll see how you do on the plexiglass and duplicator business before I risk liability for exposing a young lady to dangerous work." I eased my remarks by giving her a big smile.

So after another week we found it easy to work together. She started driving the truck around to deliver and pick up repair items. We decided to drum up more service business by running ads in the phonebook and suburban editions of the C.R. and Iowa City papers. We made joint decisions on stock replacement and decided to request extensions on the estate taxes and make partial payments from the business profits. Money was tight, but neither of us were extravagant, though I was glad to see she was gaining back some of her weight and self-esteem. The implant and nose straightening were successful and that helped I think, in giving her a more optimistic outlook. The only negative observation I had made was her avoidance of male entanglements. I know Mina and Phyllis had arranged for what they thought were eligible men for her to meet by giving evening parties, but apparently she declined to date. She was polite about it, but finally convinced them, as well as M and P to desist. I stayed out of that situation. First, it was none of my business, and second, I was sure Nan's past experience had left rather permanent scars.

As for my own affairs, it was confined to correspondence, with only the picture of Edie and me on the Josiah Snelling to keep me company. I did not hear from Mrs. Albena. The zoning board had approved some minor alterations to the Lodge: a separate parking-lot entrance to the 'Black Hand' room and the addition of a small raised stage in the dining room. That was the only news Edie had written me. I was trying to think of an excuse to see her again, but the subtle hints in my letters brought no reaction from her. Edie's insistence on meeting away from Elkton was a serious damper on nourishing our relation. While long weeks of famine followed by a few days of feasting certainly heightened the pleasures of the feast, it made the following period of famine more depressing.

I did have other things to occupy myself, however. Mercer had been pretty successful in getting orders for gazebos in the Davenport-Moline area. A few more wanted screens, so I decided Nan might just as well learn how to make those. She had a little laugh at my jig at first, but just like her uncle, she began appreciating its convenience after making a few screens. Her earlier dislike of the hardware store seemed to lessen with the realization that she was really working for herself now. Still, it seemed somehow unsuitable for her. Don't misunderstand, I'm not a male chauvinist about keeping women away from men's work. It wasn't concern about her wearing work jeans instead of dresses, or getting grease on her hands. She was not a Phyllis. She was not a Mrs. Adamson either. There was a faint look of vulnerability about her, something Mrs. Adamson never displayed, nor Phyllis Mercer probably ever experienced. She made me feel as though she needed the protection a family might provide but a hardware store couldn't.

But back to my other occupations. Mercer began sending requests to Voss for alterations on the gazebo design. My plans and jigs did allow for some size variation, not for a six-sided version, or one with a more peaked roof. At first I was reluctant to do anything about these requests, but Voss felt we'd be passing up a good opportunity to expand that business. I know he made much more out of each gazebo than I did. Actually, my share was in effect only a license fee of $200 for using my design and jigs. Still, with nothing else to do in the evenings, I decided to see what might be involved in meeting those requests.

The hexagonal gazebo really posed no problems. Just a matter of working out the cutting angles and making a new outline of PVC piping for setting the concrete blocks. The more peaked roof was a different matter. Not only did I have to redesign the roof rafters, making them of jointed planks instead of single lengths, but the hoist had to be taller and I was concerned about its stability under the considerably heavier load it had to lift. Voss and I finally resolved that issue by having Farnsworth cut a longer pipe to replace the middle piece and weld up a sort of cone shaped cage of angle iron pieces that could be slipped over that middle pipe to provide greater lateral stability. Frankly, I was hoping these added models would enable Mercer to sell a gazebo somewhere in the middle of Illinois so I'd have an excuse to see Edie, but it didn't happen.

About a week later I stopped at the lumberyard after work to give Voss my sketches and material lists for the hexagonal g. We talked for a while about whether it was necessary to build a prototype. Finally we decided that an 'architectural' sketch and floor plan would suffice for the present. If more was needed we could make a small-scaled 'doll house' model, having seen that miniature shingles and latticework were now commonly available in hobby shops in C.R.

After washing up and changing my work clothes at Mrs. F.'s, I sauntered down to the diner. Somewhat later than my usual hour. I was surprised to see Nan in one of the booths. Seeing me, she beckoned me to join her, which I did. "Not cooking at home tonight?" I asked.

"Apparently not," she answered to my rather inane question. "I decided to go to an old movie at the Art Department Theater in Iowa City, so I didn't want to get involved in cooking and cleaning up. It'll be a night off for me."

I told her I hadn't been to a movie in years. "Not sure I'd even know any of the stars today."

"This is an old, old movie, Emmett, 'My Favorite Wife'. Cary Grant and Irene Dunn are the stars. Surely you've heard of them?" Of course I had, I even dimly recalled the movie.

"A comedy I believe," I told her.

"A romantic comedy, Emmett!" she responded. "Just the thing to cheer one up on a chilly fall night. Why don't you join me? Get out of your room for a while. You probably need some relaxation."

She was right on that, I needed to get away from fussing with the gazebo changes and worrying about whether Edie's remoteness was real or imagined on my part. I accepted, ordered the blue plate special—beef stew with baking soda biscuits, and coffee. Nan was having a small salad plate. Not really adequate to call supper in my view.

I told her I didn't have my car with me, having walked down from Mrs. F.'s, but she said she had hers here and would drive. "Don't worry, Emmett, it runs fine" she quipped, seeing my skeptical look.

In fact she drove sensibly and the jalopy did in fact get us to the theater without incident. "It just needs new seat covers and a paint job. It's not the reclaimed wreck you imagine it to be, Mr. Borden."

I was surprised at the number of adults at the theater. I had expected mostly students, but then it dawned on me that they would be more likely seeking other outlets for weekend pleasure than an old movie. The adults were of mixed ages, probably mostly faculty. I looked around to see if Ridetti or Kitty Adair or Jonathon were there, the only faces I would be familiar with, but I didn't recognize anyone. Just as well, Ridetti might ask Nan how she liked the pin, and I didn't want to explain my long distance relationship to my boss.

Instead of heading straight back to Keonah, Nan drove to a little cafe' downtown. "I'd like some coffee, Emmett, O.K.?" It was O.K. with me, I could use something sweet. Maybe they had some real doughnuts here, not those cellophane wrapped abominations. I grimaced at the thought as an image of one flashed into my mind.

"Didn't you enjoy the movie?" my companion asked, mis-reading the cause of my sour expression.

"It had its funny moments, Nan, but the plot was a farce. Anyway Grant's treatment of his second wife—bigamous or not—was inexcusable."

"I guess you're just not a romantic, Mr. Borden," Nan sighed. "Haven't you ever felt romantic? Weren't you in love with your wife?"

"Of course I was in love with Fran. Have I ever stopped loving her?" I barked a little. I still seemed to resent questions about this that seemed to intrude on my private memories. "There is a difference you know," I was going to seal off any talk about Fran by expounding on a more general approach. "It seems to me a romantic is a fellow in love with love. No, that's not quite right, I think. He's in love with the idea of love." I began to warm to the subject, perhaps feeling the role of a wise older man to an impressionable youngster. "It sounds like a circular definition, a sort of love is love thing, but to me love is an emotional pleasure in the actual presence of someone. Of course it can be induced—that is, the pleasurable emotion, by remembering that someone's presence. So if you remove the sexual connotations, which are not an essential aspect, since many people have sexual relations without feeling any love for their partners, or even have such relations without partners, then those many types of love, man and woman, mother and child, friend and friend, are really all the same. Only the identity of the participants is varied."

"Goodness, Emmett, and all along I thought you were only interested in the nuts and bolts of the hardware business. And now I find you are a philosopher of life! And staying right here in Keonah so we can all have your wisdom everyday!" Nan was laughing. It was good to see her laugh, so I told her so.

The waitress didn't recommend the doughnuts as they were left over from the morning and were stale, but she had cinnamon buns which were good warmed. I ordered that. Nan kept to coffee only, so I warned her again about driving customers away by looking too poor.

"I'm surprised," she said after we were both silent for a while, "at how little this place has changed in 15 years. I used to come here often."

"Rather a long way from Keonah for coffee," I responded. I was surprised when she explained that she went to school here. When I asked her what she majored in she said she didn't graduate, she was only here until the middle of her sophomore year and hadn't decided on a field of study.

"And then you quit to get married?"

"Yes," she continued, in a sort of reminiscence, "I was staying with Uncle Elmer and drove down and back everyday—that same old car, Emmett. Jimmy Hoegh was on the football team. He was big and handsome. Not on the first team, he wasn't that good. I guess he thought he was, that was one of his problems. I was too naive to sense it then, but I found out later, unfortunately. He always seemed to feel he was better than he was given credit for. That it was always someone else that was holding him back or blocking the way ahead for him. I was swept away I guess by his self-assurance and good looks. My uncle didn't like him, told me he was vain and immature. He was right, but Uncle Elmer didn't have that many virtues of his own to convince me his criticisms of Jim were truth. Anyway, when Uncle told Jim to stop seeing me, I rebelled, and we eloped. Things were tough for us. Jim's parents were opposed to our marriage. They had other plans for him I guess, so we had to struggle on our own. Jim was working as an accounting clerk, but he wasn't very good at it. He made mistakes and always blamed it on somebody or something else. When he got fired, he blamed me for holding him back. Well you know what happened. I began to see much better after he blackened my eyes a few times. So here I am, 15 years later, back at the same cafe' with nothing I can show for all that time."

I said nothing. What could I say that wasn't preaching? It wasn't my story of married life.

Gradually, we began going out one evening or two a week. It started when Iowa and Iowa State were playing a football game in Iowa City. A practice established after I left State. I thought I'd like to see how they did and suggested to Nan she might be interested. She was. I got tickets and we drove down—my car. Of course we had to close the store for a Saturday afternoon, but we posted notice early in the week. It was a good game, but I got beaten. That is, State did, I couldn't tell if Nan's evident pleasure was in her school's win, or just being out of the store on a fine fall afternoon. We drove over to Homestead for an Amish country dinner.

"It'll be too much for me, Emmett," she protested, seeing the dishes at one of the tables all ready occupied.

"A fat wife and a big barn never hurt no man," I quipped. "Anyway you won't have to cook tomorrow, you can live on today's fat."

"You're not funny, Emmett," she groaned, but I noticed she ate adequately.

Sometimes she would suggest a place to eat. She seemed to like Chinese food. Sometimes we combined dinner with a show, a movie, or a theater at the University or at Coe College in C.R. One good result of all this was her purchase of better clothes. I shuddered the first time, shortly after I brought her back to Keonah, when she told me she was going to visit Phyllis. I was afraid of how my drably dressed boss would react on seeing sleek Phyllis. At least she had her hair restyled for that visit, and the implant in place.

Our relation was platonic on those evenings. I don't think either of us thought of them as dates. At least I didn't. But things took an abrupt change one afternoon near Thanksgiving. My friend Charlie had occasionally stopped by to talk to me about some of his school subjects. Even for the consolidated high school at Keonah, science and math had progressed from my days as a high school sophomore. I had helped him over a few humps in solid geometry and electric circuit theory. Not really deep stuff, but I could give him a second way to look at the problem, and with my experience I could quickly set up a bread board circuit to show him exactly how things worked. Anyway, that one afternoon Charlie wanted my advice about a science fair project. I suggested he might do a study of stability of the gazebo roof under wind and snow loads. We talked about it for nearly an hour at the back of the store, and drew up a schedule of experiments he might want to perform on material strengths.

"You like Charlie Voss, don't you, Emmett," Nan commented after he left. "Mina says he has grown remarkably after this past summer's work with you."

"Yes," I mused. "Charlie is a nice kid. I would have liked a son like him," I added, really without thinking, and turned to the back of the store.

"Why didn't you have a son?" I was surprised by Nan's question.

"Don't you know? My dear wife died of ovarian cancer. She had several miscarriages before it was discovered. She was operated on, a hysterectomy. For a while it seemed to have stopped the cancer, but it didn't. Some small bits seemed to have escaped and a few years later it was inoperable. That's why I have no son, no daughter either, and no dear wife, Mrs. Hoegh!" I stomped out the backdoor and into the shed. I was angry, and resentful again at why this open wound of emptiness kept bleeding at even the slightest touch.

Nan found me sitting on a bench, holding my head in my hands. She stood there looking at my misery for a while. "I could give you a son, Emmett."

I looked up at her in astonishment. "Give me a son? You don't even love me, why would you want to do that. Pity?"

"I could love you, Emmett, but you've never let love come between us. You've probably shut out others before. Please don't shut me out too. I don't pity you, Emmett, I need you."

"Need me, Nan? Nan, I'm more than ten years older than you. What can I possibly give that you need?"

She sat on the bench beside me. Not looking at me, she spoke softly. "I want what you gave your wife. I want that affection, companionship, and fidelity. I want that support and loving care for my son to be that I see you give Charlie. Oh I know it sounds soapy, but it's true."

"What support could I give you, much less our children, Nan? A clerk in a hardware store barely afloat in a dead end town? Do you think I'd be a good image to a son when he knew his father was being paid a wage by his mother?"

"I suppose not, but we could fix that—"

"You mean give me your inheritance," I broke in. "Not ever, Nan, never ever would I live in effect as a kept man!"

"I didn't mean it that way, Emmett, I'm sorry. But you were a successful engineer. Couldn't you go back to that work? Probably it wouldn't be here, but I'd go with you wherever it had to be."

So here I was facing that old dilemma again, how could I really begin life again when all I've been doing is having a momentary stay from being a drifter. It had been getting easier with each passing month of kidding myself that my life would be ended in Keonah: 'E. Borden, clerk in local hardware store, died' would be my obit in the papers. What a disservice to Fran's memory of me.

My silence must have been mis-interpreted by Nan. "But of course I may not appeal to you. I admit I haven't done much to make myself attractive—"

"Shut up," I interrupted, not too loudly. "You are attractive. I won't have you think my silence is based upon so trivial a reason as looks. Don't you see what I have been doing? I've been floundering around for years in this sea of misery since Fran's painful death. I finally landed here in this dried up old town where nothing from my past would follow me. I didn't go to work for Elmer, he was prodded by Mrs. Fashlich to hire me so all the old folks in this town could get their windows and screens fixed. I didn't offer to build Mina's damned gazebo, my dear Mrs. F. got Mina to pester me about doing it. I've just been drifting, pushed this way and that way by every current no matter how weak."

"You didn't always drift, Emmett," Nan interrupted. "You were a good engineer weren't you? Couldn't you start that again?"

I shook my head. "Please let me be, Nan, don't watch me when I'm this way."

Nan got up to go back in the store, but stopping by the shed door she said "Time is running out for me. I never thought about it before. I was glad I never got pregnant by Jimmy. I feel differently about it now. Don't dismiss our chance to start over, Emmett, without a thought."

CHAPTER XXX
RESUME'S

I finally did start to think about it, the future. The next Monday I drove into C.R. and bought copies of the Chicago and New York Sunday papers, scanning the employment ads for engineers. A few seemed to be of interest, but first I would need to prepare a resume' and try to find some sensible reason for my dropping out of the field for three years or so. Then it occurred to me to write a good friend at my old job at Electro Optics and see what prospects he might know of. Not that I wanted to go back to Mamaroneck, too close to the old pain I should have gotten over by now.

Drawing up a resume' was easy. I had accomplishments to list, patents, job titles, long term employment by only three companies to emphasize stability, and hopefully to de-emphasize my last three years in as positive light as I could: a needed recovery period from the emotional drain of Fran's prolonged illness and death. I hoped it wouldn't turn them off without giving me an interview. I was sure an interview would be favorable for me. I got a job shop printer in C.R. to make up a hundred copies. That was his minimum run, but I sure hoped I wouldn't have to mail all of them.

Trable's secretary agreed to type the transmittal letters for a small fee, during her lunch break, and to keep it confidential. I didn't want the whole town speculating on why I might want to leave. There were plenty of old biddies that could invent lurid reasons.

The replies were not heartening. "Too qualified for our position." "The position has been filled, but we will keep you in our file should something open later." And "We are still evaluating all our responses." Still, I kept track of the ads and sent off more resumes. But I did wonder why my old friend hadn't dropped me a note.

Nan and I resumed our weekly dinner and entertainment outings. Nothing further was mentioned about the conversation in the shed. We did a dinner theater evening in C.R., a blow-em-up sci-fi movie (it was a noisy bust, but we had a good laugh about its absurdities over coffee afterwards), and several just quiet dinners at good restaurants. That girl was growing on me.

Christmas was just a few days away. I had almost given up on receiving any return presents from my gift of so many resumes. Had I really destroyed my chance of a professional future by indulging my grief for so long? I hoped that was not so, but if it were true, I would have to drastically rethink my future prospects. It was not myself I was concerned about. I would survive doing something, somewhere, but could I really walk away leaving Nan adrift to manage the store herself, or stay, and remain un-entangled?

Better she should find someone as a partner for the store and for herself. Fortunately, I had not given her any hint of my intentions, at least I hoped not. Better too, if I cooled our relations a little, giving her more reason to welcome any possible suitors. I wasn't being noble, just concerned about the future of a girl I had begun to care about. If I could find no way to be a proper part of her future, at least I would not be an obstacle for someone who could.

So it was with some relief when Nan told me the Mercers had invited her to spend the holidays with them. I encouraged her to accept, saying I had made plans myself for Christmas—a lie—and assured her I could handle the store alone 'till she got back. I was confident Phyllis would see to it that some single man would also be invited.

Mrs. F. was to visit her daughter over the holiday. I had offered to drive her to their small farm nearby, but she said her son-in-law would do the ferry duty, so I was free to find my own way to wile away an evening and a day. I found myself abandoned even further when the diner posted a holiday closing notice. I thought of Nan's soup and crackers suppers. Had she spent many Christmases on that meager diet, bitter and withdrawn, nursing her wounded spirit, much as I had done after Fran's death? But it wasn't going to be canned soup for me! I'd drive down to Homestead and feast with the Amish. Some restaurant had to be open I was sure.

I had made other holiday preparations a few days before, ordering a bright bouquet of fall flowers to be sent to Edie, Christmas cards mailed to Charlie, Rosa Lynn, another to Lisa, and one addressed to Mr. Rags with a dried beef stick enclosed. I bore Rosa Lynn no hard feelings, though being dumped so abruptly seemed somewhat unchristian for one supposedly so sensitive to sin. I chose a sedate religious card for her. It had a picture of the Virgin Mary.

Nan and Mrs. F. both left on the 23rd. I puttered around the store until 7 that evening, straightening the shelves and counter goods, rearranging the holiday special displays, and clearing up the workbench in the back.

Business was brisk the next day, surprisingly. It was Nan's doing, she had stocked up on tree decorations and other holiday goo-gads, ignoring my cautions about seasonal items that have a once-a-year sales appeal, and that for a few days only. Apparently she had retained an accurate memory of Keonah Christmases past, and the old habits of decorating trees on Christmas Eve. My own experience in the East was quite different. Trees were trucked in for sale shortly after Thanksgiving and stores pushed decoration sales more than a month early. Of course the early haste was all due to commercialization of a religious holiday, but I didn't mind if Diehl's profited a bit by it.

I closed shop a little later than usual again, at 7, and drove down to Homestead. I hadn't thought to make a reservation. Christmas Eve would surely find most people at home. So I was surprised and at loose ends when the receptionist told me they were fully booked. Gazing wistfully over the tempting dishes being consumed by my more farsighted and fortunate compatriots, I was turning to leave when I heard my name called in a booming voice rising over the din of rattling plates and chatter. A hand was waving at me from a table by the far wall. This hand, I found, was attached to Ridetti, sitting with an attractive dark-haired woman, two sub-teenage girls, and an older woman feeding a small child in a high chair. The hand motioned me over and I complied.

"Ha, Borden, no room for you tonight? We have an extra chair if you're alone. Join us, I can't see a man going hungry tonight, even if he's only a cretin engineer." I accepted Ridetti's offer for the sake of my stomach, deciding to ignore his jibes.

I introduced myself to the group. The handsome woman first, as I suspected she was his wife, then the older woman and finally a general nod to the girls. The handsome woman made up for Ridetti's social omissions by giving him a frown and me their names. She was Alma, the older woman was Mrs. Estina, her mother, the girls were Adrien and Carlotta, and the child was Carlo Jr., her children.

I thanked Mrs. Ridetti for letting me join them, explaining that my usual eatery was closed for the holiday, and not expecting a crowd, I hadn't thought it necessary to make reservations. She glanced at my ring but was evidently too polite to enquire, so I volunteered that I was a widower. After that, conversation was on the conventional topics of the weather, the menu dishes, Adrien's play, and Carlotta's piano lessons. Mrs. Estina seemed fully occupied with Carlo Jr. and had little time to do more than smile and nod at the girls' description of their activities.

Dinner was good. What the food lacked in finesse was compensated by its abundance. This suited Ridetti, whose capacity for roast turkey seemed enormous. Finally, pushing his plate aside, he asked how the lady liked the pin.

"Very much," I told him. "My sister thought it was her best birthday present, but that I shouldn't have been so generous." That ought to stop any further interest on his part about my female associations.

"I hope you have more than one sister, Borden. I'm waiting for another commission from you. It will help pay for Carlotta's music lessons. You should be happy to support art, but look now, no more free welding of brackets. I had to get the priest to give my arc welder absolution for having been used for such an ugly job." He had another good laugh at this. Alma smiled and told him to behave.

"Don't worry," I assured her, "he won't be asked to do it again. I'm having a machine shop in Cedar Rapids make them for us."

"Make them? What are you doing Borden, selling them—for what?" It was Ridetti's turn to be surprised, so I told him about the first g and then about the Mercer-Voss deal to build and sell them.

"We've sold about a half-dozen already. I designed them and earn a royalty on each sale. Now that I think about it, there might be useful work some of your students could do for pin money. We don't make the weather vanes. The customer purchases them separately from a manufacturer's catalog, but there are only a few models available. Some customers might want personalized models. Not always a rooster or a horse. It would give your students something practical to do."

"Bah!" was his only comment, but I thought "Alma, his wife, showed some interest.

"Are these silhouettes, Mr. Borden," she asked? Ridetti snorted.

"They could be," I replied, ignoring her husband's disdain. "But for the better quality ones, especially animal figures, they are 3-dimensional. Usually formed with thin copper sheet. In two halves, hammered or pressed into shape by a mold of some sort, then soldered together, I imagine."

"Alma," Ridetti chided, "you don't want to do that. Chickens and donkeys! What kind of work is that for a sculptor of your class?"

But Mrs. Ridetti persisted, ignoring him, while I sketched the mechanics of how I mounted the car for Mercer and the direction letters. By this time Ridetti joined in. After pooh-poohing my scheme—which I didn't take offense at since I knew a 3-dimensional figure permitted a more satisfactory way to balance the vane yet allowing it to swing easily in even a light breeze—he offered a better method.

Mrs. Ridetti seemed disappointed when I mentioned the catalog prices, but I suggested that any original designs could be priced much higher.

By the time we finished with coffee and dessert, Alma had decided to try making a vane to see how much work was involved. Ridetti again tried to dissuade her, but she countered that she'd like to see if she could adapt a small sculpture of hers, '3 Birds In Flight', for a vane. "After all, Carlo, just think of it as another kind of mobile." Ridetti patted her arm and sighed.

I gave Alma my phone number in case she needed to get further information on mounting methods. The girls even seemed interested in their mother's project. Adrien suggested her mother do a ballerina, while Carlotta excitedly countered with big musical notes, and then in a burst of ingenuity, proposed some kind of Chinese wind chime be attached. Ridetti couldn't help but laugh at this idea, but I told Carlotta it would certainly be unique, since I'd never seen, or heard of a musical weather vane before. I wasn't sure how it might be fashioned so as to meet the basic requirement that it point the vane into the wind. Alma seemed pleased with the girl's interest in the project, and even Ridetti was amused, suggesting I buy the girls ice cream cones for their suggestions.

For Christmas day, I drove to a hotel in C.R. for dinner and then took in a movie. A McDonald's sufficed for breakfast and lunch. Another Christmas spent alone. I thought of the Ridetti's opening presents and enjoying a festive dinner at home. I didn't want to go back to my lonely room, but there was no other place to go, no one to see, and nothing to do.

On the 27th, while I was busy storing some of the seasonal items that hadn't been snapped up in our post-Christmas mark-down sale, my partner walked in.

"It doesn't look like we did too badly," she remarked, peering into the storage boxes I was packing. "But don't you think we should wait a bit? Some more sales might be made before New Year's Eve. I'll be back on the 3rd to help store anything left. Phyllis has asked me to stay for a New Year's Eve party George is giving for his employees. You won't mind, I hope, if I take another day off?"

I nodded and told her a party would be good for her, and then asked why she had driven back to Keonah. "Phyllis thought I should wear evening dress. We're supposed to go to an elegant restaurant. It floats on the river," she added. "It should be fun, but my fancy evening dress needs a little alteration and Phyllis has a dressmaker who'll do it for me in time. I came to get it. I haven't worn it for years and it probably needs a few tucks here and there."

She'll find out about my seeing Rosa Lynn I thought. It made me feel uneasy, though there was no rational reason I should. Mrs. Albena could not possibly complain about my behavior. Surely religious beliefs would not be of concern to Nan. After a few more words, mostly in answer to my questions on what Phyllis served for Christmas dinner, she waved goodbye and drove off.

I continued puttering around the shop for the rest of the day, keeping myself busy with make-work. There were almost no customers.

Mrs. F. was back and the diner was open for business, so my routine was nearly back to normal. Late the next afternoon, Mrs. Ridetti surprised me by stopping by the store. She brought her first vane, a beautiful piece of work I thought. The figure was her '3 Birds In Flight', not in silhouette, but with rounded bodies and outspread wings. There was a simple rhythm in the way the wings were placed. The leading bird was banked, one wing up the opposite down as though starting a turn. At its tail, the middle bird's wings were in the down stroke position, while the last bird, slightly below the other two, had its wings in the up stroke. They seemed separate figures, but so clever an artist, they were actually connected: tail to bill on the leading two, and left wing tips on the middle and last bird. Alma had positioned them so that there were several points of attachment to the pointer rod. I was impressed with her skill. The whole piece was quite rigid so there must have been internal bracing where the birds touched. She had a small booklet, bound sheets of sketches actually, for other vane motifs, even one on Carlotta's musical notes and wind chime.

I closed the shop and we drove down to the lumberyard. I introduced Alma to Voss. He told us Boggs was working on another g if we wished to check on how the vane mounting could be done. Alma drew some quick sketches and made measurements of the central roof bracket. Back at the office Sam and Alma discussed pricing and timing. She was relieved to find she'd have about a month from an order for one of the vanes in her sketches before it would be needed.

Mrs. Ridetti was too polite to ignore me completely, but she clearly was concentrating on impressing Sam, and quite successfully. Sam approved of everything she wanted, even her price of $500 for the completed vane. She, in turn, agreed to let him take the bird vane to Mercer, after she added the metal mounting pieces. It was clear to both of them that an actual model would be needed to justify that price. Actually, as I surmised, Sam and George would add a mark-up for their share. I, of course, got nothing since my royalty was already fixed.

Two days later, around 9:30, Sam called that Mrs. Ridetti had brought the finished vane, but that she wanted to take it to Mercer herself. I told him that was O.K. so what was the problem. The problem, he explained, was that one of us should introduce her to George but he couldn't get away at the moment. So, with business at a drag, I offered to go with her. It would be interesting to see how she reacted to the overbearing George, and how George would react to her, him being even shorter of artistic spirit than me.

Alma drove, the vane carefully wrapped and stowed in the back of an ancient but still serviceable station wagon. Our conversation was casual, mostly about her impressions of Iowa—Carlo had joined the faculty just two years before. Previously they were at Fordham, in New York City, but she was not happy raising the children in a cramped Manhattan apartment. She liked the more open spaces here and having her own studio in their rented house.

With my clear directions we arrived at Mercer's in good time. George was in his office, enjoying an early lunch. It must certainly had been prepared by Phyllis. Ham sandwiches on apparently home-made bread, a salad of chopped celery and radishes in a creamy dressing, a thermos of coffee and another one of her blueberry tarts. I gazed wistfully at its flaky crust and breathed the sweet aroma of its burnt sugar topping. I suggested to Alma we examine the completed g in the corner of the lot while Mercer finished his lunch. It would be too painful to sit and watch him eat that tart.

Alma was amused at my motorcar vane and also thought it was appropriate for the location, but vetoed my suggestion that we replace it with hers. "At my prices, Mr. Borden, the customer should be able to appreciate the workmanship up close." I had to agree. Alma asked if I would bring her vane from the car when we returned to the office.

I introduced her to Mercer, who nodded saying that Voss had called that we were coming. Mrs. Ridetti wasted no time in captivating Mercer. At first I couldn't understand why she was wasting her smiles and compliments on the big boob. I watched her explaining the several vanes she had sketched in a warm and intimate tone when I suddenly realized what Alma had understood at the very beginning. Both Voss and Mercer, but especially Mercer, had to be well motivated if they were going to urge customers to buy her vanes at more than double the price of the standard ones we had been offering. In only half an hour George was completely won over. He even suggested the sample vane be set up on a stand in his office to better illustrate the quality of her designs.

My stomach began sending me alarms about the folly of delaying lunch any longer, but without my own car I couldn't get away to eat. I had to wait for Alma to finish her conquest, and even then, after a few more effusive promises from Mercer that he'd make his best efforts to sell her designs, she thought she'd just look around the Mercer lot and see if there was a good deal on a newer station wagon.

While we were inspecting a late model van, a salesman joined us. I recognized him as the good-looking one Phyllis had flirted with some months earlier.

"Are you interested in a van, Mr. Borden?" I shook my head, surprised that he knew who I was, until he added that he handled the gazebo sales as well.

"Mrs. Ridetti," I gestured toward her, "was just looking. She is the designer of some new weather vanes Mercer's going to offer."

I started to ask his name so I could make a proper introduction, but he beat me to it by introducing himself. Alma was not a snob, she lavished her charm on the help as well as the boss. I moved a short distance away to get a better view of the little dance they were doing. Alma's was purely mercenary I was sure, having seen her do the same steps with Sam and Mercer. Steve Brooks'—that was his name—interest was otherwise. It was more than evident by the way he moved about to scan her figure. Mrs. Ridetti seemed perfectly aware of his actions but appeared more amused than offended. I suspected she felt satisfied that Brooks would be eager to promote her artwork for the possible opportunity of seeing her again.

Knowing Ridetti's temper, I was glad that Alma saw no need to work on me, since I was out of the marketing loop for her. She would be making her contacts directly with Voss and Mercer now.

"Will you introduce me, Emmett?" The request startled me. Turning, I found Phyllis a few steps away, just coming around the front of a car stopped in the driveway separating the rows of used cars. She completely ignored Brooks, except for a hard look in passing. I introduced Alma as Mrs. Ridetti, an artist who would be supplying high quality vanes for the gazebo business. After a few perfunctory remarks, she handed Brooks some keys and asked him to drive her car into the shop. "It has developed a bad tendency to drift." She continued coldly, "and it's becoming quite tiresome to be constantly alert to keep it on the road. I may need a new one. I'd better speak to George about a replacement."

Phyllis' message wasn't lost on me, nor on Alma, whose mouth was turned up at the corners in an amused smile. Brooks wasn't amused. "No doubt the linkages have become worn from too heavy a hand at the wheel, Mrs. Mercer," was his parting response.

There was an awkward silence for a good minute, finally broken when Alma said there was something she needed to measure on the gazebo, and started off in that direction. "I'll meet you at my car, Emmett. Don't be long."

"I suppose I annoyed your girlfriend, Emmett, but I don't think she was very interested in buying a car and was just wasting our salesman's time."

"She's not my girlfriend, Phyllis. Sam asked me to introduce her to George so they could agree on arrangements for selling her weather vanes. She's a very talented sculptress. Who you really annoyed was your friend Brooks. He may not forgive you for putting him down in front of another woman like that."

"He doesn't matter," she sniffed. "He's beginning to bore me anyway. Perhaps I can get George to drop him."

"Look," I cautioned her, "I don't know how far you've gone with your little games, but if Brooks was one of the players he might get even by telling George tales you wouldn't want him to hear, whether they're true or not." I left her to think that over and joined Mrs. Ridetti at her car.

"Was she very upset?" Alma asked when I rejoined her. "I felt so cold." She gave a mock shiver, "I'm not used to being undressed outdoors in the winter. She needn't have been jealous. Her handsome little puppy wouldn't interest me at all. He was much too obvious—and without taste. Doing it in a used car lot!"

"Of course," was my only comment as we drove off. I quickly turned the conversation toward finding a place for lunch. I couldn't help but wonder what she found so tastefully subtle about Ridetti. Alma asked for separate checks, so I was saved from the risk of seeming obvious by paying for both of us.

Chapter XXXI
A Boyfriend For Nan?

Life at the store was now back to normal. Nan had returned and we were boxing and storing the remaining seasonal items. I hadn't sold many after she stopped my earlier attempt to put them away. She didn't seem to mind much though. In fact, her mood seemed a bit more cheerful. I thought at first it must be due to the nearly two weeks of eating at Phyllis' table, but that turned out not entirely so. The more significant reason turned up a few days later in the person of Mr. Steve Brooks.

Assuming he wanted to discuss some modification or complaint from a gazebo customer, I started to wave him to the back of the store where I was working on a storm window repair. Instead, he turned toward the register to talk to Nan. I made no attempt to overhear their conversation, but I could tell from Nan's expression that she seemed pleased to see him. Was this a definite change from her previous reluctance to meet men?

I was still struggling with the window, trying to free bits of broken glass from the frame. some idiot had tried to repair the cracked glass with epoxy. After a few minutes, Nan called that she was taking an early lunch. I looked up to see them leaving together. So, Phyllis had palmed her handsome puppy onto my boss. Brooks was not the kind of man I would have ordered for Nan from a catalog, but he was good looking, big and virile, and about her age. He probably had some mechanical sense and could help her with the store. But was he still working for Mercer, or had Phyllis followed through on her threat to have George boot him out? I should have been paying more attention to my work instead of pointless musing about Nan's social life, since it resulted in cutting my finger on a glass shard. Disgusted with myself for being so careless, I plugged in a heat gun to soften the epoxy, which I should have done at the beginning, and resolved to add a little to the bill.

It was nearly 2 o'clock before Nan returned, apologizing for delaying my own lunch. Brooks was not with her. Mumbling something about dropping off the window repair on my way back from the diner, I left.

Brooks appeared again a few days later. Guessing this time he was not here to see me, I told him Mrs. Hoegh would be back shortly. She was depositing some checks at the bank. While he was sauntering around the shop, straightening up a few displays here and there as though he owned the place, Mrs. Ridetti entered.

Alma nodded and smiled at both of us though she must have been surprised at seeing Brooks here. "I just stopped by, Emmett, to show you Carlotta's musical weathervane. I'm quite pleased with the way it turned out. Also, Carlo suggested a better way to arrange the compass points, which he wanted you to see. It's in two boxes in my car, if you'd bring them in."

Brooks eagerly offered to help, so we each took a box from the car, though they weren't heavy. This vane was done in black silhouette. Four notes and a treble clef on staff lines. The compass points were in the second box, which Alma opened, and slipped onto the vertical rod on which the staff and notes pivoted. A simple thumb screw tightened the compass points to the rod. Neat. Completely adjustable, and much, much better than my original scheme, but Carlo had a welder to fabricate it.

She asked Brooks to hold the vane upright on the counter while she mounted the final piece: a small metal wind chime at the end of the vane. The vane swung easily at her touch, emitting a pleasant tinkling sound.

"Very clever, Alma," I congratulated. "You've pointed your art in a new direction indeed." She laughed at my rather corny play on words, but was clearly pleased with my reaction. Brooks jumped to help her repack the vane, not missing the chance, I noticed, to brush against her while retying the strings holding the box flaps closed.

I could see what Brooks couldn't, that she resented his gratuitous fondling. "I'll let you do it, Mr. Brooks, I just seem to be getting in your way," she announced, moving quickly aside. Absorbed in the little interplay with the strings, I hadn't heard Nan enter.

"Are you buying something, Steve?" Nan pointed to the boxes as he turned to face her. I answered for the startled and embarrassed Brooks, introducing Mrs. Ridetti, and explaining about the weather vanes she was making for the gazebos.

"Mrs. Ridetti was going to deliver her second model to Mercer's but stopped by to show me her husband's improved attachment for the compass points." Thinking it best to save Nan's prospect further embarrassment, I added "By the way, Brooks, you might save Mrs. Ridetti a trip to Davenport if you'd deliver the vane to Mercer yourself. You are going back aren't you?" Seeing the opening I made for her, Alma said it would be a great convenience for her if he could.

Brooks mumbled something which we took to be agreement. Alma thanked him and left. I walked her to her car, giving Nan and Brooks a few minutes to arrange whatever he came to Keonah to do. He was gone when I returned. Whatever they discussed, it left Nan in a pensive mood for the rest of the day.

My Sunday dinner of Cajun barbecue at the diner didn't seem to be quietly submissive to my digestive juices. By 9 o'clock it was in open rebellion, and I decided to take a walk to Macklinburg's drugstore for some antacid. Herb fixed me up with a concoction at the soda fountain that called a temporary truce to the war and gave me some tablets in case the battle resumed. We chatted for a few minutes while he prepared to close for the evening, turning off the neon sign and main store lights.

I started my walk back to Mrs. F.'s when I thought I saw a light reflecting off the sidewalk in front of our store. I probably hadn't noticed it before because of the brighter lights on the drugstore. Now there was no mistaking that a light was on in the shop. Burglars? Maybe, but we never left money in the register after closing, and the locks were good ones. We probably had left a bulb turned on. Still, I thought, I'd better take a look.

The light was coming from the work area in the back, silhouetting Nan and Brooks in an embrace. At first it appeared to be an embrace, but then it was evident that Nan was trying to push Brooks away. I used my own key to unlock the door, startling them.

"For god's sake, do you want the whole town to see you make love?," I scolded. "Anyone walking by can see what you're doing through that bay window."

"Don't worry about it, Borden, I'm leaving." Brooks turned to get his coat from the worktable. I could see a ledger book open next to their coats. "This store's too small to hold my interest for very long, and neither would its other assets." I could have smashed his face for that crack if he wasn't already on his way out, and if he wasn't so damn big.

I had seen that Nan's blouse was open, her slip and bra straps torn, and a breast exposed. Pretending not to notice, I turned to get her coat from the bench. "You should have made him wait 'till you got home. This isn't the place for that," I said quietly, handing her the coat, my head averted to watch Brooks hurriedly drive off.

"Is your car here?," I asked. "I can't drive you. I walked down to the drugstore for some antacid and saw the light was on."

"No, I'll walk home."

"Then I'll be off. Goodnight." I turned away to leave, but stopped when she spoke.

"You don't even care about Brooks, do you?" She sounded furious.

"I care if you're mistreated, Nan. I don't think much of him, but it's none of my business whom you date."

I felt a stinging slap. "That's for 'none of my business'. And that's for the insult of not showing interest in what you could see," slapping me on the other cheek. "God, isn't there someone between a gorilla and a eunuch for me?"

"I didn't deserve that, Mrs. Hoegh," I replied coldly. "Goodnight again." I could hear her soft sobbing as I walked out. I was going to need another of Herb's tablets.

Our relation was definitely cooler for nearly a week after that, even though Nan apologized the next morning. I told her to forget it, that I thought she was just letting off steam when the real target for her anger had scooted off.

One day, near the end of a snowy January, Mrs. Fashlich handed me a bonanza: two letters. One was in response to my resume' sent in some weeks before, which had elicited a 'we'll call' response. It was from an electronics firm in the Boston area, outlining a test engineering position now available. They asked me to call if I was interested in an interview. The other was from my friend Raymond Lorenz, apologizing for the delay in responding to my letter. The fault was not all his. He had changed companies twice and my letter had taken a long time catching up to him.

What he wrote was quite unexpected. Ray had helped form a small company, along with several other engineers from my former employer, and were doing well in design and manufacture of specialized surveillance systems. Mostly, their business was for military base security, but they had permission to market certain modified systems to key Defense Department suppliers and financial institutions. They were located in Amherst. Ray thought I might fit well in their organization as a manufacturing engineer. I knew what that was, designing specialized jigs for aligning optical elements, automating test procedures, and, probably, consulting with the design engineers on feasible manufacturing processes. I was excited. Was this the beginning of a break for me?

I had a dinner date with Nan for that evening. Nan had suggested it, saying we hadn't renewed our weekly dinner together since before the holidays. I muttered something about not wishing to tread on Mr. Brooks' heels, to which Nan miffed "Oh you can forget about him. Phyllis had finally talked me into trying on a new suit. The cut was right, but the material was cheap. I decided it wouldn't wear well. I wanted something a little sturdier and more reliable. Steve's too much like Jim that way. Good looks, but not much else. I'm long past that stage of not looking below the surface."

I said dinner, but it was really for a movie in C.R., so we would have to eat quickly. I suggested we try a little place next to the theater. Service would be fast and dinner would be cheap. Conditions that I hoped would make further conversation about the scene at the store unlikely.

The movie, 'Enchanted April', was a delight, even for me. I had trouble seeing the attraction the wives were supposed to have for their husbands, even after their metamorphoses, but the story's premise of love reborn, struck some deep chord in me. I had been accustomed to walking Nan to her door when the sidewalks became icy. Impulsively I kissed her. She clung for a moment after her initial surprise. "Goodnight, Mrs. Hoegh," I said.

"Goodnight, Mr. Borden," she replied, and then we both laughed.

I shouldn't have done that. It ran exactly counter to my earlier resolve to cool our relations in hope she would be receptive to other dates. I can only blame it on the movie and the interview offers. And, to be honest with myself, with the illogical, but satisfying relief that Brooks was no longer in her picture.

Chapter XXXII

INTERVIEWS

Next morning I called both places and arranged for an interview on the following Monday and Tuesday. I would need three days to drive to the Boston area without getting too road weary. I told Nan I would need to take a week off, starting Friday. She said O.K., repair business was slow, but I could see a question in her eyes. "It's a problem with my real estate agent in Mamaroneck. I got a letter from him yesterday, and after talking to him on the phone this morning, I decided it was necessary to drive up and settle matters personally." A white lie. No need to say anything about a job interview if nothing comes of it.

Elkton would not be a stop on the way up. Best to wait until I knew what I was going to do. I tried not to think about Nan, the hardware store, and my short life in Keonah. Also, I tried not to think about Edie as I passed the Elkton turnoff, nor Chicago, nor Minneapolis. I tried to think instead about the adjustments I would need to make to get back into the working world as an engineer, and would my absence put a severe handicap on my former expertise. I could give myself no final judgment on those issues.

The interviews went well I thought. Certainly I left feeling capable of handling either job. There was little difference in the location of the plants. Ray's was just east of Amherst proper, and the plant for Shelton Electronics, the name of the other company, was actually west of Boston, near Worcester, though the corporate headquarters I reported to for the interview was in Boston itself.

I did Shelton Electronics first, a moderately sized subsidiary of a larger corporation, hence the different locations for the plant and the corporate headquarters. They were making control panels for electric and nuclear power plants. Almost all of their business involved customizing a few of their standard designs. The work did not seem inspiring, but it would pay well and probably had built-in longevity.

Ray's company was also customizing some of their already designed modules, but each installation required some special accessory sensors unique to each job. Further new designs and procedures were needed constantly to do battle with ever more sophisticated intruders. A sort of Darwinian struggle in hardware.

Ray suggested we have lunch together after the several interview sessions were over. We went to a quiet corner at the old Lord Jeffry Amherst Inn. We reminisced over drinks about old times. I had known him and his wife for many years.

"You seem in very good health, Emmett," he said, getting around I thought to the problem on his mind.

"Put your mind at ease, Ray," I told him. "My health, physical and mental, is sound. You know how close Fran and I were and how heartbreaking it was for me to see her wasting away day by day and being unable to do anything to help. I just needed to get away from surroundings that reminded me of that, and let my memories of her be only of our happier days. I just got in my car one day and drove without stopping until, for no real reason, I reached that nowhere town of Keonah. I'd probably still be waiting for a cure to my pain if it hadn't been for the crotchety old widow woman who rented me a room." I asked if he wanted to hear all the details, then I'd tell him, guaranteeing to condense it to not more than 30 minutes while we ate.

He said he wanted to hear how a once competent engineer cured his ailment in the middle of the corn belt. I corrected his idea of Keonah being isolated in a corn field by mentioning how close it was to C.R., Iowa City, and the Davenport-Moline complex. We ordered, and I recounted the past many months with Elmer Diehl, The Snyder machine sale, and the gazebos for Voss and Mercer. I said nothing about Rosa Lynn, Edie, or the Elkton Lodge. Nor did I mention Nan. Ray seemed amused about my repairing screens and storm windows, hawking machine tools, and especially about gazebos, until I told him the size of Mina's and the design problem I had to solve making portable ones that two men could set up in one day for Mercer. He was impressed, I thought, as he should be. It was not a cut-and-paste kind of job.

But over coffee he asked the inevitable question of why I wanted to return to engineering. "You seem to have found work, or at least had it impressed upon you, and could have expanded it into a bigger job."

"I have another chance, I think, to have a family, Ray. I want them to know me as a professional engineer, not as a jack-of-all-trades. And I need to be a good provider. I got by O.K. when there was only my own needs to provide for, but you know a family has bigger demands to meet."

He asked if I was married again, but I told him I would not propose until I knew about my future. He seemed satisfied that I was mentally fit, and promised to wire me within a few days, one way or the other. I let him sign the check without the usual fuss and we parted back at his office.

I decided that I would accept an offer, if Ray made one, and the salary was adequate. It would be comfortable to work with old friends again, and while Amherst was much smaller than Iowa City or C.R. it was much bigger than Keonah, and closer to lobster dinners and quahog chowder feasts on shore vacations. I stopped at a real estate office and got some pictures and descriptions of newer homes in the area—just in case.

Although it was nearly 3:00 in the afternoon, I thought it best to start back at once. God knows what snows could pop up without much warning in that area in late January.

The interviews went well, but even so, I'd better start reviewing some of the current IEEE journals to bring myself up-to-date on the scientific front if I was going back into technical work. Waiting for a response from either Shelton or Ray would be itchy. I never could remain calm waiting for an important event. Random thoughts about electrical principles, mechanisms, and mathematical formulas flitted in and out of my mind, easing the boredom of the drive. But soon I began thinking again about how soon I could expect to hear. Ray said a few days, but it might be longer. Was there anyway I could speed things up? But of course there was! I had to laugh at the thought, an answer to my question came from among the mathematical formulas I was reviewing. By traveling west, I caused the rotation of the earth to speed up, shortening the days. How much? I couldn't do the calculation in my head, but maybe a tiny fraction of a microsecond. But would I lose the gain when I stopped? Ah! Not if I turned off the highway to the north or south before stopping. Come on, Borden, you know that's wrong. It violates Newton's laws on conservation of momentum. Had progress since then given me another way to receive Lorenz' decision sooner? No solution seemed possible, Still, I was pleased with myself for returning to scientific thinking, I stepped on the gas to eke another fraction of a nanosecond from this day at least.

Chapter XXXIII

CLARISSA

There were a few flurries on the way back, but mostly along the Erie lake front, going past Cleveland. I remembered that was where Edie said she had lived and tried to imagine what she was like as a young girl. Superficially much like Nan, to get married before finishing college, and both to macho men. But Edie was of sterner stuff I thought, with plenty of self-confidence and independence. It wouldn't be like her to waste so many years in a dead end job in Glenly. Still, she had Rodde, an old goat, but one she liked for all his quirks, and who evidently liked her, to give her a hand. Nan could have gone back to live with Elmer, finish school perhaps, and start over with a better preparation for a career or a better mate. But Nan withdrew from help rather than admit a bad mistake in judgment. A flaw in her character, or a sensitive girl abused in different ways by an uncle and a husband, I wondered?

By late afternoon the next day after leaving Amherst I neared the Interstate exit to Elkton, and precipitously, almost at the last second, turned onto it. I was not invited to visit, but surely Edie could not object to my staying at the Lodge as a paying guest, expecting nothing except to see her again and perhaps to chat for a bit about the change I was contemplating.

I could see the new electronics plant now, a few miles north of Elkton, and close by a new motel. I decided this would be much better for Edie, for me to stay someplace other than the Lodge. I could call her from there and she would be free to decide if we should meet.

There were rooms available and a small coffee shop was off the lobby. While I was checking in, a man came out of a small room behind one end of the motel desk and walked to the coffee shop. It was fortunate that I recognized him at once and bent over the sign-in book to hide my face. Robert Carlton; Edie's Robby here! Was he seeing Edie, renewing their affair? Was that why she hadn't responded to my hints about meeting again?

I checked into my room, and getting my address book out of my suitcase, I found Edie's private number and dialed. I let the phone ring for a while before hanging up. Evidently she was not in her apartment, not surprising really. I'd try again later, but there was no reason why I shouldn't treat my stomach right by having dinner at the Lodge rather than a sandwich at the coffee shop here, so I dialed the number of the Lodge and asked for the dining room.

The voice answering my call said the dining room was not open yet, but if I wished to make a reservation she could take it. I made it for 6:30, for one, and gave my name and phone number at the motel when she asked for it.

Extended travel by car, that is, something lasting more than a couple of days, is a constant suitcase business of unpacking and repacking. It seems so futile, a job that is always done an even number of times, each cycle bringing you back to the start of the next one. I was in the middle of the unpack cycle when the phone rang.

"Is that you, Emmett?" the familiar voice asked.

"Yes, Edie, it's really me, but how did you know I was here? I called your apartment but there was no answer. Are you telepathic too?"

"Clarissa took your dinner reservation—which by the way I'm canceling—and let me know you were at the motel."

"Are you telling me to stay away from the Lodge, Edie," I asked uncertainly, not sure of what she meant by 'canceling'.

"Certainly not," she laughed. "I mean you'll have dinner in my place. You are alone aren't you?" I told her I was, and she said to see Clarissa at the desk, at 6:30, and she would bring me up in the elevator. I remembered now that a key was necessary to activate a 5th floor stop to her apartment.

At 6:30, promptly for me, I was at the desk at the Lodge. Clarissa was busy registering a couple, but nodded, telling me she would be with me in a moment. I was surprised she recognized me after those many months ago when I appeared for the first and only time. We exchanged a few pleasantries on the way up to Edie's suite, and she waited a moment 'till Edie opened the apartment door. 'At seven, Clarissa," she said. "Will that be all right?" Clarissa nodded and re-entered the elevator.

Edie led me into the main room of the apartment, the parlor, and presented her cheek for a kiss. The room did not look much different from my memory of it. I think the drapes were changed but not much else that I could see. Edie suggested we have our cocktails in the card room. "No need to open the cabinets again is there? You've seen all I have to show."

"But can one ever have too much of a sensational sight, Mrs. Adamson?" We both laughed at the double meaning. Edie busied herself with the bottles and glasses in the liquor cabinet.

"Scotch on the rocks for you, Emmett?" I nodded.

We clicked glasses and I toasted her with "To a wonderful lady."

She responded "And to my gentle friend."

"Clarissa has moved up from the dining room to the front desk," I noted between sips.

"Yes, she is being trained in all aspects of running the Lodge and doing quite well, I'm glad to say. She'll be in full charge by next summer. She'll be 25 then." Seeing my puzzled look, she added, "Rodde willed the Lodge to Clarissa. I was to be trustee until she reached 25, provided she remained single until then."

"But"—Edie interrupted me.

"Clarissa is my aunt, Emmett. Well actually my half-aunt."

I must have been staring at her with my mouth open. "Your half-aunt? Then Clarissa is Rodde's daughter?"

"Surprising isn't it, Emmett?" She then told me the whole story. "Rodde had an affair during one of his treasure hunts. This time in France where he got some of the saloon art pictures". She waved at them. "Later he found out the consequences were more permanent than he had expected. But though he wouldn't marry again, he did acknowledge the child and provided support for them. When the mother died her relatives had the child raised at a French convent school until she was 14. I suggested he bring her to the U.S. but Rodde felt the Lodge and his long established bachelor behavior would not be suitable for the girl. We compromised by sending her to a finishing school and then Bryn Mawr. She graduated two years ago and I asked her to join me at the Lodge, since she would eventually inherit it."

I remarked that I hadn't detected an accent. Edie nodded. "Clarissa speaks French, English—both types, and German perfectly. She has a very good ear; an accomplished young lady."

Edie's life was more complex than I had even imagined. The revelation about Clarissa further confused the half thought out plans I had made. If Edie was about to be freed from the Lodge, the obstacles that I had thought kept us apart disappeared. My head was hot with swirling confusion from this unexpected news, and out of the mental stew my mouth blurted "But then you could join me!"

"Join you? In Keonah! What do you mean 'join you'?"

"Not in Keonah, Edie. I mean, hopefully, near Boston. I've been interviewing there and expect an offer. I'm going to return to engineering."

"And you want me to live with you there? Is that what you meant by joining you?"

"Of course live with me. Isn't that what husbands and wives do?" It was now Edie's turn to be stunned. Did I botch it? Should I have led up to the proposal in a more romantic way? Edie clasped my hand between hers.

"My dear sweet friend. If I could still bear children, I would marry you even though you need a different kind of mate than I would be."

"What different kind of mate? We went together wonderfully well those times you could get away from here. I thought about this many times, but I couldn't see a solution for us. I couldn't come to Elkton, what work could I possibly do here that would not be an embarrassment for you. Nor could I ask you to give up the Lodge and the influence and position in town that it gave you and that I know you relished. But now that isn't a problem. As for children, couldn't we adopt? Didn't you suggest that to me in Minneapolis?"

"Yes, we could, but I meant that as a last resort for you. Better for you my friend, if the child is your own. Anyway, could I be a mother again for another 15 or 20 years? I don't think I could do that. But you miss the point, Emmett. We go together very well, just as you said, but could we do so day after day?—No, don't say anything, let me finish. I've thought about this too. I'm not dependent enough for you, Emmett. You want to be needed by your wife, not just for love. I would need that too, but not for every day kind of things. You are a born protector and giver, and I, perhaps because of events, have lost the need, even the desire, for a protector. I have learned self-reliance and how to be independent and I like me like that. I know it was a novelty for you to be with such a woman. You enjoyed letting me take the lead in our relation, but I don't think you would like it everyday. There would be an empty spot in your heart, a need I could never fill because of my independence."

"You're rejecting me then, Edie," I murmured.

"No, Emmett, I'm accepting you as a dear and cherished friend, but I care for you too much to be the reason you might lose a chance for greater happiness. Let's remain friends and let our one relation as husband and wife be confined to that weekend in Minneapolis when you were Mr. Adamson."

"But what will you do then," I asked, "after Clarissa takes over the Lodge? Will you stay here, in this apartment, or what?"

"Oh I'll remain here in Elkton. I'm sure Clarissa will want my advice and help for a few more years. She's a very sensible woman. Of course this apartment will become hers. I'll move someplace else. Perhaps an apartment somewhere in town, or fix up a suite in the motel. I have a half-interest in that."

"In competition with your aunt!" I blurted. Again these revelations were making me sound like an idiot.

"No, no," she laughed. "Clarissa has a quarter share also. I convinced the electronics plant managers to let me build and operate the motel as an adjunct so to speak to the Lodge. Otherwise they would probably have to heavily subsidize an outside chain to do it. I only required a minimum number of guaranteed room rentals from them. I think it's paying its way, and it's not going to significantly affect the Lodge because we control its size and facilities.

"And you brought in Robby to run it?"

"He has the other quarter share. He's mellowed a bit, Emmett, but he hasn't finished his term in purgatory quite yet. Here's our dinner I believe." I had heard the elevator too, and in a moment, the knock on the door to the parlor and Clarissa's voice saying the table was set. I sensed Edie did not want to say more about Carlton.

The dinner was simple but elegant. A casserole of beef cubes, mushrooms and sliced carrots in a thickened sauce of wine and pan drippings, spooned over noodles that had been sprinkled with poppy seeds. It was not quite bourguignon. No bacon. The carrots added a sweet taste as well as color. It was very good. The salad, artfully arranged leaves of red lettuce, sliced radishes, and ripe olives, dressed with a little olive oil and red wine vinegar. It hadn't occurred to me before that Chef Sou might be another reason why Edie would choose to remain at Elkton.

Edie served, and we chatted a bit about the renovations scheduled for the Lodge now that the holiday events generating profitable party business had tailed off. The plans were completed for the Black Hand lounge, and extension of the dining room to create a small stage. Finally, over coffee, she asked why I was here. I told her again I had been east for job interviews. "I wasn't planning to stop since you hadn't responded to the hints in my letters about seeing you. But when I got to the Interstate turn-off I suddenly decided I needed to tell you what I had planned to do. It would be better this way, rather than in a letter."

Edie looked thoughtful. "Things were a bit hectic for me, Emmett. I couldn't break away for a week-end."

"I understand. I sensed you had a number of problems about the Lodge alterations to worry you. Elmer's death has changed the situation in Keonah. I decided to try to return to engineering. I think I may get an offer within a few weeks. If it's adequate, I plan to accept."

"You wrote that the store was left to Elmer's niece. Don't you get along, or does she want to close the store? What is she like? You had trouble locating her, I remember."

"We get along. She, her name is Nan Hoegh, is about 35, divorced from an abusive husband about 10 or 12 years ago. No children. Slim—a little too slim. A few inches, maybe 4, shorter than you."

"So?" Edie murmured.

"So the short of it is, my dear friend it seemed time to end my grieving and go back to the work I was trained for." I was not planning to say anything more about Nan, not after the gentle rebuff by Edie.

"Is she attractive, Emmett?" I could see Edie was going to be persistent in probing my relations with Nan.

"Reasonably so, after her nose was straightened and her tooth replaced. Legacies from her husband, but still there is a look of vulnerability about her." Edie shuddered. "At least she had sense enough to end it after a year or so," I added. "She did not want to return to Keonah until I told her her uncle was dead and she was the sole heir—except for my 10% share of the hardware store as compensation for serving as a trustee."

"She must have found you a most remarkable man after escaping from a cantankerous old bachelor and a brute of a husband. I assume you are the same gentleman with her as you have been with me. But perhaps you have little contact with her. She's not staying in Keonah is she?"

I had to tell her, yes, and in Elmer's house, and that Nan insisted on pulling her share of work running the store. "Of course, I don't let her do the hard work, replacing upstairs windows, or cutting glass, where she might get hurt."

"Protective again my friend. It's in your nature. I've sensed that about you from our first meeting. But why this sudden desire to leave, if you get along at work, and she's helping? Does she have a boyfriend she wants to get back to, or does she want him to replace you in the store? I don't understand."

"No boyfriend, as far as I know," I told her. "I think her experience has made her afraid of men."

Edie gave me a long searching look. "But surely not of you. No, something has developed between you, hasn't it, Emmett?"

I protested, "Nothing has developed. Of course lately we have dinner together once a week or so, and go to a movie or play at the college, but that's to make sure she eats enough and it relieves the boredom of being in my room every night with nothing to do. That's all."

"Dinner. In her house, my friend?"

"I've never been in that house since Elmer died, Edie. I've told you all that is between us. We happened to meet at the diner one evening. She was going to a movie and invited me along. It just turned into a once a week deal. She escapes T.V. dinners and dirty dishes, and I escape the routine of 3 meals a day at the Keonah diner for one night."

"If you get along, and she's not pushing you out of the store, why this sudden desire to leave?" Edie didn't really ask me that, she seemed to be musing to herself. "It's Charlie, isn't it, Emmett? It's Charlie and what I told you about having children when we were in Minneapolis."

"Yes," I mumbled, anxious to end this inquiry. "But more, the need to end the ache of this empty life. To belong to someone and have her belong to me."

"Didn't you feel that with Nan Hoegh?"

I hesitated a while before saying "A little, yes. But maybe it was more because she seemed a lost child I'd brought home."

"Perhaps, Emmett, but she's hardly a child at 35. A woman living on her own for some years. So maybe she too needs to belong. Try her out, my friend—of course, only if she can have children."

"What do I do, Edie," I replied with a somewhat sarcastic tone, "ask her to get a physical exam?"

"Just a suggestion, Mr. Borden. Follow your own path to find belonging. I would end your search here if I were more selfish or cared a little less for your happiness."

We had finished our coffee. I stood, preparing to leave, but Edie protested. "You haven't had dessert yet, fruit compote with pecan crescent cookies." Edie went to the little kitchen, returning in a moment with the fruit and cookies on a tray. She avoided a continuation of our discussion, more probing of my motives rather, and talked about the plans for the Black Hand Lounge.

We finished our dessert, and after a quiet moment, I rose and moved into the parlor to get my coat. Edie came up to me, I bent slightly to kiss her goodbye.'

"But I don't think I'm going to let you go like this, Emmett. We may not meet again for a long time if you do go back east." She pressed against me in a long kiss, and pointing to a door in the far corner, whispered in my ear, "Be a blessing in my bed for a few more hours my gentle friend."

Chapter XXXIV

Black Cloud

It was nearly midnight when I slipped back to my room, being careful to avoid being seen by the night clerks at the Lodge and the motel. I thought again about the remarkable Mrs. Adamson and wondered what would have happened to me if I had not found Rodde's left foot. But I had found it, and found a woman, perhaps the only one, that could rekindle the need for love yet recognize even before I did that there was an equal need for fulfillment that she could not give me. Perhaps Rodde's very late paternity made her perceptive of a need I was unaware of. In any case, she had given me a gentle nudge in Nan's direction without even knowing the offer made to me.

Ah, but to Edie, you've committed a sin of omission, Emmett Borden. And yet worse, to Nan, a sin of commission. Proposing to one when your whole intention was to marry the other! But was there harm done to either if they didn't know? Did the two sins negate each other? Was there some kind of algebra to certain sins permitting a cancellation to occur? Mother Borden would have chastised me for even asking such a question. Dad would have said my original intention was based upon ignorance of Edie's actual situation, and any real engineer should recognize when plans have to be altered if unexpected new facts are discovered. Besides, you owed Edie the right of first refusal. I left the ghosts of my past to argue the ethical issues. For me, I decided that those small sins will eventually fade away—if they remain hidden.

I left early the next morning and drove straight through to Keonah. Arriving at the store a bit late the following morning, I found Nan struggling over a large pane of glass on the cutting table. I could see several big broken pieces in the steel trash barrel we used for glass shards. She was nearly in tears when she looked up as I walked to the work area. "Emmett, I'm afraid I've ruined two sheets of glass trying to fix Mrs. Olsen's storm door. I just can't seem to master glass cutting."

After assuring me she had not hurt herself, I went over the procedure with her and quickly found she was using a dull cutter. "I should have thought of that, how stupid can I get?"

"Why?" I asked. "Do you think you should be able to invent the world without a few trial runs. God himself hasn't done a perfect job yet, and we don't even know how many botched tries he made before this one."

"Forget inventing the world, I should have practiced on some scrap pieces first and then maybe I'd have seen the cutter was dull. I'm glad you're back, another day alone and I'd have ruined all the glass in stock."

"But why couldn't this repair have waited until I did come back?" I asked. "I was going to get a pair of safety gloves for you to wear when you're handling glass."

"She brought the door in yesterday, Emmett. I told her you were gone. She was going to take it to Cedar Rapids for repair, but I told her I would do it. I guess I wanted to show her I wasn't as dumb as she remembered me in her Home Ec class."

"Mrs. Olsen that bakes for the diner?"

"The same. And now she'll know I'm still dumb."

I told her I didn't think she was dumb, but she might be without thumbs if she tried any more glasswork before I got the Kevlar gloves. "So that's where the svelte Phyllis learned about dough," I laughed.

I asked Nan if she would be able to put the glass back in the storm door. "Then Mrs. Pie and Cake will be satisfied you've grown smarter." Nan was sure she could. The glass was in a frame that was fitted into a channel in the door and held by four clamps, tightened by knurled screws. I knew she could fasten the clamps, I was just concerned over whether she could handle the weight of the window, being so skinny.

"You call Phyllis svelte, but you call me skinny, why we weigh almost the same!" she protested.

263

"Come now, Mrs. Hoegh, Phyllis must have 10 pounds on you."

"That's just shoulder pads—and whatever, wherever, Emmett."

"No padding on her calves and arms. A very good figure," I teased.

Nan insisted she was not skinny, and we finally drew a truce over the issue by agreeing to dinner the following Friday at a Japanese restaurant in C.R. that I had wanted to try.

I was expecting a letter from Lorenz, but it didn't come, and neither did one from Shelton Electronics. Nothing in the next day's mail either. Waiting for someone to decide my future is not easy for me. I began to think something had gone wrong in the interviews and that I was going to get a rejection notice, if they bothered to send one at all. It was hard to believe Lorenz would keep me hanging for no good reason. We had been friends for many years. Maybe I had better start thinking about alternative work, but what? Nan could see I was anxious and moody, she probably would have liked to ask what the problem was, but fortunately my sour expression stopped her. What could I tell her at this time? I had nothing to offer.

Snow started by mid-morning Friday, and I suggested it might be wise to cancel the reservation, but Nan was sure the roads would be all right, and anyway, she said she was intrigued about what differences there were between the two oriental cuisines. She was right about the weather. The snow stopped by early afternoon and the temperature stayed well above freezing, so the roads were not icy.

Nan was not much for drinking, but agreed with me that the tiny saucer-like cup of warm sake' was traditional and should be tried if she was to further her oriental experience. The weather must have deterred some diners, since there were only a few tables filled. The restaurant was tastefully decorated I thought, in sharp contrast to the too common garish red of many Chinese ones. Subtlety extended to the subdued lighting and Japanese music.

Fran and I had eaten at Japanese restaurants and sushi bars in New York and Connecticut, so I was familiar with the cuisine. I suggested, for Nan's introduction, we should try the dinner 'sampler' offer. Suddenly remembering that Lorenz' wife had an allergic reaction to shellfish, I asked Nan if she did.

She shook her head, "I can eat anything—I think I can—but no blow fish please, I'm not ready to risk that!"

"O.K.," I replied. "We'll play if safe and avoid the pleasures of dangerous living." I poured the green tea while our waitress served the soup, a red fish broth garnished with radish and scallion slices. Nan had requested chopsticks, but the soup puzzled her.

"You drink the broth from the bowl," I told her when I saw her looking for something like the porcelain spoons usually provided in Chinese restaurants, "and use the chopsticks for the solid bits."

She was fairly skillful at handling the chopsticks, but a little self-consciously awkward in drinking from the bowl. I found myself gazing at the rhythmic contraction of the muscles in her throat, exposed when she tilted her head back to swallow. I began to wonder how Nan would look undressed. I recalled that scene in the store, Nan and Brooks embracing. Then, a breast exposed to the white fluorescent light from the ceiling fixture. In that harsh light, casting no shadows, so essential in perceiving form, her breast seemed small. The skin pale, almost chaste.

She was not actually skinny despite my quips, but not svelte either. I suppose it was the impression her slightly hollowed cheeks gave of not eating enough. Her shoulders were good, not narrow, nor her chest pinched. As an engineer, I would have to say her underlying bone structure was sound.

A trickle of red broth, escaping from the tilted bowl to run down her chin, suddenly reminded me of the sensuous oyster-eating scene, followed by the rush to the bedroom, in the old Albert Finney movie 'Tom Jones'. I felt a twinge of embarrassment at being turned on by the sight, recollecting that my dinner companion was only a child when I saw that movie. Our age difference did bother me, though it didn't seem to bother her. Still, I told myself, Nan could not be much older and still bear a first child safely, if that was what I wanted. And her offer, was that something she really wanted? Doubts and questions, never occurring when I courted Fran in our youth, seemed to plague my every step in middle age.

"Where are you, Emmett?" Nan's voice startled me. "You've had a lost look in your eyes for the past 5 minutes. Your soup's getting cold."

"Just remembering an old movie." I hurried with my soup, as the waitress brought the sampler tray. Fortunately the portions were small so Nan didn't falter over trying each selection: igaguri, raw fish slices to be dipped in a spicy sauce, and a vegetable and fish mixture sushi. The igaguri especially seemed to please her with the different tastes and textures revealed by each bite. I was pleased at that, Fran was also fond of it, so I could tell her how it was made when Nan asked me.

"It's a sweetened chestnut, covered with a paste of raw shrimp and then rolled over short pieces of thin noodles, and finally deep fat fried. It's made to look like a chestnut still in its prickly husk. A cook's conceit," I explained, "but quite tasty." We switched from sea to land with our main course, a beef sukiyaki. Dessert was a simple dish of fresh mandarin orange slices and small sweet rice cakes.

On the way back to Keonah, Nan asked me what old movie I had reminisced about. "Before you time, Mrs. Hoegh," I replied, embarrassed again at my thoughts. "An English film, 'Tom Jones'."

"From the book of the same name? We still read the classics you know, Mr. Borden," she quipped. "Actually, the art theater at the University showed the film for my class on the English novel, but I didn't get to see it, I forget why. My head was full of art and literature at that time. It led to my many fights with Uncle Elmer. He wanted me to study something practical, like accounting, or nursing, or something, while I was dreaming of a romantic life, rosy and sweet, and just ripe to be plucked by my strong, wavy-haired hero. I guess I expected everything then, sure that life with him would be exciting and wonderful, in my own home away from Elmer's nagging. So much for that dream when my hero turned out to be a heel."

I didn't reply, sensing a bitter tone in her revelation. We drove on in silence for the few more minutes it took to get to Keonah. I parked in front of Elmer's house, hers now, and unlatching the seatbelt, prepared to get out and open the car door for her. Nan put her hand on my arm and asked me to wait a moment. Undoing her own seatbelt, she moved over against me.

"Aren't you cold?" I asked lamely after another moment.

"Yes," she whispered, pulling my head down for a kiss. She didn't feel cold, her breath was warm and sweet. As we lingered over the kiss, I felt her arm press against my chest, and then her elbow move furtively about my lap. I suddenly realized what my dinner companion was doing, something I hadn't experienced since I dated in high school so very long ago. She was not as subtlety adept at it as one young lady I dimly remembered.

"My coat is probably in the way, but did you find what you were looking for?" I asked, breaking off the kiss with a laugh.

"No, was it that obvious?"

"Yes, I'm afraid you haven't had much practice at it, Nan."

"I don't want to practice it, it's just that most men would have been grabbing at me by now. You haven't, so I wondered if there was something wrong—with me," she added lamely.

"Don't you mean me?" I laughed again. "Don't worry about either of us. I responded to you." She started to answer, but I opened the door and walked around the car to let her out. It had started snowing again and turning colder, so the snow on the streets which had melted earlier was starting to freeze. I took her arm and led her up the walk to the front door, gave her a quick kiss on the forehead, wished her good night and walked back to my car. I could see her, still on the porch, looking at me as I drove off. It must have been frustrating for her not knowing whether there was going to be something between us, but I couldn't really court her until I got my job situation settled. Damn it, why hadn't I heard from them.

With Brooks out of the picture and still anticipating an offer from Lorenz within a few more days, I felt my way to Nan was now clear. Edie, bless her, had stepped aside. I believed she was honest about her reasons. She had expressed in words those feelings I subconsciously perceived in me, but was too inarticulate to say to myself. Perhaps she understood me too well for me to be a long-term interest under daily contact. But surely I must still have a few mysteries to be revealed. Nan would not be as analytic as Edie. An open book to my Indiana friend, but perhaps still an interesting one to my boss.

Unexpectedly, a cloud from Nan's past jolted my pleasant musing. I had been back only a week when Jim Hoegh arrived. Nan and I were at the register checking some invoices when he entered the store. A man, somewhat seedy in appearance, big, but his frame suggested a once sturdy build had begun to turn to flab. I started toward him to ask if I could be of help but he shook his head, turning instead to the register. He stood there a moment until Nan, finally sensing his presence I guess, looked up. He must have startled her, as she stepped back, her arms raised as though she was defending herself. I didn't understand what was happening until she spoke.

"What in hell are you doing here, Jim?" and before he could reply, to me: "this is Jim Hoegh, Emmett, my ex-husband."

"Legally of course, Nan," the man responded. "But I see you still wear the ring I gave you."

"Not for the reason you may suspect," she retorted. "Now what do you want?"

I should have excused myself and gone to the back of the store leaving them in private to discuss their affairs or resume the resentments of long ago, but I began to feel some apprehension that this Hoegh might steal my Hoegh, though Nan's tone was not cordial.

"My folks wrote me that old man Diehl died, so I thought he might have left us something."

I caught his drift right away and stepped towards him. "No, he left nothing for you, if you are Jim Hoegh," I said.

"Maybe so, whoever you are, but he probably left a lot to this skinny bitch and she's going to give me a part of it. She owes me!" He started to push past me to get to Nan, so I though he needed a lesson in manners. A quick, hard, knee to his crotch stopped him, doubled up in pain. But it was only for a few moments. His face flushed with fury, he lurched toward me. I saw his right fist pulled back for a strike and I got set to parry it, but instead he hit me in the belly with his left, knocking the wind out of me. I was out of any further action for the moment, and no help to my boss, but my interference had apparently given Nan time to get the can of Mace from her purse. He tried to deflect her raised arm, but she managed to get a good part of the spray onto his face. Hoegh turned, staggering to the door, Nan screaming at him to get out.

I was beginning to come around by then. Not in A-1 shape but alert enough to grab Elmer's sickle to better defend myself. He was just too big, flab or not, for me to have much of a chance otherwise.

Nan was shaking and pale. I had not sensed so clearly as at that moment the absolute terror a big abusive male could cause in a woman.

I went to the door, but Hoegh was nowhere in sight. Nan started crying, but I thought I'd better lock the front and back doors first before trying to comfort her. I got her into a chair, still sobbing, worse maybe than before, and then dialed the police station.

In just a few minutes young Ken Randall appeared at the front door. I let him in and explained what had happened. Nan began getting a hold on herself, at least enough to answer his questions. I told Randall I thought Nan should get a protection from abuse order, though it probably wouldn't mean much to Hoegh.

"Once the Mace wears off he'll likely be even more of a problem," Randall told me. "Better if Mrs. Hoegh got away for a few days where he can't get at her," he added. "That'll give us time to get Judge Baker to issue a restraining order."

I then called Trable who assured me he could represent Nan in getting the order before Judge Baker. Nan had stopped crying, but still seemed badly shaken. "Are you all right, Emmett," she finally asked. "My god, what am I going to do? I thought I was rid of him."

I assured her I was O.K., "he just caught me by surprise. I guess I hadn't counted on him being left-handed. But what you're going to do is get out of here for a few days until Trable can see the judge. I'll press charges on him for assault, so he won't hold that against you—at least he shouldn't. But anyway the threat of a fine or jail time may scare him off. Call Phyllis and see if she can put you up for a couple of days."

While Nan made the call, I emptied the cash register, bundled up the account books and hung up the closed sign. After getting the O.K. from Phyllis, we got in her car and I drove to the house. I wasn't a boob about entering, a quick scouting verified the front and back doors were locked and the windows intact. Still, I brought the sickle with me and had it ready for use when we entered. After checking the bedroom to be sure Hoegh hadn't been clever picking the door lock and was hiding in there, I stood guard outside the door while Nan hurriedly packed a small bag with essentials. I gave her the cash from the register and told her to drive directly to the Mercer's, not to stop on the way, and not to call anyone, but to wait for my call. I watched her drive off and walked back to the store.

Hoegh wouldn't come back to the store I was sure, knowing I might expect him and be armed, either with a gun or the sickle, which itself looked pretty dangerous. But he might well break into Nan's house in the night, so I stopped at the police station and asked Randall if he could help trap him if he tried to break-in tonight. I thought I'd have a hard sell since it might be an all-night deal, but he agreed right away. It may have been the only excitement Keonah could offer him.

Hoegh didn't show up at the store and I had no idea where he had gone. Randall was to join me at Nan's around 8 o'clock. That seemed to him to be the earliest we could expect a visit if Hoegh made one. I got sandwiches and a jug of coffee at the diner, deciding to start my stakeout earlier. It was essential to give the impression that the house was not empty, so I had turned the lights on in several rooms, but stayed away from the windows. Randall would remain in his own car, not the police car, parked in a neighbor's driveway across the street, where he could keep a watch on the house but not be observed.

By 10 o'clock I had gone through the sandwiches and coffee, wishing I'd gotten a bigger jug. It was hard to stay alert and still remain hidden, so the coffee was an essential stimulant. I had turned the T.V. on in the front room to suggest Nan might be there. I was in the hallway, near the entrance to the kitchen and its back door. The T.V. was plugged into a long extension cord so I could turn it off by pulling the cord from a wall socket in the hallway without having to risk being seen going into the front room. Fifteen minutes later the downstairs was dark and only a lamp in the upstairs bedroom was on.

Hoegh was a lousy burglar. He botched his attempt to quietly break the glass in the back door, so anyone in the house would have been alerted, but he moved fast enough once he got the door opened, racing through the kitchen to the hallway and starting up the stairs. I flipped on the hall and porch lights, my pre-arranged signal to Randall, and blocked the foot of the stairs, sickle at the ready, as the dismayed Hoegh turned at the sudden light and noise.

"Oh shit!" was the best he could manage, but appropriate nonetheless. He started towards me, but when I raised the sickle he stopped. "Where's Nan dammit? What the hell are you doing in her house?"

"This is my house," I lied. "My house and my shop. Old man Diehl gave them to me. Arrest this bastard," I called to Randall, who had just entered. "I'll swear out a charge of breaking and entering at the station. That and the violation of a protection from abuse order ought to put him away for years."

"Whose order of abuse?" Hoegh challenged.

"Nan Hoegh's, creep, and stay away from her."

After Randall lead him away, handcuffed, to his car, I called the Mercer's. George answered, and when I identified myself, he put Nan on the phone. I thought it best not to tell her about the break-in, it would only add to her scare. Instead, I told her to stay with Phyllis until I called again that Judge Baker had issued the order.

The next morning I asked Randall if I could talk to Hoegh for a bit. He was reluctant to let me see him, as Hoegh hadn't been to court yet, or obtained an attorney. However, I managed to persuade him it might be in Hoegh's best interest as I might not press the breaking and entry charge if I could get him to leave the state.

I moved a chair up to the cell bars. I sure wasn't going to go inside with that gorilla. The puffiness on Hoegh's face had mostly disappeared by then, but his manner was still sullen. "What do you want, you bastard?" was the only greeting he had for me.

"I'm going to do you a favor," I responded, and then made my proposition. I had thought about the situation during the night and felt the only practical way to get him out of our life was to get him out of Keonah and out of expectation of getting any money from Nan. So I told him I'd not press the assault and breaking and entry charges if he left the state and kept away from Nan. I told him she had no money to give him.

"She's got the house hasn't she?" he retorted.

"Look, mister, I told you before it's my house. I'm just letting her live there, it comes out of her wages at the shop, and it's a convenience for me, if you get what I mean." I put on the best leer I could and hoped he'd get my meaning without my having to make still another explicit lie.

"The fact is, Hoegh, if I press charges on you they'll put you in the county jail and I don't want you around, messing things up for me by scaring her away. So I'm going to offer another incentive to get out of our life and stay out. You plead guilty to the assault and breaking and entry charges and I'll get the judge to give you a probationary sentence. And just to show you what a good guy I am, I'm going to give you $100 as a going away present." Interrupting his response I warned him that if he bothered us again he'd probably go to the state penitentiary.

"That's just talk, dammit. I didn't steal anything. And as for assault and battery, you hit me first, and a cheap one at that."

"Well, Hoegh, you think you know best, but remember there was another witness in the store. I think she'll agree with my version. What do you think, Nan Hoegh is going to do you a favor after you knocked out a tooth?"

"I've got to get more than that mister. I can't get anymore from home, that's why I came here when I got the news about Diehl. I'm in trouble and I need a lot more than a hundred bucks."

"You're a greedy bastard as well as a creep," I told him. "You're in trouble and you came here to get more of it? All right, I'll give you another fifty, otherwise you can try your luck in court. And pay for an attorney also," I added.

"I need a grand. The county jail may be a safer place for me if I don't get it. And when I get out I'll be a little more clever about how I put the squeeze on your playmate."

I didn't like that threat. I could give him the money, but how could I be sure he'd leave us alone? "Hey mister, for a little more than a thousand dollars I can arrange for an accident and be rid of you for sure. A hit-and-run specialist, or maybe a little cyanide-laced cocaine if you're a druggie. I can even save the money by having Nan lure you to the house and shoot you myself. No risk for either of us since you're already on record for breaking and entering, as well as violating the protection from abuse order." I grinned at him, hoping he'd realize I had the upper hand. "Anyway, what do you need the money for to take such a risk?"

He finally mumbled it out. He'd welched on a gambling debt, $4000 some dollars, and was warned to make good in two weeks. He tried his dad, who refused, but his mother gave him $3000. With no other source, he thought he'd bully Nan into giving him the rest when his folks told him about Diehl's death. When I asked him how he knew she was here, he said he didn't, just chanced it as he had no other place to look for her. He was reluctant to tell me who held his IOU, but finally spilled it when I suggested he was a swell storyteller, but not too believable. He had drifted about after Nan left him, ending up in Baton Rouge. He actually had a job, a stock clerk at a grocery wholesaler.

Randall came in to cut the meeting short. I told Hoegh I'd see him in court and left. I hoped he was stewing in his own juice.

Mulling over the get-rid-of-Hoegh problem between bites of Mrs. Olsen's mincemeat pie and gulps of coffee at the diner that evening, I finally decided to risk the grand on his story. But to make sure he couldn't bilk me, I figured out how to give it to him by long distance. I'd wire the money to Baton Rouge and he'd have to go there to get it. Satisfied with the scheme, I called Nan from Mrs. Fashlich's hoping to keep her spirits up, but no one answered at the Mercer's.

Sleep gave me an even better arrangement. It often happens that way. You work on a problem with no success during the day, or maybe you get a not too perfect solution and put it out of your mind. Somehow your subconscious works on it while you sleep, and unfettered from outside distractions or preconceived approaches gets a better solution. I hurried through the morning wash and shave so I could get to Hoegh again before his scheduled hearing with Judge Baker.

I told Hoegh what he had to do to get the rest of the money to pay off his gambling debt. He was to give me the $3000 he already had, I'd add a $1000 and wire it in care of the gambler's name he gave me in Baton Rouge with instructions to the Western Union clerk that the money was to be turned over to the gambler only when both were present and signed for it. I'd drop the burglary and assault charges, but he'd have exactly 24 hours to get to Baton Rouge to collect the money.

The poor bastard couldn't do other than agree, but Judge Baker insisted on an explanation of why I asked him to drop the charges when the police caught him in the act. All I told the judge was that I was most concerned about getting Hoegh out of the state where he could not further harass my business partner. Judge Baker warned Hoegh about any further contact with Mrs. Hoegh or me, signed the protection from abuse order and gave him a suspended sentence.

An hour later we wired the money, I gave Hoegh an extra fifty for expenses in getting to Baton Rouge and watched him drive off. Was it worth it? I hoped so, confident that I'd get an offer from Lorenz in a day or two more and we'd be out of Keonah for good, and Hoegh wouldn't be able to find us.

I opened the store for business again and placed a call to Davenport. Phyllis answered and I asked for Nan.

"Isn't she back in Keonah yet?" She sounded surprised. "She left yesterday Emmett, while I was out."

"Yesterday? I told her to stay with you 'til I cleared things up with Hoegh." A picture of Nan's car crashed and hidden in a ditch flashed into my brain. "Have Mercer check on any accidents on the road right away and call me back." I hung up and called Randall to see if he could get any accident reports.

An hour later Phyllis called. "No accidents reported, but I found an item in yesterday's Cedar Rapids paper about a burglar arrested in Keonah. Could that have scared her? She just scribbled a thank you note and said she was leaving."

I was barely polite in thanking Phyllis and asking her to let me know if Nan contacted her. I hung up. Damn that skinny bitch, echoing Hoegh's comment that seemed more appropriate to me now. She probably panicked reading about the break-in and scooted. But to where? I had no clue on how to find her again. I could ask the state police to be on the look-out for her car, but Davenport is just across the river from Illinois. She could have gone there and the Illinois police wouldn't be that enthused about looking for a car not involved in a crime. Still I had to try it, there was nothing else I could do. Now I was sorry I had let Hoegh go. I was so mad and frustrated I'd have asked the judge to give him 20 years at hard labor for messing up my plans for the future.

I kept bugging Randall for the next few days to see if any sighting of Nan's car had been reported. We had extended the search request to Missouri and Minnesota, both within easy reach from Davenport. I even checked with her former landlady in Glenly, though I thought it unlikely she'd go back there when Hoegh might have gotten that address from papers in her house.

Winter weather wasn't the only gloomy thing in Keonah. Nearly a week had gone by with no car sighting reported. No letter from Lorenz either, for which I could be thankful now. What could I do if an offer came through with no Nan to propose to and no one to run the store if I left. I stopped at the bank late Friday to deposit the register receipts and cash my weekly paycheck, which I had to make out myself again. Mrs. Bonnestahl, head cashier at Farmers and Merchants State Bank of Keonah—all of that on the bronze plaque by the door—called me to her desk.

"Is there some problem at Diehl's, Mr. Borden?" she asked. "I got a call from the Fort Dodge State Bank wanting to verify a personal check on our bank for $2000 by Mrs. Hoegh, and to transfer the balance of her account to them. Of course, there's enough money in the account and they verified that Mrs. Hoegh herself presented the check—driver's license photo and a credit card. Still we'd like to know if there was some dissatisfaction with our bank and whether the Diehl account will also be changed."

Found at last! After I explained that Nan probably panicked after the break-in, Maggy B. agreed to delay transferring the account until I could reach Fort Dodge, and to call the bank back and get an address for Nan.

An hour later I was on my way to Fort Dodge as fast as I could make my Chrysler go. 80 West to Des Moines, then 35 North to Blairsburg, then west on 20 to Fort Dodge. I didn't even pause for a nostalgic glance at the university as I sped through Ames, so anxious to pin down my scared butterfly within the Keonah town limits.

By mid-evening I parked in front of the address the bank had given Maggy Bonnestahl; a rooming house much like the one in Glenly, except I didn't need to get the landlady, the rented rooms had a separate entrance from the street. She was on the second floor, at the rear. I could see light under the door, so she was probably in. My knock was answered after a long moment by a wary "Who's there?"

"A special delivery, Ma'am," I said trying to sound official, "from the Keonah State Bank." I could hear a sigh of relief as she pulled back the door bolt and let the door open a crack, as far as the chain allowed.

"Emmett!!"

"Yes, Emmett, and I ought to—well never mind what I ought to do. It's enough I've found you after a week of worry and having the police in half a dozen states on the lookout for you." Relief and irritation were playing tag in my head, so my exaggeration seemed warranted. "It's too damned late for us to get back to Keonah, but first thing in the morning. Now I'm starved, I haven't had supper and drove all the way here without stopping. What did you do, go back to soup and crackers?" I saw the hot plate and an open box of saltines on the table.

She was starting to cry again, but I grabbed her coat and handbag and handed them to her at the same time pushing her out the door. She struggled into the coat on the way down the stairs and I herded her into the car. Turning the car around, I headed back towards the center of town where I had spotted a diner.

By the time we had gotten settled in a booth she had regained some control over her emotions. She looked a sight with her makeup streaked and her hair tousled from the wind, but she was still my Nan. I ordered for both of us and asked for coffee right away to settle my nerves and hers.

"I don't know what rules your landlady has about guests, but you'll have to put me up for tonight. I'm too tired to search for a motel and I don't trust you to stay put by yourself."

"It's just a single bed, Emmett, and only one room." She seemed nervous and unsure about my statement.

"Don't worry, I've slept on the floor before. The mood I'm in right now, I'd much rather paddle your ass than pat it, so you needn't worry about your virtue. Better if you explain to me why you ran off and what were you planning to do by trying to transfer your bank account. Though if you hadn't tried that I might never have found you." The waitress brought the dinner plates at that moment. I held up my hand to stop her explanation, telling her to save it for dessert, that I was too hungry to listen with a calm frame of mind. We ate in silence, but I can't remember what I had, I was still agitated with a strange mix of relief and exasperation.

With the second cup of coffee, it all came out. When she read the brief newspaper report about the break-in, she panicked and scooted, but ran short of money. In order to cash a check she had to establish an account at the bank so at the bank's suggestion, she authorized a transfer of her account. As to where she was going and what she was going to do after that she had no clear idea at all.

"I was just trying to get away from him, Emmett. It didn't matter where, just someplace where he couldn't find me."

"Well he's gone now and I don't think he'll try to get back. I talked the judge into a suspended sentence and gave him money to get back to Louisiana."

"You gave him money?" Nan was incredulous. "Why, and why the suspended sentence?"

So I had to explain to her that if he was sentenced, it would probably be only for thirty days at most and in the county jail, and then he'd be free, and in Keonah, and probably bent on revenge. "As for the money, he was trying to pay off a gambling debt and chanced that you were back in Keonah and he could browbeat you for it. So I arranged it so he had to go back to Louisiana to get the $3000 he'd got from his mother and the $1000 I gave him. That way, he'd keep his job, stay in Baton Rouge, and as a condition of his suspended sentence he was also to stay out of Keonah. So I think you'll be safe from him. And as for the money, we'll put it in the books as a business expense. We can charge it to maintenance, or maybe loss due to damaged goods might be more fitting. Anyway, why couldn't you rely on me to protect you?"

"By day—and in the night too, Emmett?" I had no answer to her retort.

We drove back to her room in silence. I waited in the hall until she undressed and was in bed, then took off my shoes, stretched out on the rug, a couple of throw pillows under my head, and our coats for a blanket. I did make sure however to position myself next to the door so there would be no chance for her to leave without waking me. In almost every thing she had done since deciding to stay in Keonah and help run the store she seemed rational and reasonable. But for this Mr. Hoegh she seemed permanently scarred.

I rose early the next morning, stiff and cold. A glance showed my boss still asleep. Some towels were in a closet. Grabbing one, I went quietly down the hall to the bathroom. A quick rinse on my face, a plain water gargle, and my morning cleansing, such as it was, was done. No shave, no toothbrush, and no soap. I hadn't prepared for this trip, being anxious to reach Nan before she took another notion to scoot.

I knocked before re-entering. "Emmett?" she asked and when I responded she said I could come in. "I guess I look a sight. Just give me a few minutes to wash up and we can start back."

She did look like she'd been tumbled in a clothes dryer. Her hair was uncombed, cheeks still streaked from last night's crying, and her lipstick blotchy. Still she looked good to me, even wrapped in a wrinkled bathrobe and wearing some scroungy bedroom slippers. It occurred to me that I had never seen her in her bedroom outfit before, and I thought I'd buy her a welcome home present of some new slippers and a robe of more feminine cut and definitely of a brighter color than the faded green which I detest. As she started off to the bathroom, I called after her that I'd settle with her landlady and to start packing when she returned.

Mrs. Haskins was surprised to see me when she opened the door at my knock, telling me I was pretty early to be looking for a room. I quickly straightened her out, found out that the room had been let by the week, paid in advance, and that nothing was due and nothing would be refunded.

An hour later we were on the road. Nan driving in front and me immediately behind. I spotted a truck stop diner up ahead and tooting my horn, motioned for her to turn in. My metabolism must be set a little on the high side because I get hungry so much. Especially in the morning, and especially this morning when my waking-up habits were broken.

"You're still mad at me, Emmett?" she asked after we had been seated and I had studied the menu in silence. I told her no, that in fact, I was glad I had found her within driving distance and in one piece, having worried me and Phyllis that she's been wrecked and lying hidden in a ditch on the way back from Davenport.

"But please don't do this trick again. The majority partner at Diehl's can't run off and leave me to explain what happened, and maybe put under suspicion that I murdered her to gain full control over the nuts and bolts business."

She gave me a promise with a weak smile at my attempt at humor. But after a whole pot of coffee, hash browns, sausage, two large eggs, dry toast and jam, and fresh squeezed orange juice she regained some color in her face and seemed in good spirits again. Not that she ate all that, not even half, but I did.

Chapter XXXV
Black Velvet

Jim Hoegh was out of the picture, at least I hoped my arrangements would hold, but what other unexpected catastrophe might occur. I hadn't probed any of Nan's past. Were there other men that would come between us? I needed a commitment, but how could I ask for one with my future in limbo? I had almost resolved to call Lorenz and Shelton Electronics and try to find out what my situation was. Could Lorenz have decided not to make an offer and been too embarrassed to tell me? It would be easier for him, with me a thousand miles away, to simply avoid further contact and save himself from having to tell an old friend that he wasn't needed anymore.

I went back to scanning the employment ads in the Chicago and New York newspapers. I should have been more discreet about it, waiting until I was back in my room. Nan couldn't help but notice, and asked what I was looking for. I muttered something about looking for a used glass cutting jig we could use, and hurriedly turned the pages to the for sale sections. For sure, Mother Borden had probably given up in exasperation at all the lies I told in the last month, but it was past bothering my conscious anymore.

We had been back at Diehl's—we'd decided finally to leave the name unchanged—for about a week. My anxiety about not hearing from Lorenz was becoming unbearable and I resolved to call next day.

I did not sleep well that night. My mind kept going over the interviews, looking for something I had done wrong. Was I considered too old for the job, or had being out of the field for several years made me obsolescent? I woke late, for all of that pointless worry about things that could not now be changed, and even extra coffee at the diner didn't revive me. I felt tired and dispirited when I got to Diehl's. I mumbled good morning to my boss and partner and headed immediately to the back of the shop.

There wasn't any work actually, but I puttered about straightening the glass shelves and sweeping the floor. I could hear a few customers come in, but Nan didn't call me so I suppose they wanted some things that she could handle. I heard the front door close again and in a moment Nan appeared. "A telegram for you, Emmett." She waited a moment while I hastily tore open the envelope and scanned the message.

"Good news?" she asked, hearing my sound of relief.

"Yes!" I folded the wire and stuck it in my pocket. It was from Lorenz, apologizing for the delay—it was necessary to recheck my security clearance he wrote—but it was a solid offer. $50 K to start. Not as much as my last professional position, but I had not expected to reach my old level again immediately. It was enough for two to live decently, and I had income from my own investments and the house in Mamaroneck I could sell.

I could see Nan wanted to ask about the wire, but I thought I should wait a bit. I would give Shelton Electronics another day or two before deciding to tell her. Lorenz had given me a week to decide. Generous of him, I thought. My mood perked up considerably and the rest of the morning sped by quickly. Business perked up too, but mostly because of last night's snow, not because of my wire. Snow shovels and salt were the big items the rest of the day as the optimists realized that winter would not be over for yet a while.

Poor Nan, she couldn't help but wonder if this wire from Massachusetts was related to my newspaper search and whether it might mean bad news for her. I knew she could hardly have imagined running the store herself. We had gone over the books together during probate and the estate tax filings, and it was clear to both of us she could not make ends meet if she had to hire a full time experienced helper to replace me.

Later that afternoon, Mrs. Fashlich dropped in. "Special delivery letter for you, Mr. Borden. Thought I'd better bring it over on my way to the grocery store, though it doesn't look like it's from your spittoon friends." She had her laugh and left, still amused at what she thought was a good joke.

It wasn't from Indiana of course. Shelton Electronics had responded at last, and it was also positive, and about 10% more than Lorenz's offer. After a night of nagging worry I now had a tough decision to make. Earlier, on my drive back from the interviews, I had planned to accept an offer from Lorenz, I needed to think again about the pros and cons of both jobs, and more importantly, assuming she would accept my proposal, which I hadn't yet made, get her views on each. I decided to wait until tomorrow to ask her. That would give me the evening to mull over which was the better offer for the two of us, or if it should come to that, for me alone.

My anxiety relieved, I slept soundly that evening, even though I couldn't fully resolve the question of which offer to accept. I felt more comfortable to go with my old friend Lorenz, but also recognized his company was smaller and riskier because of its reliance on military contracts. Shelton offered more money and perhaps greater stability, but the job would not be as challenging. I ended-up deciding not to decide, but to wait until I knew what Nan would say.

I opened the store the next morning. Nan hadn't arrived by the time I had finished bacon and pancakes at the diner. A call from a Mr. Rawlins, one of Elmer's old pinochle crowd, asked if I could replace a storm door glass and latch mechanism that had suffered from an accident. He seemed embarrassed to tell me that he and his wife had gone out the night before to a movie, but the latch on the storm door, which had been acting on the tricky side for sometime had finally given up. Apparently the spring operating the push button on the outside of the latch rusted out and jammed the lock so the button couldn't be pushed to release the catch. He had to break the glass in order to get back into the house. I told him I was alone, but would try to get out today to fix it.

Just as I finally decided to call my partner to see if she was coming in, she showed up. She seemed a little down and listless. Shaking her head when I asked if she felt sick, and again when I asked if she had eaten anything, I wondered if this was going to be a good time to propose. Telling her about Gus Rawlins' call, I said I'd be back shortly.

Mrs. Rawlins was home when I knocked. "I'd been after Gus for months about that latch, Mr. Borden, but he's a great one for procrastinating. Now he's got to pay for the glass too." There was a lot more, but it was all on the same frequency. Gus was a clerk at the municipal building, and I remember from Elmer's comments, a little lazy, more so when Mrs. Rawlins pestered him. It seems like so many marriages have rough edges that never get worn away, just gouging deeper with time. I'm sure, except for her disease, Fran felt, as I did, that at least we had a happy and loving marriage. I hoped that would be true again with Nan.

I had decided to take the old latch off and bring it back to the shop with the glass frame. There are several mounting styles for door latches and I didn't know, nor did Gus when he called, what type he had. On the way back to the shop I stopped at the diner and got two large coffees and sweet rolls to go. Nan still looked like she hadn't seen a blue sky for months. I handed her the sack of goodies and carried the frame to the back of the shop.

"Thanks, Emmett, but I'm not sure I can eat this." Nan gave me a wan smile when I returned.

"Sure you can, we'll have a picnic here at the cash register. This job will cost Gus Rawlins extra for the two trips and my having to listen to Mrs. Rawlins' complaints. Serves him right though for being so slow to fix things."

"Yes, I suppose there are many men like Rawlins who are slow. One shouldn't wait forever to do things. Sometimes it may be too late by the time they get around to it."

"Not me," I replied, getting the message I'm sure her remarks intended. "I try to act on things as soon as possible. Now please drink your coffee and eat that roll. I want to check you out on replacing Gus' storm window."

She did seem to perk up a little after that. The glass wasn't too large, there were two panes in the door and Gus had the good sense to break the smaller one, so Nan could handle it with no risk. While she fitted the glass in the frame with new gaskets, I poked around in the latch bin for a matching unit. I couldn't find one with the same appearance, but the mounting holes were the same and that was the main thing.

An hour later I was back with Rawlins' check—written by Mrs. Rawlins— for $75 plus tax. I entered the transaction in the daybook and rang up the check in the cash register. It was going on to 1 o'clock so I suggested Nan have her lunch and then I would go. She said she didn't want lunch, so I headed back to the diner.

There were a few customers when I got back. One who had me scurrying around the stock bins and up and down the ladder until I found the cabinet hinges in the style he wanted. Elmer might have lived 10 more years, I thought, if he'd only organized his shelves in a more sensible manner, saving himself from climbing for small items. By 4 o'clock it was starting to get dark, the early twilight that comes on an overcast winter day. I decided not to wait any longer. I called to Nan and suggested we close early because I needed to talk about something important, but not here in the shop. I think she had been expecting this. She nodded and hung up the 'closed' sign on the front door and got her coat.

"Will you ride with me?" I asked. "There is a quiet little place just on the outskirts of C.R. that will do. No crowds and no music." We didn't talk during the drive to the small inn. I had discovered it many months ago. The dining area was tiny perhaps 5 or 6 tables, closed of course as it was still early for dinner, but adjoining it was the bar, also tiny with only four booths. We took one tucked away in a corner. Nan wasn't sure she wanted anything, but I ordered a good dry sherry for both of us. Nan took a sip, looking questions at me. It was best, I thought, to just plunge ahead. There really was no point in trying to creep up on the matter, we were both adults, and certainly had been through this before.

"I got a job offer yesterday. Two of them in fact, both engineering positions some 50 to 100 miles west of Boston—"

"You know I can't offer you more money, Emmett," Nan interrupted. "The store just doesn't earn much."

"I'm not asking for more money, silly. I'm asking you to go with me, if you'll let me finish, I'm asking you to marry me." It took a moment for Nan to realize what she had heard.

"Now who's silly! Of course I'll marry you. Didn't you realize I proposed to you months ago?" Was it a miracle? The whole area suddenly became lighter. No miracle, the bar man had just turned the lights on, but to me, and I'm sure to Nan, gray doubts and black anxiety faded away even without the help of Edison's invention.

"But why did you wait so long to ask? I was sure within a few weeks of coming back, that you were what I really wanted." It came tumbling out as though my proposal had pulled a stopper from her thoughts. "Seeing you with Mina's son showed me I had something more I could offer you as well as love and affection. Something you had probably given up hope of having. Something I could give to fulfill both of us."

I had to raise my hand to stop her. "How could I ask you before? Yes I wanted a son, and I wanted a good wife. You offered both to me but I had nothing to offer in return. A clerk, working for my son's mother, and barely able to support them! That may be all right for some men—I'm not a snob—but not for me, not for my wife, not for my son. So I had to find work that I was trained for and was good at."

"And that was why you went east, not because of a problem with your house?"

"Yes, for an interview. I couldn't be truthful to you, suppose I was turned down. I'd have upset you for nothing and would have to begin my search all over again, and it might take months before I found a suitable job. But that is all over, Nan, it's behind us. Now we have to plan for the future and I'm afraid decision time is very short on the job offers, just a couple of weeks at most. But first, sherry won't do to celebrate." I gathered our glasses and went to the bar.

"Didn't the lady like the sherry?" Nan's glass was still half full. I could see the bartender's name tag on his jacket.

"The sherry was fine, Mike," I replied. Then, leaning over the bar and wiggling a finger to bring him closer, I whispered in his ear "I proposed and she accepted. Now I want something suitable for celebrating. Champagne or sparkling rose' or something."

Mike took a good look at me. "Married before?" he asked.

"I'm widowed, she's divorced. It's a late romance if you really need to know, but I'm feeling good to my fellow man, so I don't resent your question."

"No offense, sir. I only asked to make an appropriate suggestion. Champagne is too prosaic for the second time around. Shiella's my second too. You don't want something that could bring back memories of other mates. I'll find something special for you, trust me."

"Good," I responded, "but better give me something for her to nibble on, she's had no lunch yet." He puttered around the cabinets under the bar for a moment, then gave me a bowl of crackers and cheese, which I carried back to the booth.

"You'd better eat some of this, Nan, this is not the time to get sick. Our philosophic bartender is going to fix something special for a toast." She nibbled on a cracker before speaking.

"You could have had the hardware store yourself you know. Uncle Elmer really left it to you."

"I'm the trustee, Nan, I know what was in the will."

"Yes, Emmett, but you made him change it. That was my first—no second—clue to the kind of man you were."

"I'm sure Trable didn't tell you that, it must have been his secretary." I wondered if she had told Nan about my other letters. "Anyway, it was only right and Elmer agreed that if I provided financial guidance to you the store wouldn't be thrown away. You know, Nan, he never really forgave himself. He felt he drove you into a marriage that you wouldn't have made if he had let you have more time to see Hoegh's character. And speaking of character, I know I'm just what you see, but what, out of curiosity, was the first clue you mentioned?"

"Telling me I was smart to get Trable's phone number from the long distance operator instead of using the one you gave me. So I knew you were honest and could be trusted. Reinforced, of course, by the fact that you didn't make a pass at me that evening."

Mike's special arrived. Three pilsner glasses filled with a dark bubbly mixture I remembered from long ago. Nan looked hesitantly at the glass, but Mike and I clinked ours and held them for Nan's.

"To the happy couple," he said.

"To my Love," I replied, and we all clinked again and drank. Mike swallowed half his, I took a healthy gulp, and Nan a swallow.

"What is it?" she asked. "It's very smooth," and took another swallow.

"Black velvet," Mike replied and took his drink back to the bar, having another gulp on the way.

"It's Guiness stout poured together with champagne," I explained. "Elegant and smooth as I'm sure we'll be with each other. But better eat more crackers, and try the cheese." I helped myself as well; black velvets can be lethal on an empty stomach.

Later we moved to the dining area. Small filets of beef; a small round of fried potatoes, crisp on top but soft on the bottom; Jeanette, the chalkboard menu said; and green salad. Nan was too full for dessert, so I skipped it. We had coffee instead. The main topic of discussion was when and where to be married. I wanted it done before leaving for Massachusetts. This meant within a couple of weeks. Where, I left to Nan; she could have it at a church, a J.P., or a pastor in her home. I didn't care, it was the bride's prerogative I felt. Nan opted for a church wedding, but private, for just a few friends. She'd get Mrs. Olsen to cater the reception at her home. Nothing was settled about which job to take, we'd talk about that tomorrow, along with what to do about the store and house.

Nan gave up her seatbelt to snuggle against me on the drive back to Keonah. I bent to kiss her goodnight at the door, but she ducked to open it, and taking my hand, led me inside. "I'm not a virgin, Emmett, so there's nothing to save for our wedding night."

It was well after 10 o'clock when I left Nan sleeping peacefully, and sneaked back to my room. After all, my toothbrush and razor were there, and why cause comment before we went public.

CHAPTER XXXVI

MRS. BORDEN

I opened the store at 9:00, Nan usually did, but she hadn't arrived yet. My first job was to call Trable's office for an appointment, and got one at 11:00. My partner, boss, and fiancé (mutually agreed to but not announced) finally came in at a quarter to ten. I was in the back, busy with Dave Perkins' cabinet door. He came in while I was on the phone with Trable's secretary. His little one had banged a toy against the glass. Fortunately for Dave Jr. the glass cracked but didn't shatter.

"Sorry I'm late," she murmured, giving me a quick kiss on the cheek. "You should have given me a nudge. I was going to fix your breakfast. I don't usually oversleep. When did you leave? You must have been very quiet about it."

"I guess around 10:30. I didn't want your neighbors to start gossip just yet."

"Last night! Good god, I didn't hear a thing. I must have fallen asleep right after I--." She stopped, flushing with embarrassment.

"Yes." I laughed and kissed her again, on the forehead. "You went out like a light. I'll have to be more careful next time." Fortunately, Mrs. Olsen came in looking for a knob to fit the lid of her large steamer. Nan went to help her, thus avoiding further bedroom revelations. I continued to fuss with the cabinet door.

By the time I removed the wood strips that held the glass in place, being careful not to damage the finish, it was close to 11 o'clock. Nan was still chatting with Mrs. Olsen. I put the letter from Shelton Electronics and Lorenz's wire by the cash register, along with a map and the house listings I got in Amherst. I called out that I would be back shortly and that she should look at those papers. I pointed to them and left.

Carol Brindly was Trable's secretary. "So you told Mrs. Hoegh about the change Elmer made in his will. Was that proper?" I chided her.

"Nan Hoegh is a friend of mine, Mr. Borden. I thought she should know what kind of man was going to watch over her. You couldn't possibly resent that," she said with a smile.

"And I suppose you told her about my job inquiry letters, too?"

"Certainly not. That was your business only. I knew you would tell her, if and when it was necessary. If she knew about it, it certainly wasn't from me!"

"It's O.K., she didn't. As for the will, it turned out to be a good thing she did know. I thank you for that, and rest assured, Mr. Trable will not know. Now, is he in?"

Trable was not totally helpful, but promised to get a definitive answer for me in a few days. He needed to talk to a tax consultant in C.R. My problem was to determine if I could use the capitol gains in selling my Mamaroneck house to buy a new one without incurring taxes on them. It was my renting of the house that caused my concern. Nan would probably want to sell her house, but there should be no added capitol gains after the estate tax valuation was made. Keonah wasn't a boomtown, more of a bust town really.

Nan was still studying the letter and house listings when I returned. "I can't decide on the job for you, Emmett. It's your field of work and you know the people involved. They both sound all right to me, but that is nothing. Both locations seem O.K. too, but Amherst seems a little quainter than Worcester—I have trouble saying that name, I have to remind myself it's like the sauce. As for the money, when I add my bond interest in, it seems we could live very comfortably on either salary. I don't see the difference in pay as too important, especially if you take a third off for the extra tax."

So it was agreed that I would decide, and I decided then and there to go with Lorenz.

Nan suggested I move into her house, but I refused. "Not until we're married, so you better arrange it quick. Why be a constant temptation to my sense of propriety." I did agree to let her cook dinner for me on Sunday.

I finished the glass repair for Perkins and called in an acceptance telegram to Lorenz. We were married the following Monday. A private ceremony at the Lutheran Church. Nan wanted a church wedding this time, not that she was very religious, but she felt a formal ceremony in front of her friends would bring dignity to our union that her hurried elopement with Hoegh had not. At least that's what she told me. I believed her. As for me, the religious words meant nothing, but our vows meant everything.

Nan wore an old dress of her mother's she had found in an attic trunk. It required a few alterations. A tuck or two in the waist and a shortened hem for current fashion.

Mina and Phyllis were there, as well as Carol Brindly and Trable. Mrs. F., of course, and Charlie. Mrs. F. told me it was about time I did something good for women besides fixing broken glass, then, pulling me aside, asked what she should do if my Indiana friends should call. "They won't call, Mrs. Fashlich," I whispered. "I sent them an announcement, and anyway, they encouraged me to get hitched with some young one again."

"Well, she must be a strange one to let you go so easy. Why if I was twenty years younger I might have set my bonnet for you myself, and given Nan Hoegh a run for the money. Having a repairman always handy would be worth some aggravation." She gave her little broken laugh and started to move off. I stopped her and gave her a good kiss on the cheek and told her if I was 20 years older she'd have to run hard to keep away from me. So Mrs. F. and I parted friends. I knew she'd miss the room rent, so I had paid for the following month as well, saying it was in lieu of the short notice that gave her little time to get a new renter.

Charlie was another matter. I had told him on Saturday that I would be leaving. He took it harder than I had thought, hoping we would be able to work together again the following summer. I tried to let him down easy. "You've proved yourself now Charlie. I'm sure your dad will want you to help build those gazebos and work on designing new ones for your uncle Mercer. You know, young man," I added, "you are to blame for this, because you showed me how much I was missing by not having a son like you." Not really a maudlin sentiment, however it may sound to you. It meant something good to me and I'm sure to Charlie too.

We had just two weeks of quiet pleasure and contentment left before leaving. That warm companionship I had previously experienced with Edie on the riverboat for only a few hours was now nearly continuous with Nan. We seemed to fit together naturally in our moods and habits. Not that we didn't have disagreements at times. Mostly about how we were to handle the house and other property in Keonah.

We had agreed about the store. That would have to be sold to pay off the remaining estate taxes. And anyway, it couldn't be profitably run from Amherst. Sam Voss seemed the most appropriate prospect to buy it and we broached the idea with him immediately after the wedding. He agreed it would complement his lumber business, but he wasn't sure he'd want the hardware part in a separate location. We finally agreed to sell the stock and goodwill to him and put the building up for sale separately. I also convinced Nan to sell her car, promising to buy her a new one in Amherst as a wedding present. It wasn't difficult, as she didn't relish the thought of the two of us driving east separately in the winter. The house was the big sticking point. She wanted to sell, but I thought she should rent for a while until we settled on a new home and could get a better handle on the tax liabilities on my Mamaroneck house. Nan's argument was that selling would give us money to buy the new house sooner. My counter argument was that a husband should provide the home for his wife. She countered with the desire for us to be equal partners for the rest of our lives and that we should pool our assets. Eventually she agreed to rent for a while until we determined what we might find for a permanent nesting place in Amherst, and I accepted the pool concept.

The tedious property details finally settled, at least temporarily, the hardware stock transferred to the lumberyard, the building given to a realtor for sale, her jalopy disposed of to Jake Garnishe's garage and used car lot, and arrangements made to store selected furniture and houseware items until sent for, we were free to go.

There was naturally one more nagging problem left, which bothered me more and more as we sped along the interstate. Should we stop at Elkton? I had written Edie that I was marrying Nan, but received only the laconic reply 'Congratulations and best wishes', and signed 'Your old friend.' Edie was being her discreet self in case someone else should see the letter. But would appearing at the Lodge risk discretion for both of us, for I had never told Nan, nor did I intend to, about my relation with Edie. Nan resolved the problem for me, by suggesting we make our evening stop near Cleveland so she could have her secret wish to spend a night at Niagara Falls, which would only be a few hours drive the next day from Cleveland. "It's still winter," I reminded her in astonishment. "The Falls will be as cold as the devil. It's next door to Buffalo you know, the icebox of the east."

"You'll keep me warm, honey," she countered, and, laughing: "I want to feel like a young bride, at least for a night." So we whizzed by the Elkton turn-off a little after noon, adding 'too early to stop' to the reason for waiting for another time to introduce Nan to the woman that brought love back to my life.

Ian James Borden was born in early November. Named after my father. I sent Edie a picture of Nan and the baby.

About the Author:

The author has previously published a technical book on computer design, was a contributing author on other technical books and numerous in-house training manuals on computers at Univac (now Unisys). He has been an adjunct professor at Drexel and Penn State Universities in their graduate evening schools for many years. Writing this novel was one of the several hobbies he enjoys in his retirement. It contains snippets from the many experiences in travels and dining.

TIME LINE FOR KEONAH DAYS

1994--   Emmett goes for interviews, late January '94

Drive to Glenly, mid-October '93
Diehl dies, early October '93
Date with Rosa, early September '93
Barking Dogs chapter, late August '93
Gazebo finished and Mina's picnic,
mid-August '93
Minneapolis weekend, late July '93
4th of July picnic at Voss's
Chicago weekend, late June '93
Deal wth Snyder, June '93
Emmett finds Rodde's left foot, May '93

Emmett starts at Diehl's, March '93

1993--   Start of story. Emmett drives west, he is 47, Edie is 49, Nan is 36

1989--   Francis dies

1987--   Rodde dies

1981-   Edie widowed at 37

1977--   Nan marries at 19

1973--   U.S. Draft ends   )
             Emmett is in defense work   -)
             and draft exempt   )
)   )

1969--   Man on moon   ) peak of)
1968--   Emmett graduates at Iowa State   ) - Vietnam)
) war

1964-   Edie marries at 20   )

1963--   JFK shot

1958--   Nan is born

1953--   Emmett is 7
)
) -- height of Korean war

1950--   )
1946--   Emmett born at Beverly, Iowa in N.W. corner of
         the state. Father is the Water Commissioner
1944--   Edie born, August 10, 1944